MOTHER OF TREES

STEVEN J. MORRIS

Mother of Trees

Book 1 of Thaumatropic Roots
Steven J. Morris

ISBN 978-1-956105-19-3

To Supportive Friends and Family

The Fortezas & my wife cheer me on,

Edie (not Eddie) makes my books better,

My mom & now my kids are reading,

Eugene & Brett (who question what's going on in my head at work... oh, and thanks for telling my boss not to touch my ears because I have a weird elf fetish),

Angel, Briana, & Brittany – my most active social media supporters/questioners

Books by Steven J. Morris

The Guardian League series

The Guardian of The Palace

Stars in the Sand

We're Going on an Elf Hunt

The Song Unsung

Thaumatropic Roots series

Mother of Trees

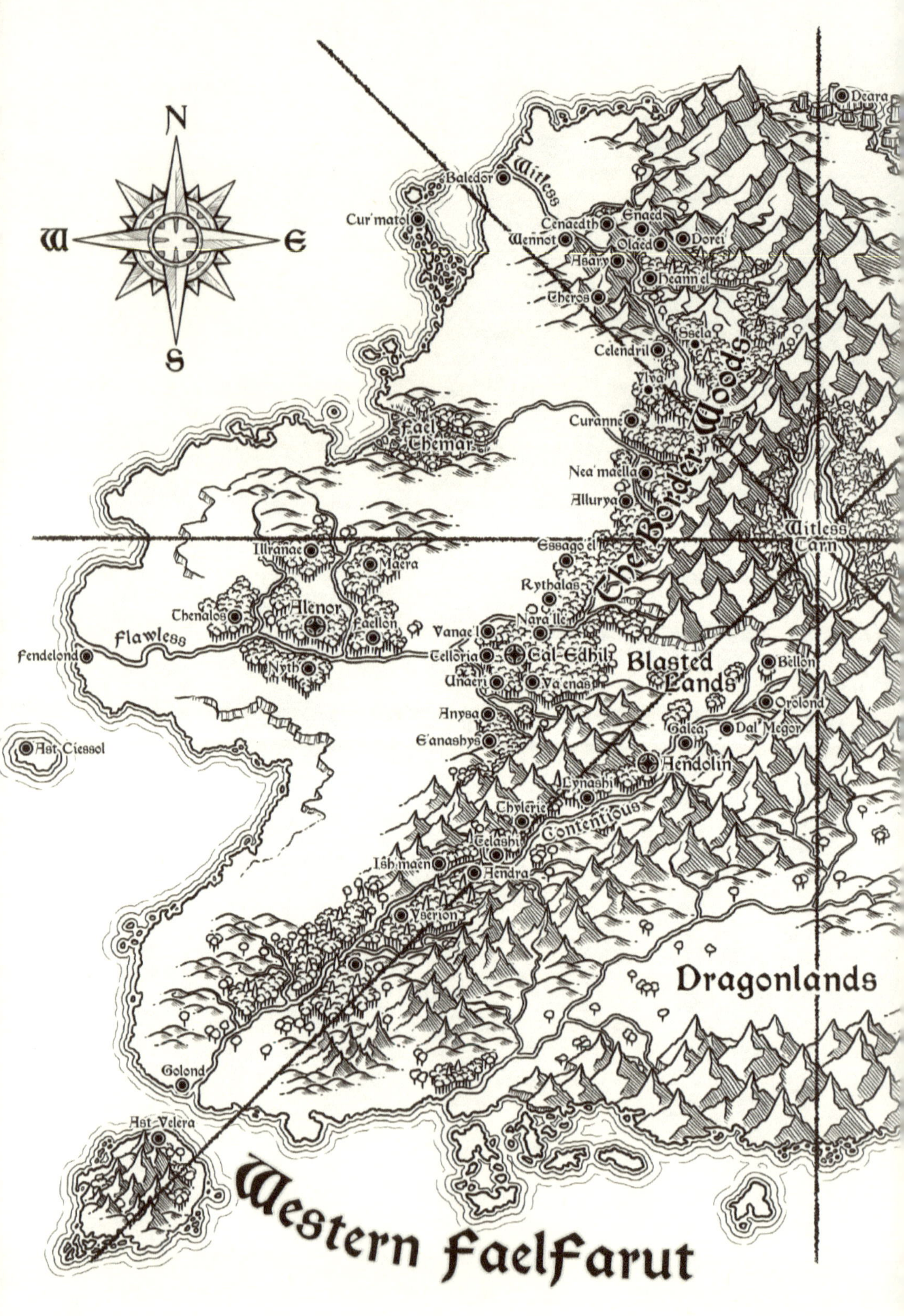

N
W
E
S
Deara
Baledor
Witless
Cur'matol
Cenaedth
Enaed
Wennot
Olaed
Dorei
Asary
Heann'el
Theros
Ssela
Celendril
Ylva
Fael Themar
Curanne
Nea'maella
Allurya
Essago'el
The Border Woods
Witless Carn
Illranae
Maera
Rythalas
Thenalos
Alenor
Faellon
Nara'lle
Vanae'l
Cal-Edhil
Blasted Lands
Bellon
Flawless
Telloria
Fendelond
Unaeri
Va'enash
Orolond
Nyth
Dal'Megor
Anysa
Galea
Ast-Ciessol
G'anashys
Hendolin
Lynashi
Thyleire
Contentious
Telashi
Ish'maen
Hendra
Vserion
Dragonlands
Golond
Ast-Velera
Western Faelfarut

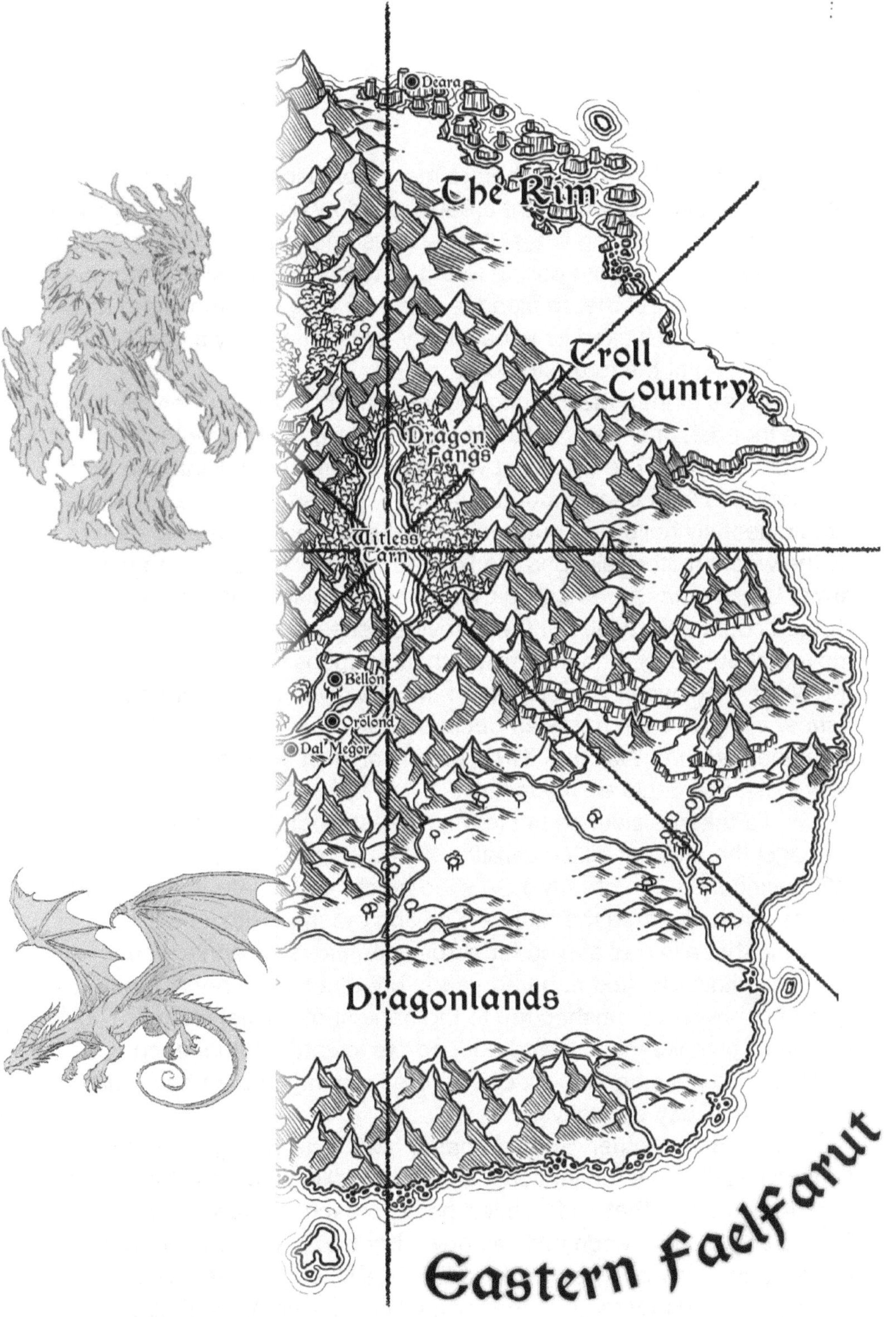

Deara
The Rim
Troll Country
Dragon Fangs
Witless Tarn
Bellon
Orolond
Dal' Megor
Dragonlands
Eastern Faelfarut

Prologue

On a night much like the one before me, I would lose everything. The gentle undulations of wisp-light created shadow dancers from the bared branches of surrounding limbs. It wasn't just the evening, with its unusual mid-winter's warmth calling forth the wisps… the vision echoed an elf, climbing to meet me, to plead… I Saw nothing past that time, and my twilight Vision lacked its usual clarity, presenting only a pond's rippled reflection of the future to come.

Elves birthed their young infrequently, but not so rarely as to call on me for each one—entreaties to me implied something either very good or very bad. The applicant who approached me fell into the latter category. Did I not bear enough burden? My heart grew heavier while simultaneously hollowing out, ready to give up. I knew what to expect as the weary mother climbed the Rooted with her babe nestled in her arms. Lacking, the elves called them. The title disturbed me. The Rooted could not travel, but they provided shelter, while the Roamers moved about freely, and their titles, though opposing, did not bother me. Why, then, was I so opposed to the title given to the Lacking? *Because*, a tiny voice in my head declared, *the moniker defines them by what they are not.* Was that it? Or did my disgust arise because their very existence declared my failure?

I'd taken residence not in the highest Rooted of the forest, nor amongst the elves at all. Separation kept me from falling into the trap of influencing them too greatly. I Saw too much, and of late, the weight of the loss overwhelmed me, at times driving me mad with its burden. Knowing that all I had strived for across countless millennia would crumble within the next hundred years, but that I could not see how, could not prevent it, pushed me to the darkest of mental realms. The evening's glimpse into the end nudged me toward another such episode. Would I even come out of it before I met my fate, or had today been my final day of sanity?

"Please, Mother. Should I name her?" The young elf startled me. I'd lost myself in my ruminations, so near to falling into the chasm of my dark forebodings, that I'd forgotten her approach. Her dark brown hair flowed unbound to reach halfway down her back. That and her sunkissed skin marked her as a Wood Elf. Of all the elf races, the Wood Elves remained most true to the form I'd crafted, covering their bodies with thin material that left much of their skin exposed. Her desperation beat at me like waves hitting a shore as she pulled her baby from her bosom, holding the infant out to me like an offering.

Should I name her? What she really asked was whether her baby would live. Whether she should let herself get attached to the gift bequeathed to her.

It hardly seemed worth it. Her child would never live to be an adult. No newborn elf would. We neared the end times, when magic would cease, and life with it. To make things worse, her child already lacked magic. I felt it even as the mother had carried her up the long wooden landings that led to my home. The Father had touched her, though I knew not how, as he'd done with the Stone Brothers and an increasing number of elves over the last thousand years.

I regretted my apathy the moment I looked into the anguished mother's eyes. She deserved better. Children with no magic lived short lives, even when well cared for. She didn't comprehend that it mattered not whether her child held magic or lacked it—the reaper would take the wheat with the chaff.

"Hand her to me." I held out my hand. I would hold off my plunge into darkness. While it ultimately wouldn't matter, I could pretend. No matter the fate of the child, I would comfort the mother. That kindness was mine to give… a parting gift to the last of my first creations who were built to create.

She hesitated. Was she dreading the answer she would hear? Or did she fear letting me hold her baby? My fingers, covered in dark gray decaying bark, were as long as the mother's torso. Using a touch of my old magic, I grew vines over them, producing a bed of fresh, soft leaves. Yet the elf still balked.

"Illiara." I spoke gently, pulling her name from her with a part of my magic that still worked. "The time given her is the same, whether I speak of it or not. You can enjoy the time you've been given, no matter how short."

I'd meant that to convince her not to pursue an answer—to my mind, the knowing made things worse. At that moment, I reconciled myself to a lie—I would comfort Illiara if she asked.

She handed the little mewling babe to me.

I wrapped the baby with vines, cradling her in my fingers, not wanting Illiara to fear for her child's safety. Illiara smiled a sad smile, seeing her newborn cradled—a mother's worry to which I related all too well. I closed my eyes to See better.

I struggled to find her gossamer thread. Like a spider's first silky creation, it would glimmer in my vision and then I would lose it.

But I did finally latch on.

Once I connected to the gossamer fiber, I crept forward along the slender silk. *Spider-like,* I thought with amusement. I moved slowly at first, searching for its untethered end, afraid I might slip off the thread or slip past its end, and not recognize the difference. To my surprise, it continued on.

I sped up, Seeing in the distance what I recognized to be coming for us all. She crossed others' threads, touching them here and there as all threads do, weaving into the pattern of a generation.

Ahead, the end loomed. The end of us all. I could not See past that point—my own final ending. And I'd Seen all the other threads… I'd followed every elf that lived. None continued past a knot in the pattern… a knot formed around the gaping hole of my disappearance.

I followed her spiderweb-thin thread in, noting that it had at least thickened from when it had begun, though still not as big as the threads of most elven newborns. I smiled at her resilience as I pulled into the knot…

… and out the other side.

I'd gone through the knot.

I'd never Seen the far side of the knot. Threads ran everywhere, but they weren't elven. Those strands belonged to the children of Stone. Their Father-tainted threads eluded my magic, though I recognized them for what they were.

The child's elven thread, to my astonishment, was not alone.

That was impossible.

I'd followed every elf. None got through.

I jumped to one of the other threads and followed it backwards until I found a point where the newborn's wisp of a spider's thread touched. At their intersection, I moved back to the spider-thread, found another point where it touched yet another elf. That one went through the knot as well.

None had gotten through the knot before. Her thread—her gossamer strand—changed things. Sight, the ability to See the future, was a dangerous ally—the act of observing could affect the outcome. It was a paradox I'd lived with long enough to accept the truth of it. Would the baby's strand have made it through the knot had I not Seen it? Was it possible to save even more elves? Was it possible to save *myself*?

In the physical world, I choked out a sob, opening my eyes. Illiara lurched forward, reaching for her baby, but I held up my free hand, forestalling her.

In her sleep, the little whelp gnawed on the bark of a finger. Tears flowed down my wooden cheeks and dripped onto the limb of the Rooted I sat upon, and small sprouts of green emerged at the points of contact.

I settled back in, closing my eyes to See, quickly finding that precious diaphanous thread.

It continued to move forward through time, a collection of threads growing around it. The threads of the children of Stone still abounded, and in the distance, another knot approached. Even if that marked the End, I'd already been given a gift—the elves would continue, at least for a time.

I hit the second knot, the babe's thread finally becoming the size of a normal elven adult. Its size made it easier to follow when it appeared on the other side.

The threads of the elves were mostly intact. It was the threads of the children of Stone that had diminished. I paused a moment to look around.

It wasn't there.

I backed up before the knot to make sure. It had been there, and after… gone.

The Father of Stones' thread had disappeared.

I laughed aloud.

Illiara reached into my palm, intending to rescue her child, but with only a fraction of my attention, I grabbed her with my other hand, holding her screaming form away from her baby, and I traveled forward on her thread once more. The thread stretched on… and on. It gained color, something else new to me, a light green. I sped along it and missed the point when it disappeared. I sighed—I'd Seen all I hoped for already. I widened my view, searching for the lost thread, just to See where it had ended.

It had grown large enough to stand out.

What I Saw from a distance confused me even more. The thread had ended… there. Then it started up again, over there, like someone had chopped a piece out. I followed it again and, once more, it disappeared.

I widened my view further, and I realized segments of her thread existed in multiple places. Thicker, deeper green, it wove into patterns as intricate as my own.

Then I lost all trace of it. Fooled before, I searched broadly. But I did not See it. Something else new—my Sight had never before let me See past the end of a thread.

I moved forward, curious where my magic would stop me. Threads around me blackened. Not ending, but corrupting. It wasn't elves, but one of my later creations. Short little threads, but dazzling. Unless they blackened—the blackened ones stretched on and on, never doing anything.

The threads of the elves knotted, a deep black thread drawing them all tight.

It horrified me. The whole pattern, everything the little babe had created, going black and patternless, or knotted up and unraveling.

I slowed as the pattern began to disappear, sadness beyond what I'd experienced going into the effort overtaking me. The elegant weave had come so close. So much like mine.

Then the threads of the elves also blackened, and finally, all at once—vanished.

Sadness overwhelmed me, but I marched forward, and a moment later… her thread popped back! Twice the size of when it had disappeared, it glowed with a rainbow of colors.

The blackened threads rapidly ended, a kaleidoscope of threads forming a new pattern. Few elves entered the pattern—in fact, I recognized very few of the threads. But one I did—a child of Stone had weaved in. Their threads, I'd only ever seen as destructive, but one worked into the tapestry, and others joined it, not destroying but embellishing. It was wondrous to my eyes.

The blackened threads continued to end, and crying with joy, I halted my vision into the future. *Let her patterns be her own.*

The floor around me swayed with branches sprung forth from my tears, and the little mewling had chewed off the tip of my finger, and worked to shorten it further.

The mother stared into my open eyes, frightened but hopeful, as those without hope cling to their last branch.

"Well?" she begged.

"By all that's green and growing, name her!" I choked out.

The mother put her hand to her mouth, half laugh and half sob, at my little profanity.

She picked her mewling from the vines of my palm, letting her continue to gnaw on the nub she'd chewed off—it would grow back. It all would grow back.

The baby, freed from my vines and taking my finger's tip with her, found itself thrust aloft, and its eyes flew open in surprise.

"Elliah," the babe's mother announced. "I will call you Elliah."

The mewling closed her eyes and screamed her disappointment, the chip of bark she'd taken from me falling from her mouth to the Rooted below and blending in with the other bark. I leaned back against the trunk of the tree, tired, as I always seemed to be, haunted by the future. The joy of seeing a path forward couldn't compete with the weariness. But I smiled as I settled in, wondering how, exactly, a child without magic would save it.

Witless Tarn
Nara'lle
Cal-Ehdil
Faeltic Forest
Bellon
Hendolin
Contentious
Dragonlands

Zoras * 1

The ground shook beneath my feet as I stared in awe at the Roamers battling waves of enormous trolls. I couldn't make out the details from our perch on the hill, but my father had told me the Roamers would wrap the rocky monsters in their limbs and squeeze until the trolls' stone hides shattered, spewing putrid green blood and guts. Yet the sheer number of trolls… fear squeezed my heart, a fear entirely different from the one I'd had when riding in with my fellow recruits under the cloak of night. Yet my excitement had not entirely vanished—my eyes sought out Her.

"They're sending us children now!" the Alluvium spat. My eyes shot back to the dark-skinned commander standing beside me. He scrutinized us with tired, angry eyes. "How old are you?" he asked me, his tone softening.

"Eighty, sir." Not true. I had just turned seventy, but as a High Elf, I was taller than many of the recruits and hoped my height created the illusion of age. From the look on the commander's face, it didn't work.

"Them," he said, "I have use of." He nodded to the two Wood Elves. "They can climb the Roamers and guide them." He waved at the young Warder who stood as tall as me with shoulders that spanned twice the girth of mine. "He can join the battle, taking out the trolls who get past the Roamers. She," he said, pointing at the bone-white Salt by my side, "can move the winds."

The Salt shook her head in concerned denial.

"Call lightning?" the commander asked.

"Rain, sir."

"Rain," he repeated, sighing. "I can use that too. But you, an underage High Elf, do you plan to *talk* your way into the good graces of the trolls?"

I understood his point, but, ironically enough, I had no rebuttal. So I kept my mouth shut.

"A High Elf who holds his tongue—a treasure indeed. May it always be so. But I must know, what strength do you bring us?"

"I'm good at solving unusual problems, sir." I cringed as I said it, but I wasn't physically strong, and I didn't wield powerful magic. I just... didn't think like everyone else.

The commander grunted, disappointed, then he barked out orders, and officers stepped up to pull my fellow recruits away, leaving me standing there, a lone recruit with Wynruil, head of the elven army, and a smattering of officers, all ignoring me.

I did not understand what they intended. Was I turned away from the army? Well, if that was to be my fate, I would at least take advantage of the time before me. I scoured the battle below, searching again for Her. My father had told me I would struggle to find Her. Not always—sometimes She stood as large as the Roamers. But most times, She was no bigger than the largest troll. That said, the largest troll still towered over an elf—even a tall Warder didn't reach to their waists. Yet I could not find Her on the battlefield.

The trolls streamed past the Roamers—not a mere trickle that the Warders would fend off, but hordes of them. They didn't charge toward our outpost, though I had to imagine their clan lords recognized the elven command center, and I cast my eyes to the south, searching for their target based on the direction of the trolls' charge.

My breath caught at the first sight of Her. My eyes would have drifted right past, had it not been for the movement of the trees themselves, branches flailing as though the very forest had come alive. In their midsts stood a two-legged tree, like the Roamers but smaller—troll height at that moment—surrounded by a cadre of Wood Elves. I squinted, desperately wanting to be closer, to see Her work. The trees around Her bent and swayed, in ways trees were never meant to. Earth and rocks flew as their roots tugged from the ground. The roots knotted together, pushing the trees even higher as the Wood Elves ran *toward* the convulsing danger, hopping onto the roots and climbing!

As the first of the trolls neared them, the Mother of Trees grew, joining her small army of newly created Roamers. Still, the number of trolls... hundreds of them... and She had only a dozen Roamers. I flicked my eyes back to the original line of Roamers—they'd had twice as many and the trolls had broken through. What chance did only a dozen have? Even though the original line marched in mighty strides toward the Mother of Trees, She would be overwhelmed by trolls before Her defenders arrived.

A giant red shield appeared around the Mother of Trees and Her squad of Roamers—a translucent dome of magic. Trolls slammed into it and stopped. I nodded my head, appreciating the fact that the Roamers closing in from the outside would make easy targets of the ignorant trolls who flailed uselessly at the Mother's magic.

But then… a troll broke through. And another. Five… ten… twenty.

The Roamers inside fought, tangling and crushing their foes, while the ones outside did the same, pushing their inexorable way toward the red shield.

"They broke through the shield," I muttered to myself.

"Elven magic grows stronger with each generation," Commander Wynruil growled. I hadn't realized he stood on a rock behind me, watching the same battle from a higher vantage. "But the trolls' resistance to magic grows as well. And they breed faster." He grunted in disgust. He whispered, and I, the person in front of him, would be the only one to hear. "That… is why we will lose."

Not many trolls made it through the Mother's shields. The Roamers inside handled them. The ones outside slowly decimated their enemy.

As if by sudden agreement, the trolls turned and ran. Cheers went up among the officers nearby, but Wynruil remained silent.

The trolls ran back to the mountains, Warders and Roamers pursuing them to pick off as many as possible

Wynruil startled me, his voice right in my ear—when had he moved? "They ran because we killed their Warlord. You arrived on an auspicious day—we will have relative peace for a time. Until another Warlord is born. With the Father of Stones bending their ears, there is no reasoning with them. Not that there's any point in reasoning with a normal troll—they can barely pour water from a cup with instructions on the bottom. The Clan Chiefs are smarter, but not smart enough to organize an effective assault. But when a Warlord is born, the Father takes interest. And He will not rest until we are destroyed."

I scanned the battlefield but did not find any sign of the defeated Warlord.

He pointed. "Right next to the Mother."

My eyes darted back, finding the Mother of Trees. She knelt over a figure I could barely make out, Her arm of wood on his chest. Was She speaking with him? "You want to help?" Wynruil said, interrupting my thoughts. "Solve the problem with magic. It might take a thousand years, but once the trolls outgrow us, we're done."

Beldroth : 1

The Mother has a plan for everyone, I reminded myself from my hiding place, though I suspected She'd cast me in the auspicious role of a dragon chew toy.

"It's not normal to find a dragon with trolls, is it?" My son's question brought a crooked smile to my face. His mind astonished me under most circumstances. He devoured books like sheep devoured grass, spitting out quotes and formulas like cud to be mangled for further nutrients. How he'd come by such smarts, only the Mother could say. He certainly hadn't inherited his brains from me. And his mother had avoided libraries like the plague. But then again, he'd spent the last decade stuck in a cave, regurgitating ancient knowledge while I'd performed my Luminary Vigil so that I might move on. It was a wonder he wasn't broken.

"No, son. It is not normal to find a dragon with trolls." Frowning, I considered my words carefully. "Though who knows 'normal' anymore. Historically, trolls kill everything they encounter, and dragons don't associate with *anyone*."

"Devorak's Compendium of Lore retells many stories where dragons and elves—"

"Don't!" I cut him off. It wasn't the first time he had brought up stories that preceded the Breaking. If dragons had once worked alongside elves, then it made their betrayal all the more painful. I preferred to think of them as monsters. How could he feel anything different than I?

I shut those thoughts out. A decade was long enough. For the sake of my son, I would move on. I would…

I sighed, realizing how contrary to my intent my response had been.

"I'm sorry," I said. "In all of your reading, did you ever encounter anything about dragons and trolls interacting?"

I took my eyes off the distant scene to examine my son. As I expected, he took my question seriously, thinking through the volumes of tomes he stored in his mind. He hadn't deserved to lose his mother. But even more, he hadn't deserved to lose his father, who'd been *right there*, drowning in anguished appeals to The Mother.

"There are stories of dragons *fighting* trolls." He grimaced. "To help the elves."

My eye twitched, but I smiled encouragingly.

"None where dragons cooperate with trolls, though," he said. "Nor the other way around."

I pondered that. It meant something, a dragon with trolls.

No trouble with the trolls ever began without a Warlord.

"Why are they building that wall?" I pondered aloud. How did the pieces fit? A dragon and trolls. A clumsy wall of stone around the southwest side of the Tarn, blocking the very place from which the trolls typically attacked. It made no sense for them to block their own way.

"Maybe they have something to hide?" my brainy son answered.

Something to hide. Some kind of plan. My conviction that our stony enemies had birthed a Warlord increased.

"I can't help but notice…" My son peeked around the rock that hid us from our distant enemies. I stuck my head around and followed his gaze. "They've dug massive holes to build those walls."

He was right. I'd fought there before and should have noticed, but the wall had distracted me so much that I hadn't really pondered what lay on the far side. Wide holes. Many of them. The occasional troll that popped out and cast a boulder to the top made it clear that the holes were deep. Other trolls carted the boulders down the line of the wall, taking them out of sight with swift marches born of legs bigger than an elf.

I'd never been inside a troll's cave. To my knowledge, no elf had. But I'd seen them pour from the caves before us when we'd mounted a counter-offensive during the last troll uprising, so I suspected they lived there. They'd pushed us back, ultimately leading to the destruction of my home.

Still, so what if they dug even bigger holes?

I looked at my son, realizing he looked not at the holes he had pointed out, but up at the mountains beyond. At the Dragon's Fangs with their glacier-capped peaks.

"I read something from Wynruil Warweaver—"

"Wynruil *Embergrove*," I grumbled, but his eyes didn't leave the white tips of the Dragon's Fangs.

"Wynruil Warweaver…" he began again. I grunted, but didn't stop him. How had he even found books that told of the war master before he'd lost his mind? Not for the first time, I squirmed under the thought that, if that poor lunatic had held on to his sanity for just a few hours longer, my world would not have fallen apart. Still, as The Mother wills.

"...he remarks in an old journal that half of the boulders in the Contentious were once trolls."

I wondered how true that was. Any time we fought near the Contentious, we drove them to the water. The river penned them in, as they were reluctant to cross the swiftly flowing water. I shivered, thinking of how many times I'd walked into that river without considering that the rocks beneath me might once have lived. The very floor of the river might once have been creations of The Mother.

Still, even The Mother had destroyed them when it was necessary for the survival of everything else. I closed my eyes and said a silent prayer, asking her for the love and patience She had shown me as I'd struggled through my resentment. I asked Her again why She'd brought me there. Why She hadn't let me die with my friends when our home was destroyed, or die with my wife when her time had come? But I received no answer. I supposed it still wasn't my time to know.

I opened my eyes to the icy Dragon's Fangs, glacial remnants of a time before the Breaking, perched atop the tallest peaks in the world. So much ice that it made the mountains unclimbable due to unpredictable avalanches, if one were fool enough to risk the trolls on one side and the dragons on the other, as my dear wife had done the one time.

With a happy surprise akin to hearing the bleat of a lost sheep you suspected to be forever gone, my prayer was answered.

Elliah ~ 1

My mother told me many times that all adolescents feel like they don't belong, but… I really didn't. So I spent my free time away from other elves, on my own but for the animals… they didn't understand how broken I was. And I was quite pleased with my current find, so I snarled when a noise behind me scared away the drakeling that had settled in my hands. Black with a pattern of red scales along its spine, its body the thickness of my finger, it took flight with a flurry of thin leathery wings and disappeared behind a massive brown trunk.

"The real ones are much more intimidating," said an unfamiliar voice.

Time slowed as I tensed to run, shocked that I'd let my guard down so much that anyone had gotten that close. How many lurked behind me? On the outskirts of town, in the thick of the woods near the river, I had expected solitude.

"Stay, Bereft. I am not afraid," said the voice. His words provoked me.

"No one's *afraid* of me," I blurted. Bitterness stained my words as surely as the pollen of the bloodcups had stained my ragged clothes.

I turned away from the vanished drakeling to focus on the intruder who'd scared it away. A man. *No*, I corrected myself, *someone my age*. Someone not quite old enough for adults to consider one of their own, but too old to call a child.

But not Bereft. No other elf shared that with me.

The newcomer was slightly taller than me with a thin frame, his light hair hanging long, wild, and tangled. He was new to the village—I would have noticed an elf with skin so light. I'd heard whispers of him at school. Kethryllia had called him Salt-kissed, and I'd wondered what that meant, but his light skin answered that question. He'd undoubtedly caught whispers about me, heard of my… condition. Bereft. Yet at that moment, I thought only of the hours of coaxing I'd spent to draw the little drakeling into my grasp, and that the stupid elf had scared it away. I wanted to punch him.

"Maybe they should be," he said, taking a step back, though it would have taken me two leaps to get to him, and he'd have me pinned in one, if he had any skill with magic at all. But I'd prepared a leap already, only not in his direction. As I sprung away, he continued, raising his voice, "And you're right, they're not afraid of *you*."

I landed with a tree between us. His magic wouldn't be able to snag me there. Unless he was very good at it.

"They're afraid of what you represent."

Angry at myself for not hearing his approach, at the boy for scaring away my drakeling, at the world for what I *was*, I shouted back. "Troll-scat! They don't give a hellkite's hairy eyeball about what I *represent*!" They simply understood I couldn't fight back.

With my full attention, I had no trouble hearing his approach, and I started toward the next tree that would block his sight of me, recognizing I moved more stealthily than he.

"I've seen many," he said, making so much noise with his movements that he must have been doing it on purpose. "Dragons, I mean. And more than my share of Ancients."

I slowed, even though he had to be lying. I'd put another tree between us and scampered up. He would have more trouble restraining me in a tree... unless, of course, his magic bent toward that. The noise stopped, as though he rested, even though I continued on. Then the odd man-boy started telling me a story!

"Where the Frigid feeds into the Contentious, I once happened upon a red diving into the river." The Contentious? That was far to the east, where the Warders called home, but the Frigid meant nothing to me. His voice faded as I moved farther away, leaping to the next tree to gain more distance. "So big, and yet it split the water like a gannet."

I paused, wondering what a gannet might be, and just a little curious about his story. I enjoyed both reading and hearing tales of other places.

"Father said it caught a riverwhal, but I could only tell that it crunched on *something* after its head and neck popped to the water's surface."

I waited, listening hard, but did not hear the boy move.

"It climbed out the side of the river, pumping its wings, then glowing like a wind-blown coal, and finally taking back to the winds. I'll never forget that."

The pieces clicked—I'd overheard conversations. Son of a Warder... or something similarly outlandish. Salt-kissed son of a Warder, up from the Contentious. I'd never seen a Warder, or a Salt, though I'd read about them, and I'd hoped to catch a glimpse of the travelers…

but not be caught alone in the woods with them.

"What's your name?" he asked, his voice distant, but sure. Sure that I heard. That I hadn't fled him entirely. He wasn't dumb nor oblivious.

But would I give him my name? I'd heard adults say names had power. But did mine? Plus, he could learn mine very easily from others. He probably already had. I clutched my bone dagger, a gift from my mother, finding comfort in an old habit and familiar contingence.

"My name is Hughelas," he said, as though offering his name had any import, when he'd already dubbed me Bereft. "Hughelas Do'wood."

Yet he hadn't drawn closer.

"Elliah," I said, barely loud enough for even the tree I perched upon to hear.

"Just Elliah?" he said, and I heard the smile in his question.

And I suddenly felt I'd said too much. So I ran. As I always did. As I always had to do to survive. I ran.

"I don't like it when you disappear." My mother's reproval rang hollow, a liturgy cheapened from repetition.

I gave thanks to the tree and walked past her to the space I'd claimed as my own, caught up in daydreams of a drakeling snuggling in my arms, my imaginings of a red dragon diving for its meal, and a knot of worry about the intent of the newcomer to our school.

"Did you hear me?"

"I'm not a *child*," I blurted, irritated.

"You're *eighty*," Mother responded. "You *are* a child. *My* child."

Eighty hard-earned years *entitled* me to my little freedoms. No one else had to deal with such overprotective parenting, so much confinement. "I'm *not* a child!" I insisted… childishly, even to my own ears. Refusing to let her get the better of me, I slowed my ragged breathing.

I tucked away my fantasies of dragons and Warders, buried my worry about Warders' sons, and stepped back to the common area we shared, where my draconian mother sat, surrounded by the tools of her trade.

"Troll warner," Mother said, who hadn't stopped writing since I'd entered our home. Mother wasn't old for an elf… but her ability to multi-task belied her age. Probably because she'd always had to keep one eye on me. And used the other to watch out for danger.

The setting sun lit the room through vine-draped windows, but the light would fade within an hour, forcing her to stop working. Writing scrolls required too much concentration for her to summon a magelight, and fire proved a false ally to scroll-creation.

"Troll warner?" I asked, curious about both her words and why, if I'd understood her correctly, she would create such a thing. The Roamers kept us safe from trolls. I'd never even seen one.

"I hear there's a Warder about, come from the Contentious." She winked. "Know your market."

She wasn't wrong—I suspected I'd met one. Warders had a reputation for benevolence. Still, weren't Warders supposed to be huge? The man-boy in the woods had been tall, but not heavily muscled. Stories I'd read of lean and pale Salts would fit him better. He had cast no spell—that I'd witnessed—yet he'd known I was Bereft. That suggested kindness, or at least the lack of cruelty. *Or*, I thought cynically, *extreme manipulation.*

"You've learned about Warders in school, haven't you?"

I blushed, realizing I'd become lost in my thoughts, standing there like an idiot. But she misunderstood my embarrassment to be a lack of knowledge.

"They are elves that fight the trolls along the Contentious River. They're a heartier stock than us Wood Elves."

Exactly! The boy hadn't been big.

"Lighter skin," she continued.

His skin *had* been light, and his hair too, though not white like I'd heard the hair of the Salts to be.

"What magic they have tends toward defense, meaning—"

I tuned her out. If she'd paid any attention to me, she would have known I'd read Talena Talonforged a million times. The stories of Warders might have stretched the truth, but I'd read of them. They'd also taught us of them in school, but that hadn't gone so well. That had been many years ago and several villages back…

***

"What makes a Warder a Warder and us Wood Elves?" I'd asked, drawing a look of affronted superiority from my teacher.

"What?" he'd said, and with total clarity I realized that I'd overstepped my place.

"I mean, we're all elves," I said, looking down and biting my lip. He waited for me to continue. "But we call them Warders because of what? Their skin color and where they live? What about the Salts, the Alluvium, the High Elves?" I'd already read much of Talena's adventures, and marveled at the idea of other races of elves. "What about us?"

Snickers disrupted the outdoor classroom, stretching out for far too long as the teacher waited, staring at me like I was a particularly repellent bug.

"I," said the teacher with snotty pride, "am a Wood Elf. These," he said, indicating the other children with a grand sweep of his arm, "are Wood Elves." Why hadn't he included me with them? "*We* use magic oriented around life."

My cheeks burned when I realized he excluded me from their company because I couldn't use magic.

"Warders use less magic, and the ones who wield it are very practical about using it for fighting. Shields, Strength, Speed. They rely more on their physical size than their magic."

Elves who rely less on magic?

"You," he said, and his lip twitched in the same way it did when he'd watched Soliana shake her dandruff onto the table and then eat the flakes. But he caught himself and said, "*You* are derailing the lesson."

But I knew… everyone knew… what he'd stopped himself from saying. I was Bereft. I was *not an elf at all!*

I might look like a Wood Elf, but I'd never *be* one of them. So, I'd shut up, hearing his unspoken words as well as his spoken ones. I didn't belong. *But maybe*, I'd thought, *among the Warders, who use less magic… maybe they wouldn't care about my condition.*

***

Though it had happened years before, the beating my fellow students delivered after school had burned the lesson into my mind. *I don't belong.* The village had even valued my mother as a Healer, but not enough to ignore the parasite she brought with her.

"I wish I knew what went on in that noggin of yours." My mother's voice snapped me out of my reverie.

"Nothing," I said, irritated at the way she attempted to pry into my life. I didn't need another lecture meant to either make me feel normal… or try to convince me my condition made me *special*.

"I'd be a fool to believe *that*," Mother said, sweeping her penfeather across the parchment with a final swoop, then sighing. She rolled her shoulders and began the work of cleaning up, putting away her paper and ink, casting a cantrip of a Healing spell to undo the damage of the ink on her skin, and I helped her clear the table.

"Meditations," my mother said, welcoming me to join her, and we went through our ritual mindfulness exercises. While I didn't see the point, given my condition, I'd stopped arguing with her decades prior. Rituals, I'd decided, had a power of their own.

My trek to school provided daily opportunities for disaster. Whether I hopped from limb to limb, used well-traveled bridges, or crept through the brush on the ground, many points left me exposed, a target for children half my age. Spells to trip, to snag, to burn or freeze, to blind or numb, to sting, pinch, startle, slow, confuse, scare… whatever they needed to practice, knowing they wouldn't invoke retribution. Most of their direct spells failed, but enough did not, and nothing stopped the indirect spells, so I avoided being seen as much as possible.

That morning, I'd opted for ground cover to avoid others. An open patch of ground lay between me and the next coverage, and I watched the bridges and branches above me until movements stilled, then darted across. My swift movements landed me behind my next targeted hiding space, the lee of an enormous conifer trunk.

"Morning."

I jumped, spinning, throwing my arms between myself and my attacker. *You have a dagger, you idiot*, I berated myself. But drawing a weapon, when the enemy had magic and I had none? That offered a frightening next level of cruelty. Plus, my mother had gifted me the dagger… I didn't want to lose it.

The light-skinned boy from the day before stood before me, arms crossed, looking at me like I was a flower that had bloomed out of season.

"What are you *doing*?" I hissed, throwing my arms down, looking around for other attackers, but finding none.

"I was just puzzling out how I would get to the school, if I wanted to sneak in." He smiled briefly, like *he'd* said something embarrassing.

"What? *Why*?"

He grimaced. "I don't know. I get these ideas, and then they nag at me…" He trailed off, then shrugged, unable or *unwilling* to justify his actions. "Can I join you?"

My mouth worked, but no words came out. Was it a trick? *Should I run?* He'd already found me twice—that was more than coincidence. But if his intent was to harm me, he already had me. No one would see us from above, and so few trod the soil to reach school… except High Elf Varitan, who behaved as though jumping through the trees or traveling the hanging bridges was beneath him.

The boy started off toward the school, and waved me to join him. Flabbergasted but curious, I followed. The learning tree sat on the west side of E'anashys, just like my home, but the abundant elfbloom near the school signified its sitting *inside* the town, whereas you would need a keen eye to spot the plant near our dwelling place.

"Have you lived here long? What's the school like?" he asked.

I narrowed my eyes at him, though walking ahead of me, he wouldn't see it. Why all the questions? "Why are you here?" I asked. "Why were you waiting for me?"

After a few steps, he answered. "My father sent me to gather… information… from the kids of the town." His pauses worried me—what was he hiding? "They… mentioned… you."

"And you wanted to see the oddity for yourself?" I couldn't keep the sneer from my voice. *Come see the freak! Witness the Bereft!*

"My father wants to speak with your High Elf teacher." The boy's shoulders fell for a moment, some silent inner conversation he chose not to share. He'd completely ignored my tone and implication. "But I told him I would meet him at the school. I *hoped* I might run into you."

I stopped.

The boy walked on a few paces, then halted as well. He looked back, raising an eyebrow at me.

"Why?" I asked, ready to dash off.

"Why are you always alone?" he responded, his tone holding nothing but curiosity.

I drew my dagger.

He looked sheepish. "I have my reasons. You're safer if you don't know too much." Then he turned and started walking again, waving me to follow.

I let him go. Why did he hope to find me, a Bereft, lurking in the underbrush?

He walked a few more steps, then turned back and gave me an awkward and hesitant wave and a smile. "See you at school," he said, pausing before he added, "Elliah," and he continued on his way, casually disappearing into the foliage.

I waited, confused. Confused by my fears. He hadn't attacked. He hadn't confronted me at all.

I returned my dagger to its sheath, looking at the space where I'd last seen him like the foliage held answers. I replayed the events in my mind. He'd made no frightening moves at all. In fact, he'd smiled…

a lot. Was it possible… that someone might want to be my friend? I doubted it with every fiber of my experience, but desperately desired it. *Don't be stupid, Elliah,* I told myself. *He was playing you. Why else wouldn't he tell you why he was looking for you?*

Yet, I followed the boy. Hughelas. He'd called himself Hughelas Do'wood. Do'wood… not of the woods. He'd named himself a foreigner, though with skin and hair so light, it was evident anyway.

I traced his footsteps, not trying to catch up, until they disappeared into the mess of countless days of children's tracks at the base of the stairs spiraling up the learning tree, an ancient silvervein that had endured much from its occupants. Silverveins formed the core of every Wood Elf town, the thousand-year-old trees stood taller and wider than any others, and elves whose magic tended to nature worked with the silverveins to form homes, stairs, and bridges to other trees.

Elves had grown the wooden stairs of the learning tree through magic and care, and the tiny white elfbloom that dotted the railing that time of year made it particularly eye-catching. But Hughelas wasn't hard to spot, conversing with a hulking elf that the smaller children stared at with mouths agape. The large elf's arms looked bigger than my legs… maybe my waist. A thick tunic covered his chest, leaving the light skin of his muscular arms bare. Those massive arms were decorated with patterns of artwork, blue swirls and symbols that looked familiar but meant nothing specific to me. His blond hair reached almost to his shoulders, and I marveled at the hair on his face, also blond, and about half a finger long. I'd not understood what I'd read about Warders having hair on their faces; I'd pictured it looking like animal fur. But the hair didn't cover his whole face—just under the nose and chin and along the jawline. No other race of elves had such a thing. He'd covered his legs with a tough-looking hide that also covered his feet—poor clothes for jumping around in trees… but his people didn't live in trees. They fought trolls along the Contentious River, a waterway that plowed through canyons between the mountains that separated elves from the dragons. A wooden handle poked above his wide shoulders, and a knife, or perhaps a short sword, sat holstered at his waist. The broad and encouraging smile on his face, as he listened to his son, confused me—it belied his mountainous form in some elusive way.

The warrior elf spoke with his comparably diminutive son, and I avoided their attention. Unfortunately, they created a problem for me—there was no way around the crowd of gawkers. I first thought to wait them out, but the crowd only grew as more students arrived at school and whispered words drew them down from above.

I couldn't wait forever—my stomach knotted at the idea of yet another detention where I sat with Professor Varitan, doing nothing of consequence in silence. Should I climb another tree and cross on a bridge? With the crowd being drawn to the stairs, that might have proven the safer choice. I looked up at the myriad limbs and hanging bridges that enabled passage from nearby trees. I sighed—it would still make me late. So I chose an angle of approach that would bring me in behind most of the children. With their eyes glued to the Warder, I would pass many of them unseen, though the smaller children who had lingered on the stairs to see over their fellows' heads would notice me.

"Leah Lacking." The whisper started in front of me, though I didn't see from whom—someone young.

But children's whispers spread like flames on dry kindling. An unorchestrated chorus of "Leah Lacking" informed me that even those behind me had turned. Such a stupid nickname... it didn't even sound like my name, not that it mattered to *them*.

"I failed my magelight exam because of her."

"She ruined our whole cantrips lesson."

"Gorre died because Mylaerla's Heals wouldn't land."

I nearly missed a step at those words. That was the type of rumor that would force us to leave town. We'd done so well in E'anashys that I'd begun to think we might hide there forever. But any unfortunate coincidence with magic always found its way home to me. My mother would want me to tell her.

I climbed the stairs, having navigated the crowd successfully, half in a daze, wondering how quickly my mother would want us to leave town while also pondering the intent of Hughelas Do'wood. He hadn't behaved like the others. Did he plan some elaborate trap, or was he being... kind? Experience taught that the former was the more likely. *But... what if?*

I was so lost in daydreams of maybes, I failed to dodge when someone charged down the curved stairs, knocking me on my butt. I looked up into the wide eyes and fear-filled grimace of Kethryllia, a girl roughly my age who I'd avoided like poison-berries since the day she'd "helped" me down the stairs with a gust of wind. But, in a heartbeat, her grimace became a sickening smile.

She pushed herself off me, then jerked me upright, whispering, "You better run, Bereft!"

I stood there for a moment, confused. Why help me up if she

meant to punish me? But her smile foretold her intent to see me suffer.

And then she cast a spell.

Frightened of the possibilities of her casting, even though it might not take, I fled down the stairs. I heard her attempt a spell, but nothing happened, and I kept running, targeting the inside of the circular stairs both to jump down two at a time, and to cut off her view of my retreating form quickly.

More chanting, louder and urgent, pursued me, and my foot snagged. I would have fallen hard, but instead of hitting the solid wooden stairs, a bed of vines met my nosedive, tangling my arms and legs even as I struggled to rise.

"I got her," Kethryllia shouted, and I froze. Not, "I've got you." No, she'd said, "I've got *her*." I squirmed until I could see to whom she spoke.

Our teacher, the High Elf Professor Varitan, stood at her side, breathing hard, staring at me, his sour visage puckered tighter than ever before. "How *dare* you," he snarled, his fury loosely reined.

My relationship with the school's High Elf teacher had always felt like a stroll over a rushing river covered with thin ice. My mother had rarely allowed me to attend school before we moved to E'anashys. In previous towns and villages, I'd been a visiting student who would move on in a month... a week... a day. I'd assumed she wanted to keep me away from other children, but E'anashys had shed new light on that belief. When we'd first arrived, we'd chanced upon the teacher, and instead of scurrying me discreetly out of sight, she'd narrowed her eyes and stalked directly over to the High Elf. I would never forget how his eyes had widened when he'd found her standing before him, and despite his being more than a head taller, he'd looked frightened, like a cornered animal. They'd exchanged words, and she'd returned to me with the declaration that I would be attending school in E'anashys. And yet, despite whatever past she wouldn't share with me, he had always treated me with scorn, looking for any excuse to criticize my efforts. I cringed at the familiar ease with which he accused me.

Yet I was unable to answer. Vines covered my mouth, and... I had no idea what he was talking about. Professor Varitan slinked down the stairs, his dark blue robes revealing the tips of his lighter slippers each time he descended a step.

"We let you into the village, into the school, and you repay us with *treachery*."

The scurry of little feet sounded behind me. We had an audience. I looked past Varitan at Kethryllia—her facade of shocked innocence was briefly betrayed by a grin that fled as quickly as it had arrived.

My view became the bottom of a blue robe, and I noticed the black fabric that formed the neatly sewn hem, as well as the wave of black I'd previously missed on his slippers. He crouched down and yanked my bag free of the vines, his merciless rending of the vine causing a retreat of small feet.

Then he jerked upright at the echoing clomp of a heavy tread ascending the stairs behind me. I tried to turn but could not—the vines had secured their grip on me. They clutched me tight enough to hurt.

The look on the professor's face—somehow both superior and intimidated—reinforced my suspicion that the Warder stood behind me.

"Can I help you?" Professor Varitan asked, his voice cracking.

"I'd hoped to talk with the High Elf my son told me he had the pleasure of learning from at this school." Though the Warder's face was outside my field of vision, I heard the smile in his words, his voice surprising me in its pitch, nearly matching that of Varitan, where I'd expected it to be much deeper. "I see I have the great fortune of arriving at an opportune moment—I get to see the wisdom of a High Elf in a difficult situation." Something prodded my back through the foliage. His boot?

"She was caught stealing *this*!" I heard a sloshing noise like a decanter of juice.

"Scrollwriter's Ink?" said the Warder.

Scrollwriter's Ink! He'd pulled that from my bag? He was framing me! Then I remembered the cruel smile on Kethryllia's face. *She'd* framed me. She'd put that in my bag. But I hadn't been anywhere near the scroll room. I'd been with Hughelas. All I needed to in order to be redeemed was for him to speak up.

"Yes," agreed my teacher. "She *stole* it from the school," he spat.

"And what," the Warder said, almost cheerful, "will be done with the culprit of this pernicious crime?"

"She will be banished from the school," Varitan declared.

Of course Hughelas wouldn't speak up for me, even though he could have vouched for my whereabouts. It was his chance to show he was one of them.

"High stakes indeed," responded the Warder. "May the Mother

of Trees grant you wisdom in abundance." *Mother of Trees…* he invoked the name of the legendary goddess as though he expected direct intervention. Despite all the legends about her, or because of them, I suspected she was no more real than Talena Talonforged. And my mother's only mentions of her sounded more like curses.

Banished from the school? I laughed under the mask of vines and leaves, tears escaping my eyes at the mix of pain from the ever-tightening grip of green cords and the relief at the teacher's words. Mother and I moved from village to village whenever my condition drew too much attention. After the incidents of the day, I would be as glad to leave E'anashys behind as they would be to see me go. Still, the false accusation stirred my anger, and my self-loathing burned as I considered the daydreams that had distracted me as I'd climbed the stairs— I'd believed Hughelas might *like* me. *Stupid, foolish girl*, I berated myself.

I realized that the pause in their conversation had grown long, and through my shrouded ears, I heard whispering. Small children murmuring their awe at having witnessed the entrapment of a thief. But also…

"My son believes you have provided him, in your wisdom, a test," the large man said, stepping around the vines past my head and entering my small field of vision. My teacher climbed up a stair and moved toward the center of the spiral, relinquishing his spot to the bigger man. Yet I saw only the Warder's boots and pants, the thick leathers that didn't fit in the woods—one would never be able to feel the limbs beneath one's feet in those. The boots were huge—befitting of the behemoth Warders I'd heard and read about.

The teacher stammered, fumbling in a manner I had never heard in his authoritarian rule of our classroom. In his way, he'd been so much worse than the teachers in the other villages, always full of himself and critical of any lack of understanding. But he'd also been abundant in knowledge, and not as quick to judge and cast me away as other teachers had, ready to get the Bereft out of their midsts. The latter, of course, had changed in the last few minutes.

"He points out that Scrollwriter's Ink stains the flesh—rather quickly, in fact. I can already see the touch of it on your fingers." A pause, presumably while Varitan examined his hands. "The girl wears no gloves, and yet her hands…" The large man knelt and tore vines away from my hands. "They remain unmarked." Fingers wormed their way between a vine and my chest, momentarily hurting me even more, then blessedly freeing me as the vine snapped in two. I took a deep, intoxicating breath.

No one spoke, and I could only imagine what took place. An examination of my hand. A search around the crowd. What if Kethryllia had the brains to wear gloves?

"Kethryllia." Varitan sounded surprised. "Why do you hide your hands?" Because I lay on the stairs, I felt the vibrations that accompanied the clomp of booted feet that climbed up, but the Warder's mighty boots stayed put. "Show them to me. At once!"

Varitan growled with disgust, and the remaining vines dissipated, slithering back into the step from which they'd sprung. Strong hands grabbed my arms, first preventing me from falling as the vines released me, then lifting me and setting me upright.

He let me go and reached out an arm to Hughelas, who approached his father. The Warder had righted me two steps above him, placing my eyes more or less even with his. Twinkling blue-green eyes and smiling lips made the huge man unexpectedly approachable.

"Well," the large man said, turning his attention to his son and losing his smile. His father placed his hand on Hughelas, his palm spanning his son's entire shoulder. "You made an enemy today, my son." Then he pulled his son in for a hug. His smile returned with contagious ferocity. "I couldn't be more proud! Mother of Trees," he said to the air. "Thank you."

Zoras * 2

700 years before

"Welcome back to the front," Wynruil said, nodding at me.

It was a different hill, a different land altogether, but wherever war went, Wynruil would be. And no matter where one traveled in the Border Woods, if Wynruil was there, one had found "the front."

"I am pleased to return." Partial truth. I had work to do, and the interruption slowed progress. But news had reached the Heartlands— another Warlord had risen. It pleased me that Wynruil thought to summon me.

"I doubt that." He stood, laying a pen on the table before him, and approached me. "I've heard about your schools and libraries, the cities you've seeded. You aim at understanding the fundamentals of magic."

"I try, sir. I am not so egotistical as to believe I must solve the problem you've given me alone. Thelian has written a remarkable treatise on magic in nature—"

"I've seen your fingerprint," the commander interrupted, "on elven culture, my solver of unusual problems."

I blinked at that. I'd spent decades with Wynruil, learning strategy and tactics. Watching him organize troops, learning how to motivate people, and training with a sword enough that I at least wouldn't impale myself. But after seeing firsthand how the trolls resisted our magic, I'd taken my leave, intending to tackle the problem he'd presented to me. My solutions would only work if people didn't realize they were being manipulated. Did he really know?

He walked back to his table and fished through a box, coming back with a bottle and two wooden cups. "The Wood Elves seem particularly influenced," he said, handing me the cups with a twitch of a smile. "They will get a reputation." He poured the contents of the bottle into the two glasses and set the bottle on the table, taking a glass from me and drinking.

"We can only hope, sir." So he understood. "You were right that magic grows with new generations. Gorson's trials documented the phenomenon very clearly." I sniffed at the cup. Elven wine, but strong.

Speckleberry? "Though it manifests differently in each race. The Alluvium create spells of greater potency while the Wood Elves regenerate mana more quickly. The High Elves—"

Wyrnruil cut me off. "But only *you* would think to influence our morality." He looked up at the stars. "Children on the war front. Children having children." He sighed, and we stood in silence. I'd long ago become accustomed to awkward silences… even enjoying the quiet. I'd gotten good at creating a show, but the commander of the elven army didn't need a show. He poured himself another drink and with a twitch of his head, he asked me whether I wanted more. I shook my head no.

"The Salts have abandoned the front," he said.

That was news to me. Why would they leave? How would we fight without them?

Wynruil sighed. "I had wondered when it would happen. Salts don't have the heart for war—they were made for peace."

"Made for peace?" What did that mean?

"Salts for peace, Alluvium for protection. Wood Elves, life and beauty; Warders for Truth; High Elves," he said with a wink, "for solving problems. You see, your little manipulations played right into their strength."

With that confirmation, I knew he'd seen how I'd encouraged promiscuity among the Wood Elves. But I'd never heard anything like what he'd said about the races, characterizing them. Salts for peace? I appreciated peace, but we needed them to fight. If that was their nature, I'd need to find a way to steer that. But of all the attributes, one stood out as the most unbelievable.

"Warders for Truth?" I asked. "They're so big… and simple!"

"So is the T," Wynruil answered with a smile.

That wasn't right. The Truth was complicated—that's why it required so much research, so much effort. Warders were built to fight, just like the Alluvium. Through work, Truth would belong to the High Elves.

Wynruil again refilled his glass, then held the bottle out to me. I shook my head—I wanted to think.

"You are very annoying," Wynruil finally said.

"So I am told."

"But your cold calculations and manipulations may save us."

"So I hope."

He grunted. "It didn't use to be like this, you know."

"What didn't?" I asked, curious.

"Any of this. The trolls, the elves…" His tongue stumbled. Not his first bottle to open that evening? He pointed at the Witless Mountains. "The *mountains*!"

Wait? Was he saying…

"These were plains when I was a boy. Sure, mountains existed, but not here. Trolls existed, but they weren't a problem. Then, *They* arrived."

I realized my mouth hung open and I closed it. He spoke of a time of legend, before the Mother of Trees and Father of Stones, before gods walked the world.

"Sure, we had a thousand years of peace, while the world healed. Dust clouded the sun for a century." He spat like the taste still lingered on his tongue after countless years. "Pockets of elves survived. So many died. Almost everyone. And ever since the world recovered, life has been nothing but fighting."

He'd lived through the breaking of the world. Old guard. Stories told of a cataclysmic event that transformed the world, and legends of elves who had lived through it.

"You're thousands of years old," I said, uttering the unbelievable. If he told the truth, I'd squandered a valuable source of information, learning only battle tactics from him.

"Everyone used to be. What's remarkable is how few of us are left. Maybe five?" He made a disgruntled noise. "They might all be gone. I don't keep up." He waved at the battlefield. "Been busy."

Busy. Busy being the front.

"What was it like? Before the Breaking." How would I know whether he spoke the truth? The truth was never simple.

"Easy," he answered. "So easy." He downed his wine and poured another. "The Warders believe the Mother of Trees came to save us. She talks to them the most, you know." I knew. He shrugged. "Kindred spirits perhaps? Hopeless dreamers. She kept the Wood Elves and you High Elves alive during the days of the dark, but with the Warders, she *shares her stories*."

Had she ignored the other races? "And do *you* believe the Mother of Trees is our savior?" I wanted to steer back to that topic.

"I believe…" His eyes flashed. Anger? Madness? He continued in a fierce whisper. "I believe she came to *punish us!*"

I crinkled my nose at his words, or perhaps his vehemence. I'd done things in the last centuries that I hadn't liked, and I heard a hint in his voice of what that might do to me over a thousand years. I squirmed, trying to wriggle away from my internal echo of his madness. "She fights for the elves." I tried to sound calm and reasonable, but I heard the defensiveness sneak out.

"To punish us for our sloth, our laziness, our privilege." He waved me closer, as though the hillside, emptied because he'd sent his captains away, might have hidden ears.

I obliged, closing the distance between us.

"I once overheard her telling the Warders," he said, "that she'd created elves to be her helpers, advocates of magic and life throughout the stars. What do you make of that?"

I didn't know what to make of it. But I vowed to myself to spend more time among the Warders. I'd focused primarily on educating the High Elves and growing the population of Wood Elves. Schools and libraries for the first, and tales of romance and debauchery for the other. Some, I'd written myself. *Spellbound Scandals: Tales of Temptations* had proven a big hit among our nature-loving cousins. It wasn't that the customs of the Warders, Salts, and Alluvium didn't interest me, but there were only so many hours in the day. I'd spent decades sending them all to battle, but I hadn't learned more than I'd needed to make good use of them. Warders were brutes who were good with shield magic. Salts manipulated the weather. Alluvium had mastered fire. Wood Elves were strong Healers. High Elves cast mind spells—almost useless against trolls, but we could bolster the courage of those fighting.

My brain spun on how to put measures into place so that I could step away from my ongoing efforts and learn more of the other races. I would need to accelerate my endeavors to enable magic which allowed communication over distances. That mystery, that *truth*, had hidden itself well. A Warder would never discover it.

"I think we failed her." He pulled me back from my musings. "And She manifested in Her current form to punish us, or to cleanse us of impurities."

His words still made no sense, yet there was *something* there. If the world had lived in lazy peace for as long as the old guard insisted, why would She disrupt that? But I also wondered, how much of what I was hearing was just the mouthings of speckleberry wine?

He slammed his cup to the table, emptied, then lifted the bottle and found it empty as well. He spun and threw the bottle with some anger, and I saw a glowing molten blob of glass fly out of sight.

"I have two problems for you this time." Wynruil, mercurial, spoke calmly, like he hadn't just melted glass without any sign of casting a spell. Generational magic resulted in increased potency among Alluvium, but only experience brought such finesse. "The first, this Warlord. He's crafty. They're all crafty, but this one…" He shook his head, then his shoulders, like a wet animal shaking its fur dry. "What's worse, I fear the Mother intends to use the same tactic she used on the last Warlord. I dread to see how many trolls would break through her shield. Zoras, you can't let that happen."

"How…" but my mind was already calculating possibilities, and Wynruil wouldn't have asked if he'd found a solution to that problem. So I changed what I was going to say. "And the second thing?"

"I'm weary of fighting, young Zoras. I want to rest, in a nice cave, far from the front. I want to *leave the front!*" He spat the last out with a vehemence that made me question his grip on sanity. Was he dramatizing—I had become better at that myself—to prove his point? He needed a change. My gut clenched with worry—did his grip on reality grow tenuous? What would elves do without Wynruil?

Perhaps it was because he presented the two problems to me at once. If he had presented me with either of those problems on their own, I don't think the idea would have popped into my head. Or perhaps the notion occurred to me because of the way he'd behaved in our private meeting, with his fits and emotional outbursts. The solution was crazy, and it would have its repercussions, but I believed it would accomplish his goals.

I put a hand on his shoulder and asked, "Can you find peace in a world that believes you've lost your mind?

"I am Beldroth, little princess. My son tells me you and he are friends."

Hughelas scrunched up his face, embarrassed. About which statement? His father's appellation of *little princess*, which admittedly, had made me squirm on the inside, or his declaration of our friendship? We'd barely talked.

I needed to get home—we would have to move again, and Mother would want to act quickly. My feelings on the subject had grown more complicated over the last decade. As a younger girl, I'd either liked a place or I hadn't, and I'd responded with a child's emotion about my preferences—not that any display affected my mother's choice to leave, though I suspected my outbursts influenced our destination. But as I'd aged, I found myself more conflicted. I'd never made friends, so I'd never minded leaving, but I had of late wondered if leaving explained why I had no close companions. If I had stayed in one place long enough, would I have found someone willing to befriend a Bereft?

"Thank you for helping me," I said to the Warder, out of an unfamiliar need to return his kind words and friendly tone. I turned my eyes from Beldroth to Hughelas, wanting to be sure they each understood that I thanked them both. "I must return home now."

"Home?" the Warder said, his eyebrows bunching, but his smile remaining. "School has yet to begin!"

I couldn't explain how dangerous it would be for me to stay. Hughelas might have made an enemy, but so had I, though I'd done nothing. When I became an object of fascination in a village, we moved on. Sometimes we stayed only days at a new place, sometimes we managed years, but as I'd neared adulthood and become more independent, I'd had to learn the signs to watch for, as my mother was not always by my side. I wondered, not for the first time, though I'd never asked, if my mother resented the life my existence had forced upon her.

I simply repeated myself, "I must return home. Thank you again." And I left them behind, something inside me tightening at the thought of never knowing whether Hughelas might have become a friend.

Within seconds, Hughelas caught up, and I turned to find his father as well.

"We will make sure you get home safely," his father said, his smile buried under something harder, something that suggested ferocity without being fierce. Something unstoppable. Something… protective? I could not think of anything that would change his mind or alter his course of action. A fleeting thought crossed my mind that I should be worried—that I had reason to distrust the two visitors—but that idea caught no purchase. I nodded once and set off.

I tried to convince myself that my mother would not be angry about their following. She had, after all, wanted to sell him magic scrolls. I winced at the irony of being accused of stealing Scrollwriter's Ink, when my mother had, in fact, been trying to create scrolls to sell to the very Warder who had championed my innocence. Scrollwriter's Ink was expensive and not a luxury mother could afford. She had to use normal ink, which decreased the efficacy of the scroll. A scroll written with the special ink would sell for more, making it possible to buy more of the expensive ink, but if one had no money to start with…

I took the land route home—the idea of the large Warder hopping from limb to limb was laughable, and the trees didn't deserve such punishment. But with him for a guard, I didn't have to skulk in the underbrush or dash through the clearings. I led them straight toward our tree on the outskirts of E'anashys… as straight as one can travel in the woods anyway. Hughelas walked beside me, and his father trailed behind. When I'd look back, he'd be smiling but alert, a hand resting absently on the handle of his blade, the wooden haft of another weapon bobbing over his shoulder.

"Are you okay?" Hughelas asked me. "Do you need any Healing?"

I rolled my shoulders, then twisted my body from side to side as we walked. "All good," I said. "Besides, it wouldn't help."

"It wouldn't help?" Hughelas's eyes weren't on me as he spoke, but bounced around, as though hoping for answers from the underbrush and trees.

I had learned to be cautious with information, so I didn't tell him that spells didn't always work on me. External manifestations caused by spells… sure. But ones meant to operate directly on me via magic? They might not land. Like with trolls.

Instead, I kept my mouth shut and marched on, unconcerned about upsetting him with my silence. I would, after all, be gone before the sun bid the trees good morning.

"Why?" I asked, desiring to change the topic. "Why didn't you just vouch for me? You didn't have to pin the blame on Kethryllia. You could have just told Professor Varitan that you'd been walking with me, that I couldn't possibly have stolen the ink."

Hughelas shrugged, as uncommunicative as I had been. I returned the gesture.

Fair was fair.

We walked on in silence, but when I glanced sideways at him, I caught a grin that had escaped from his feigned disinterest.

Unable to help myself, I grinned too.

And the next time I glanced his way, the grin had etched itself firmly onto his pale face. *Is this what friendship feels like?*

"We are staying at the mill," he offered, presenting neutral ground. The mill—at one time it had probably been simply a mill, but over time it had grown into a conglomeration of land-bound wooden structures along a stream that ran through the north-east edge of E'anashys. In addition to the mill itself, storage rooms housed trade goods—mostly speckleberry wine making its way west—and lodgings provided rest for weary traders. The entire collection of buildings had earned the appellation "the mill." I had spent little time there, as it was far from our tree and the school, but I had seen the buildings in my explorations of the town's perimeter, and I'd wanted to inspect them more closely.

"What is it like, sleeping inside of dead wood?" I wondered aloud. The elfbloom thinned in the space between the school and my home, though a discerning eye would still find it. When we traveled, we used the small white flowers of that vine as a barometer to know when we approached an elf village.

Hughelas cocked his head to the side, giving my question genuine consideration, though I hadn't meant to do anything but continue our conversation.

"I've never slept inside one of your rooms grown onto a tree," Hughelas said. "So I can't compare them. But I can say that the room at the mill isn't as comforting to me as a mountain cave. The walls feel… thin." A mountain cave. My mother and I had sometimes slept in small caves when we'd moved between towns, but I suspected Hughelas spoke of something much more grand. Talena Talonforged had traveled to the stone gardens of the Warders as well as the labyrinthian tunnels of the Alluvium. My excitement bubbled up at the very idea, but unfortunately…

"This is it," I said, halting and pointing at the silvervein tree before us. We didn't live in the village proper, but a small cluster of abandoned silverveins clung to the west side of E'anashys, and we had chosen one for lodging. Our silvervein had no stairs nor ramp—I had often imagined some long-forgotten battle between elves and trolls had demolished them—only a rope ladder that disguised itself among the vines clinging to the ancient brown and green behemoth. The ladder was not a necessity for me, as I could scale the tree easily enough. Mother climbed even better than I. But it came in handy when we needed to carry bulky items, like the carcass of a big game animal.

I looked askance at the large Warder and back at the rope ladder. The ladder had met its match.

"Thank you for walking me," I said to them both, then turned to Hughelas. "I'm sorry for the trouble it has made for you."

"I thank you for the opportunity to do the Mother's work," my pale could-have-been-a-friend answered, looking askance at his father as though checking whether he'd gotten the words right. Apparently, he did, for it brought not just a smile to the Warder's face, but a single bark of laughter.

To do the Mother's work? The Warder had referred to the Mother of Trees as well. They were religious fanatics?

A pinch of worry nibbled at me for having led them to my home, but I also realized it probably didn't matter—we wouldn't live there much longer. My smile became thinner, and I jumped to catch a higher rung of the ladder and scrambled quickly up.

"Elliah?" my mother's voice called from above, and I paused, looking down at the two figures below who had not yet left, then up to my mother, who peered out over a branch. I didn't want to yell up to her, to explain the situation within earshot of the two who had followed me. So I resumed my climb, hurrying my ascent.

When I reached the top, I found my mother not just waiting, but waiting with an arrow readied. She'd kept it out of sight, but she'd not left my climb to chance. She raised an eyebrow in question.

"It's okay," I said, deciding it was. They hadn't followed me up the tree, after all. And I didn't know what was normal for Warders—perhaps they regularly littered their vernacular with phrases about the Mother. Then I thought about my words in the context of being home rather than at school. "*They're* okay. But it's time for us to… go."

She grimaced, but nodded. "Pack," she said. "But first, let me see if I can sell the Warder the scrolls I've been working on. We need the money."

She turned and shouted down to the Warder and his son. "Prithee hold fast thine…" and she fumbled for a word and waved her hands, undoubtedly revealing her bow to those looking up. "… spot," she finished feebly.

Had she gone mad?

"What?" she said in response to the look on my face. "Warders talk all… formal," she explained to justify her behavior. That hadn't been my experience, though my sample size was admittedly small, and he *had* uttered a higher count of references to the Mother than I heard on an average day. She waved for me to go inside.

She stopped at the table, sighing and handing me her bow and quiver as she looked over both her finished works and the unfinished mess, and began rolling the completed scrolls. We had only one proper scroll case, and she would want it to carry her papers to our new home. Would she use it to sell the finished scrolls to the Warder, or keep it for herself? My gut tightened with guilt for the trouble I created… how difficult my mere existence made her life.

"Cover me," she said, heading back out.

Wait… what?

She looked back at my stupefied form and opened her eyes wide, then looked meaningfully at the bow. "Cover me," she repeated and disappeared through the mossy overhangs we used as a door.

I looked at the bow, a well-carved piece of wood, but nothing fancy. I'd used it before, hunting for dinner with Mother. But… I'd never used it to *protect* her. Elated but worried, I dashed after her. She'd already leapt to another limb, pulling the attention of the two waiting below, giving me a chance to move without being watched.

As quiet as a mouse, I leapt the opposite way, knowing intervening limbs would cover my movements, then scurried to another tree and dropped from limb to limb, finally stopping, elevated but close enough to the ground to hear their conversation.

I aimed for the Warder's chest as my mother dropped from the trees, landing near them. I had a clear shot, though I was a little askew to the Warder, which made his massive chest a slightly smaller target. But it also gave me a clearer view of what belonged to the handle that appeared above his shoulder—a war hammer. I pictured it being swung against a rocky troll. *Are all Warders so big?*

My mother approached them, holding the scrolls above her in one hand, and I realized they were only at the Warder's eye level. I was a little taller than my mother, though scrawnier—I hadn't filled in to my height. For some reason, the height difference between the Warder and my mother seemed greater than it had when I stood before him. "Scrolls," she said. "To aid thee in finding trolls most foul."

Beldroth and Hughelas exchanged a look, and Beldroth answered, "I mean no disrespect… my lady. But there is no such spell. And if there were, I'm not sure I would have a use for it. Trolls are not the most secretive of creatures. I've had no trouble spotting them. And, again, no disrespect, but the efficacy of scrolls, even from the hallowed halls of Alenor, leaves much to be desired." He looked up at our shack, indicting my mother's work based upon the quality of the facade of her workshop.

My anger flared for my mother's sake. She had a gift for festooning spells to parchment, even without the expensive ink that made Alenor's scrolls so pricey. In a flash of a daydream, I let an arrow fly…

"I find I must leave town quickly," my mother said, interrupting my dark vision, and dropping all pretense of grand language. "So I'll make you a deal. I have five scrolls here. Five copper for each, if you cast the first one and it works. If it fails, you get them all for free."

The Warder had stopped smiling. Without his smile, his countenance was like a mountain boulder, hard and cold. "As I said, I have no need for such a spell."

Changing tactics again, Mother said, "Then help a grieving widow with the poor orphan she's brought into her home?"

Widow? Orphan? I almost giggled, thinking my mother recognized she'd lost the sale, and might as well spit out the last seed.

Oddly, the Warder's face lit up, and Hughelas deflated. "A widow in need? I thank the Mother for crossing our paths. I'll gladly donate—"

But as he reached for a belt pouch, my mother flew into a rage. "I don't need your *charity*!"

A groan escaped me, my shoulders slumping, though I didn't dare lower the bow. Hughelas's reaction clicked in the context of my own. We both suffered from the same affliction: parental embarrassment.

"I have perfectly good scrolls *for sale*!" She wielded them like she intended to beat the Warder to death. "How dare you insult me with…"

As she railed on, the Warder went from light-skinned to blood red. "How *dare* you lie to a *Warder* about *widowhood*!" A part of me absently questioned the legitimacy of emphasizing three words in one sentence, but he made it work.

They continued yelling at one another, and I worried about my mother. Not just that he towered over her and had both a short blade and a massive hammer on his back, but also that I'd so shocked her with my sudden need for departure that her temper had frayed in an instant.

"If I may," a small voice squeaked.

Neither squabbler halted.

In a move that surprised me, Hughelas looked directly to where I hid in the trees and waved for me to come down. I thought I'd snuck into my hiding place unseen. Then he yelled, "IF… I… MAY!"

My mother and his father quieted, looking at him. I didn't leave my post—even if he'd seen me, my vantage point still served to protect my mother.

"I would like to take your deal," Hughelas said. He reached for his own pouch. "But at three coppers per scroll." He held out his hand. "It is all I can afford." He grinned and closed his hand. "Should the scroll work, of course."

Tiny insects buzzed in the silence that followed. My mother lowered her impromptu scroll-club and smoothed out the wrinkles where she had gripped them too tightly. Then she pulled one off the roll and held it out to Hughelas. The Warder's complexion had faded back to a light pink, and a smile cracked his stony visage.

Hughelas took the scroll and studied it, while the rest of us waited.

Scrolls activated upon incineration. Even I, Bereft, could activate one, though their chance of success diminished under a flame lit by me. In theory, even trolls were capable of using them, though the practical circumstances that would lead to such an event occurring had a tree's chance in the deserts of the red dragons.

"When you trigger it, look at Elliah," my mother said.

Look at me? Why?

But Hughelas just nodded, glancing up in my direction, though I should have been damned hard to spot. Then he returned to studying the scroll, as though reading it… as though *memorizing* it.

Nobody hurried him. My mother and Hughelas's father stared at one another with a heated wariness, two timber wolves squared off for the alpha position. The Warder's size looked like a clear advantage, but Mother had a fierceness—and brawn rarely dictated leadership among elves.

Finally, Hughelas lifted the scroll with one hand, murmured an incantation and gestured with the other, and a flame tore through the parchment.

Mother had told me that sometimes she observed a faint aura when scrolls released their spells. Some hint of almost-light. I'd never seen any such thing, and I wondered if she'd seen her tell when the scroll ignited.

Hughelas squeezed his eyes shut hard, rubbed them with his hands, then opened them and blinked rapidly. He squinted in my direction. "What in the…" He rubbed his eyes, looked at his own hands, then back up at me. "Oooooh," he murmured softly.

Oooooh? What is he seeing?

Hughelas turned to his father, then gasped lightly. He squinted and approached the Warder slowly, tilting his head from side to side like a curious bird. He circled his father, and the Warder turned his head comically in order to monitor his son. Hughelas looked back toward the direction of the school, squinting, then back at his father.

"I think I know how they're finding us," Hughelas said, and his father's eyes widened in interest.

As though on cue, the forest erupted with a screeching roar on the other side of the elves. All three of them spun, and I stared, trying to make out anything through the foliage. It was *not* a noise I recognized. It was not a noise of the forest.

The Warder had drawn a weapon—a war hammer so large I doubted I could lift it—while I'd searched the woods. Hughelas and my mother wielded knives, and she eyed the longer blade the Warder had left in its sheath.

But nothing stirred. Maddening seconds passed in the suddenly and disturbingly quiet forest. But I kept an arrow drawn, still squinting into the trees.

My ears perked with the sound of movement beneath and behind me. I was reluctant to turn away, leaving my mother exposed to unknown danger.

The distant forest emitted the screeching roar again, and a second later, another screech came from the forest to my left… and a third from below me. Unable to ignore the nearest threat, I peered down after the roars quieted, pointing my weapon as I heard something move rapidly through the forest beneath me.

A reptile with the bulk of the Warder charged forth, bee-lining toward the elves. It ran on all fours, covered in light green scales with stripes of yellow and black that ran from its head down the length of its body to the end of the long tail that whipped in small side-to-side movements as it ran. It dwarfed any drake I had ever seen, but was not so large as to fit my imagining of dragons, and it lacked… elegance.

I wanted to shout, to warn my mother, but I froze, afraid… afraid that if I called out, the fearsome creature might turn its attention to me, or that there might be more. No one had my back, and though my height should have comforted me, I had nowhere to hide. Paralyzed by fear, I missed my chance to fire at the second reptile that appeared, one that burst from the foliage very close to the woman I wished I'd never let climb down our tree.

Jenat, the First of the Lost

Ten years prior

Not because of what you are, the Wood Elf hissed. *Or not* just *because of what you are,* she amended. *Also because of* who *you are.*

The words whispered in my mind, not meant for me, but ringing with truth.

Threading the needle.

Dragons collect their dead.

It seems I've run to my death! The odd joviality in her voice finally made sense. The conclusion of a hard-fought struggle, the end of the pain of loneliness.

No… that was the past. One problem with Seeing—the past and the future were twines of the same rope, and I sometimes struggled to separate one from the other.

It seems I've run to my death! A Salt wandering the cold peaks my sisters and I called home. At first, I'd supposed her to be a bear as she marched through the blizzard, a bear who my younger sisters had chased from its home to obtain their shelter. But a bear would have more sense than to walk right into my den. Though Lost, I had learned enough history to realize my kind had never been charged with the care of her race—Salts were under the care of the blues—yet curiosity got the better of me, and I let her speak.

"It seems I've run to my death!" she'd said when she spotted me, her voice oddly jovial.

When nothing else happened… when she offered no other words, I prompted her. "Explain."

She jumped back, startled. Dragons and elves had not interacted since the Breaking, not in any meaningful way. But surely they knew we spoke their tongue. *Many of us don't anymore*, I reminded myself. I banished the stray thought; it had been *my* choice to pull my siblings and children into the lonely snow-capped mountains. The Salt began a rambling tale, and jumped again when I lit a magical fire—I didn't need it, but she did.

My wing spasmed, jerking me momentarily back to the present. If I hadn't already been beaten near to death, I might have been able to pull the details of the Salt's story to mind. Something about being trapped on an island and a daring escape, trolls and dragons and other adventures.

The particulars didn't matter so much as the fact that she drew me in; she made me care. And so I let her live, helped her on her way to those once under my custody. And I paid the price with my Sight. And we would both pay the ultimate price for my Sight. *Observation affects outcome!*

Not because of what you are, the Wood Elf hissed. *Or not just because of what you are. Also because of* who *you are.*

A young elf—one of the green's charges—threaded the needle of a future so fragile as to be a wistful dream. It was one of many crucial forks in her future, one I Saw through threads intertwined with the Salt who'd wandered into my cave, as lost in her own way as I. But it was a fork which resonated profoundly with me.

After a life of being Lost, of being the very first of the Lost, I realized—finally—that I was who my mother meant me to be all along. I had shared my understanding with my daughter, Arsyli, since I was cursing her to the same fate my mother had bestowed upon me. I had very little to give her, but sharing my Sight was like letting her smell a tasty meal without eating it. Was it good fortune that I had birthed her early, or was that also a chain reaction from my mother's Sight? Regardless, my daughter had her role to play, but was too young to work her Sight. I had shown her how my fate was sealed, not just because of what I was—the first of the Lost and a powerful Seer—but because of who I was: the abandoned daughter, the mother who would abandon her daughter, the dragon that didn't kill a lost elf.

I had arrived. Unfortunately, the lost elf hadn't been wrong; it had just taken longer than she expected. The act of Seeing had intertwined our fates, and our journeys would end together.

It seems I've run to my death!

Elliah ~ 5

Unlike me, the Warder did not freeze. His face reddened, veins flaring, as he swung the war hammer, slamming it into the side of the charging reptile's head.

But a second scaly beast bowled him over from behind. The Warder spun and jammed the shaft of his hammer like a wedge into the creature's snapping jaw. Hughelas, closest to me of the elves, plunged a knife into its flank, while my mother jabbed at an eye socket from the opposite side. The dazed lizard that had taken a blow to the head clumsily pulled itself up, and I finally unfroze.

I let an arrow fly. I'd hunted with my mother often enough, and the reptile stood relatively still as it regained its senses. The arrow flew true, into the eye, and presumably, into the reptile's brain. The beast froze, then dropped.

But I shouldn't have been watching my arrow and its effects. I had wasted time, being sure my shot reached its target, and I'd thrown away precious seconds enjoying my victory. I drew my next arrow, desperately hoping no one paid a price for my stupidity.

The Warder had regained his feet and scanned the forest for more danger alongside Hughelas and my mother, standing by the corpse of the reptile they'd all attacked.

Where's the third one?

From my perch, I had the best view, and I used it to search the forest floor in all directions. Nothing. I looked back at the other elves. They'd formed a triangle with their backs, still poised to defend their position, and my mother finally sought me out.

Her widening eyes gave me just enough warning to duck. My arrow flew wildly away as I rolled off the wide branch with the weight of a boulder slamming into me, teeth snapping in the space my head had occupied moments before. I grabbed desperately at a branch as I flew past, snagging it with one hand as searing pain burned the length of my torso. Clinging desperately to the tree limb, I spun back to grab the same branch with my other hand, recognizing that it should have held a bow and not remembering when I'd released it. I wondered at how much trouble I would be in, even as I heard branches snap below me, and I secured my grip just as a sickening *splat* reached my ears.

From the pain in my side, I imagined the lizard had raked a claw across me. I pictured the blood soaking my shirt, spreading, dripping down my leg to plop onto leaves or the forest floor. *Stop! Focus! If any more lizards appear, I am dead meat hanging on the tree, ripe for the picking.*

I could have dropped to the ground and lived, at least on a good day. Growing up in tall trees supplied an early and abundant education in falling well. But my side hurt immensely, and I closed my eyes hard, the world spinning and twisting while I clung tightly. Even if I lived through the fall, I would worsen my injury. So I pried open an eye and pulled myself up, surprised by the difficulty and pain involved, climbing from the lesser branches until I reached a solid limb to sit on. The spinning world had slowed as I'd exerted myself, but then a wave of dizziness threatened to cast me back off my hard-won perch, and I grabbed on with my legs and squeezed my eyes shut until it passed.

"I'm here, Elliah," came my mother's soft voice from nearby. I opened my eyes, fearing I would trigger another dizzy spell, but risking it for the comfort of seeing my mother. "I'm here," she said again, closer. I tried to roll my head back for a better look behind me, but the world performed an elegant pirouette just for me, then everything went dark.

Zoras * 3

"Sir…"

I waved off the interruption—establishing strong leadership among the Wood Elves would be key to enabling them to move from small villages to proper towns. These little parties I hosted seemed frivolous, but they let me watch people, determine their strengths and weaknesses, and grow them into what their people needed. With my campaigns to encourage same-race breeding, it had become increasingly difficult to attract a crowd of both Wood Elves and High Elves. In fact, I feared I'd lost control of the reins—the height and golden hair of the High Elves far outnumbered the occasional glimpse of the far more dynamic blond, red, and ebony hair colors the Wood Elves sported. Not one Alluvium nor Warder had joined the party, though they still appeared on the front, and I'd yet to coax a Salt off of their ships to mingle with us. For the most part, that served the need of increasing our racial specialties in magic, but it raised concerns about the unity of elves.

"Sir," the voice insisted. Maintaining my smile, I leaned slightly to indicate to Axilya she should whisper in my ear. "It's your crystals, sir."

I didn't like having an in-person conversation interrupted by someone trying to reach me through the communications crystals. An odd mix of pride and irritation swept over me. Pride that I'd driven the creation of the magical crystals to fruition *and* understood the magic enough that I grasped the mechanics. Irritation because I didn't like how reachable I'd become. The advantage of quick access to distant information had a price. "Which?"

"Several, sir. *All* the red ones and one white."

I furrowed my brows. "If you'll excuse me," I offered my guests. Within a few steps, I'd already forgotten about them. *All the* red crystals lighting made no sense—Axilya must have made a mistake.

I avoided conversation, weaving through my party with my focus elsewhere. Another Warlord—it was the only explanation. But it didn't account for *all* the crystals which lit. One particular crystal I would not have expected to light with the others.

I climbed two flights of stairs and cast a spell to remove the trap I left on the door. Even Axilya didn't have permission to enter my communications room; though from her room she had a small window to observe whether any crystals lit up. Why had she been in her room in the middle of the party? Well, I suppose I couldn't promote promiscuity and not expect my staff to respond. I took note of my double entendre to save for later use.

One white and all the reds; Axilya hadn't been wrong. A green lit up before my eyes, and on its heels, a red went dark. That wasn't good. Sighing about the lack of sleep portended by the crystals, I closed the peephole to Axilya's room. Sitting at my desk, I found the next blank page in my notebook, unstopped my ink, and cast my spell.

***

Hours later, I was startled out of my ponderings by a rapping at my door. By its insistence, I assumed it had gone on for some time.

"Yes?" I shouted, standing and stretching my back and neck. My desk was a mess of maps and notes, some torn from my notebook and held in place by small clips of my own invention.

"Would you like a drink, sir? Or any food? Your guests have retired."

My stomach growled in response. "Thank you, Axilya. You are a wonder."

"I know," she shouted back, and then silence.

A Warlord had attacked. There'd been feints all along the Borderlands, but he'd driven the real thrust just south of the Wood Elf town of Allurya, pushing west hard. That meant he was headed to the Heartland. I assumed his target was the Mother of Trees, whom we'd moved for her own protection after the previous Alluvium commander lost his mind and burned the entire forest southwest of Bellon. Crazy, that business. But it achieved the desired goals.

To think the Warlord's target might be me was narcissistic to the extreme—I had no such illusions. Yet that hadn't stopped some from suggesting as much. Millennia of stories told of the Mother of Trees saving the elves. I knew—and I'd guarded the secret well—that *we* protected *Her*. The trolls targeted *Her*. I had only suspected it before, but the information I'd gathered that night was incontrovertible.

Every Alluvium commander spoke of trolls, and I'd had to gather information from the leaders and then circle back through them all with explanations. One thing I'd failed to appreciate about Wynruil when he'd commanded? He was not suicidal. Hot tempered? Sure. But he erred on the side of living to fight another day.

Not so with the Alluvium commanders I'd spoken with through the night. We'd lost one overenthusiastic leader who'd decided to die before letting the trolls get past, though I only received that report second-hand, from a commander ready to follow his leader's fate. I had no official role on the front, but since enough information flowed through me, I influenced the elf war force more than anyone realized. I just needed to decide which direction to push them.

The Mother prized life. Even in the oldest stories, she never took the offensive. Never pounced after the periodic Warlord met its fate. She left them to rebuild. Grow stronger. But we were losing. Would ultimately lose. What would it take to convince the elves to change? Losing the Mother? Would elves attack the trolls to save Her?

As they usually did, an orthogonal idea popped in my head—did we have other allies? Enemy of my enemy?

Axilya returned with a tap at my door, interrupting my reverie, but handing over a much desired tray of food and an open bottle of wine with a glass. I followed her interested gaze back to my desk. *Ah, yes.* I hadn't responded to all the jewels. One had turned off and on all night.

Shutting the door, I readied my food and wine, taking a couple of nourishing bites before tackling the last red. I'd saved it because it made no sense—Wynruil wasn't on the front.

I cast my spell and my mind connected with another. The relay through a communication crystal didn't come through as clearly as casting the spells directly with another mage. One couldn't see properly while communicating through the crystals. Instead of what actually lay before my eyes, I found myself lost in a fog.

"Wynruil," I said in greeting—he would hear my voice through the fog, the same as I would hear his.

"Took you long enough," he answered testily.

"There's trouble on the front," I replied, though he would have heard that through other sources. So why contact me?

"There's more trouble than you realize," he replied. The shadows in the misty semi-reality surrounding me darkened.

"Lay it on me," I said, though I didn't feel capable of tackling another problem. The mist closed in around me.

"A baby died," his voice called out from the shadows.

The darkening mist lightened, became less dense… backed off. Tragic? Sure. An addition to my burden? By no means. The lighting had reflected my relief, though I felt bad that Wynruil would have seen the same. Still, I recognized that a show of sympathy was required. "I am sorry for your loss."

"There was something wrong with the baby, Zoras. We couldn't land spells on her. Despite our best efforts, we… lost her. It was as though she was a… a troll."

In a heartbeat, the mist darkened. The trolls were winning. On the front, and within the elves. Somehow they'd struck a blow, countered our increased breeding. I'd been wrong. It *was* my problem.

Elliah ~ 6

"By the Fruit of the Mother, why isn't my Heal working?" A voice, male, grunted in frustration.

"It's helping," answered my mother. "It's just not responding the way you expect. Keep at it." Then I heard her cast her own Heal spell. And again.

It was a ritual I'd lived through before.

"I don't have the mana to keep this up," the familiar male voice muttered. My brain wouldn't fire—I couldn't place the voice.

My mother paused between castings—her endurance was amazing, but even she needed breaks. "Buckle up, buttercup. You've got a long night ahead of you." She chuckled and resumed casting.

The male grunted again, but I heard amusement in it.

And the spells *were* working. What began as a sluggish return to consciousness became a rapidly clearing head. A mind unclouded to *all the pain* burning in my side. I gasped, opening my eyes to the sight of the huge Warder sitting at my feet, his legs crossed underneath him. Blood stained the ground by my feet. Hadn't we been in a tree? Scrolls and Warders and giant lizards. I'd fired an arrow. Had I fallen? I tried to sit up, but my mother restrained me, cradling my head in her lap.

"Welcome back," my mother said between castings. Then, "Take a break, big guy. She's stable, and your passing out helps no one."

The Warder blew out a sigh and nodded slightly.

I craned my head enough to see the blood trickling from my side through the hole rent in my flesh and clothes. I also found Hughelas perched by my side.

Hughelas closed his eyes and began chanting and waving his hands. I waited for him to finish, then asked, "You… know… Heal?" My raw throat wouldn't cooperate. Had I been yelling?

Hughelas opened his eyes. "I think so," he said, then grinned a little. "I can't tell if I cast it wrong, or it just didn't take because of… well, you know." He blushed slightly.

My mother stopped casting. "Try again," she said, and he closed his eyes and followed orders.

"Open your eyes," my mother said when he finished. He did.

"You are close." She held out her hands in a pattern, then moved a finger slightly, pushing them toward Hughelas. Hughelas looked puzzled, then nodded with an, "Oh!"

He closed his eyes and cast again, after which my mother said. "Better. Keep your eyes open when you cast."

"It helps me concentrate." He blushed and grimaced.

"It's a bad habit," my mother said. "You don't want to close your eyes in battle."

His father chuckled appreciatively.

My mother resumed casting, and Hughelas joined her. The pain in my side gradually eased, and the Warder swapped back out with Hughelas after a few minutes, returning to Heal duty.

Eventually, I moved my sore arm, then ran my other hand down my injured side. "I'm good," I said.

"You'll have a scar," my mother warned, not ready to halt her repeated castings.

I pushed myself into a sitting position, and she didn't stop me. I sat there, remaining still, letting my head stabilize. My mother climbed to her feet, and I saw how much blood stained her outfit. My blood.

The Warder stayed fixed beside me, looking as tired as I felt. "Thank the Mother that worked. But… I may just rest here a bit," he mumbled.

My mother's eyes darted to one of the reptilian corpses, then returned to the Warder, pinched.

"They won't attack us again anytime soon," he said.

My mother approached the Warder, holding out a hand to help him up, asking, "How do you know there won't be more of those things?"

The Warder looked at my mother's hand like it was a strange bug. Then he sighed and took it, his massive fingers going past her wrist. "They've come in waves." He got his feet under him as my mother leaned back and pulled, while he pushed off the ground with his other arm. "Days apart."

"Why?" my mother asked, trying to steady the Warder. Hughelas did the same from behind the large elf.

He shrugged, but he hid something—his honest face was not built for secrets.

My mother studied him, waiting for more. He looked uncomfortable, but didn't offer an explanation. My mother pursed her lips in irritation. "Well, best of luck with that." She turned and put an arm on my shoulder. "Let's go get packed." She helped me to my feet, and we started toward the rope ladder. Blood on the ground around it suggested how I'd gotten down from the tree.

"Wait," Hughelas said.

My mother rolled her eyes, but only I saw it.

She turned around and found Hughelas fishing coins from a coin purse.

"The spell worked," he explained. "Here's your money."

My mother seemed to weigh something, grinding her teeth as she considered the coins. She scanned the forest floor, and I followed her gaze. Along with the reptilian corpses, the scrolls lay on the ground, scattered but unharmed.

She turned back and accepted the coins.

"You're leaving town?" the Warder asked. She didn't reply, and after a pregnant pause, he added, "There's safety in numbers."

"Only when those numbers are on your side," my mother replied. "We are too easily targeted." She meant *I* was too easily targeted. "For us, there's safety in anonymity."

She took my arm and turned me away from the Warder and his son, helping me start up the rope ladder—the Warder would be too heavy to follow.

"Travel with *us*," the Warder said more loudly. "We never intended to stay. You would be safe with *us*."

Mother didn't turn around, but she paused. "With those things chasing you, coming in *waves*? That doesn't sound safe to me." But she'd stopped. We'd never traveled with anyone before. My whole life I had never had what most people would consider friendship, and I thought… maybe…

"True enough," he said. "But their attacks are days apart. We can escort you to the next village or town without fear of attack."

My mother still didn't turn around. She ground her teeth, considering. And I hoped for just a little more time… in the company of Hughelas.

Abruptly, she spun around. "We leave at dawn. Can you be ready?"

The Warder seemed more himself, smiling at her vehemence. "I am afraid I need a day. I came here to speak with the High Elf, but our meeting was interrupted."

He looked over at me, and I blushed. He'd walked me home instead of meeting with Professor Varitan.

"That erudite prick? What for?" Mother's filters had never worked well, but I winced at the insult. I supposed it didn't matter since we were leaving town, but I wouldn't want those words to reach my teacher's ears if I were staying.

Yet the affront brought a grin to the Warder's face, quickly hidden. "We are headed to Alenor." My mother's shoulders twitched. "I wanted to speak with the High Elf to learn what I might of his homeland."

"You just want information on Alenor?" my mother asked.

"Yes, generally. If the Mother smiles upon us, I would like to learn more of a rumor regarding the Mother of Trees." My mother raised an eyebrow, inviting more. "That a hundred years ago, she stirred and spoke."

"Why?" my mother asked. "Why that rumor?"

"I am a Warder," the large man said with pride. "We live on stories of the Mother."

My mother narrowed her eyes at him. Seconds ticked by. He kept smiling, a blissfully simple smile, and my mother continued her glare. Finally, she sighed and spoke. "Varitan won't know more than he's heard from passing storytellers. He left the Heartland well before the event you speak of. It was eighty years ago, not a hundred. I lived in Alenor at the time. If you want *that* story—" She pushed me to climb and started up behind me. After we were well above the Warder's reach, she turned and shouted back, "If you want to know *that* story about the Mother of Trees, I can tell you. But you better hurry, because we're leaving town at dawn."

What?

I stood there, stunned. On occasion, she'd stretched the truth to make a sale. But saying she'd lived in Alenor? Did she have more scrolls to offload? Did she want the protection the Warder offered? What was she after?

I looked behind me at the Warder and his son. I locked eyes with Hughelas.

"We better pack," said the Warder to his son. "The mill!" he shouted at my mother's back. "That's where we're staying. But we will be back! At dawn!"

Hughelas shot me a conspiratorial grin that made my skin tingle in unfamiliar excitement.

We packed, silent, each of us taking care of our own things. We'd done it enough, and, in fact, had become quite proficient at it. I packed my small-clothes and my alternate shirt, along with our sewing kit that I'd need to mend the rent in the top I wore.

I had just one prized possession I carted along: *The Tales of Talena Talonforged*, a child's story that chronicled the tales of an elf who traveled the world, having grand adventures. The tales were silly and made up, but the places she went were real, and I liked to find other books that talked about her travel destinations. From her stories, I had formed my mental map of the world and the elves and creatures who inhabited it. The book, clearly stolen—the craftsmanship of the leather-bound cover with its map of the world outshone any of our other possessions—had traveled with me for as long as I could remember.

My mother usually took care of packing the hard tack we might eat for sustenance, but when I left my room, I found she'd abandoned our abode, so I began packing provisions. She reappeared through our vine-covered doorway, her bow slung over her shoulder. I grimaced, but she comforted me. "Dropping the bow saved your life. I know I've scolded you for not taking care of our things, but that's about raising you not to be careless. Ultimately, *things* are just things… they're re-placeable." She leaned in close, resting her forehead against mine. "You're not."

The little girl in me rose to the surface. She hadn't shared a speech like that in a couple of decades, and it pulled at my memories and my heart, making me choke on my next intake of breath, drowning in nostalgia. Back before I understood my condition, what I *was*, I as-sumed everyone moved about as we did. My mother's reassurances had dropped like rain in the spring, providing love and life.

A chasm had formed when I'd started asking questions. Why did other children stay put? Why do other kids have fathers? How did elves work magic? My mother's reassurances lost their power to comfort, and we'd fought increasingly over the years… until her solaces had stopped, and her reassurances dripped on parched earth.

I hadn't realized how much I'd missed them.

But the gulf had become wider than a single nostalgic moment had the power to close. I put a hand between us, holding her there. A small part of me wished to be that little girl again, but more than years separated me from that girl. A chasm of fear and anger, doubts and in-securities, pain and loneliness, kept us at arm's length.

"I've packed our food," I said, pulling away awkwardly. I fumbled for something else to talk about. "Will the dragons collect the ones we killed?" *Dragons collect their dead.*

She didn't take the bait. She wrapped a hand behind my head and held me there, as though I just needed a little more time. And I let her, not entirely wanting out.

"Those weren't dragons," she said. "We won't be visited by dragons securing their corpses. Wolves or wildcats will feed on them."

Then she released me and looked around the room. She'd liked the place, a habitat larger than we'd usually found, far enough from oth-ers that we could live as isolated hermits, but near enough to the village where I attended school and she traded with the townsfolk. Wood elves grew their homes into the silvervein trees, using magic to form rooms of bark, with doorways and windows of vines. The family or families that built our current home must have been large, or eccentric, or both. My mother and I had enjoyed separate rooms, a shared living area, and an outdoor area for cooking. In most places we'd stayed over the decades, we'd had to share a single room and cook on the forest floor. I read into her frown the disappointment of having to leave the veritable castle be-hind, and also her dismay at abandoning all we'd collected.

As though our appetites had expanded to fill a larger stomach, we had filled our space with accouterments that had spoken to us. The wooden table had occupied the home when we'd stumbled upon it, but we'd polished it up, and my mother's scroll-writing paraphernalia deco-rated it. We'd brought up stumps for chairs, and cushioned them with feathers packed in skins. A nook in the wall held a collection of large snail shells we'd accumulated without ever speaking about it, each of us silently adding our findings. They surrounded what we presumed to be a seashell that, like the table, predated our moving in. Dried flower wreaths brightened the room, with ivy woven around them on the walls and ceiling. Makeshift cooking utensils hung from the wall near the exit that led to the cooking area.

Wooden arrows camped near every window—we would leave them until morning, just in case. Even then, we'd created more than it was reasonable to carry. We had a handful with flint arrowheads, but most were simply well-carved wooden shafts with pointed tips. Sometimes I thought my mother was a touch paranoid, with arrows decorating every hole in the wall, but she would laugh crazily—to my ears, purposefully crazy—at my accusations, and tell me that only the paranoid survived.

For reasons I couldn't explain, our packing up meant more than I expected, more than any of our past evacuations. It was like those reptiles we'd battled had latched their teeth onto my emotions and fought to pull off the meatiest chunks—I was wracked with angst whose source eluded me. It wasn't simply that we'd stayed longer than usual, put down more roots. It was me. With maturity, my attachments had grown more nuanced—that table was the first place I'd realized my words cut my mother deeply, and by that window I'd learned a heartfelt apology healed like magic. In the past year, I'd realized I bordered on old enough to live on my own. That had unnerved and excited me, but warred against a fear of complete isolation. I wanted to hide under my covers; I wanted to scream at the world; I wanted to cry; I wanted a hug from my mother.

Beasts pulled my emotions apart, leaving me raw as I gathered my things.

Still, we were bound by what we could carry, so it didn't take terribly long to pack. My mother secured her scroll-writing equipment, leaving behind several bulky ink pots. We would abandon all the decor we'd collected—prizes for the next hermits that found our shell.

Not *our* shell… once the sun reappeared.

"Well," she said, looking around, "I guess we're set." Her eyes lingered on the arrows, then the nook containing our treasured shells. My guilt over what she sacrificed for me swelled.

"I'm eighty years of age, Mom. Maybe it's time we stood our ground. Or," and she cocked her head at me when I paused, "maybe it's time I went away on my own."

Truthfully, the thought scared me. But I'd daydreamed of running off often enough. I'd lived a hard life, and I was more mature than others my age. Elves believed a century defined the point of becoming an adult. Only twenty years shy of that, there wasn't much that an adult was physically capable of doing that I was not, though I was not as strong or as fast as my mother.

I'd heard often enough that my brain hadn't completely matured. In normal elves, that was reflected in their feeble magic, but in my case… well, my mother would say that I "burned the tree down to kill the moss." She was one to talk, with her mercurial temper—I had seen no evidence to suggest I would grow out of mine.

But I had learned enough that I recognized how hard it would be to live on my own. In our travels, we had occasioned upon orphaned elves. Unlike trolls, elves had only one child at a time, and waited for that child to fully grow before having another. Elf babies were helpless, mewing, empty-bellied time-leeches for at least ten years. Orphans not picked up by a family member had little chance of survival. At my age, with all my mother had done to prepare me, I would survive, but it would be rough.

My mother walked over to our collection of shells and picked up one of the larger ones, filling her palm. She walked back over to me, smiled wistfully, and crushed the shell. "Even nice homes are temporary," she lectured while I cringed. "*You* are the treasure." She pulled me close while I struggled with my own emotions, saddened by the loss of the shell and leaving our home, joyful from a desperate longing to be protected, and anxious with the need for independence.

Patting my back, she said. "You could make it on your own, and I'm proud of that."

I smiled and sighed, grateful for her approval while also wishing I'd taken control, whether she'd liked it or not.

"But I think I shall manage one or two more adventures with you before you fly the nest," she added.

One or two more adventures? Well, tomorrow would start the first. That meant a year. At most, a few years, but no more. With excited fear, I took refuge in the idea of my looming independence. We settled into our meditation rituals, the intensity higher than most nights. I'd realized several exoduses prior that my mother's exercises increased in vigor around our travel. I associated her stress and worry about our travel with a need for more mindfulness, and I attempted the same, letting my fear melt away in our ritual.

Zoras * 4

180 years before

I groaned, unsure how we would survive another Warlord. We hadn't defeated the last—we'd barely held it off while *time* did the job we could not. Why had the gap between Warlords decreased? Just ill fortune? Or did we near a time when Warlords would be birthed so frequently that we would never see a day without them?

"You're certain it's a Warlord?" I asked into the fog of magic that connected us via the crystals.

During the last incursion, we'd used information gathered through communication crystals to pin down the Warlord's army. It had cost us a shocking number of Wood Elves and Warders to box them in. Less Alluvium perished, but only because there weren't as many amongst our forces. I hadn't counted on losing Alluvium recruits when Wynruil… retired. But I was glad the Wood Elves had multiplied so successfully—they constituted the bulk of my army.

My army. It wasn't supposed to be my army. But the Salts had fled the battlefield and refused to do more than carry supplies upriver. The Alluvium leadership had gradually diminished, and without new people of their race joining the fight, High Elves had moved up and taken control. Someone had to. Warders held the Blasted Lands, though they'd had to do so without the aid of the Roamers, which meant the Wood Elves were only good for Healing them. So the army had morphed a great deal. Warders on the southern front, where Wynruil had destroyed the Faletic Forest, with a smattering of Wood Elves, while Wood Elves and Roamers held the Border Woods, with a similar small number of Warders to aid them. The High Elves used their mental spells to embolden the increasingly demoralized Wood Elves.

"You don't trust me?" asked the voice from the other end.

"I'm not questioning your loyalty, just clarifying your certainty. You saw this Warlord with your own eyes?"

Despite having trapped his army, the Warlord had somehow escaped. At the time, I'd feared he had traveled on to the Heartland on his own, but I'd heightened security around the Mother of Trees for naught—years later we discovered he'd returned to the mountains, gathering a new force which he used to create constant trouble. Still, I preferred skirmishes east of the Border Woods to the alternative of his skulking around the Heartland.

The response did not come immediately. "No." Another pause. "Perhaps I'm seeing shadows and monsters because my heart is black with rot."

I smiled. "You've just had a baby. Very likely, one with quite a lot of power. Rejoice!" But even as I dismissed her morose demeanor, I took comfort in the thought that she might be reading a Warlord into her depression.

The fog darkened. "I can't believe I gave my heart to a fool. And my body to his ambition."

I froze. She'd wielded power, and we needed power. I'd liked her… more than *liked*… I truly had. Something about her appealed to me in a way… new to me. But she was a Wood Elf. Studies showed that half-breed children did not bear as much power as their parents. So I'd arranged a better fit. A leader among the Wood Elves took notice of her, and I'd believed she'd come out none the wiser regarding my involvement.

"Your husband is no fool," I responded.

"*I'm* not a fool," she growled. "I saw through your manipulations." *Interesting… few did.* "Or maybe I am. I hoped to make you choke on your own poison."

I hovered in the fog, silent. Regretful. I'd given her up for the greater good… but I'd done it. I'd believed I'd only damaged myself, and that had made the pain bearable. I quickly dismissed my spike of anguish—one can't grow crops on salted ground. *She'd borne his baby, for the love of words.* The irony hadn't escaped me either; after centuries of steering the races not to crossbreed, I'd given my heart to a Wood Elf. Still, I'd done what was right for the future. I'd given her up.

At least there wasn't a Warlord; she'd just needed an excuse to reach out. How old was I? Six hundred? Yet I'd acted like a hot-blooded youth and provided her an exorbitantly expensive crystal because I couldn't let her go. Even with the realization that I wasted my time in the conversation, I could not pull myself away, cherishing her hateful declarations for the seed from which they sprang—she'd cared too, even while playing out her role. She'd wanted to be mine.

"While in my darkest hours, I believe your poison sits at your core and spews out through even your most casual words…"

I smiled at her poetic picture, even though it painted me deplorably.

"... I cannot hold that visage when I see the trolls prepare for battle."

"Wait," I said, startled. "You saw trolls *yourself*?" Celendril lay far from the mountains that spat out the waters from the Witless Tarn into the Witless River.

"I traveled to the mouth of the Witless. Climbed the mountains."

"While carrying a child?"

"Wood Elves are hearty stock." The fog lightened, her mirth genuine. "It is almost amusing what you know and what you do not." The clouds darkened slightly as she grew more serious. "The trolls gather. If not a Warlord, then what?"

"Are you there now?" I shuddered at the thought, even though logically it made no sense—she'd been with child on the trip, and it was past time for her child to have been born. Surely the self-proclaimed queen of Celendril hadn't birthed her baby on the edge of the Witless Tarn?

"I just returned. I didn't bring the crystal with me. So you had to wait."

I scowled in annoyance. Those crystals cost an astonishing amount—one flawless crystal that had to be split in two by a skilled gemcrafter while our spells sat upon it. They couldn't be used again. I had a pretty collection of cold red jewels that used to connect to Alluvium leaders. They weren't meant to be left behind. She'd taken a jab at me... distancing herself from me. I reconciled my irritation quickly— I'd deserved it, particularly if she'd recognized my machinations and had still gone along with them.

"How long has it been? When did you see the trolls amassing?"

"Weeks ago," she replied.

"I'll move troops." We hovered in the silent fog. I didn't want to let go. "I am... sorry... things couldn't be different."

"That is... comforting," she replied, sounding anything but comforted. "Though I am pleased to know I did not give my heart to one who lacked a heart of his own. More the fool I'd be." The fog swirled. "It is ironic that your flimsy excuse for providing me a communication crystal actually resulted in locating a troll army, when really... you simply couldn't let me go."

"Yet it paid off," I replied.

She sighed, "Which will further confirm your wisdom and detract from suspicion. Does everything work out for you, Zoras?"

I'd tackled many difficult problems in my lifetime, but I did not think any of them had particularly "worked out" for me. Always for others, or the greater good. I did not like to dwell on that.

"How is your baby? Girl or boy?"

"Girl—" the fog scurried away, signaling the end of our conversation, then halted and pulled back together. "Speak of the Father and your magic runs dry—she's awake and crying. I don't want to do this. I'm not ready for my life to pause." The clouds swirled, twisting into funnels.

I needed to ground her. For her and her child. "What's her name?" I'd raised my voice, fighting over the storm.

"Illiara."

I wanted to say more, hoped to reel her in, to give her some kind of comfort, but the fog vanished.

Elliah ~ 8

"Weren't we leaving at dawn?" I groaned, not seeing a hint of light from the window in my room. Why had she awakened me so early?

"Change of plans," my mother said, summoning a dim magelight she'd left in the living area to follow her into my room. It dashed in and I turned my head away, letting my eyes adjust while I wanted to close them and settle back into slumber. But she wouldn't have allowed that. "Do you remember Rythalas?"

Rythalas? Wasn't that the town… "There's a mob?" My eyes opened wide. Rythalas was the town where Gorre had died from an accidental fall after the town healer couldn't land her spells. Mother had argued, confident she would have saved him. The villagers had turned against my mother and her Bereft child with the swift certainty of a wolf pack finding a doe alone with her fawn.

"But how will we tell the Warder?" I asked, swinging my legs off the feathered mat I slept upon. I grunted at the jolt of pain in my side, the quick movement a stark reminder that I'd injured myself the day before, and hadn't let the others completely Heal it. "How will he find us?"

"He won't," she said, grabbing the arrows near the window and shoving them into her quiver.

Alarm rang through me, launching me into wakefulness, but not clearing my confusion. "But *why*?" I wailed, feeling like a hunter's snare had flung me into the air. I immediately regretted my tone, sounding childish to my own ears, especially since she'd already told me why. I hopped up and rapidly readied myself and my pack, not waiting for an answer.

What did it matter anyway? What had I thought would happen? That Hughelas would befriend me? That he felt the same burbling… something… as I at the idea of spending more time together?

The whole idea was ludicrous.

My mother continued to stock up arrows, sighing quietly, and wistfully murmured, "We're safer on our own."

I wasn't sure what had changed her mind, but I didn't argue— we had always fled towns because of elves, so bringing some with us rather defeated the point. Only… these elves seemed *different*.

But in the scant minutes it took to wrap up our packs, I did not formulate an argument to justify waiting for the Warder and his son. Particularly if a mob were on its way. "How do you know there's a mob coming?" I asked, looking out the window and seeing no sign of light.

"I went into town to procure some last-minute items," she said. I wondered, did she steal them? I wouldn't ask. Did she get what we needed?

After one last look around, we left our home of the last several years, our favorite shell, behind. It hurt more than I expected.

I climbed down the ladder first. With our heavy-laden packs, the ladder was the only manageable path. My whole side was stiff and sore as I stretched from rung to rung, but I coped. I hopped from the last rung and waited at the bottom, in darkness broken only by the dim moonlight peeking through the trees. But even that soft glow provided sufficient illumination to spot what stalked from the nearby foliage.

I was already smiling as my mother dropped from the bottom rung.

"What?" she asked, looking like she couldn't imagine there being anything worth smiling about.

I nodded behind her. She turned and froze.

"I said dawn," she said critically. It was a tone that typically made me feel small, but the Warder only smiled.

"I was worried about finding our way back in the dark," he said, "so we left early." Hughelas and I grinned like a pair of forest cats who'd spotted a hare.

"A Warder… afraid of getting lost?" my mother said dubiously, but she looked somehow less like a mighty ironwood.

The Warder's smile grew. "These trees all look alike."

Completely untrue, but the statement made my mother roll her eyes and almost smile. Then she turned and stalked away. I looked at Hughelas with wide eyes and started after her. The bulky tread of the Warder followed behind.

Elliah ~ 9

When the sun at last broke the night, the direction my mother led us became clear. North by northwest. Northwest was significant. It meant
we'd exhausted our decades-long southbound trek through the western
rim of forest villages of the Border Woods. We'd stayed far from the
east side—away from Roamers and trolls and fighting—but always in
the woods. Northwest brought us closer to the Heartland—it meant a
reset, a change to our normal routine, with larger towns, different customs, unexpected pitfalls. Why was she taking the risk?

     We had other options. We could have headed east, deeper into
the Border Woods, to a life of fewer elves and more physical danger. Or
the homeland of the Warders to the southeast offered a similar fate.
West to southwest would take us into untamed woods—a hard way to
live, but isolated, where we would not have had to worry about reproof
from our people. Why head deeper into civilization?

     We walked in silence, stretched out in a line. Hughelas had
fallen behind me, having paused to cast a magelight while the darkness
still reigned. His father struggled in some of the more overgrown sections, his bulk a hindrance, but he never fell out of earshot. We hit a
section of thick-trunked sheetleaf trees whose massive height and ap-
propriately named leaves darkened the ground, keeping it clear of com-
peting foliage. I spotted no elfbloom in the large open area before us,
so we were well beyond the village outskirts. Even sheetleaf wouldn't
have stopped that mischievous vine. The Warder took advantage of the
open ground and, with long strides, caught up with my mother.
Hughelas jogged to catch up with me, and I slowed to meet him sooner.

     When he caught up, I glanced sideways at him, and he smiled
and nodded his thanks, but all notions of what to say suddenly vanished like the memories of a dream upon waking. I slammed my mouth
closed and spun my head forward, locking my gaze on the backs of our
disappearing parents, whose voices whispered through the forest,
though their words eluded perception.

     How did one even greet a friend? I'd heard it often enough when
other children had met at school, and daydreamed of it a million times,
and yet my thoughts had darted away like frightened finches set upon
by a mountain lion.

"I'm glad we arrived early," Hughelas offered.

And with his words, my thoughts coalesced into something dark. Why had they arrived early? Why were they so intent on traveling with us? What had he seen when he'd looked at me after triggering my mother's scroll? *What are they up to?*

"This takes us deeper into the Heartland, yes?" he asked. "Father believed you'd head south or west."

"If we're taking you in a direction you don't want to go, you should find your own way."

"No," Hughelas answered, peaceful, despite the bite I'd put in my words. "This is actually where we wanted to go. He'd assumed we might lose some days traveling with you, but this works out well."

They wanted to head into the Heartland? He'd stopped in E'anashys to speak with our High Elf teacher, but a Warder wouldn't leave the Contentious just to seek a lonely town on the edge of the Border Woods. They'd been heading into the Heartland all along, looking for answers amidst the High Elves.

As though reading my mind, Hughelas continued his explanation. "My father thinks the trolls are up to something big. And he's got this idea in his head…" I glanced over at him—his light skin made the blush of his cheeks apparent.

Familiar with the feeling of wishing a parent would behave like a normal person, I threw Hughelas a rope. "Why does he think that about the trolls?"

"Because they scarcely fight us any more. 'Peace and prosperity have broken out like a plague,'" he said, imitating his father, pulling a giggle from me.

"So…" I said, laughing despite myself. "You are on a quest to halt a ne'er-before-seen level of peace?"

"Quite so," he chuckled back.

"I've never seen a troll," I admitted. "We've stayed mostly on the west side of the Border Woods, well away from trolls and Roamers. We've been as far east as Nea'maella, and I *did* see a Roamer there. That was something—a walking tree."

"I've never seen a Roamer, but I've seen Warders fight trolls. Taking on the really big ones is like attacking a stone fort. A fort that punches back." Hughelas stomped on a decaying branch from a sheetleaf, creating a soggy broken mess. "I hear the Roamers are taller than mighty oaks, but I don't understand how wood fights stone."

"Well, how do the Warders fight them?" I asked, trying not to equate trolls and elves with Hughelas and the splattered log… but failing.

"Brute force plus Shield and Heal spells, mostly. Some Wood Elves stayed behind when Bellon burned—they handle the more serious injuries. But if there's a Clan Chief organizing the trolls, then we have to set up some kind of trap. Once the Clan Chief is taken out, we can separate the rest and pull them apart little by little."

We? Hughelas had fought trolls? "Do you suppose Roamers do the same? Heal and Shield and batter them?"

"I don't think so," he said. "And a stone is much stronger than wood. I just find it hard to believe the Roamers are a threat to trolls."

"You've not seen a tree split rock with its roots?" I asked. "I've seen that in many places. though it takes decades."

"Hmmm," he answered, considering my words. "I suppose you're right. They must grow *very* quickly, these walking trees. Amazing."

"Is it possible," I suggested, "that the trolls simply grow weary of fighting?"

He blushed again. "I proposed the same and received a firm rebuke for my presumption. And believe me, that's a sight you really don't want to see." I remembered the red, vein-popping visage of his father's face as he swung his hammer into the side of a reptile's head. No, that wasn't something I wanted cast in my direction. "But evidence suggests my father's concerns are valid."

We exited the shadows of the sheetleaf grove, returning to single file as the brush surrounded us in its inexorable pursuit of light and water. Suddenly self-conscious of Hughelas's view as he trailed behind, I found myself unable to walk normally, jerking about like an inexperienced puppet-master yanked on my strings.

"For one," Hughelas said, interrupting my preoccupation, "there have been rumors of a young Warlord spotted at battles for the last several decades. Of course, as near as I can tell, rumors of Warlords dot our history like… black sheep."

What did that mean?

"But also—"

I stopped, startled by an unexpected noise from ahead. It had been years, but I immediately recognized my mother's laughter. Memories flooded my mind: tickle-fights, dancing and music—when had there been music?—and silly costumes made from plants and skins.

Hughelas pushed through to stand by my side. "But also," he

started again, "my father and I crept up to the Witless Tarn. On the far side, between the Witless and the Dragon's Fangs, we found the trolls digging. Humongous troll-sized caves sloped into the earth, with mountains of rubble creating a makeshift wall that stood taller than most trolls, with segments rising all around the Tarn."

He gestured for me to lead the way, and I followed the signs of our parents' passage. My thoughts danced away from fleeting memories of my mother's laughter, replaced by visions of places and creatures I'd only read about or heard of in tales.

The Witless Tarn, a mountain lake that the Salts estimated to be almost a full day's sail at its thinnest, and more than a two-day sail from north to south. Of course, none had actually tested that, as trolls occupied the surrounding mountains.

I'd read as much about trolls as I could get my hands on, ever since I'd learned that magic didn't work on them. With skin like stone, many grew to three times the size of an elf. While brutally strong, they were dumber than the striped swamp toad of Fael Themar, a species which forced itself into the mouth of the predatory lockjaw gator as part of its mating ritual. How they'd survived as a species remained a mystery. But some trolls didn't grow as big, and the smaller ones were smarter. Clan Chiefs organized small raids. Warlords, still taller than an elf, but half the size of the biggest trolls, were highly intelligent, and had often organized the whole species to concerted attack.

A wall suggested more than a few trolls. But elves didn't want those mountains, or the Witless Tarn. Why build a wall? Truly a strange change of tactics.

My mother's whistle urged me to catch up, forcing our conversation to a halt. Visions of Warders and trolls ran with me through the forest, like I lived a chapter from *Talena Talenforged*.

We had halted for the evening, and my mother hunted with Beldroth while Hughelas and I set up camp. Unless Beldroth fouled it up, my mother would return with meat, so I prepared a fire. I struggled more than many elves, but I was not alone in being unable to invoke fire. Flint and knife worked reliably.

With the fire started, I set off into the trees, taking Hughelas with me. Fingers of the Amyla river reached throughout the woods, and we filled our water-skins from it, then I foraged for berries and edible roots. I'd gathered fruits and vegetables even at our last home. The only difference on our trek was that I needed to be more aware of my surroundings—many things were capable of taking out a lone elf in the forest. Less could take out two elves. Except…

"Were those dragons?" I asked. "Those things that attacked us?"

Hughelas glanced at the root I'd plucked, then turned his eyes back to our surroundings. I wasn't sure he really understood what to look for in our forest, but the extra eyes comforted me anyway. "No. We call them drawgs. They're trainable, even by elves, but the dragons keep them as something like pets."

Pets? Those things? They weighed as much as I did. Probably more. But I assumed dragons were much bigger, so for them, the drawgs would be relatively small. I loaded a bag with more wild edible roots while I contemplated the scale of scaly things.

"Dragons send them to retrieve their dead," Hughelas said. "I've seen packs of drawgs carting bits of dragon corpses like they intended to find a nice spot to reassemble them. In our case, I think they're tracking the hammer."

"The hammer? Why? How?"

I grinned at his smirk. "Your mother's spell. It helped me see the hammer in a whole new light." Her spell had also revealed to him something about me, but what? "I suspect the dragons, or the drawgs—or both—have the same vision. And the hammer shines under that spell. What if they can even see where it's been? Follow its trail?"

"You've told your father all this?"

Hughelas nodded his head. "Last night. But he won't leave the hammer behind."

"You've been fending off drawg attacks your whole life?" I would think that would make one… rather twitchy.

"No," he admitted. "I mean, yes, there have been occasional attacks, as far back as I can remember. But they've always been… circumstantial. Coincidental. It's been different ever since our trip to the Witless Tarn."

We moved on to a cluster of under-ripe berries, and I opted for a few choice picks. The light dimmed as the evening set in. Possibly, Hughelas could cast a Magelight, but I certainly could not. I would not forage much longer before heading back to camp.

"Since then, they're on us like blood bugs. I think the dragon, the one near the troll caves, either spotted us, or… somehow saw the residue of our passage? And it sent the drawgs after us."

"Sure," I said, standing and stretching, because I'd gathered enough. "Why not? If the drawgs can see the hammer, then why shouldn't the dragon see the hammer's residue?"

I was being facetious, but Hughelas missed it. "Yes, that was my conclusion too. But did he send the drawgs to prevent us from relaying what we saw of the trolls? Or was it just a matter of principle?"

"Principle?" I asked, confused.

"That's what I think too," he said, misunderstanding me again. "Why would a dragon care if anyone saw the trolls digging? Dragons don't care about elves—or trolls. But they care about themselves. So, yeah, principle."

What in the world was he talking about? Principles of dragons? Tracking hammer residue? Would I even be listening if he weren't the first cute elf ever to talk to me like I was normal?

Then my mind seized up. When had I let myself think Hughelas was cute?

"How did you recognize what comprised the hammer?" he asked.

Scrutinizing him, I decided he was younger than I, and that he would continue to grow, where I had more or less tapped out in height. I would fill out in the next twenty years, but I didn't expect to get taller. I couldn't imagine him ever putting on the girth or height of his Warder father, but he would stretch past me over the next decade. Muscle tightly knit his lean arms—not at all unpleasant to look at. But that wasn't the root of his appeal. He listened; he talked; he treated me like I was normal. He was even a little curious about how I was different. About what made me tick.

"That's okay," he said, smiling with sympathy. "I don't always know how I know things either."

Only then did I remember that he'd asked me something. About the hammer? *Shoot.*

"Sometimes my mind jumps ahead to the answer, and leaves me struggling to reconnect all the pieces." He looked up at the sky and said to no one, "It would be a great gift... if the answers I jumped to were always right."

While I'd been lost in my own musings, Hughelas had moved the conversation forward without me. I hunted through my memories of the last moments to piece together his monologue. Something about dragons and the hammer and how I knew? I was so lost.

"The hammer..." I stammered, not even sure where I intended to go with the sentence.

"Sorry," he said, blushing again. He was definitely cute when he blushed. My cheeks heated, flushed, but I suspected it would not be so apparent as his. Still, his blush deepened. "It's so rare that anyone listens to me—I'm... babbling." He turned away, staring at the ground so intently that I half-expected something to burst from it. "Yes, we were talking of dragon bone." His gaze returned to mine, his blush fading as he picked up his thread of thought. "The dragon bone hammer glows under your mother's sight-shifting spell. I wonder if dragons see each other's bones as glowing." He cocked his head at me like I might supply the answer.

"Maybe?" I offered, still trying to piece together his message. Someone had crafted his father's hammer from a dragon's bone. Said hammer would glow under the spell that my mother had provided. Further, he believed the drawgs somehow tracked that glow. The *consistent* attacks had only begun after their journey to the Witless Tarn. His logic made sense. But...

"What about me?" I asked, afraid of the answer, but needing to know. "What did you see when you looked at me?"

"The spell shifts your vision, attuning it to magic. The trees, the grass, the flowers, they appear as a soft glow. With care, one might walk through the woods without running into anything, though distance was confusing. The hammer, it shone like a flame. No, more like a magelight—steady, not flickering." Whatever he saw on my face, he paused before continuing. "You… were the opposite."

"I flickered?" That wasn't so bad. I'd been afraid it would be much—

"You devoured the light."

—worse.

Elliah ~ 11

I stormed my way through the dimly lit brush, ignoring the cacophony of my passage and the abuse of the plants in my way. Dark thoughts chased one another around my brain, repeating litanies from my life. *Bereft! Lacking. You devoured the light.*

"Elliah!" shouted the presumptuous boy-Warder from behind. But I didn't stop, even as his footsteps sped up. "Elliah!"

Bereft! Lacking. You devoured the light.

When he grabbed my shoulder, I spun, forcing him to jerk back to prevent a collision.

I didn't shout, but my words spewed out loudly, bashing their way out. "I thought you were—" I locked my tongue, not sure what word would have popped out if I'd let it. Different? Kind? A friend?

"Elliah," he said again, closing the distance between us.

I turned my back on him, shoulders slumping. Defeated. Bereft. Lacking. Devouring the light. I didn't cry. I wouldn't cry. But it was a battle I won by not showing up on the field—I disengaged from my emotions and stood, hollowed out, Bereft of magic and bereft of feelings.

"There's nothing *wrong* with what you are, Elliah."

His gently spoken words cracked the barrier that kept my emotions at bay. Why the compassionate message from a stranger struck me more deeply than similar phrases from the woman who'd raised me, I could not have said. I choked back a sob. I didn't want to cry.

"You aren't lacking magic, Elliah." I wasn't? Yes I was! *Bereft* couldn't cast spells. More often than not, spells didn't work on me. While his gentle words and the repeated use of my name continued to fracture my soul, what leaked through—what poured through—was not sadness, nor relief. Anger streamed in, and I soaked it up like a sponge.

I spun back around. "You have no *idea!*" I hissed. "No *concept* of what it is like to be me. We run from town to town, *hiding* from our own kind. They think I'm *cursed.* They fear for themselves that my *disease* might spread."

Hughelas shook his head no, but I didn't know whether he meant they need not have worried, or he denied that any such events could have happened.

"They *do!*" I insisted. "And my mother—she has had to hide me, has had to live on the run ever since I was *born*." And there, my anger made room for sadness. It wasn't right, after all that she'd given up for me. But my anger quickly regained its throne. "She shouldn't have to do that. I shouldn't have to do—"

I found myself unable to talk because of a sudden blockage over my mouth. His *lips* covered mine, his head tilted sideways to make the geography work, and his hand held the back of my head to keep me there. It caught me so unaware that, for several seconds, I had no reaction at all.

Then I shoved.

He fell back a step and caught himself.

I covered my mouth with my hand like I would feel something there, like swelling after a bug bite or insect sting. But they were just lips. Hughelas hadn't moved from where he landed, but even in the dusk, the blush growing on his cheeks grew more profound.

"What…" I fumbled, just as he mumbled something apologetic.

He was embarrassed? Something deep in my core cracked, and a single giggle burst from behind my hand.

Hughelas smiled sheepishly at my outburst. "I'm so sorry." He searched the forest floor for a way out of the conversation, but found no escape. "My mother, she had a temper, and when she went on a terror, my father would halt her with a kiss." He waved his hands like they would help explain, but they didn't. "I'd seen it so many times. It just…"

He'd kissed me. Like he'd seen his father kiss his mother. Like I'd seen other adolescents kiss at school, or skimmed over descriptions of in storybooks. Had my mother done that at one time? Had she ever joked with someone… yelled at them… found a partner who stopped arguments with a kiss? Maybe. But he'd abandoned us after learning what I was. So my own direct experiences in the conditions leading up to a kiss were quite limited. Still, while I suspected we'd fallen rather short of the ideal, my heart danced at the idea of the role he'd cast me into.

"It just happened," I finished for him. It was nice. Even if he'd meant it just to quiet me or calm me—which on its own I imagined I would find abhorrent—it had been an act he'd seen in his family and reenacted. Not an act of meanness, but one of love. Maybe passion, maybe care, but familial love. And he didn't fear me, didn't worry about *catching* my lack of magic. Mother of Trees, he'd *kissed* me.

"What's she like?" I asked, my thoughts skittering about like leaves in the fall. "Your mom."

Unable to stand still, I nodded my head for him to follow and turned back toward our camp. I treated the forest more respectfully as I hiked through it.

Hughelas quickly caught up and moved to my side, not touching me, but by necessity of the forest confines, staying very close, pushing through the foliage where he had to in order not to drop behind me. Night moved in, but an early moon reinforced the fading sun as the air cooled. "She died years ago. She was a Salt, 'as mercurial as the sea', my father would say. 'Some days, allowing tranquil passage and others a raging tempest set to wrack the boat.' My father doted on her in his way. I look like her, though my skin is darker, like my father's." Like his father's? His father had light skin. Salts skin would have to be as white as snow! "But my build is hers, my face is hers, the curls in my hair, hers. I'll never have my father's bulk." After a brief pause, he smiled and added. "I didn't get either of their tempers. And *your* father?"

"I didn't know him." Presumably, I'd laid eyes on him as a baby, but I had no memory of him. I wasn't even sure how to interpret my mother's statement about his having left us when I was born. Perhaps I'd never even seen him. The few occasions where I'd broached the topic had sent my mother into a brood with no answers. "My mother raised me on her own."

"Oh. I'm sorry. What was he?"

"How do you mean?" I asked. Surmising his intent, I answered, "I'm told he was a teacher."

"No. I'm asking what race your father was. He obviously wasn't a wood elf."

My eyes pinched in confusion. I continued walking, but looked down at my arms, my hands. "I look like my mother."

"Your body does, sure. Just like *my* build takes after *my* mother. But your face… it's got something else in it. Surely you're aware of that."

In fact, I was not. I'd seen a mirror once, when I was little, in a town we'd traveled through, but I couldn't remember what I'd looked like, and I'd been little anyway. I'd seen bits of my reflection in knives, puddles, rivers, ponds, but never clearly. The bits that I didn't see, the parts that rippled in the water, I'd always mentally filled in with my mother's features.

"You didn't know," he concluded. "Surely you realize that, when you move to a new town, the other elves can't see that you lack magic. I understand that little cantrips are cast everywhere—I'm sure someone eventually uses magic that doesn't work on you, and your cover is blown. But your protection from spells doesn't show up on your face. Your face is what shows up on your face. You look different from other wood elves. More elegant and at the same time more wild. You're cut from a different cloth."

Many things ran through my mind. Confusion about what I looked like. Excitement that he thought I looked more elegant and wild than other wood elves. But most of all, "You said 'protection from spells.'"

He looked at me and grinned. "You're special, Elliah. Like the trolls, you're protected from magic. You absorb magic instead of emitting it."

He said it with such conviction that it sounded good, even though he'd compared me to a troll. I grimaced, trying to wrap my mind around being protected from magic. Trolls were hulking monsters with skin like rock. But elves, we were fragile buckets of blood wrapped in skin—we needed magic to defend ourselves. How could resistance to magic be good for an elf?

"The really interesting question," he said, looking up into the trees like they carried the answers in their moon-drenched arms, "is where does the magic go?"

The mouth-watering scent of cooking meat wrestled my mind away from our conversation, hastening my steps even as weariness from a day of travel settled in.

"... but she was so covered in juice from the berries, she was purple for a week!"

The Warder's barking laughter cracked through the night while my mother's softer purr of amusement encircled it. "Oh," he began, "that reminds me of the time Hughelas tested his theory that wine would be made stronger by boiling it. You should have seen the explo—"

"Dad!" Hughelas barked, charging into the small clearing. "I wasn't *boiling* it, I was *distilling* it, but there must have been a leak." At least we'd missed the beginning of the story about my childhood misadventure, though the awkwardness of knowing someone else had heard it settled on me like a cloak as I joined Hughelas and our respective parents.

The Warder smiled and waved his son's concerns away. What story had my mother told about me? I was purple? What else? I exchanged a look of concern with Hughelas.

"Are we swapping stories?" I asked, then looked at my mother pointedly. "Did you tell the one about bathing in the stream and a passing kingstag hooked your clothes on its antlers and carted them away?" Turning to Hughelas, I explained with a smile, "We chased it for at least an hour, and she ran through town without a stitch of clothes." I turned to my mother. "We weren't in *that* town for long."

Hughelas grinned. "We have a similar story with a fireworm that set my father's clothes ablaze. Removing flaming clothes while continuing to fight—"

"Enough," the Warder said, though he chuckled. "I take your point. Though I do, in fact, remember that battle with an odd fondness. Fighting in the clothes the Mother gave me was... liberating." Hughelas smacked his hand over his face and kept it there.

My mother chuckled and said, "Streaking through the town on the heels of a kingstag is one of my fonder memories."

I squinted, trying to decipher the look exchanged between the two adults. They were turning the tables on us... weren't they?

Sighing, my mother said, "But I promised you my story about meeting with the Mother of Trees."

The Warder's eyes lit up.

"Over dinner," she said, forestalling him. "Elliah, prepare the vegetables, please." Her mention of vegetables reminded me of my hunger. One of them had made quick work of skinning a gametail fox and something smaller. My mother would have done the skinning elsewhere, to reduce any unwanted predators. A larger group required more food, but it also brought the opportunity to eat better and relax.

I looked over what I'd gathered and chose a combination I hoped would go well with the meat, then began cutting, crushing, and mixing my choices with water to make a paste which I used to coat the meat, while using a small metal pan to boil water for the tougher roots I'd acquired. The meat spun slowly over the fire, secured on a spit by a pronged branch with tiny wind-catchers. One of the adults had bespelled it with a tiny swirl of wind to keep it rotating.

An enormous conifer had collapsed within the last year, not only creating the clearing, but providing a natural barrier to the east with a trunk thicker than the Warder's height. Fallen limbs provided natural benches.

It crossed my mind to feel self-conscious as the others watched me work, but I'd done similar preparations so many times that my concerns scampered quickly away. My mother pulled out our bone dice, occupying the others with a game of clans. The traditional six-sided die marked Warders, Salts, Alluvium, Wood Elves, High Elves, and Trolls, and one rolled them to obtain matches. I wondered whether our new companions would know the game, but they jumped right in.

Without thinking, I took over the meal preparation, including what my mother had begun, listening with half an ear while the others played clans. Several minutes into my work, without realizing it, I'd started humming an old tune my mother had sung when I was little. When actual words escaped my mouth, I halted, suddenly self-conscious.

To my surprise, Hughelas started singing. He picked up the tune where I had stopped, singing quietly as he continued to roll the dice in their game of clans.

"River Queen, River Queen,
Dancing down the silver stream,
Fiery hailstones hissing steam,

She'll not reach sea by morn'.

Rocky shores did stay her berth
The Queen plowed on, fer all she's worth,
Longing for to lie on earth,
Her heartland did she mourn."

As he repeated the chorus, I pondered how his version differed from the one my mother had taught me. Fiery trees stayed the River Queen's birth in mine, not rocky shores. Had the Warders altered it to make sense for them? Had *we*? And then I wondered who I meant by *we*. Was I entirely a Wood Elf?

My mother jolted my meandering thoughts by joining in for the next refrain.

"Push and wail, cry and flail,
The Queen fled on through fiery hail,
And duet screams soon marked the tale.
Her baby girl was born."

The Warder joined in, his tenor belying his size, though it was still the deepest of our group. Was it odd that we all knew the song, albeit with slight differences?

"The silver vein in a fiery heart,
Led the Queen to her life's new start,
An island not on any chart,
Her heartland had been torn."

I joined them for the final chorus.

"River Queen, River Queen,
Dancing down the silver stream,
Fiery hailstones hissing steam,
She'll not reach sea by morn'."

When all of us sang together, I had the oddest sensation, like I'd gotten away with something naughty. I'd always been an outsider, unwelcome in group festivities. At best, I'd watched from the shadows. Singing with Hughelas and the Warder... I'd stolen a kiss. Why had that tune popped into my head in the first place? Something about traveling?

"That smells delicious," the Warder said.

"And it looks to be done," my mother added.

I smiled. "It should be palatable. I lacked spices." Though, in truth, I'd foraged a rather tasty collection of fruits, vegetables, and herbs. "Let's eat."

My mother had already moved to the fire to steal some meat, but she froze when the Warder chanted, "Thank you, Mother, for your glorious blessings. For providing the animals to hunt, for Illiara's keen eye and swift arrows, for the rivers that bring us water to drink, for watching over and guiding us. It is under your protective branches we find rest. We pray your blessings upon our quest, and I thank you for those you have sent to our aid. Amen."

I exchanged a look with the woman who'd raised me, one of my eyebrows rising while her lips pursed, a look not missed by the Warder's son, judging by his slight blush. But she resumed her intended goal, using her dagger to carve off a piece of meat, then impale it, stabbing some sauteed roots and walking back to the log she'd chosen as a perch.

The Warder watched her intently all the while, then turned his stare to me.

I blanched, wondering what he expected of me.

"Among our people," Hughelas said, "the one who prepares the food eats first."

Ah, so the Warder waited for me. I looked at my mother for confirmation. It wasn't like we had guests or occasions where *we* were guests. Had she done such things before I was born? But my mother simply shrugged, not caring about their customs, or explaining ours.

Hunger was winning over curiosity. I carved off a hefty chunk of the smaller animal—probably already a victim of the larger beast that we dined upon when my mother had found them. Following my mother's example, I skewered some vegetables and joined her on her log.

I savored my food as the Warder and his son served themselves, following us in our haphazard dining etiquette. My mother got up and sliced off a little more meat, not sitting back down as she enjoyed it near the fire. "Time," she said between bites, "for a little honesty. You're a Warder," she stated, "traveling to the Heartland. You hope to see the Mother of Trees."

"Not just *see* the Mother of Trees," the Warder confirmed. "I intend to get her Blessing!"

My mother closed her eyes, hard. "Of course you do."

The Mother of Trees? The being to whom he gave thanks for his food? Who fable spoke of as our Creator? Who legend said fought Warlords to protect us?

"I hear she has grown a town around her, but she keeps herself apart. Meditating." The Warder said the word *meditating* like it was the answer to his prayers.

"A town has grown around her…" my mother mumbled, like the picture in her mind discomforted her

"Do not all things grow through her?" The Warder said it like the answer was obvious.

The conversation perplexed me. While I'd seen Wood Elves who worshiped the Mother of Trees, some even with the enthusiasm of the Warder, my mother had never been one of them. She'd as often as not invoked the Mother's name as a curse. At some point in my eighty years, I'd decided the Mother of Trees was just a story. My mother's muttered statement, *a town has grown around her*, was not the kind of thing one said regarding an imaginary being. Unless she meant a town had grown around the *idea* of her?

Sighing, my mother said, "I would steer you from your path. You won't… you won't find what you seek."

"I will," the Warder said.

"You *won't!*" My mother's vehemence shocked me.

Crickets chirped, ignoring the tension.

My mother looked me in the eye and broke the silence, "The day Elliah was born, I gained an audience with the Mother of Trees."

Beldroth gasped. "It is so easy, then?"

I scrunched up my face, blurting, "The Mother of Trees is *real*?"

"Of course she's real," the Warder responded, his face blotching red in the firelight. "She created us and provides for us."

I wanted to yell back at him that his indignation was unfair—my mother had treated the Mother with scorn and derogatory remarks my entire life. My finding out she'd actually seen the Mother was a shock.

Was she lying? Did she have some motive to lead the Warder on? That… made a lot more sense. I didn't know what she was up to, but I held my tongue.

My mother blushed. "It was not so easy. Alenor guards her well. But that's a tale for another day. I gained an audience." And *that* was unlike my mother—her typical story would happily follow a story-hare off into the brush, not always returning! Her tale was too direct—surely she was up to something. But what?

The Warder sucked up her words, nodding for her to continue. But Hughelas and I exchanged a glance—he wore doubt on his face like a mask. I had my own doubts. Alenor? She'd never told me of visiting Alenor, the very capital of the High Elves and the seat of control for all elves. What if the Warder had visited Alenor? Would she be able to preserve her lie?

"My baby… my newborn… lacked the ability to… enjoy magic's protection." She fumbled for words.

Bereft, Mom… I'm Bereft.

Hughelas opened his mouth to speak, but I shook my head. It wasn't the right time for his theories on how my condition made me *special*, that it *protected* me *from* magic. Oddly, my mother's fumbling words rang true. Why did truth lack words while lies flowed like a river? The fact that she weaved something true, my lack of magic, into her tale lent it credibility.

"I sought…" and her eyes flicked up to mine, seeking something. "I sought the Mother's Blessing."

"And did you get it?" the Warder asked, his eyes wide.

"She responded," my mother answered.

The Warder jumped to his feet. "I knew it!" he shouted, pounding a fist into his other palm. "For a truly righteous cause, she stirs." He spun to his son. "She will bless our endeavor." He paced before the fire, occasionally tearing a bite from the meat affixed to his dagger, his eyes seeing some future not shared.

If she'd truly sought to steer him away, she'd made a fine mess of it. Had she wanted him more determined? Was she trying to steer him away from us? Send the Warder and his son on their way?

"She responded," my mother repeated, "but it wasn't a Blessing."

The Warder stopped his pacing, turning his head slowly to meet my mother's eyes. But she looked only at me, creating a tunnel between us. If she was lying, she was doing a very good job at it. "She stared at you. For a long time. Then she cried." Was she serious? What would it mean, that a god cried? "Finally, she told me to name you."

The loud clap of the Warder's hands echoed through the woods, drawing our attention. His eyes practically glowed. "*That* is a blessing," he declared, then danced, some crazy little jig with his arms flying and hips gyrating, drawing a laugh from my mother and a groan from Hughelas.

"Is it though?" my mother asked the fire, her smile remaining, but her eyes haunted. "I thought it was, at the time." She looked at me and said with a smile, "And I count you as a blessing." She turned back to Beldroth. "But the stories of old speak of the Mother's Blessing like it was a prayer answered. I wanted the Mother to grant Elliah magic. Somehow, the words didn't come out. I asked a god if I should name my child, and she said yes. Nothing changed. I still had to flee, to hide. Is that a Blessing?"

The Warder stalked over to my mother, then crouched down so that their heads were level. "*That* is a Blessing," he repeated, smiling contagiously, and my mother fell victim, her lips stretching in a grin.

***

My mother and I did our mental exercises silently that night. The Warder had offered to take the first watch, and she'd nodded, sat down, then closed her eyes and meditated. Seeing her, I followed suit. I wondered what the Warder and Hughelas thought we were doing, but cleared that from my mind. I struggled more to vanquish the evening's conversation. A story I'd never heard before... a story *about me*... and she'd shared it with near-strangers. Why? In the end, I decided she'd intended to steer him away from his goal. I decided she hadn't lied, hadn't tried to maneuver them in one direction or another—she'd meant to be genuinely helpful. She hoped to save him from pain. Yet he wouldn't hear.

"*That* is a blessing," the Warder had said.

But, as she'd said, "Nothing changed." We'd been running my whole life. But—it settled on me for the first time—*she* hadn't been running her whole life. Before I was born, she'd been someone else. She hadn't been running, hadn't been hiding. What a blessing I was! *Mother of rotting Trees.*

Elliah ~ 14

The next morning, I pulled my mother aside, away from the camp, while the Warder and his son cleaned up. "Mom, the story you told yesterday…" *Was it real? If it was real, why had you kept it secret? Why had you never talked about the Mother of Trees like she was anything more than a legend? If she wasn't real, why did you make up that story? Why string the Warder along? What did you hope to accomplish?*

The questions had plagued me through the night, despite our meditations where I had, in fact, managed to clear them out, at least temporarily.

"It happened," she said, sighing, leaning back against a tree and rubbing her eyes. On closer inspection, they looked red and strained—she'd struggled as much through the night as I had. "You have to understand, Elliah… I broke the law. There's a reason the High Elves keep us away from the Mother." She sputtered to a halt, and I sensed there was more to the story, but she pursed her lips and barreled ahead. "We've been chased ever since. I couldn't tell you that when you were little. Couldn't have you repeating our story. And… I don't know, I *missed* the opportunity." She waved at me. "You grew up, and there was never a right time."

I wanted to ask so many things—in particular, *so you tell me in front of others?* But first, I had to be sure. "So there really is a Mother of Trees. She's not some made-up story for children?" Because some of the things she'd said throughout my life were pretty blasphemous if there really was a goddess walking the land.

She grimaced. "There really is a Mother of Trees. And I imagine the stories of her are true. Or at least some of them are based in truth. But to see her now…" My mother's eyes gazed into the past, haunted. "Gods shouldn't… shrivel." She returned to the present with a shake of her head. "Whatever she is, she isn't what we've been told."

Hearing that the Mother of Trees was real didn't make her feel any more real to me. I tried to imagine how I would react if my mother told me Talena Talenforged was real. The stories about her were children's stories, fanciful and fun. Yet, they were grounded in real places, and her adventures merely stretched credulity—I think I would more easily accept Talena had walked the land than the Mother of Trees.

We didn't have much time before we had to rejoin the men. So I jumped ahead. "So, what are we doing?" I asked her. "Where are we going?"

"Celendril. Maybe all the way north to Heann'el. We'll cross the Flawless at Nara'lle. We can either skirt Cal-Edhil or walk through it, if you'd like to see it."

My eyes widened. We'd spent the last couple of decades avoiding Cal-Edhil, the capital city of the Wood Elves. It was too crowded, too easy for my condition to be noticed, too dangerous. The nature of that danger transformed in my mind—had we run because of what would happen to a magicless child on the playground, or did we flee so that my mother would not get caught for the crime she had committed? "What's changed?"

"You're an adult. Or near enough one. We lived in E'anashys for five years. Va'enas for three years before that. Those are long stays. You've become adept at taking care of yourself. I think you can handle a journey through the big city."

I smiled, inside and out, like a flower opening its petals, welcoming the sun and the admiration of those fortunate enough to see it. But…

"And the Warder?" I asked.

"We travel with them until we don't," she said, shrugging.

I had mixed feelings about her statement—I'd never had a friend before, and I was loath to lose my first chance at one so quickly. The touch of his lips on mine popped into my mind, and I recognized I lied to myself—I wanted time to explore *that* sensation. But the Warder intended to see the Mother of Trees, so he would head to the Heartland. "What if we cross the Flawless at Vanae'l instead of Nara'lle?"

She smiled. "It is nice to have company, isn't it?"

I smirked—if she only knew—but then frowned at a sudden idea. "You're not buying into the whole grand *quest*, are you?"

She rolled her eyes and shook her head. "No, sweetie."

Sweetie? She hadn't called me that in years.

I crinkled my nose at her, about-faced, and headed back to camp to get my pack.

A faint sigh and a mumbled remark reached my ears, "But I want to."

I didn't pause, didn't want her to know I'd heard, but I thought I understood. There was something about the large man's excitement that, despite sounding crazy, also appealed. We'd encountered religious fanatics in villages before. They'd been some of our shortest stays, as religious dogma and tolerance did not travel together, and my very existence did not fit the standard of elvin beliefs about magic. Babies born without magic were a punishment! That was why the babies never lived. No town or village that unabashedly worshiped the Mother of Trees would suffer a living embodiment of sin in their midst. Perhaps that was why I'd grown up questioning the reality of the Mother—my mother had avoided any communities that would have promulgated the idea.

And yet the Warder comprehended what I was, held strong convictions about the Mother of Trees, and looked at me with a smile, called me blessed. Hughelas had done more than that, and maybe... would do so again?

Suddenly, the blond, lean object of my daydream appeared in front of me, smiling wryly. "You ready?" he asked. I blushed, nodding my head yes, though with his pack on, I grasped that the context of his question was entirely different from where my mind had gone. I was ready all right.

They'd cleaned the camp, having doused and buried any remaining embers, readying their gear, and I wondered with a small, stupid thrill whether Hughelas had handled mine.

My mother pushed through from behind, striding past us and into the clearing. The Warder smiled at my mother. "To where do we journey this fine day?" he asked. My mother stopped and squinted at him with suspicion. "We decided," he said, "we shall accompany you to your destination before we take our leave."

"But you seek the Mother's Blessing," my mother countered.

"And you already have it!" he said with a smile and a laugh. "What a fool I would be not to see you safely to your destination."

My mother closed her eyes hard, then rolled her shoulders and stretched her neck from side to side like she was preparing for battle. "What if we journey to Baledor?" Baledor was a Salt-run city at the mouth of the Witless, known to house a more reckless breed of elves than the norm. A town of runaways and criminals. My mother had no intention of going there—she'd yelled at me vehemently when I'd brought home the idea from a book, thinking that in a town of runaways, I might fit in. "You've committed no crime," she'd snapped. Then she'd softened her tone. "Besides, you have the heart of a mother brown-tailed felling." I'd half smiled at her reference—those small, cute furballs with the long tails became stupid regarding their children, starving themselves to bring their offspring food. But her tone had turned dark again after that. "They'd eat you alive."

Still, that had been twenty years before. She'd just told me that she thought I could handle Cal-Edhil. I'd toughened up, grown up. Was she serious about Baledor, or just testing the Warder's conviction?

"Then Baledor it is," the Warder answered. "By land or by sea?"

My mother pondered a second, then picked, "Sea." She turned to me. "Unless you wanted to see Cal-Edhil?" she asked.

I did. The capital of the southern Wood Elves held a strange allure, even if I would have had to skulk about it in the shadows. But going by sea meant we would follow the Flawless out to open waters. And the Flawless traveled through the Heartland and Alenor, the capital of the High Elves. It was the seat of power for the High Elves, who influenced all the other elf races. Plus, I had a new curiosity. If the Mother of Trees was real, seeing her was an even grander prize than Cal-Edhil.

Zoras * 5

"Do I call you Uncle Zoras?"

Illiara. She'd shown up on my doorstep with a letter from her mother, though Elitha and I hadn't spoken once in the fifty years since Illiara's birth. Not that I hadn't tried, but she'd refused to respond to the crystal.

Zoras Keawynn of the High Council,

I send my daughter, Illiara, to you. I hope you can house her for a season. Headstrong for a child, we think she would do well living a time with one similarly inclined. Rock breaks rock, but only a chisel creates a statue.

Elitha Silverheart, High Lady of Celendril

Fortunately for them, the Warlord she'd reported had never manifested, for a troll army would have torn their fair city asunder. Yet my gut told me a Warlord lived. I suspected he found the ranks of trolls too thin from the attacks of the previous Warlord. I wondered if he'd started his own campaign of breeding, and suffered from missteps... his own Elitha Silverheart. Whatever the reason, the troll army had vanished by the time the elves arrived. The trolls had headed south, but on the west side of the Witless Tarn, which set them up for attack anywhere in the Border Woods. Yet, in a hundred years, they'd never sprung forth, save for the random troll now and again—creating either the illusion of no Warlord leading them or... or perhaps even Warlords struggled to control all their subjects. Or perhaps the Warlord had died, and we kept troops prepared for no reason.

"Uncle Zoras is fine," I said. I'd raised children, and I'd had nieces, nephews, and more distant relatives who called me Uncle.

I'd learned that Elitha had born a second child, a son, before Illiara even came of age. It was unheard of to have a second while weaning the first, and yet she had. Others informed me Illiara's parents treated their son with a warmth that had never surfaced with Illiara. Same father, same mother, but one child they doted on, and the other they wanted to be rid of.

"Why don't we look anything alike, Uncle?"

She'd already dropped the "Zoras" from "Uncle Zoras"? Casually Impertinent. I believed she would grow up to look much like her mother. Same hazel eyes, same cheekbones. Her chin was stronger than her mother's. She reached out and took my hand as we walked away from the ship.

"My guard, Jerithon, wasn't my uncle, but he looked a lot more like me than you do." She reached out for Axilya to take her other hand, and after a moment of bemused uncertainty, Axilya took it. "I tried to get Jerithon to teach me to fight with my dagger, but all he wanted to do was chase around the Salt women on the ship. Such a silly way to spend your time. Why do you do that?"

An ironic question, given how I'd encouraged promiscuity, particularly among Wood Elves. The Border Woods needed an army. But chasing elves of a different race? The council had made a mistake enacting the racial purity laws. "Forbidden fruit is all the more cherished." Clipping funds and military support to towns that housed half-breeds had caused new towns to spring up all around the Border Woods. Fiercely independent groups created their own militia to defend themselves. Armies outside of my control did me no good whatsoever. I looked over at Axilya, who wore the ghost of a smile.

"How far is it to your home? Not that I'm in a hurry. Will there be anyone else my age? I hope they don't look like me—I've quite enjoyed seeing the Salts and you High Elves. Are you really my Uncle? Will there be any books where we're going? I do like books. Do you like books, Uncle?"

Startled that she had actually stopped talking, I realized I wasn't sure what question she hoped I would answer.

"He has many books," Axilya said, and the child turned her hawk-like attention away from me. "I take care of his library, and several of the books in it he wrote himself. We are already on his grounds, and his actual home is not far. There are a few children your age visiting, and you'll find them in the commons, but you'll be staying with us at the manor." She would be? "He is not really your Uncle. As you noted, you are a Wood Elf and he is a High Elf. But I believe all elves are related, so Uncle works just fine."

The young girl smiled, taking in everything, though I was slightly aghast. "Thank you, Auntie…"

"Axilya." Axilya was definitely smiling.

"Axilya," repeated the girl. "That's an interesting name. It's short like mine. I like short names. Why do some elves have such long names, and then add titles to them, so that they go on and on and on? Do more words in your title make you more powerful? My children shall have short names. But I shall have sons, not daughters. I don't understand why titles are passed through boys and not girls. Do you? But I don't like being raised to be a broodmare, and I shan't have daughters and subject them to the same. I'm excited to see the library. Will I be allowed free access? We have a library in Celendril, but Father banned me from it because I spent too much time there." She whispered loudly to Axilya. "I would send others to get books for me, but it's not the same as being there."

Axilya giggled—a sound I couldn't remember ever having heard before. I found it calming, in an odd sort of way. It took away the sting of panic from the onslaught of questions. "Indeed," she replied. Indeed she would have access to my library? Indeed asking for books to be brought home was not the same as being in the library? Indeed it was a shame to be a broodmare? It seemed an all-encompassing answer.

"I hope I will be allowed to learn more than clothing and flirting and other such nonsense here. I want to learn to fight. I want to learn how money works. I want to learn different kinds of magic. Mother says I have a knack for Healing, and my mana charges 'with particular haste.' I am fairly good with a bow already. I traded a boy some kisses for a lesson in tracking. It sure was stupid—the kisses, not the lesson. That's why Mother sent me away, I think, when she found out. But I don't understand. 'For anything worth having, one must pay the price.' She got angry when I said that, and the next thing I knew, I was boarding a ship with Jerithon."

For the love of words, this girl can talk! I'd met my match. Illiara didn't stop talking, but I stopped hearing. That phrase, "for anything worth having, one must pay the price," was a quote from one of my books. It must have caused Elitha a special kind of pain to have her daughter, the product of my own effort to strengthen the elves at the cost of breaking her heart, fling that in her face.

The chatter went on and on as we made our way back to my manor house, but my mind drifted. Logically, I recognized that, if I'd kept Elitha by my side, we would not have had the same child as the one before me, but Illiara was the byproduct of my decision, and, of course, Elitha's. She was so much of what I would have asked for in a child: curious, bright, interested, willing to make sacrifices for what she wanted. Those characteristics reminded me of Faelern, the High Elf who I'd recently sent off to gather more information and establish regular communication with the Warders. But she railed against the very things I'd promoted to save the elves: promiscuity to create a faster-growing population and racial division so that magic increased though the strength and purity of each race.

While not the product of my loins, she was a result of everything I'd done. That made her mine in a very profound way. Plus, raising a Wood Elf would counteract the growing racial disharmony. I needed some way to unite elves, something to counteract the trends that had taken efforts too far. She was just what I needed. I squeezed Illiara's hand with a smile, letting magic trickle into the touch, encouraging her to trust me. She would be interesting to raise… for a season.

Elliah ~ 15

We headed northwest, intending to skirt the west side of Anysa and then follow the Amyla River until it joined the Flawless, then… well, none of us knew the routes from the south end of the Border Woods to the Heartland. Were there trails that followed the Flawless through the grasslands? Did one need to book passage on a ship?

Either way frightened and excited me, but all of it scared me less for being in a group. We traveled for three days, spending the daylight hours hiking, the evenings peeling off to forage, and the nights swapping stories.

And I took advantage of the foraging time, alone with Hughelas. We became two completely different people—laughing, sharing what we'd learned from books we'd read, ideas we'd had about why things worked the way they did, and… and a tantalizing physical closeness that, if I'd stopped to label it, I would have called playing with fire. His fingers grazed mine over plants we handed one another. We walked too near and from time to time stopped too quickly and caused a collision. We whisper-sang songs, under the auspices of not scaring away food, so that the other leaned close to hear.

I almost hated the idea that we had to rejoin society. I lay awake on the ground that third night. My mother had first watch, and having drawn closer to her as we'd traveled than I'd felt in years, I decided to cave in and ask for some maternal advice. I mean, I understood the… kinesthetics… of sex. We lived in the woods—I'd seen abundant examples. But books had hinted that there was more to it with elves. Courtship rituals? Those books had not drawn my attention, much to my regret at that moment, so I hadn't paid particular attention to romantic stories.

So once I was sure the men were asleep, I quietly rose and crept to the edge of the clearing where my mother leaned against a tree, her back to the fire.

"Mom," I whispered nervously.

Some watch guard!

"Mom!" I whispered with more vehemence, drawing closer, but still she remained unmoving. I had a moment's fear that something was desperately wrong, but then decided she'd simply dozed off. I'd give her a good teasing about her dereliction of duty.

"Mom," I said, gently shaking her arm.

She collapsed to the ground.

"Wake up!" I shouted back to camp, drawing my dagger and searching the shadows.

Something hissed and a cool mist swept over my face. I jerked back, glimpsing my assailant clutching onto the tree my mother had leaned against.

"Gah!" I yelled, jumping away from the tree.

The Warder's yell as he charged made it very clear he headed my way. I presumed Hughelas approached as well, but more quietly, dwarfed by the noise his father created.

But before the cacophonous warrior reached me, an ominous thump, followed by silence, declared me alone in the fight for my mother's life.

I didn't move. Possibly Hughelas was still out there, biding time as I was, eyes darting to search the shadows.

Something big if it took out the Warder, I thought, imagining what size such a creature would have to be. All my instincts screamed at me to run, but I couldn't. I wouldn't leave my mother there.

I jerked away from a hiss in the tree near me, and a mist drifted over me again. Backing away from both trees, I homed in on the noise and movement I'd glimpsed before and spotted a creature scurrying to hide behind the tree.

It wasn't big at all. The length of my arm. And the way it moved… reptilian.

I eased back over to my mother, dagger ready. When I reached down to roll her onto her back, the creature charged from the tree, hissing and spitting its mist at me.

I thrust my dagger and caught it right in the neck, my blade slicing clear through its small frame. In the dim light, I couldn't make out its color, but its body was as long as my arm, with some wing-like structures on its back that looked decorative and not usable. It had similar decorations on its head, the flags drooping in death.

Without pause, I grabbed my mother by one arm and dragged her a tiny distance toward the fire, while another lizard charged after its prize. I ended its charge and its life as quickly as I had the first, then continued dragging my mother over the dirt and brush to get her close to the light, passing first the prone form of Hughelas, and then the Warder.

I dropped her close to the fire, quickly throwing on more wood to grow my light. Then I returned for the others. Dragging the large Warder looked… daunting, so I moved on to Hughelas.

A lizard sat on top of him, snacking. The light of the fire revealed colors—the lizard was tan with thin red stripes running down its back. Hughelas's arm was a bloody mess. The creature flared its wings, both on its back and its head, spraying me with a fine mist. It looked fierce and the mist was disconcerting, but I was shocked by how little it dodged my attack. It died quickly. I dragged Hughelas close to my mother by the fire. To stanch his bleeding, I haphazardly wrapped his arm.

Finally, inch by excruciating inch, I tugged and rolled the Warder back with the rest of our crew. No more lizards appeared.

Settling in, I unwrapped my makeshift bandages from Hughelas's arm. The lizard had torn a strip of flesh from his forearm. It oozed blood, but there was nothing I could do but clean and re-bandage it, hoping the others would wake and Heal it.

Exhausted, I plopped down near my mother, back to the fire, staring out into the night for any sign of lizards.

It was more than an hour before my companions stirred. The Warder was the first to wake.

"Gwaaaah!" he shouted, popping into a sitting position like seeds bursting from a dried bluecap pod. Once my heart resumed beating, I rushed over, grateful that I'd remained frozen for a few seconds, because he vomited with a vehemence I'd never seen.

"Ugh," he muttered, looking around with bleary confusion.

"You're okay," I assured him, moving close enough to pat his back while avoiding the remains of the night's meal he'd regurgitated.

"Sweet Mother," he moaned. "How much did I drink?"

"Drink?" I asked, wondering why he woke first. Size?

My shoulders clenched at my mother's scream as she also bolted upright. Because of my experience with the Warder, I waited, and, though less violent, she also spat up her dinner. I worried that we'd undercooked dinner and I would join them… my stomach was not happy with the visuals.

I rushed to close the small distance between us and comforted my mother, looking sideways at the Warder and his still unconscious son. The Warder crawled over to his son as my mother moaned and held a hand to her head.

"What… happened…" he choked out, looking at the bandage on

his son's arm.

"The lizards," I said. "One bit him. It's ugly, but it's not terrible. He'll be fine once you're in a good enough state to Heal him."

The Warder nodded once, then put a hand to his head and groaned. Hughelas twitched, then shot up like the others, gasping. He didn't scream. He scrunched up his face, and I did the same, knowing what to expect. His father was in the danger zone.

"You might want to move back a—" I started.

Hughelas let out a gurgling belch and groaned. *Well, that wasn't so bad.* My dinner would stay down.

The lot of them were a mess. I supplied drinking water and babied them into sleeping positions, reconciling myself to guard duty for the rest of the night. I worried about Hughelas's arm—I'd hoped that one of them would be capable of a Heal, but none of them could have poured water out of a bowl that had instructions on the underside. I worried—what if a night without Healing was all it took to ruin his arm permanently, or take his life? My meditations helped me focus on the things I could control and recognize those which I could not, and though my worries remained, they didn't suffocate me. I spent that night keeping my companions alive, thinking that in the morning, one of them would Heal him… or they wouldn't.

After all, in a world of trolls and dragons, elves needed magic to survive.

Elliah ~ 16

When sleep had threatened to consume me, I rose and restocked the fire with nearby wood. In my search for ways to remain awake, I pulled out the shirt torn by the drawg, and mended it in the poor firelight. My shoddy repair work would be more visible than my scar.

"Ugggh," my mother groaned, the first to wake. The sun had not risen, but its glow brightened the sky in the clearing. She sat up, scrunched her eyes, and put both hands to her head. "My head… what hit me?" I had little sympathy. A day of hiking and a night without slumber left me dull and weary. The others stirred, the noise waking them.

"That," I said, pointing with my dagger to a pair of small corpses roasting over the fire.

"It packed quite the punch," she said as the others sat up and showed similar displeasure about the brightening sky and the prospects it brought. "But it smells good enough over a fire." My stomach tightened and I bit my lip, blinking back the threat of tears, as I watched Hughelas. While one hand rubbed his eyes, his other lay useless in his lap, purpled and swollen like overripe fruit.

"As soon as you are capable, he needs a Heal," I said. That woke the Warder further. He crawled over to his son and carefully unwrapped the wounded arm. "I cleaned and bandaged it," I said, to which the Warder grunted. The grunt could have meant anything, but I heard an indictment about my inability to Heal his son.

The Warder sucked in his breath at what he found. I closed the small distance and looked over his shoulder. Yeah, it was ugly. The skin was swollen and angry around the missing strip of flesh, and purple lines wandered across his skin. The Warder sat back on his heels, closed his eyes, and began casting.

Nothing happened.

"Dad," Hughelas said, but his father ignored him and tried again, to the same effect.

"Dad!" Hughelas insisted. "It will be alright. Calm down, eat some food, get your head on straight."

My mother wandered over, drinking water from her flask. She knelt opposite the Warder and sighed. "You did good," she told me, gently prodding the young Warder's inflamed skin, causing him to gasp, and earning an angry glare from the larger man. She ignored both of them and lightly massaged the flesh of Hughelas's arm. To what intent I was not sure. "This won't close on its own, and a simple Heal won't fix it at this point. Leave it to me."

She stood and walked to the fire. "This is what attacked us?" she asked, looking at the corpse I had not cooked. "What magic do they use?"

"Basilisks," the Warder said. He pulled a pack over and propped Hughelas up. "They paralyze their foes."

"Luckily," Hughelas said, and, despite his pain, he flashed me a smile. "We have you."

My mother froze, and the Warder looked at his son quizzically, then at me.

"She resisted their magic," he explained. "If not for her, we'd all be dead."

"But, I couldn't Heal you," I said, defending my long-held negative image of myself. *But why am I undercutting my role?*

"You wouldn't have been able to Heal me if they'd paralyzed and eaten you either," he said with a mischievous grin. "I much prefer this outcome."

The Warder chuckled, then put a hand to his head like it hurt him. "Agreed," he said, as my mother prodded at the meat over the fire. She looked at me and half-smiled.

My face burned with internal heat that came from my very core. Why couldn't I accept their praise? Her half-smile… it was like she also struggled to find any advantage in my being Bereft, to see a good side. We'd been running and hiding for eighty years. I cut her some slack— overcoming decades of preconceived notions would take time. And in cutting her some slack, my own discomfort waned.

"Edible?" my mother asked.

"Quite tasty," the Warder answered.

My mother carved off a piece and headed out of the clearing. "I need some herbs," she declared. "I'll be back."

The Warder looked at me, eyes haunted, and said, "Keep him safe." Then he quick-stepped to catch up with my mother.

"You get any sleep?" Hughelas asked.

I pulled some meat off the basilisk, then dragged my weary body over and crouched next to him. "No," was all I had the energy to explain. I handed meat to Hughelas, and we nibbled on our attackers. The Warder was right—quite tasty.

"They're creatures of the dragon side of the Perils," he said, looking at the corpse I hadn't cooked.

I scrunched my face, unfamiliar with the name.

"The Perils?" he asked, and I nodded. "That's what we call the mountains on the east side of the Contentious. The mountains that separate us from the dragons. Well, mostly separate us."

I didn't recall ever having seen the mountains named on any of the maps I'd encountered. Other than the Dragon Fangs near the Witless Tarn.

"They're quite deadly, despite their size. A large enough group of Warders can handle them. They can't paralyze everyone since their magic is in their spit. Keeping it off your skin helps, though it will soak right through cloth."

"Their magic is in their spit?" I asked, the oddness of that concept drawing my attention despite my tiredness.

"They transfer the *spell* through their spit. I imagine they contain their magic through something internal, just like we do."

I growled at him.

"Sorry," he said, scrunching his face in pain as he raised his arm in apology. "What I was trying to get at is that the magic has to be constrained to a target, or it is useless. I mean, if basilisks emitted their magic continually, then how would they raise their children, even if they managed to mate?"

He blushed, and the image of basilisks in petrified acts of reproduction made me smirk. "Okay, so they need to contain it, but not all creatures' magic is like that. The wisps just glow... all the time."

"True, but that's not exactly harmful to the species, unless they're attracting predatory birds, I suppose."

"Nothing eats wisps," I said, dismissively. "There's nothing to them. No substance worth eating."

"If you say so..." Hughelas said with a smug smile that said he knew better. "But my point is that certain spells need boundaries, containment, to be useful. Unbounded, there's no gain to the species."

That rattled around in my brain, his final words finding no purchase. "I don't understand." Tired as I was, I almost dreaded asking, "What does the species gaining something have to do with anything?"

"Oh! I have this theory. I call it flourishing suitability."

I rolled my heavy eyes. "Flourishing. Suitability?"

Hughelas didn't have the decency to blush. Instead, he grinned, and I recognized in that moment that, despite his pain, despite the open wound of his forearm with its swollen flesh, he attempted to put me at ease with humor and distractions. He perceived my worries. Maybe more than I'd admitted to myself. Everyone had almost died, leaving me on my own. I was exhausted, scared, lost.

Thoughts flooded my mind—all the fears of the night, the way Hughelas tried to tend to *me* when *he* was the one injured. My blood burned and my pulse quickened, laughter and tears all wanting out at once. The next thing I knew, my mouth was locked onto his, a purring hum coming from somewhere deep inside me. I gasped, coming up for air, wondering how long I had been... preoccupied. I'd literally rolled over on top of him, straddling his body.

I pulled away, my cheeks burning and my stomach knotting, climbing to my feet and taking a step back, breathing hard while I kept my eyes pointedly on the fire. What had made me do that? Through lowered lids, I stole a look at Hughelas. He turned his head from side to side, studying the woods.

I blushed—he was looking anywhere but at me.

"Have you seen any more basilisks?" he asked.

I shook my head no, too embarrassed to speak. What had I done?

"Too bad," he said, drawing my eyes to his with his stare. "I was hoping to get my other arm flayed and earn a second kiss like that one."

Zoras * 6

100 years before

"Yes, I assure you, we have them. They're just smaller than you describe, and they lack horns. One could never ride them—they're not big enough for that." While I had long recognized the importance of establishing a personal connection, I was shocked by just how much time we had spent discussing sheep!

"So they just walk around getting eaten then?" Since it was a connection through communication crystals, there was a little more to it than words. I sensed the rolling of eyes behind his words. Tassarion Balceran of the Black Ram Magi: the result of sending Felaern to establish a connection for me, to contact a Warder leader along the Contentious. Felaern assured me Tassarion was an authority of some weight among his people, but I had yet to understand why. I would be able to ask Felaern himself soon enough; I expected him back at any time.

"In fact, they do. We have elves who shepherd them, keeping them safe from predators. I suppose we've bred whatever defenses they had out of them." That was speculation on my part—I'd never paid particular attention to sheep. They probably had some kind of herd defenses, but why else would they need shepherds?

"Holy Mother of Trees! You breed with your sheep! Don't your women get jealous? Or are they happy for the break?"

While I sat, stunned, trying to process that, a mountain of suppressed mirth pressed in from the other side.

Hmm. "If we do it right, they drop their coats, and our women like the clothes we make from them."

Silent laughter flooded the connection. "Aye, but you've got a circular problem now. If you could get your wife to stop wearing clothes, you wouldn't need the sheep in the first place!"

Communication crystals were strange. With most elves, I saw a haze, and what little communication occurred was done by something like a mental shout, barely discernible at the other end. That's how my connections with Wynruil always worked. With others, the connection was clear, and might even include a sense of the emotions behind the words.

With Tassarion, I sensed images of great devotion and dedication to one woman. He joked, but he meant none of it. Oh, he meant liking to see his wife naked, but none of the rest. I'd never had a connection that involved so much nuance. Thus far, all spent on sheep. Well, not *just* sheep. I'd learned that the mountains west of the Contentious contained sheep with horns, both long pointy ones and rounded ones meant for battering; sheep that jumped, some with horns; giant sheep for riding; meat-eating sheep that surrounded their prey and attacked as a pack; some kind of monster that looked like a Warder during the day, but changed into one of the carnivorous sheep during a full moon. With the amazing connection, I anticipated I would sense a joke, but I hadn't. I'd just seen, with almost the clarity of being there, an image of a large man with a full moon behind him, becoming something with horns and teeth that bleated like a scream into the night.

I guarded my thoughts, using techniques I had learned and even taught others I cared about. I didn't want Tassarion to see how much the life I'd led differed from his expectations. Through the magical binding, I'd sensed a centuries-long devotion to one woman, a devotion that permeated every aspect of his life. I didn't think he would appreciate the centuries I'd devoted to encouraging promiscuity.

"I'm afraid I must go," I said, hoping my suddenly obscured thoughts would look like an interruption. "Someone is here. I look forward to our next conversation."

I ended the spell, sighing. What had Felaern been thinking? I needed someone who would help me keep the pulse of the Warder nation. Not someone obsessed with sheep whose morals wouldn't let him make short-term allowances for long-term gains. I immediately regretted my attitude. Hadn't I chastised myself for my negative influence on the world? Why did I think I needed more elves with the same predilections?

Sighing again, I left my communication room to find sustenance. I descended the stairs in something of a trance, a heaviness weighing on my heart. I intended to preserve the elves, but what was I preserving when I twisted them all up for the sake of saving them?

I was neither surprised nor concerned to find light streaming through the windows—I'd lost the night, but it had happened so often the sensation was a familiar balm. The tinge of a dream-like state nestled in my mind.

Noise from the kitchen alerted me that we had company, and though it occurred to me to turn back, I wanted food badly enough to brave another conversation. My protege, back from his adventure, was a sight for sore eyes. "Felaern! I'm pleased you've returned." Felaern reminded me of myself when I was younger, a problem-solver eager to make the world a better place. I'd lived through too many problems to believe my efforts had done anything more than shift the world's troubles around. I wondered if that was how Wynruil felt when he'd found me—it was oddly encouraging how naivety stripped away bothersome wounds. In that moment, I realized that I'd taken refuge in Felaern's innocence and energy, and had even groomed him to replace me. Would I need a Wynruil-level disaster to step down?

Illiara stood opposite the table from Felaern. It struck me that though she was fully grown, she didn't even reach Felaern's shoulder. Axilya, short for a High Elf, still stood half a head taller than Illiara. But the Wood Elf had muscles where Felaern's arms were twigs. She looked so much more vibrant and alive than he, and the ghost of what attracted me to her mother arose. It had been almost a century, but I thought her mother had been taller. Guilt whispered epithets of devotional love being eternal.

"He's returned with an appetite," Axilya touted, placing a platter of cheeses on the table amidst a small collection of books. I took in the unfamiliar books, then looked up at Axilya, who smiled and nodded toward Felaern—they were from him, not from one of her arranged exchanges. Felaern looked gaunt, skin and bones, but with fire in his eyes, and I took comfort in the latter.

Household staff cooked and cleaned, worked the grounds, repaired damages, and Axilya managed them all, in addition to caring for my semi-private library. Yet, when we hosted no parties, and the main house stood empty save for me and Illiara, I often found Axilya in the kitchen, preparing simple meals for the three of us. The lack of kitchen staff informed me that Felaern's visit was unexpected. I'd kept so busy, I wouldn't have been surprised to descend into chaos, having forgotten about some event I was meant to host.

"He's come from the Contentious," Illiara blurted, holding her tongue from further elaboration with some effort. Of course, I'd already known that was where he'd come from. Had Felaern been entertaining them with tales?

The Contentious—the river fought over by Warders, trolls, and dragons alike. When Warlords spilled from the mountains, they'd historically entered from that area. *Until the last century.* Wynruil had burned the forest below those mountains—it had secured his "retirement" and forced the Mother off the battlefield, all to the good, but the Roamers would no longer defend the treeless land. That unexpected outcome had increased the burden on the Warders. Their pilgrimages to the Mother had subsequently decreased, though I wasn't certain why. I suspected they grew disheartened by finding Her comatose, but that meant I had even less opportunity to cross paths with them. Hence my need to connect with Tassarion. The Wood Elves and Warders were all that stood between the trolls and the High Elves.

"Did you see signs of a Warlord?" I asked. I had never stopped looking after the report from Elitha and the signs near Celendril.

He cocked his head. "No." Then he considered it more thoroughly, honoring me with a deeper study of his own memories. "No," he repeated.

Where in the fires of Cenaedth had the Warlord gone? I hoped one day I would learn he had fallen victim to a deadly rock fungus, or whatever freak accidents killed trolls, but that was unlikely to happen.

"Why—" Illiara blurted, then closed her mouth, shaking her head to deny she had a question when I raised an eyebrow. While she'd changed in the three decades she'd spent with me, she hadn't entirely gotten hold of that wild tongue of hers, particularly when excited. It wasn't like her to remain so quiet. Was she nervous in front of Felaern? She'd known him for thirty years. I silently cast a spell to calm her. Like Wynruil melting a bottle, I'd become quite experienced at very subtle spellwork. But she scowled and shook her head. I felt a moment of pride that she'd noticed the spell; I'd trained her well.

I returned my attention to Felaern—he definitely looked gaunt, his golden skin tarnished. But the bags under his eyes didn't mute the light inside them—he had something he wanted to share. For a time, I'd wondered whether he might have been a descendant of mine from my early days of bending our culture toward having more children. Even if he was, five or six generations separated us. Yet we were kindred spirits, and I was more attached to Felaern and Illiara than any of my own children. Possibly I misremembered; I had sired no children in several hundred years. I didn't want my weaker magic diluting new generations. We needed stronger magic to survive.

"So tell me what's happened since last we spoke?" I'd talked to him through a communication crystal about a month before, and that had been in regard to leaving a white crystal with Tassarion for him to work the spells at his end. Axilya had spoken with him more recently, but reported only that he was on his way back. I couldn't remember how I had managed the crystals before I'd let her pick up calls. "Convincing the Warders to keep holding the Blasted Lands, I hope."

"I hope I pushed things in that direction. Befriend Tassarion. He will prove useful. Learn everything you can about sheep," he said, wide-eyed and solemn. "But the Contentious was only a waypoint. I continued farther east."

Farther east? The only thing east of the Contentious was…

"Dragon Lands," he confirmed.

Why? What problem had I mentioned that drove him there? Warders fought the dragons over the Contentious. We understood very little about dragons beyond the constant effort to keep them from spilling over the mountains into the Contentious and beyond. Spilling over was the right metaphor, as the dragons did not appear to have a true desire to expand into the Border Woods.

Wynruil, one night long after he'd removed himself from power and responsibility, had reached out through the crystal while heavy with drink, barely able to hold the connection, going on about life before the Breaking. It was difficult to tell how much the wine spoke for him, but neither could I dismiss every story. Among other wild tales, he'd claimed dragons were fewer before the Breaking, and played games with the elves! He'd said the Breaking hadn't devastated them the way it had elves, but rather had merely cleared out space for them to grow. He also claimed, with drunken vehemence, that they'd gotten meaner. That made no sense, and Wynruil had ended the conversation in a depression about the state of the world that left little doubt that at least some of his stories should have been ignored.

Had I mentioned those stories to Felaern? Perhaps I had. Some elves believed I was capable of remembering everything, but the truth was, I took good notes and filed them well. I'd let Axilya in on that over time, and she'd even taken to compiling some together into well-indexed tomes. But I'd found—in referencing old notes of conversations I'd forgotten about—several instances of repeating the same diatribe multiple times. I was old, and though my body didn't feel its years, reading my oldest notes brought the sentiment home sharply.

"Dragons can talk," Felaern interjected, and I realized I'd created an awkward pause while my thoughts had darted into rabbit holes.

That brought me back. My eyes grew wide as I tried to recall the stories from Wynruil, and why Felaern would have returned with that information. As usual, the pieces snapped into place before I completely understood how they fit together.

I snatched the last piece of cheese from the plate before Felaern grabbed it. I smiled as I uttered my conclusion. "You found us an ally."

Elliah ~ 17

Elliah

The camp kept us hostage that day, though I suspected the town of Anysa lay only hours away. We didn't get time to find a basilisk and test Hughelas's theory on amorous responses to excoriated skin, nor even a simpler trial of more spontaneous repeatability. I loved the way Hughelas spoke of everything as an experiment!

Our parents had returned all-too-quickly with a collection of herbs. My mother understood more about herbal remedies than most elves. She'd often had to turn to them for me. And Hughelas's situation differed from mine: she needed to beat back the infection that had taken root, and then a Heal spell would land. An educated enough Healer would know spells specific to fighting poison and infection, but my mother's strength was in her fortitude and persistence with a basic Heal.

So we stayed put, my mother ministering to Hughelas's wounds. I dozed for a time in the embrace of a hollowed out tree until a change in lighting disturbed my slumber. The sun beamed down proudly into our clearing, but small clouds rushed briefly to intervene, and bigger, darker clouds moved in slowly, intending to reinforce them.

I didn't enjoy being on the ground during a storm. Silverveins grew with metal venations snaking through their wood—not entirely silver, as their name suggested, but with silver aplenty. It gave them a pliability that enabled the weathering of fierce winds and morphing from magic, but more importantly, it allowed them to embrace the dance of lightning.

"Elliah," my mother said, hearing me stir from the hollow and halting her sing-song spell-casting. "We won't be traveling today."

I stretched and walked over to get a better look at Hughelas's arm—in places it looked healthier, and my mother's spells had latched on; the skin reaching for its companion shore across the wound. But other stretches still puffed out, and the infection fought back with ugly tenacity.

In the end, my mother would win. She'd had decades of practice with sedulous Healing—she would not stop, using but a trickle of mana with each casting so that she did not deplete herself. She'd become a master of endurance.

"Why don't you two go find us food," she said. "And a shelter from the coming storm." From the way the Warder loomed, I suspected my mother desired a break from scrutiny as much as she wanted food and shelter. But sending me off with the Warder… that also illustrated a level of unprecedented trust. I could not dig up a single memory of my mother trusting another elf with me, though occasionally she found out after the fact that I'd had detention alone with Professor Varitan. She would scowl and usually say something flippant about my teacher.

Without a word, I took up my mother's bow and quiver, checked my knives and trap strings, and started toward the woods. I shouted over my shoulder, "I think she meant you, Warder."

Walking slow enough for the Warder to catch up, I scanned over the trees for signs of a silvervein, determined to be worthy of my mother's trust in me. We'd headed far to the west of any known grove, but it wouldn't be out of the question to find a younger silvervein, even so far from their primary cluster. I just wouldn't see it towering over the other trees because of its youth. It took them close to a thousand years to grow so vast as to house elves; and too far from other silverveins, they succumbed to forest fires long before gaining the height and strength they needed to withstand a blaze.

"Are there any caves nearby?" the Warder asked, catching up.

"I've never been here before," I said. "Just seen it on maps. But nothing I'm seeing suggests caves." Truthfully, it hadn't occurred to me to look for caves. It made sense that the Warder, having lived in the hill country, would think to shelter underground. Caves would protect us from a storm as surely as a silvervein.

"How about near the river?" he suggested. "Sometimes the shifting waters will carve out a shelter. But we won't find your silverveins there. They don't grow along rivers."

They didn't? I'd never noticed that nor read it. But thinking back, the silvervein groves which formed the heart of any Wood Elf town might be *near* a river, but none sat right *on* a river. How had the Warder learned that when I had not? I was a Wood Elf! I mentally kicked myself.

"Though anything we find here would be more of a rivulet anyway," he mumbled to himself.

True enough. In that part of the woods, we would only find small streams that one could wade across. Some of the towns we'd lived in had such rivulets. In retrospect, I wondered whether they were natural, or diverted from rivers to add to the beauty of the town.

His idea was better than mine, and as much as that rankled, what really mattered was finding shelter. Hughelas needed it. "Wait here," I said, scampering up a tall pine. I looked out over the tree-line, then returned to the ground. "There's a break in the trees to the west that suggests water. Let's head that way."

"As the Mother wills," the Warder responded, almost absent-mindedly, like a phrase spoken out of habit. Religious kook.

I kept my eyes open for signs of prey, but ignored their trails as I headed for the stream. Finding shelter worried me more than finding food—game abounded in the forest. Within minutes, we hit a stream bed that headed north, the water low and sluggish, though the bed was deep—exactly as I'd hoped. The spring rains had not hit in earnest—or the water would have been bold and determined—but the relatively dry winter had left wide and walkable swaths of smooth, gray rocks on either side.

"Yes," the Warder said, nodding his head and looking both up and down the stream. "There will be a cave here somewhere."

"Which way?" I asked.

"Those trees over the horizon," he said, pointing downstream. "They suggest a hill, and so, possibly, a cave."

The darker clouds masked the sun, and a whip of wind sent a chill down my spine. "Go," I said. "Get them and bring them back. I'll head downstream. When I find shelter, I'll signal you with smoke, if it isn't raining."

"Caves are not always empty," he responded with skepticism. "And if you don't find shelter?" He shook his head. "I don't think Illiara would be happy were I to leave you alone."

Illiara? My mother's name was foreign to my ears. Hearing it made my gut tighten protectively.

"She should worry more about your being defenseless should another basilisk appear on your return trip," I said, curt. "That is, if you can even find your way back to camp on your own."

His gaze sharpened, his eyes boring into mine, then a smile spread across his face. "You are your mother's daughter."

I had no use for his pointless statement.

"If you will let me," he said, nodding toward the dagger at my belt, "I will teach you to fight with that blade."

"I do well enough," I said.

"Well enough," he agreed. "But those basilisks have me spooked." He didn't look spooked. "I would see you excel... to keep me safe."

I narrowed my eyes at him with suspicion. Was he more clever than he appeared?

"Find us shelter!" he said, turning away and chuckling. "Mother, keep her safe!" he shouted to the sky as he walked—then jogged—away.

Nut-job Warder.

I set off alone down the stream bed, gloriously independent and relishing the trust imparted to me.

***

We sheltered in the lee of a corroded cliff, burning wood I'd collected before the rain dropped. The overhang provided shelter from the downpour, though the carved-out nook did not stop the occasional intrusion of wind-driven splatter. We caught no meat, but we had plenty of trail food. I'd stood taller as everyone had arrived, proud of accomplishing my goal. I mean, it wasn't like we were skulking through troll country, running for our lives, but we were relatively dry during a storm that would have soaked us. We passed the time with my mother singing over Hughelas's wound, beating back the infection with her poultices, and advancing the skin growth through Heals with each minor victory against the infection. She was winning.

Meanwhile, the Warder attempted to teach me combat skills. The idea had excited me while I'd searched for a haven from the rain, imagining glorious battles against rocky trolls and scaly dragons. Instead, he had me practicing how I stood and moved, with no weapons at all.

"Am I going to be fighting with my fists then?" I said, belligerent. I changed my stance to one more natural and comfortable than the unfamiliar pose in which he had placed me.

The Warder turned slightly, knocking me on my butt with an ease that irritated me.

"There is no weaker foe than one who has lost a weapon that he depends upon," he said, the message sounding like one he had repeated many times.

I turned my scowl to Hughelas, embarrassed at being knocked

down so casually and expecting to see him laughing. Instead, he grimaced.

"I know how it feels," Hughelas said with sympathy. "It isn't fair that he weighs three times what we do."

"Three times?" the Warder scoffed with mock offense. "I'd wager I'm roughly twice your weight at best." Then he laughed his joy-filled laugh that somehow took the sting out of everything. "But yes… sometimes size matters."

My mother let out a chirrup of laughter, her eyes studiously focused on Hughelas's wound, though her song paused while she regained control of herself. I had a guess about why she laughed, but I didn't think it was what the Warder had meant. And while it was out of character for the woman who'd raised me, decades of stern control had sloughed off over just a few days of travel. She even looked… younger.

And so we passed the storm, amidst drizzle and fire, Heal spells and fighting—or training to fight at least. My mother continued her inevitable march against infection in Hughelas's torn arm, and by my guess, the morning would see her victory complete. She even paused and pulled the others into our nightly meditations, walking them through the basics of breathing and clearing one's mind. Beldroth showed a natural aptitude for both.

***

I awoke, my darkened spirit echoed by the overcast morning that outlined the overhanging rock. A chill hung in the air from the night's rain. What the light did *not* outline was any sort of sentry watching over us.

"Gruh," I muttered, painfully leveraging myself up on stiff arms. How could all of that *standing* produce such soreness?

"Gruh yourself," Hughelas muttered, stirring from his spot near me, the embers of the night's fire separating us from the vacant entrance. I'd fallen asleep watching the lines of his face in the flickering light, and our heads had lain near one another through the night. A devilish thought of what we'd missed by not shifting closer in the darkness slipped through my mind, and suddenly my brooding spirit flitted away, my momentary alarm at our missing parents becoming an… opportunity.

"How's your arm?" I asked, crawling closer to Hughelas as he examined it himself.

"Good as—"

He stopped as I ran my fingers down his forearm, lingering on the spot where there should have been a scar. Damn, my mother was fantastic at Healing for an elf who hadn't made it her vocation.

But I smiled at his broken statement. "New," I said, inching even closer as he wriggled his way into a sitting position without removing his arm from my touch.

"What?" he asked, his face inches from mine, my hand reaching across his seated body so that I leaned slightly over him. Needles of anticipation pricked my skin.

"Good… as… new," I whispered, moving my hand into his, where eager fingers intertwined with my own.

He scoured our small overhang, like his enormous father hid behind a pack no larger than my torso. Or my mother lurked among the embers of the fire. Then he looked me in the eye, slid his hand from mine and slipped it behind my back, pulling me close… and he kissed me.

Time sped up and slowed down all at once, and I was unsure whether our lips had just touched or I'd lingered on the kiss for too long. The needles poking my skin melted from the heat coursing through me, and I… I hungered… but it wasn't for food. I didn't know what I wanted. Had I held the kiss too long? Was I being weird?

I pulled away and sucked my lips into my mouth, my desire for something clear, but its aim elusive, wishing to be bold, but immersed in uncertainty. He purred, his eyes closed, then he grinned, slowly raising his lids.

"Mmm," he hummed, and I smiled. Embarrassed that I'd smiled in response to his appreciation, I looked down and blushed. *How do elves get through this?*

My mother's laughter jerked me back to reality.

"… never seen an elf swim so fast!" came the booming voice of the Warder, his voice fading in from some distance away, but I still stood and backed away from Hughelas like I'd been sitting too close to a viper. Hughelas didn't rise. Instead, he sighed, then scooted forward and reached into the ashes of the fire and plucked out an ember, which he juggled from hand to hand.

"What are you—"

"Shhhh!" he shushed me. "Stop reminding me you're here."

"Did they follow him?" my mother asked, laughing. They were coming closer, their voices clearer.

I watched in confusion as Hughelas sucked in his breath and dropped the glowing red bit of wood. He blew onto his hands, said, "Throw some kindling on the fire," and then plucked up the ember and began again.

Confused, I followed his orders.

"They didn't come out of the water," the Warder said, ever nearer. "But we were much more careful about where we swam after that."

Hughelas dropped the bright ember back into the ashes just as our parents, laughing, turned the corner and came into view.

"Oh, good," the Warder said. "You've rekindled the fire. We've got breakfast." He held aloft a few fish strung up on a short string.

Hughelas huffed on the glowing ember and a flame licked onto the wood I'd thrown into our little pit.

My mother and the Warder busied themselves with preparing our meal. With them preoccupied, I leaned toward Hughelas, who finally climbed to his feet. "What was that all about?" I whisper-hissed at him, mimicking his juggling.

"I had to put a fire out," he whispered back, throwing some larger branches on the fire.

"What?" I whisper-shouted, loud enough that my mother and the Warder paused to look at us. I smiled stupidly and picked up more wood; my mother rolled her eyes and resumed her work and conversation.

"Trust me," Hughelas said, reaching for the wood I held, but overshooting and running his fingers down the exposed flesh of my forearm, setting my skin aflame as he grabbed the log from my hand. "I had a fire to put out."

I blushed as realization dawned on me.

Beldroth : 2

The overcast sky did not deter us from moving on. The clouds, as yet unprepared to deluge us again, still prevented the sun from drying out the foliage and ground. It made for a mucky trek. The stream had grown overnight, fueled by the Mother's gentle tears. I chose to ignore the Bereft's mumblings about the storm being the "Mother's tantrum."

"Tell me about where you're from," Illiara asked, as we followed the river along its bank.

"Bellon?" I asked. "Or life along the Contentious in general?"

"Why not both?" she responded with a wry smile that brightened the gloomy day.

I laughed, enjoying a tranquility I'd sought on our journey, but hadn't truly expected to find. "I've only been as far south along the Contentious as Aendolin, the capital of our people. That is, before this trip. We took the old mountain pass between Lynashi and Thylerie to enter the Border Woods—traveling down the Contentious is faster and less dangerous than going overland in the open area that was once the Faeltic Forest." The mad Alluvium, Wynruil, had consumed it in flames hundreds of years ago. The forest never regrew; trolls made sure not to lose that foothold.

"I saw quite a bit of new growth from the river," my son offered.

I nodded my head, conceding his point. "The trolls have turned their attention elsewhere." That wasn't a good thing. They were up to something.

"But, yes," I said, "perhaps the Faeltic will regrow. Maybe we will see Roamers at Bellon again. Wouldn't that be something?"

I'd never seen a Roamer. I hoped to see one in the Border Woods, but I'd realized it was unlikely. Still, as the Mother willed…

Illiara made a clicking noise with her tongue, and I smiled at her redirection of my attention. "Bellon," I explained, "is the first city south of the mountains that separates us from the trolls. I'm told it was once a glorious fortress, but that was well before my time. Bellon is a set of caves and collapsed buildings occupied by determined Warders. The rest of the Warder cities: Orolond, Dal Mego, Galea—and I imagine all the towns along the Contentious—have to deal with dragons venturing out of the Dragonlands over the Perils. But those fights are sporadic at best, so to stay sharp, most Warders come to Bellon for mission work."

"Fighting trolls is mission work?" the Bereft asked. *Elliah*, I corrected myself. I'd already marveled and thanked the Mother for the precious Bereft *survivor*. But she'd shown herself to be so much more… timid with people yet bold in her actions, caring despite a lifetime of incomprehensibly poor treatment from her fellow elves, and filled with a determination that she inherited from her mother. Or the Mother.

"Of course," I answered, smiling at the thought. "But I was *born* in Bellon. As was Hughelas. It was our home. New missionaries, we would teach how to fight if needed, where to hide, how to… stay alive."

Our trek took us upward, the little stream growing into a tiny river as the bank pulled higher and higher. I paused as we navigated a steep cluster of rocks.

"Returning veterans we just organized," I said, offering Illiara a hand. Which she took! "We sent them on campaigns to clear trolls from the Faeltic."

Releasing her hand with reluctance, I continued to follow the edge of the increasingly dangerous edge. The trees thinned out ahead, revealing some kind of gorge crossing our path in the distance.

"We had a resident Wood Elf Healer," I said, with an acknowledging nod to Illiara. "Anlyth. He claimed to have been there since before the Faeltic burned." With a smile to Illiara, I added, "But he couldn't hold a candle to your endurance." Anlyth had pulled off some complicated Heals. No doubt he had experience and would have finessed Hughelas's arm wound, but he wouldn't have kept Elliah alive.

"And Hughelas's mother?" Illiara asked.

My smile broke. *That's not okay,* I told myself. I plastered it back on. "A Salt. She worked water and wind spells like no Warder or Wood Elf. I'd never seen a Salt before I met Lyrei." We walked on in silence for some time. Her fate weighed heavily on me. "We married," I finally said. "And she died."

I'd performed my Vigil. Why did it still trouble me?

"I spent the last decade performing the Lamenter's Vigil." My voice sounded heavier than I liked so I perked it up. "I still trained raw recruits and organized efforts from my Vigil. I just couldn't participate."

"I've never heard of Lamenter's Vigil," Elliah said quietly. "What is it?" she asked Hughelas.

"After a spouse dies," he answered, "the one who lives spends a decade mourning for their loss. You do not have such a thing?"

Elliah looked at her mother in question, but Illiara shook her head no.

Hughelas nodded and continued. "Some isolate themselves completely. Others give up something. He gave up fighting. It's meant to help one process grief... but it seems to me it just compounds it."

I frowned. The Vigil had helped me focus on my loss, and surely that mattered. Beluar Zinric recorded many of his infamous Lamb-entations during his own vigil, and while I personally did not see much use for sheep beyond a source of food and clothing, his words pulled on even my heartstrings.

We traveled in silence for some time. It eventually became clear that the gorge held a river, one the fledgling river we followed would feed into. Even before we crested the hill that defined the corner of the two chasms, we heard the murmur of the water.

"The Amyla," I stated. Other races believed Warders had a supernatural sense of direction. We didn't. It was not one of my finer skills. But I'd studied maps thoroughly for our endeavor, and I was relatively confident I grasped where we were. More importantly, the Mother would lead us truly, even if I was wrong about our location. "We follow this east to Anysa?" I looked to Illiara to confirm.

"I think so," she said. "I've never been there. We crossed the Amyla farther upriver when we moved to E'anashys."

I looked over the edges of each cliff. The Amyla lay very far below. It looked much more angry than the Contentious, trapped between the walls of the canyon. The pretty name did not do it justice. The rivulet we'd followed was not as long of a descent, but it ended in a waterfall that spilled into the Amyla. Most of the noise was from that tumultuous cascade. Crossing the rivulet would be treacherous; we would have to walk for at least an hour back upstream to be sure of a safe passage.

Nodding, I set off east by southeast, following the Amyla. "The Mother willing, we will board a ship in Anysa," I said.

Elliah's eyes widened. "Boats will travel on *that*?" The river moved swiftly, and while it had the width to support a boat or three, the protruding rocks suggested treacherous passage. Upon closer examination, I spotted the wooden hull of a boat wedged into one such excrescence.

"I feel certain they do," I said, looking to Illiara for confirmation, and she nodded.

We crossed rolling hills as we followed the river, most valleys draining tiny bits of water off the edge of the cliff. I steered us away from the edge where the trees grew thicker. The terrain was what I expected. After all, the Border Woods nestled in the foothills west of the great divide. The day was too cloudy to see them, but the mountains overlooked us to the east. I longed to see them.

I wasn't certain how far away Anysa lay, nor truthfully, if we were even headed in the right direction. But campsites abounded, so we could let the sun descend quite far before settling in, and it was just past midday. Still, we were not particularly in a hurry—even with the Mother's Blessing, it would take us months to accomplish my intent. It wasn't clear when Illiara and her daughter would part company with us, but finding them had clearly been the Mother's plan, and I intended to convince them to travel with us. Another night camping with them would draw us closer.

So I was prepared to call an early stop and spend more time talking, when we crested a rocky hill that bore few trees, and found a wide valley between the rolling landscape that led to the river. The valley must have once, eons ago, been the natural path for the river. Something upstream had shifted and redirected the waterway to its current course, creating the perfect spot for a town. Until the Mother moved the river back. I shivered at the idea.

Nestled along the shore lay a town that outsized what I'd imagined. Buildings of wood, and even stone, held fast to the shore and lined a path shooting away from the water and into the trees, which themselves held their distance. Silverveins towered a short hike from the river, declaring Anysa a Wood Elf town despite buildings affixed to the ground. I expected such things in the Heartland, in High Elf territory, but not in the Border Woods.

"Mom…" Elliah muttered. "Look at all the *buildings*." *Ah, so it isn't common.*

Illiara cocked her head at her daughter, then pursed her lips like she wasn't sure she should speak, but she did. "You were too little to remember, but it's not the first time you've seen such buildings."

"Buildings are so rare?" Hughelas asked softly, recognizing Elliah's offput state.

She nodded her head.

"We have many along the Contentious," Hughelas responded. "Well, and caves too. No silvervein grow there." He eyed the towering trees with something like awe, and his wonder relaxed Elliah. As he'd probably meant it to. He was a good lad.

Still, my idea of spending another night camping was shot. I started downhill, Illiara by my side.

I'd seen boats before—small floating hollowed-out trees that could hold a person, or pieces of wood bound together to form a raft that might hold more. The largest boat I'd seen might have held two people and a bit of cargo at most, using wooden oars to get around.

Comparing the boats from my past to the ships in Anysa was like comparing elfbloom to a silvervein. Sure, they were both plants, but the scale! The ships in Anysa looked like they could hold twenty people, maybe more. And they had wooden poles jutting into the sky, with large stitched canvases held to the posts with ropes. The harbor didn't hold many that size—four in the river moorage and one up on shore undergoing some kind of work. But among those large ships, one stood out. Its size matched the others, but its colors were sharper, its lines more graceful; and even among its magnificent brethren, it stood proud. Though it bobbed up and down with the others, it looked more eager to get away, to detach from its moor and play in the river proper.

But to reach the ship, we had to get to the *road*. Paved passages for travel were not a common occurrence in Wood Elf towns, or at least not in the smaller towns we had lived in. The one in the valley below, which carved a straight path between the river on our left and the deeper woods on our right, looked smooth and wide enough for two carts to pass. As we approached it, an enormous cart, at least the length of two people, lumbered from the river to the woods, pulled by a creature I'd never seen. An enormous hairless bear? I hurried to the road to get a closer look, Hughelas on my heels.

The beast and its burden crawled past. On all fours, it still stood at least twice my height. The head, gray-skinned with enormous black eyes and yellow tusks, paid us no attention. I'd been wrong about it being hairless, but only wispy gray threads clung sparingly to what looked to be a thick leathery skin. I wondered what terrain its flat feet were built for.

"What is it?" Hughelas shouted up at the elf who held a rope that ran through the creature's mouth. I'd never seen such a thing, even in the stories of Talena.

"Bumpkin," I heard the elf mumble, and I blushed slightly.

But the reprimand did not discourage Hughelas. "What is it?

Where is it from? It's beautiful!"

Beautiful? Interesting, for sure. But beautiful? However, the comment drew a smile from the driver. "We call it a garonaut," he said to us. "They live around the Faelian Swamp, in the brackish waters."

"Amazing," Beldroth said, having caught up at his more leisurely pace.

"You should see them when they fight," my mother said. "Or mate." I shot a look at her… why would she bring up mating? But she wasn't looking at me, just the garonaut.

"I imagine that is quite the sight," Beldroth said.

"You've seen these before?" I asked, ignoring the inappropriate mating comment and taking offense at the fact that my mother had never mentioned giant gray hairless tusked bears.

"Yes," she said, looking at me and turning suddenly reticent.

"Where?" I demanded.

She looked away and sighed, like she'd slipped up. Which she had. "In the Faelian Swamps. Come," she said, cutting me off. "Let's get to the moorage." And she stalked off, the Warder following behind with a shrug. Hughelas looked at me with an eyebrow raised, then nodded for me to move.

Irritated, I started after our parents, who had stepped onto the smooth yellowed-stone road and traveled toward the river. Even after I could no longer see the hulking swamp creature my mother had never mentioned, the road shuddered beneath my feet with its slow rhythm.

The road ran straight through a small arrangement of wooden buildings that smelled of fish. It ended in planks that hovered over the water, with piers jutting into the river like limbs of a tree reaching into the sky. Small waves lapped against hull and beams, while a stone's throw away, the river rushed past with quiet, but not silent, determination. Hungry birds patrolled the docks and boats, while others glided above us on cushions of air that I imagined being natural creations of the gaps in the hills.

But all of that was mere background, new and impressive enough on its own, yet nothing compared to the bustle of elves busy with burdens of various sizes moving about the docks and on the ships. The busiest cluster was around the ship I'd spied from atop the hill—the one that stood out with its clean lines and sharp colors, not to mention its peculiar calmness, as though it didn't deign to notice the swirling eddies that wandered the river.

Beldroth headed straight for it, but stopped without climbing the plank that led up to the ship. "Faeyoo!" he shouted, earning rough looks and a wide berth from the elves working around him. I shot my mother a look of concern, but she seemed unfazed, and I found Hughelas's eyes danced with mirth.

"What—" My question was interrupted by a second bellow from the Warder. "Faeyoo!"

The gap between us and any other elf grew. The noise from the deck quieted, and a face poked over the railing of the ship—a face with skin as white as snow. Alabaster hair, decorated with shells and gems, cascaded over bared white shoulders. I'd never seen the like, but I instantly realized that I looked upon a Salt, an elf whose people roamed the waters.

"Faeyoo," the elf said, the voice feminine. She looked from Beldroth to the rest of us, her gaze lingering on Hughelas. Then she turned back to gaze at something I could not see. The river?

"Have we met?" she said, spinning around to look at Beldroth, who maintained his maniacally good-natured smile.

"We have not," he said, placing an arm on Hughelas's shoulder. "But the mother of my son was Lyrie, Daughter of the Nine Winds."

The woman's gaze lingered on Beldroth, then languidly moved to Hughelas. "And your name, son of Lyrie?"

"Hughelas." He smiled as he answered, an echo of the Warder's overpowering beam slipping in. I realized, looking at the two, that though Hughelas's skin was light, it was darker than the Salt's.

"I am Edraele, captain of the Knoll. And where is your home, Hughelas?" the captain asked Hughelas.

"I have never had a home," he answered, and his father nodded proudly.

Their words, I finally realized, had a tenor or ritualism, and I mentally repeated the conversation. Faeyoo… water is life, or life is water. Where is your home? *I have never had a home.* They spoke of the ship. Hughelas Do'Wood. Not of the woods. Half-Salt without a ship. Half-Warder, but no brawn. He smiled as he declared and defined himself by what he wasn't. While my whole life I had hidden what I was.

I stood straighter, and the eyes of the captain flicked to me, then my mother, then back to the Warder. "Why do you call on me?" she asked, direct and simple.

"We seek shelter on your home for a time."

"From whom do you flee?"

"All Warders have enemies, but our haste births from that which we seek rather than those who chase us. We seek the Blessing of the Mother."

The captain's eyes narrowed. "Then you are a fool. She has slept nigh on a hundred years."

"Eighty!" Beldroth cheered. "To be exact, eighty years, not a hundred. I bring that which last broke her slumber. Perhaps it is a fool's errand, but I would count myself the greater fool for not trying."

The captain's eyes danced around the Warder, cocking her head in curiosity at his hammer. Which was all just as well, because I imagined my face scarlet from the realization that he believed *I* would *spark the Mother of Trees,* whom I had long believed to be fictionalized, into Blessing whatever mission his son had warned me about. Why hadn't I used any of my time alone with Hughelas to understand his father's goals? When had I become a girl who would lose her way like a buck following the scent of a doe into a hunter's snare?

"And Lyrie, Daughter of the Nine Winds?" the captain asked. "Where is her home?"

"She and her home have both returned to the Mother," Beldroth answered.

"Together?" The captain's face remained neutral, but her raised eyebrow and held breath conveyed weight to the question.

"Her home departed first." Even the Warder's eternally congenial face became dour with his proclamation. The captain frowned and let her breath out with disgust. The Warder continued. "She lost her home, the Quiet Storm, while trying to reach the back side of the Two Fangs." The captain's eyes flashed with surprise, then she nodded her head like she'd heard a familiar story. "She spent decades without a home…" The captain pinched her eyes closed. And then the Warder's smile returned. "But she made the best of her predicament." He patted his son's shoulder. "In the end, that which she'd searched for found her. Faeyoo."

The captain inhaled, looked up at the sky, and breathed out slowly. What had Hughelas's mother searched for? But it wasn't the time to ask. The Salt nodded her head. "Faeyoo," she uttered in conclusion. Then her tone changed to business. "There is no room on my home for louse-abouts. If you would board, then you must work."

The plank leading onto the boat bowed in despair when the Warder grabbed a barrel and crossed it. But it held—a task doubly impressive given the way the Warder's muscles bulged under the weight of his burden.

Hughelas grinned and, winking, walked to another barrel. "Well? Help me out." Between us, we could not lift it—his father's strength astounded me.

"Come," said the white-skinned captain. "There are many other things you can help with. In fact, you are better suited to some tasks. Below deck, the space is tight. The Warder would not even be able to stand up straight. Join me. We have cargo to secure."

My mother led the way up the ramp, and I followed, Hughelas trailing behind me. I suddenly forgot how to walk. How did he keep ending up behind me?

Somehow, I climbed the plank without an awkward splash into the river moorage.

Zoras * 7

Felaern grinned like he'd pulled off a masterful feat of magic… which, perhaps, he had. Dragons had fought elves for as long as I'd lived, but they'd indiscriminately fought with elves and trolls alike. Dragons considered everyone else an inconvenience. If Felaern had secured their help…

"I found records in Aendolin of a white dragon who appeared multiple times in their history. There's even a statue in their famous stone gardens that has a dragon sitting on eggs while fed by elves. Not eating elves, mind you," he said with a grin. "The statue is old and worn, but it looks like elves are bringing the dragon some of those mountain-climbing sheep that everyone along the Contentious fights over." Felaern shook his head, like he thought something in all of that was stupid, but he didn't explain. I imagined that, like me, he struggled with how integral sheep were in the culture and lives of the Warders. "Some of the older elves remembered stories—legend says it would birth its young in a cave where the ruins of Bellon now sit."

"Bellon?" It sounded familiar, but a name from a different time.

"We lost it when Wynruil set that part of the Border Woods afire. It sat very near both trolls and dragons."

Ah. Bellon had once been an integral part of any plan of Wynruil's. Its decline after the fire had brought Wynruil to tears. "It existed before the Breaking," he'd wept. "One more piece of our past… gone."

Felaern turned contemplative. "It made me wonder if an Ancient influenced the city's origin." Hadn't Wynruil suggested as much? No, no, that wasn't it. He'd said something about a dragon *protecting* the elves in those mountains after the Breaking, like the Mother had sheltered the Wood Elves and High Elves. Might that not have looked much like influencing the city's origin? Unfortunately, Wynruil only talked of the Breaking when his tongue loosened under copious amounts of drink, so the stories didn't knit together as much as they merely clung to the same tapestry. One thing I'd never managed to pry from him, even when he was well-lubricated, was the name of any other Old Guard.

Felaern returned to his narrative before I did. "I searched for the Ancient for several years."

He paused, and I dutifully returned to the story at hand and asked, "How does one even go about searching for a particular dragon? Especially without becoming a snack?" I granted him that pat on the back for the effort he'd put in and to recognize his cleverness. Illiara's saucer-like eyes drank in every word from Felaern. Axilya returned from the kitchen with more cheese and a bowl with nuts, then put an arm on Illiara's shoulder. Illiara jumped, then smiled at Axilya as her cheeks reddened.

Felaern smiled at my setup. "*That* is an interesting dilemma. The Warders mostly fight with greens that spill over mountains to get to the Contentious. Occasionally, reds or blacks cause trouble." He was enjoying the opportunity to display his gained knowledge. "However, despite the old records, white dragons were not a familiar sight for recent Warders."

I raised an eyebrow, inviting him to reveal his mysterious plot twist.

"But the *Salts* knew where to find white dragons."

"The Salts?" I said with the proper amount of shocked incredulity. In truth, it didn't surprise me. Salts sailed the world over, so unless the white dragons resided with the trolls in the Witless Tarn, the Salts would have seen them.

"On the far side of the world, south of the Rim and its boulder-hurling trolls, there's an inlet that weaves right into the smaller mountains east of the Two Fangs."

How ironic! White dragons actually *did* live near the trolls. "The Salts go there? Why?"

Felaern shrugged. "It seems they go anywhere the oceans reach. They're drawn to learn its secrets. I traveled to Ast Velera, their island home south of the Contentious." He paused. "I believe we have very much underestimated the Salts. They're quite secretive, but the knowledge they've amassed rivals our own."

Secretive, yes, though I couldn't believe the Salts' collections *rivaled* those of High Elves. Undoubtedly, Felaern dramatized for effect.

I wished I could say I'd corrected my mistake nearly five hundred years before, when I'd recognized how little I understood of the Warders. Though Wynruil had helped me connect with the Alluvium military, it had taken centuries to form my recent connection with the Warders, and though I had good intentions, I'd made no connections with the Salts. In fact, Axilya had proven more effective than I with the water-bound elves. I didn't understand how she accomplished it, but I'd noticed changes in my library—in particular, detailed maps—and I suspected some books and accouterments had found their way to Salt libraries. She spoke of libraries in the major Salt cities, and a mysterious island with a library greater than the one I'd created in Alenor, in a town nobody ever left. I remembered smiling indulgently and asking, "And how, pray tell, do you know of it if no one has ever left it?"

She'd harrumphed and flung the knife she'd been cleaning. It stuck in the nearby cutting board she'd used to carve us a snack, ending our conversation with a *pointed* reminder that she had more than culinary and diplomatic skills.

"The Salts have a library in Ast Velera," Faelern said. Axilya had already shared that information in the context of maps that had appeared on the walls of the dining hall. "It didn't compare to the ones you've created in the Heartland," he said consolingly. "Very different from our libraries, but quite impressive." I sighed inwardly, thinking of the hassle involved were I to venture out to see those libraries, though I had no doubt they would appeal to me.

"The Salts are experimentalists," he declared. "Think of it this way—we High Elves have pondered deeply about many things, recorded our thoughts, and built upon that knowledge. The Alluvium are all fire." He smirked at his little joke. "They use the same spells, incrementally adding a bit here and there, but overall they just get stronger and better at combat spells."

I nodded in agreement.

"The Salts… they don't think through every potential piece to its logical conclusion. They try things, and then build upon failures, until they eventually succeed."

The conversation had gone quite sideways, but it fascinated me nonetheless. "That sounds very dangerous."

"There are few old Salts. Not by our standards. But they understand magic that we've never considered."

"For example?" I asked, ready to counter any evidence with my accumulated centuries of knowledge.

"Half-breeds," he answered, puzzling me. What did that mean? He smiled. Patronizingly? Illiara fidgeted. "You believe the offspring of two races weakens the magic of the children." I nodded. The data of Farryn and Aien showed that the spells of half-breeds were at best equal in strength to that of their parents, but almost always weaker.

He tapped a book sitting on the table. "Read this and then tell me you still believe that."

I squinted at him like he played some trick, but flipped the gray-covered book open to take a look. Scratchings. Scribbles. Someone's journal at best.

"Just read it," Faelern repeated.

I didn't want to—if it showed what he claimed, that half-breeds had stronger magic than pure-bloods, then everything I'd steered toward over the last several centuries had been wrong. What's more, I'd given up a relationship for incorrect data. I'd tasted it before, the bitter mouth-drying tang of my own manipulations twisting, creating problems instead of solving them. It wasn't my first encounter with the experience, but it was the first time I truly understood Wynruil's mad exit from leadership, burning the entire Faeltic Forest just to stop fighting for them. What had Wynruil done in those centuries that he'd regretted? How many lives lost? What ate at his soul? And if I'd been wrong, hadn't I influenced all elf culture to take the wrong direction? Would not my mistakes cost ten times any of Wynruil's? In that moment, I wanted *out...* so badly.

My eye twitched, a rare loss of control that I kept from repeating itself by taking a slow breath. I removed my hand from the book—I wasn't ready. "For the love of words," I mumbled. "And the Ancient?" I steered us back to this original story; my doubts and fears always waited patiently for my return.

"I traveled the mountains east of the Witless Tarn. Troll territory. Though I spotted whites flying, I failed to reach any of them. I did not find her." Her! Well, he had mentioned a statue of a dragon sitting on eggs, but for all I knew, the males did that work.

Faelern had not finished his story—he would not be smiling in my kitchen if the story ended there.

"But the effort was not completely fruitless—I found an Ancient *red*. Or she found me. I was scaling one of the Fangs, hoping to find a white, and I slipped. The red plucked me from certain death. And she spoke to me, Zoras! She spoke Elvish!"

So dragons *could* speak. Some of the oldest tales suggested as much. I didn't want to reveal how much I didn't know about dragons, so I simply nodded for him to go on, saying, "And she wants to help us? She wants to fight the trolls?"

He hesitated. "Neither, specifically. She wants to help magic and her offspring, and I convinced her that helping the elves was the best way to do that."

As allies went, the one Felaern chose cast ten shades of doubt on a clear day. A red dragon, an Ancient, who would side with the elves? No, no, not even that—a red dragon who wanted to help *magic*, an intention which might, temporarily, coincide with aiding the elves.

I considered what little I knew of dragons. Dragons collect their dead—a saying that predated even me. That was about it. For the most part, dragons ignored elves. Dragons did what they wanted, whether an elf was in the way or not. Dragons ignored the *concerns* of elves.

There was a saying as old as Wynruil: "a bandage and sword for my enemies' foe." But dragons, to my knowledge, treated trolls with the same irrelevance as elves. They were not foes of our troll antagonists. We had no common ground with dragons. Faelern had talked a dragon into something… or the dragon had talked its intent into Faelern.

I must have paused for too long, or perhaps I failed to conceal my doubt. But when I prepared to ask further questions, I found something harder than I expected looking back at me. It was like the first bricks of a wall lay between us. Faelern's eyes, cold and calculating, invoked a fleeting memory of a parallel from my past—a day I'd told Wynruil he was wrong and forced a change in his battle plan. Faelern believed he held the future in his grasp, while I desperately wanted *out*. Was it a cycle without end? In Illiara's words, "New growth sprouting from fallen trees." What disasters would Faelern create in his certainty?

Despite the flipped circumstances, I had no mad plan ready. I had no Faelic Forest to burn, and wasn't sure I could light the fire if I did. What would that even look like for me? How did one burn down centuries of social conditioning? It would take a catalyst in the same arena… something drastic would have to inflame the hearts of elves. Was I ready to give up the ghost of the fight and let the new vine strangle the old? I'd caged a god to preserve a memory, steered social convention to create an army, and amassed knowledge to gain power for the good of elvendom. But my hand rested on a book that suggested at least one of my efforts had done naught but harm, and if even one, why not all?

Before me stood my protege, intent on moving forward with plans of his own… schemes based on the self-assurance of youth and doomed to the same fate as my own well-meaning but poorly founded intentions.

Though I'd lived a long time, I'd never felt so… old.

I groaned quietly as I stretched and realized just how many muscles hurt. My shoulders, my legs, my back and stomach… even my fingers hurt! A dim glow crept in from above. The square of light, along with the gentle rocking, reminded me I rested in the hull of a boat. *A ship,* I corrected myself. When I'd asked about the difference, I'd practically started a fight among the existing crew.

"A ship has three or more masts," one snow-colored elf had said.

"What of the Deliverance then?" asked another. "She is a *boat*? She could *swallow* this *ship* we're loading."

"Big the Deliverance may be, but a ship she is not," claimed the first elf, bowing up for a fight.

"The difference—" interrupted a younger elf, female and closer to my age, silencing the fight. "The difference between a *ship* and a *boat* is that, if you call the captain of a ship a boat-captain, you will have a fight on your hands, but if you call the captain of a boat a ship-captain, she will buy you a drink."

Laughing, the crew resumed loading and securing their cargo.

We secured the freight for many hours, slight cuts and bruises popping up on my fingers like cracks on the sun-baked ground. The ship's crew did not have similar struggles. They navigated the narrow confines without looking, where I kept backing into things. Their fingers had callouses in all the right places to protect from the ropes. They had practice at grabbing the boxes and barrels without slicing themselves.

And why so *many* casks? It was more wine than I imagined ever being able to drink. Hughelas and I found we could roll them, but it earned us a quick reprimand for the risk that we might cause it to open. I thought that unlikely—elves had magically grown their seals. But, apparently, it had happened once, and the risk wasn't worth the advantage.

At one point, my mother pulled me aside to Heal a finger I'd smashed. The Salts eyed us askance as she quietly repeated her spell until it took hold.

"Wood Elf thing," Hughelas had mumbled to one sailor. "Prayers to the Mother."

If I'd had any energy, I would have laughed. That was his father's thing, not ours. But the Salts shrugged and carried on—we didn't linger so long as to shirk our duties.

I learned a great deal about ropes, knots, and tying up goods. Finally, the Warder had come below deck to sleep, and the *ship's* captain had been right—he was unable to stand up straight. Hughelas, my mother, and I fit in the tight quarters without trouble.

Still, all in all, the work had made for one almighty body ache. I remembered starting my meditations, but not finishing them. Nothing appealed to me more than the idea of rolling over and closing my eyes for just a bit longer.

I bring that which last broke your slumber, the Warder's voice intoned from the surrounding darkness.

A skeletal hand as large as my body, composed of rotting wood, reached out to enfold me…

My eyes flew open. I still lay in a hammock strung between two posts in the hull of the Knoll. No hand reached for me. My heart raced. After *that* dream, sleep and I had nothing more to say to one another.

What was that dream all about? Did I trust the Warder or didn't I? He'd done nothing untoward, but the way he'd lit up at my mother's story about the Mother of Trees… I had a feeling he would discourage us from parting ways. Probably that was all the dream meant—some lingering fear of being used. My mother's words from the woods came to mind, that she *wanted* to trust him, and I understood her sentiment. While the Warder was extreme, he was also kind, and his earnestness had power. I wanted to like him. And I definitely liked his son. Did that play into my feelings toward his father?

Slow and quiet, I eased my way above deck. The captain stood with her back to me, peering over the edge of the ship to the north, where the rolling river waited, patient and exuberant.

"I'm surprised you're awake," the captain said, not turning to see who had arrived. "I did not work you hard enough."

Groaning, I rolled my aching shoulders, and the ship's captain chuckled quietly. "I wished to sleep more," I told her.

She turned then, looking me over. "You are young to be troubled by dreams."

She wanted something. An explanation? A story? But I'd built my life on secrets, and despite my admiration for Hughelas's declarations of who he was or was not, my tongue lay heavy as a stone in my mouth. *How does one say,* "I've had the best time of my life traveling with a Mother-revering nut and his son, despite multiple attacks… or possibly because of them… I'm not sure. But I've ignored the fact that the lunatic thinks I'm going to trigger the holy awakening of a slumbering god. I've pretended that I might travel on with Hughelas forever, instead of being discarded faster than the shell of a bandaru nut after I fail to achieve the Warder's prophetic vision. And even if they succeeded in awakening the Mother, why would they keep me around?"

"I'm just excited to travel on the water," I said, avoiding a discussion about my feelings, like I always did, glad when the captain looked the other way so she would not see the lie on my face.

"Do you have an affinity for water?" she asked, raising her hands and gesturing an unfamiliar spell. A ball of condensed mist floated above her hand. "Or perhaps air?" The mist swirled away over the edge of the ship, getting lost in the dim light.

"I like them both well enough," I said, making a joke and guarding my secret. "But I do not know their spells." Not a lie. Not *exactly* a lie.

"If you stay long enough, you will learn."

No. No, I wouldn't. I would never cast a spell. "The river downstream looked really rough," I said, hoping to change the topic. "We came from that direction for a short way."

"Yes, the water is high right now, after that quick storm, but the Amyla is always dangerous, and it will grow unrideable when the true spring rains fall. High or low, it holds perils. But we have coursed through this vein of FaelFarut often enough."

"FaelFarut?" I inched closer and almost got smacked by a dramatic wave of the captain's arm as she spun to face me.

"FaelFarut. It is Salt slang for everything not ocean, but more literally—"

"AllForest," I said.

"Silly name," said Beldroth, startling me. I hadn't heard him come up behind me. For such a large man, he moved quietly. "I told Lyrei the same. Plenty of things are both not ocean and not forest."

"Indeed," the captain said with a dangerous smile. She closed the distance between them, moving with the grace of a dancer. "Rocks, for instance? I am told Warders have impressive stones." She cocked her head and looked up at him, and I blushed, catching her double-meaning. I wanted to protect him, to defend him from a predator he didn't see coming, but I had no clue what to do.

"Oh, yes! You should see them if you get a chance." From his innocent tone, I didn't believe he was on the same page… or in the same book!

But the captain nodded her head once, then turned and walked into her above-deck cabin, saying, "I plan to do more than see them."

"Well," the Warder said, childlike wonder in his smile as he moved to look out over the river, "I hope she gets the chance."

I stood there, blushing bright enough that I wondered how the sunrise outshone me.

The ship rocked about on the rushing river. Hughelas taught me that it technically pitched, rolled, yawed, heaved, swayed, and surged. All I could say for certain was that the boat moved unpredictably. Or rather, *I* could not predict it. The Salts had no trouble, and stood in place as though they had roots running into the ship.

Fifteen minutes into the trip, the Warder's face turned green, and one of the crew promptly escorted him below deck, where he remained for much of the day. The rest of us did fine, and the captain let us stay above deck, out of the way near the captain's cabin.

Soon after the Warder's departure, one of the crew pointed to the cliffs on the southern shore above us, calling out, "Captain!" It didn't sound like a worried yell, just loud enough to be heard over the wind and water. I followed where he pointed. Something ran along the edge high above. Several somethings.

Hughelas appeared by my side. "Drawgs," he said, grimacing. There must have been at least five, maybe six or seven—from our angle, it was difficult to tell their number.

I watched and waited, my imagination allowing the creatures to jump from the cliffs and target the Knoll. But they weren't dragons. They didn't have wings. The cliffs were as tall as a silverleaf in that section of the river—jumping would be suicide.

I released a breath I hadn't realized I'd been holding when we passed the intersection of the stream that created a waterfall into the Amyla. We left the drawgs trapped at the corner of the two cliffs. Hughelas exhaled and chuckled lightly. "That was close. But this should throw them off the scent."

"Because it is so hard to tell which way the river goes?" I asked him with a nudge.

"Fair, and I don't know how they track us. Do we leave some kind of magical residue? They won't see where we will leave the river, so it at least buys us some time, and it's possible we've lost them altogether."

I grunted my acknowledgement. I was glad enough the drawgs couldn't get to us, particularly with Beldroth sick in the hold of the ship. But if they'd tracked him from the mountains, it seemed unlikely they would give up. Dragons collect their dead.

Liandra, the young woman who'd prevented a fight among the crew the day before, stayed near us much of the day, explaining bits of what the captain and crew worked through. "The woman at the bow is reading the water." Liandra pointed to the front of the ship, where a woman leaned over the rail, casting what I thought of as a continuous spell. Such a spell didn't require repeated casting the way my mother had to do when Healing me. Rather, the spell would be cast once and last as long as the caster maintained mana for it. "Her spell lets her see into the water, warning us of any upcoming rocks." Soon enough, I saw the woman hold her right hand out, and within moments, the ship veered right. "Look closely at her waist. Ghirsel is quite experienced, but for safety, we clip her to the hull." With Liandra's prompting, I spotted the two ropes and metal clips preventing her from a perilous journey over the front rail.

"The sails are working to slow us during this leg of the journey. Kharis and Thallan there," and she pointed at two men standing on opposite sides of the deck, a little behind the Mizzenmast. "They catch the wind in the Mainmast, which has a special configuration to enable catching a reverse wind." She pointed at the mid-ship mast, where I spotted a canvas sail configured to drop to either side of the mast. "That rigging's unusual—something Captain Edraele devised for rivers. Think of it like a brake on a cart. They're ready to resist the draw of the river current. Of course, we have anchors we can throw overboard as well, in an emergency, but the controlled wind-break enables more finesse."

"But there's no wind in the sails," I said, confused. The wind from our passage down the river made my hair dance, yet the canvases sagged.

"That's *their* doing. Their spells are killing the wind around the sails. We don't need to slow right now."

The two men spoke casually to one another near the mast. How did they maintain their spell or spells? How would a spell like that work? As the boat traveled downriver, wasn't it constantly hitting new air? Liandra laughed at my confusion. Hughelas looked around the boat at the sky like he would spot some trick.

"Their spells are critical when we travel upstream. We still have to tack, but between Captain Edraele and their wind, we can manage even these floodwaters." I turned to look behind me. The captain stood atop the platform over her cabin, casually steering the ship from a wooden wheel as large as one would find supporting a cart. "She looks at ease, but she wields spells as well. Hers works the water, smoothing our passage. Moving upstream is an entirely different spell."

Hughelas, clearly insane, slowly carved a circle in the air with a finger. Then he did the same with his other hand. Liandra laughed at his instability. "You've got the right idea," she said, disproving my belief that, like me, she thought he'd lost his grip on reality. "Otherwise, the expenditure in magic would be too great." I didn't like the way she looked at him as she added, "You are a clever one."

"My mother," Hughelas said, oblivious to the calculations of Liandra, "never taught me any shiplore… isn't that what you call it?" He didn't wait for an answer. "The Contentious, as disagreeable as the name sounds, is not nearly so wild as the Amyla, at least where I grew up. But any ship larger than a raft gains unwanted attention from dragons, so there wasn't much opportunity. She'd always intended to take me to the ocean, but she died before we had the chance. Ironically enough, from a dragon attack."

"How old were you when you lost her?" Liandra asked.

"It was a little over a decade ago now, so I would have been in my seventies, I suppose."

I had a clear view of the captain's raised eyebrow, though she didn't pull her gaze from the river. The captain angled for the Warder— was a decade long enough that she could move in? It almost certainly was. My mind went to my mother laughing with the Warder in the woods, and my gut tightened at the thought of the captain's interests.

Liandra, on the other hand, looked confused. "That's more than old enough to start learning shiplore."

Hughelas shrugged. "Looking back, I believe a part of her wanted to get me to a ship, but there's something… enticing… about being needed. Her skill with water helped win many battles. And she loved being with my father. And me."

It seemed like a good explanation to me, but Liandra looked doubtful. I suspected she'd spent most of her life on a ship, and didn't understand any other way. But I didn't have any trouble grasping the draw of being useful and loved.

Still, I couldn't puzzle out the finger-circles. I refused to ask and display my ignorance. I looked forward to questioning Hughelas in private.

***

Because of the rapid speed of our travel, after several hours we had gone a great distance, and the river calmed. The work on the ship had mesmerized me—Ghirsel scanning the water, Kharis and Thallan on the sails, and the captain manning the wheel. Liandra supplied food to her shipmates at midday, and when Hughelas noticed, he helped her. That put a damper on my enthusiasm, but before long, he brought me some salted meat and cheese, and his smiles for me drove any jealous thoughts from my mind. I settled back into watching the crew work, even as the river gradually widened and slowed. The Warder stumbled above deck, still green, but healthier than when he'd secluded himself.

I caught the look of scorn from the captain. After her aggressive statement from the night before, I wondered what she was thinking. She clearly thought less of him for becoming sick from the motion of the ship on the river. Did that diminish her desire for the Warder enough that she would leave him be? Did I care?

I did. But I didn't know why. He was a good man. I didn't want her to think less of him. Ironically, and inexplicably, I also didn't want her attracted to him. Something about the captain rubbed me the wrong way.

"Are we there yet?" the Warder asked Hughelas, the ghost of his usual smile flitting across his bilious face.

"Did Mother know about this?" Hughelas said with a grim smile that held back a torrent of laughter.

"*I* didn't know about it," he admitted. "Never been on a ship. I've rowed boats often enough."

"It is hard to become sick from the motion of a boat," Liandra said. "It has to do with what you see versus what you feel."

Hughelas cocked his head, suddenly deep in thought.

The Warder groaned, stretching. "I feel better already," he said. "I just needed some fresh air." Then he belched and grimaced, revealing the small lie of his story. "Do you travel during the night?" he asked, looking at Liandra for an answer.

"Not in the Amyla. Once we reach the Flawless, we could, though I doubt we will. The Amyla, even in this more gentle stretch, holds too many dangers, and changes often enough to trick even seasoned crews. No, we will moor as the day wanes, at Telloria'ahlia."

"Telloria'ahlia?" the Warder repeated. "That's a mouthful."

"Half Telloria?" Hughelas asked.

"Very good," Liandra said, nodding approval at Hughelas with a smile that made me want to claw at her face. "It's not technically half. Telloria, the true wood elf city, lies in the forest, a full day from the port. But Telloria'ahlia gets its name for another reason." She approached Hughelas, confident and full of grace, and put a hand on his chest. "They're like you, part one elf, part another. Mostly High Elf mixed with Wood Elf, like your friend. Never seen a Warder-Salt mix like you before."

Like his friend? Me? Wood Elf mixed with High Elf? Was she saying I was part High Elf? That my father was someone like *Varitan*? My mother had always refused to talk about my father, but I'd assumed…

I stood dumbly, offended, as Liandra inched uncomfortably close to Hughelas.

He tried to retreat, but Liandra moved with him, sliding her hand up to his cheek as his back hit the rail of the ship, preventing further movement. Her fingers slowly moved up to his hairline, catching an errant curl, then brushing the bottom of his ear.

She laughed, pulling her hand away and spinning to turn her back on him, finding, to both of our surprises, that I stood in her way. I didn't know how I'd gotten there, nor what I'd intended to do.

Liandra raised an eyebrow at me, and confused by my own actions, I took a step back. She laughed again and strode past me.

"Liandra, come take the helm," barked the captain.

"Aye aye, captain," Liandra said, sauntering up the stairs and relieving the captain. The smug elf leaned against the wheel, pushing her body against the wooden spokes as she bit her lip and kept her eyes on Hughelas, holding the wheel steady while she cast a spell. Hughelas, for his part, stared with wide eyes.

My blood boiled, but torn by whether to slap Hughelas or Liandra, my feet remained planted somewhere in between.

"Careful not to get a splinter in your cleavage," my mother called out. The captain halted and the crew froze. "A small prick is irritating, particularly in a tender spot."

Mortification instantly replaced my fury and indecision, keeping me frozen. Seconds ticked by. Just when I thought my unbelieving soul would ignite in flames, taking me from my wretched body of furious embarrassment, the captain laughed.

And not a tiny laugh. She barked a laugh that would have made the cawing cry of a vulturous death-feeder proud.

The rest of the crew joined with guffaws and chuckles. Even Liandra. And I stood there baffled, unsure of what had taken place around me. My concerns melted away as the captain and crew resumed their activities, the captain talking with the two crewmen working the wind, before she marched to the fore of the ship to speak with Ghirsel. I peeked at Liandra, but she no longer leered at Hughelas. Her eyes were glued to the river.

Hughelas, for his part, had untethered his eyes from Liandra, and he listened to some joke being shared between the two men supposedly working the wind.

"I know it's hard to believe," my mother said, her voice quiet, pitched for my ears only, as she put an arm around my shoulder, "but I was a young woman once too." Though I tried to pull away, already irritated by whatever nugget of wisdom she had prepared to drop before me, her grip had turned to iron. "I remember what it was like for the blood to run hot. Don't let those emotions control you, Elliah." She nodded toward Liandra. "They won't steer you true."

"Oh?" I asked, irritated with her, with Liandra, with Hughelas. "When we get to Telloria'ahlia," I said, mocking the singsong sound of the town, "am I going to find it populated by elves that look like me? Because they're half Wood Elf and half High Elf, Mother." I bit the last word hard. "So when you caution me about my *blood running hot*, do you speak from experience?"

Her grip on me released, and she headed toward the Warder who had joined his son. But I still heard her whisper, "Just so."

From the description, a half-town full of half-breeds, I expected something shabby or ramshackle. But Telloria'ahlia put the small quay of Anysa to shame. A pair of towers, one on each side of the river, stood guard over the region, their tops visible above the trees from quite a way upstream. At first, we saw a few dots of stone or wood buildings among the trees. As we neared, the trees thinned out, though even in the town, some remained, but the number of buildings blanketing the hillside down to the water shocked me. Stone and wood structures, proper structures, not ramshackle nests, decorated the town, forcing me to realize how tiny E'anashys had been. Telloria'ahlia dwarfed any place I'd ever lived.

The harbor itself comprised more stone than wood—long, rectangular slabs of gray rock carved a calm mooring into the slope of the land. The city lay largely on the north bank, though the south bank echoed the structures in diminutive form. I'd never seen a stone building in my life, though I'd read about them and even seen a drawing of one several years before. I *marveled* at the stone quay, the occasional multistory buildings and towers built on the climbing hillsides, driving into and blending with the trees. And in the river…

"What is that?" I asked.

In the distance, a stone pylon poked into the sky from the water near each end of the river.

"They are building a bridge," Liandra said, once again freed from the helm and returned to her role of trip narrator. "You cannot tell from here, but that isn't a single column. You'll see when we get closer that it's a row of columns, but the ones on the ends are much taller. I don't understand how they plan to reach between those columns though. Insane."

I had to agree. Five ships the length of the Knoll would fit between the two sets of columns. Nothing could span that. And why make the end columns in a row so tall?

Still, they looked impressive. As the sun sought its escape, the columns created long shadow-fingers that reached into the northeast bank.

I looked up the hillside as we drew closer, fascinated by the stone walls and structures, enchanted by the permanence of it all. I stared and ogled the buildings… until we neared enough for me to do the same with the *people.*

How had I not seen what I was before? Their skin color ranged from the light and dark browns of a Wood Elf to the golden skin of a High Elf, and their bodies spanned the spectrum of the small but fit dwellers from the woods to the tall and elegant erudites of the cities. When we floated past a woman with golden freckles, my hands shot to my cheeks. "Fawn spots," my mother had called them when I was little. They'd faded about a decade before, but I caressed my cheeks, imagining I felt them there, under my skin.

I'd definitely landed on the Wood Elf side of the spectrum. But I thought back to our most recent winter—we were roughly the same build, but my mother's clothes didn't quite reach my wrists or ankles the way they should.

"I'm sorry," she breathed by my side. My pent up anger from earlier had faded, even before the town had entranced me. I'd been remorseful about my angry words, but still bothered enough that I didn't approach her. She'd lied to me my whole life!

Her hands gripped the ship's rail next to mine. With our wrists in the same place, my fingers stretched out longer than hers. I'd seen the same as she'd held her hands over mine to instruct me on using the bow, but I'd never thought anything of it. I glanced up and quickly confirmed that High Elves had longer fingers.

"For what?" I asked, my voice calm, hoping to convey my contriteness, my question stemming from genuine curiosity.

"Never bringing you here," she said. "It wasn't because I wanted your heritage kept secret." She grimaced for a moment, putting a lie to her words. "At least not from you. I was worried about…"

My condition. Bereft. Lacking magic.

I looked at her and smiled, putting all the confidence I could into it. "I absorb magic. That makes me special among elves." *There, I've said it.* Saying it aloud gave it a power I hadn't expected, making it more true than it had been only minutes before. *Words have power, Eliah,* my mother would tell me after I'd said something particularly nasty. *Be careful how you use them.* Of course, the same woman's favorite song, which I'd heard quite often, told of a bee that got drunk and mated with a cactus. It wasn't even remotely anatomically correct—

"You've always been special," my mother said, reaching a hand to my cheek and capturing my wandering thoughts. "No matter what your relationship to magic." She smiled. "But I think I erred. A city scared me. More people. More magic. But you would not, I think, have felt so out of place."

She wanted to reconcile. I understood where her heart had been, trying to protect me. Yet it hurt. I wasn't completely ready to let it go, but I could at least make a return gesture. Grinning, though she wouldn't be able to see it, I said, "Please tell me Varitan is not my father."

My mother choked and made a disturbing growl of disapproval. "Mother of rot-infested Trees." I smiled at her profanity, particularly since I had only recently learned it was legitimately profane. "No, Varitan is not your father." She stilled, her gaze distant. "Your father was worse."

"Okay, you two," the captain interrupted. "Time to earn your ride." She nodded to the hatch.

Really? Right now?

"Tonight," my mother promised. "When we're done, I'll tell you about your father. About why we've hidden your whole life."

Not much of the cargo had to be unloaded, but neither was all the merchandise meant for Telloria'ahlia situated closest to the hatch. So it took some shifting and maneuvering in order to remove what they meant to be sold at that port. None of the wine casks left the ship. While still exhausting work, it wasn't as bad as loading all of it.

I had a lot to think about while I worked. I wasn't who I thought I was, and my father… he might as well have been a troll. I shouldn't have been so negative—I judged a whole race based on children's tales and my experiences with one nasty teacher. Yet I couldn't help myself. I turned my mind to something brighter: Telloria'ahlia. It was full of mixed race elves… elves like me. Well, not Bereft, so not *exactly* like me. But, if nothing else, it was a place for people who didn't fit in elsewhere, and that was soil I could grow in.

I found myself getting more and more excited about the idea of exploring Telloria'ahlia. I even started to daydream about staying there. *Living* there. It was silly, but I had an imaginary argument with the Warder, who wanted me to continue with him on his quest to see the Mother of Trees. Hughelas, torn between duty and love, chose to stay behind with me.

A whistle from above brought me out of what had become an inexplicably long kiss on the edge of a cliff overlooking the Amyla, sunset pinks and purples lighting the horizon. *Gah! What is* wrong *with me?*

"That's it!" shouted the captain from above. "Secure any loose cargo and the evening is yours."

A quick cheer erupted from those of us in the hold, and we got back to work consolidating and binding what was left. When the time finally came, when we were free to go ashore, the evening was deepening to night, and the quay was alight with torches, while magelight dotted the city proper, like wisps had settled in.

"Come," Kharis said, "there's a good tavern up this way. They always have a song and a dance."

Thallan grimaced. "Not 'Into The Wind' again. Who wants to dance after all that lifting? I'm going to The Stowaway, and will enjoy a drink in peace."

"Oh, and it has nothing to do with that pretty barmaid with the ivy-green hair?" Kharis threw back.

Thallan shrugged, grinning.

Kharis laughed. "I'll choose a dance, with a woman in my arms, over something pretty just to look at, any day."

"We sail at dawn," the captain said. "Anyone not returned gets left behind. Warder, would you stay and help me guard the Knoll?"

"I would be honored," Beldroth answered happily, and the crew laughed, most of them hopping off the ship and splitting up to head opposite directions on the quay.

"I want to see the city," I told my mother. "Can I go?" I asked, knowing that she would tell me it wasn't safe, but armed with arguments that I'd crafted while we unloaded the ship.

Liandra grabbed Hughelas's hand and pulled him to follow her. My blood went cold, freezing me in place.

"I'll go with her," Hughelas told my mother, pulling away from Liandra. A brief smile snuck onto my face. Liandra cocked her head at me, and I swallowed my smile, regretful, like I'd done something awful. But she simply shrugged, then with a wink and a laugh, ran to catch up with Kharis.

"I'll join you," my mother said. "I don't want to be on this ship tonight. Our fearless Warder fails to understand his situation." She trekked across the gangplank and I followed. I turned back to see Beldroth standing near the umbilical cord between the ship and dock, an imposing figure with his hammer cradled to his chest, but I giggled at the idea that he looked like a child clutching a stuffed toy for protection.

"Do you want to follow the dancers or the group looking for a quiet drink?" Hughelas asked.

"Neither," I said. "I want to walk through the city, see the… the *everything*."

Hughelas smiled.

My mother nodded, dropping behind us as we started up the stone stairs leading away from the quay. Because they'd carved the harbor into the hillside, the initial climb took an effort, making me grateful for the rope-based lifts set up to bring cargo out of the ships. If we'd had to carry our heavy burdens up the stairs, it would have worn me out—I would have been too tired to explore the city. Though it made me wonder why they didn't offer the same means of reaching the shops to people. Why did we have to climb when the cargo got hauled?

But the question fled from my mind when I reached the first city street. *My first ever city street!*

Single-story shops lined the avenue, with signs bearing pictures that showed, presumably, what each one sold. Based on that evidence, most of the stores sold fish, though the smell was strong enough that I wondered why they bothered with signs.

We continued up a much gentler slope to reach a wider variety of shops. Cobblers, clothiers, varieties of food vendors… *is that a bookstore?* I exchanged a look with Hughelas and we bee-lined toward the shop with a sign that bore a shelf of books. Sadly, no light seeped between the vertical shutters covering the windows, and I realized even before we reached the door that the shop had already closed. I kicked lightly at the door, irritated because we would leave at dawn, before I would have a chance to return.

But many shops remained open, so people walked the streets. A golden-haired man paused and said, "The Ahlia Library stays open all night."

Hughelas and I exchanged another look, and my mother laughed. "Where might said library be?" she asked the retreating form. "We are new to town!" she shouted, for the semi-helpful person kept walking away. She sighed and turned back to us. "So we are in a town, the likes of which you've never seen, with dancing and music and magic… and you want to find *books*?"

My cheeks blushed slightly. With all the options before me, I'd navigated toward the one that kept me the most isolated. Yet, despite all my years of daydreaming about joining in on a dance, the idea of ac-tually *doing* it scared me.

"Won't we see the town as we search for the library?" Hughelas asked.

Yes! Thank you Hughelas!

My mother laughed and waved her arm for us to proceed.

We wandered uphill. When we walked to the side of any level, we found houses and less magic to hold back the night. But if we kept moving up, occasionally circling a fountain or statue, the streets re-mained mostly lit by other elves with magelight to guide their feet. The floating lights cast long shadows from those walking near the mages who summoned them. It made for a strange dance of light and dark.

I couldn't imagine what they were all doing. Some had clearly been drinking. Others moved with haste to reach some destination. Still others seemed to be out simply enjoying the atmosphere.

The buildings became cleaner and larger as we climbed. The stone structures reached two, then three stories high. While still short compared to the size of a silvervein, I'd never seen a building constructed so tall. The artistry continued to increase as well, with carvings on the walls and crenellations appearing on more and more buildings. Parks provided gathering places and foliage, and it was early enough that even some older children still scurried about them, making alarming amounts of noise for their size. The early night with floating parental magelight created the perfect ambiance for games of hiding and finding.

But watching them dart from tree to shrub reminded me of my own, earnest hiding from other children. Instead of playing games with others, I'd had to conceal myself out of fear. My heart, hollow as a rotted log, beat its lonely rhythm as I witnessed a normal part of childhood that I'd never experienced. Hughelas laughed beside me, watching them dart about, and I understood that his was the correct elven response to children playing. I tried to dig it forth, to do more than intellectually appreciate that children playing was a good thing. But no tree would grow where a seed had not been planted. I walked through the park, thankful that the night and shadows hid my sour look.

"That must be it," my mother said from behind us.

I hadn't forgotten she was there. I'd even wanted to turn back and check… did she wear my same sour look, or did she smile when she witnessed frolicking children? But I hadn't wanted to reveal to her my struggle, and she would have read it on my face. Still, her voice startled me, and I realized I hadn't really been looking where I walked as I played a game of hiding from my emotions.

Before us stood a statue of a book. Hughelas cast his own magelight and illuminated the gray stone book, half-an-elf taller than us, opened for reading, with the chiseled message, "Beauty is found in knowledge applied to improve the elven condition." The base of the statue bore the words "Ahlia Library."

An enormous building perched behind the statue. Light emanated from within through…

"What *are* those?" I asked.

"I don't know," my mother said.

"Nor do I," said Hughelas.

The light shined from the building through colored material where shutters should have been.

"Let's find out," I said with a laugh. I took Hughelas's hand and pulled him forward.

Zoras * 8

I'd warned him. I'd warned her. *Nobody listens!*

"That journal was garbage," I'd told Felaern. "Crazy ideas concocted to explain the unprovable."

He'd just smiled. "The ideas make sense."

"Orthogonal vectors of magic? What does it even mean to be orthogonal in five directions?"

Felaern had actually laughed. "That's not even the hardest part to wrap your mind around. They argue about which sets of orthogonal vectors best explain magic."

"But you can't prove or disprove *any* of it! Illiara, please tell me you're not listening to this fool."

I'd introduced Illiara to Taegen, an up-and-coming Wood Elf leader who sought to tame the swamps north of the Heartland. I counted myself an excellent reader of emotions, particularly in younger elves, and I recognized that they made a connection; they were a good fit. Yet she'd left him and returned to Alenor and the politics around the High Court… and Felaern.

"I try not to listen to the fool, but I've only found one way to shut him up!" She smiled adoringly at Felaern, with a hand on her belly, and I realized my argument came too late.

I growled. Over the years, I'd lost my repose more and more frequently with Felaern. He enjoyed getting under my skin, ever since I'd first questioned his ideas of working with the dragons and encouraging half-breed magic.

I'd watched the relationship between Illiara and Felaern bloom. I blamed myself. For one, Illiara's nature tended toward the rebellious— my growing tension with Felaern had increased his appeal. Second, as much as I hated it, Felaern and I were much alike, and I'd become the father figure Illiara lacked in her biological father. Her season in my home had stretched on to a second and third year; before I knew it, thirty years had passed and Illiara had become a grown woman. Elitha's communication crystal had never lit in that time, though Illiara had sent and received missives by bird. I sent a few such letters as well, thinking her parents would desire updates, but I'd never received any response whatsoever. Regardless, Felaern's nature, so similar to mine, made it easier for him to charm her.

They were certainly a pair—how was it that the two people I'd put the most effort into had turned out the most difficult!

"Breeding across races for power is insanity!" I blurted. "You want data? Go ask midwives how many half-breeds are Bereft!"

They both scowled at that, and Illiara's hand returned to her belly, protective.

"You didn't know that," I said, my calm returning as their worry increased. "I read your book, Felaern. It came from you, so I didn't dismiss it lightly." I needed him to grasp that I cared, though I had a bias against the contents. "I read it more than once. But in the end, I couldn't see how it mattered."

"But breeding for stronger magic—"

"It makes no difference if the stronger magic isn't tangible!" I didn't shout, but my voice had energy behind it, and I backed my tone down. I wasn't looking for a shouting match. "Which is what those formulas argue. Greater strength, but only in the entire set of vectors, some of which may not manifest in the potency of a spell."

Oddly, what I'd found in the journal Felaern had brought from the Salts was not what I expected. He'd described the Salts as experimentalists, but the book was all theory, and quite speculative theory at that. It referenced experiments, but I'd heard of none of them.

"But if it could be—"

"Felaern! It doesn't matter. Whatever your book says, it isn't what we're *seeing*. I'm sorry. Half-breeds bear more Bereft. Their magic isn't growing, it weakens… it breaks. The entire theory in that book is bunk." We all scowled in equal measure. "Have you even considered what it would do to you to birth a Bereft?"

I meant the question for Felaern, who endeavored to enter the politics of the High Council. A Bereft offspring would hamper, possibly destroy, that climb.

He considered my insinuation. Puffing out his chest, he spoke. "I would take care of it myself if our baby were born Bereft." It was the reaction I'd sought; like me, he would not shy away from harsh practicalities. However, I'd miscalculated, for Illiara looked at her belly with eyes wide as saucers.

Still, it might do the trick; a sacrifice like that might prove his dedication to our people and to the High Council. But what would it do to him? To Illiara? It would break them both. And though it was *their* stupid mistake, my heart chilled. I hoped, even prayed a little to the Mother of Trees, that they weren't destined for that road. My stomach twisted at the thought of my role in it.

Glass. The light we'd witnessed had shone through windows filled with *glass*. I'd seen it used to create pretty beads I'd longed for as a child. But someone had placed small panes of it, each piece about the size of my palm, in a wire mesh. You couldn't see through them with any clarity, but a plaque near the entrance explained that "Xirafel's Glassiers intends to create flat panes of translucent glass to decorate any window, keeping the elements at bay while allowing light to enter." Artistic examples of multi-colored bowls, globes, and swirling patterns of glass decorated the entrance to the library.

Beyond the entrance, more books than I had ever seen lined shelves that stretched into the distance. *That's not saying much*, I thought to myself. The largest library I'd encountered in my schooling, always in the smaller towns we'd adopted as temporary homes, had at most a hundred books. Many had far fewer. Not all Wood Elves even bothered with learning to read. But for long stretches of my childhood, books and my mother were my only companions. So when I got my first glimpse beyond the displays of glass, I'd nearly choked on the wealth of paper-bound friends stretching off in all directions.

I lost my mind for a while—Hughelas asked people questions, learned how to find books on specific topics, learned the organization of the library. But, overstimulated, I let him pull me along, enjoying his hand in mine while I also reached out to touch certain volumes and convince myself they were real. *If this is a dream, may I never wake!*

Alcoves sat at the ends of many of the aisles of books, and unlike the quiet stretches of books, several alcoves brimmed with noise. All of them held displays of one kind or another: paintings, statues, histories of different aspects of spellcraft or buildings or wine… or anything! Elves freely discussed what they saw, what they liked and what they didn't, ideas they wanted others to consider, things they wanted to try themselves but desired advice.

We stumbled through all the halls of the first floor, then climbed stairs to the second. The alcoves were less crowded, less boisterous, the sparse magelight creating deeper shadows, the tomes whispering promises of secrets. Impulsively, I tugged on Hughelas's hand, and when he stopped, I kissed him. He grinned like an idiot and I laughed quietly. So many books! I left him, grinning myself, walking the aisle with a hand dancing across the spines and my eyes darting to books in other rows.

I smiled when Hughelas grabbed the hand I'd kept free for exactly that purpose. He pulled me into a dark alcove filled with models of constructions that I couldn't make out from the dim lighting streaming in through the doorway. He stepped behind the door jamb and stopped abruptly, making me collide with him as he did a sudden about-face. I jumped back, but he'd wrapped his other arm around me and kept me close. Eyes wide, I glanced behind me. We'd lost my mother, but I looked for any other signs of an audience. I found none, but without magelight, my sight couldn't pierce the depths of the room. When I turned my head back, I found lips ready for mine.

I pressed in, hungry for more.

A city of half-breeds like me and Hughelas.

A library I could spend a lifetime in.

A man who wanted me as much as I wanted him.

What more could anyone ask for?

His hands searched for the hem of my shirt, and finding skin, worked their way up my back, creating a tingling heat that begged for more. I didn't know where we were going, but I wanted to *get there!* I found the edge of his tunic and pulled it up, forcing him to relinquish his hold on me as I pulled his top off over his head. Tossing his shirt aside, I ran my fingers over his chest and stomach while he picked frantically at the buttons on my top. Though he didn't have the muscle of his father, he was lean, fit and… yummy.

My blouse's buttons finally relinquished their charge, and Hughelas's fingers caressed the skin beneath as I pulled him close and resumed exploring the landscapes of our mouths and bodies. He ran a thumb up the hairline scar that stretched the length of my torso—the one I'd earned on the day of our meeting—sending tingles through my skin and mind as the shared knowledge of its origin sizzled. He reached the wrap that bound my breasts and dug under as much as the tight cloth allowed. I pulled him close, the skin of his stomach pressed against mine, our hands wrapped around—

"Elliah?" My mother called from far away, breaking the stillness and quiet of the second floor.

We simmered down, but remained quiet, hidden, soft kisses exchanged like bees hopping gently between flowers. Magelight sifted in through the entrance, though from a distance. It bobbed along, undoubtedly tracing aisles of books, my mother looking for signs of her miscreant daughter. "Elliah, are you up here?" She didn't sound particularly worried, but she would keep looking until she found me. With quiet and reluctant sighs, we pieced our clothing back together, using my mother's own faint magelight to align buttons and, in Hughelas's case, get his shirt right side out. It was hard not to laugh.

I tried to think of some excuse to explain our silence, but I failed to come up with one. *We didn't hear you*, while not convincing, would probably earn us just a scowl. It might provoke more questions on what we were doing that drowned out her calls, but she might decide she didn't want the answer, and so withhold the question.

The light had stopped, and I wondered whether she would give up on her search after all.

"Elliah!" she shouted. I froze, because her voice held a note of panic. "Elliah! We have to go! Now! Are you here?"

Stunned, wondering what had happened, I reacted too slowly, and with loud footsteps, the light quickly faded with more shouts of "Elliah!"

I darted out of the alcove in time to see my mother's light disappear down the stairs at the opposite end of the aisles.

"What was that about?" Hughelas asked, still fumbling with his final buttons.

"Cast a magelight," I said, demanding. Then grimaced and added, "Please."

He did as requested, and I quickly scanned the room, wondering what had frightened her. Aisles of books, alcoves at the ends. Above some were symbols, shields, pictures, one had wheels… none of them meant anything to me.

Shaking my head, I gave up. "Come on," I urged, jogging through the aisles to reach the stairs. Hughelas let the magelight go as we drew near the better lit first floor, and it wasn't hard to spot my mother from the stairs, darting from alcove to alcove, no longer shouting, but scared.

Scared myself, I didn't call out, but I ran a path to intercept hers. Once off the stairs, I'd lost sight of her, but I stayed true to the path I'd intended… and collided with her as I exited the aisle.

She jumped back with a hand on her knife and fire in her eyes, breathing like someone on the verge of tears. "Mom!" I whisper-shouted. "I'm okay. What is it?"

She choked back a response, then took a deep breath, her eyes calming. She looked around, and though several people stared, they all just appeared curious, not threatening. She held out a hand to forestall me, then waved for Hughelas and me to follow, and she walked, as calmly as a woman with a hand on the hilt of her knife could walk, toward the entrance.

Her composure improved with each step. But while her shoulders relaxed, and her grip on her knife eased, her hand didn't release the hilt. She stopped near the entrance, getting the attention of the librarian we had talked to earlier, who still sat before what looked to me like the same cart of books he'd been with when we'd entered.

"Excuse me," she said politely, a friendly smile once more on her face. The librarian put a finger on the page he'd been reading, setting his feathered pen in the inkpot and looking at his notes once more before looking up at my mother. "On the second floor, there's an alcove with a coat of arms above it: a 'Z' with a silverleaf on either side…"

"Yes, Zoras Silverheart. Several alcoves are dedicated to him." The librarian's smile asked whether there were any more questions.

"I'm surprised," my mother said, feigned innocence radiating like magelight. "I'd read that he enacted the racial purity laws. I would have thought that would be a somewhat unwelcome subject in this town."

The librarian's indulgent smile looked thin. "That's partly true. While the racial purity laws are widely credited to him, he didn't actually create them. Regardless, those very policies define Telloria'ahlia. It wouldn't exist without him. So he's fundamental to our history."

"Ah," my mother said, genuinely relieved. "So those alcoves document the history of the city." Her hand finally slid from her dagger. "Bad blood and all."

"Mostly," the librarian answered, taking his pen back to hand. "Though there's little bad blood with all he's donated to the city. He's in the library quite often, staying at the place he built downriver—"

The librarian fumbled to a halt when he realized that my mother had disappeared out the doors, and Hughelas and I exchanged a worried look and departed on her heels.

Elliah ~ 24

Our journey back to the ship began in silence. The night had truly set-tled in, draining the streets and parks of people. We moved swiftly downhill compared to our uphill slog. My mother jumped at breeze-stirred noises, and she pulled ahead any time I attempted to catch up.

"Mom," I called, but she shook her head and walked on without looking back. "Mom!" I insisted, but she simply carried on, shooing me with the hand not on her dagger. Finally, I simply stopped.

"What—" Hughelas blurted, startled when he almost collided with me.

Unlike my mother, I answered. "She wants to be alone." I didn't speak loudly, but there was little enough noise that I didn't have to be loud for my mother to hear me.

She jerked to a stop. For several seconds, she just stood there, breathing like a trapped animal. We'd stopped in the middle of one of the little parks where children had chased each other around at dusk. Insects buzzed and ticked in the trees. Windows glowed beyond the edges of the park. I imagined eyes everywhere, but saw none save the stars above. Finally she turned, stalking with such a look of madness that I took a step backward despite my best intention.

"I don't know what I'm doing," my mother blurted into the chill of the night, planting herself in place. I looked at Hughelas, and with a nod of my head, indicated he should keep going. He grimaced and walked down the hill.

My mother waited for him to clear out, battling her own demons. "When we left E'anashys, I'd intended to do what we'd always done—find a new hiding place. Yes, I truly meant what I said about going back to the north, finding another small town we could disappear into for a few more years." She looked behind her—trying to determine whether Hughelas was out of earshot?

"Then Beldroth and Hughelas showed up that morning. I'd planned to leave them behind, but it had been so long with just the two of us. So, so long. And I let myself enjoy the company a little too much. The idea… *his* idea… of going to the Heartland?" My mother looked up at me. "I don't buy what the Warder says… about the Mother's Blessing enabling a quest to succeed." She looked back down and continued in a quiet voice, choked with emotion. "But I so much wanted to believe."

She sniffled and carried on.

"I can see you want to stay here, and I want you to be able to. I truly do. But… if Zoras is here…" She shrugged. "He's one of the elves we're hiding from." She rubbed her eyes. "I thought this city would be safe—the people here have *every* reason to resent him." She growled under her breath. "But I should have known better. He's always a step ahead. Of course he would ingratiate himself to any place that could have been a haven. We have to go, before he learns we were here. And he *will* learn."

"I don't understand," I said, her fear palpable and making me itch to move. Shadows moved in the distant windows and I wondered if they tried to listen in. "Were we never going to the Heartland with the Warder?"

"I don't know!" she shouted. Hughelas looked up at the shout, then returned his gaze to his feet. "I had ideas—I hoped we might stay *here*. I wondered if we might learn that things had changed. Maybe Zoras or your father had died—people die sometimes. I didn't have this figured out, Elliah."

Wait. We ran because people blamed me for bad things that happened in their towns. We ran because I was Bereft. Right? She made it sound like… "Are we *hiding*? From my *father*?"

My father. While my mother paced back and forth in a tight line several strides long, I marveled once again at how little I knew about my life. "You said you were going to tell me about my father."

She didn't stop pacing. "Your father was a monster who would stop at nothing to gain power. Just like Zoras."

I'd had enough. "Then why have a baby with him?!?"

That stopped her in her tracks. After several seconds, she answered, her responses jagged, like her breathing. "I thought he was different. He opposed Zoras, offering something new. He broke the racial purity laws. In the Heartland. That felt *important!*"

"Then why does he want me dead?" I practically whined, but I already knew the answer.

"Not because of what you are," she hissed. "Or not *just* because of what you are," she amended. "Also because of *who* you are."

Her answer surprised me. *Who am I?* I was Elliah, a Bereft mixed-breed elf who had done nothing but run her whole life.

My mother looked down at her hands. "I've been a fool," she said. Her voice had calmed, but her tone sounded defeated and tears leaked from her eyes. "There's no way we will outmaneuver Zoras. Lying low has kept us alive, and it remains our best bet. We should leave the Warder and his son, set north by foot, and put as much distance as we can from this town."

"No!" I blurted, more loudly than I'd meant. Her eyes shot up to mine. I looked around, but the park remained empty. "No," I said again, more quietly, but firmly. "I won't keep running." I didn't even know what I was running from. "Hiding." I hadn't realized we'd been hiding. But I refused to let my recent taste of life be snatched away. "There's got to be a way to *fight* this."

My mother stared at me, her face blank. She'd had some kind of idea, but was reluctant to share it.

"What, Mom?"

"Running is a better idea," she said.

"Tell me what you're thinking."

Still she hesitated. Finally, reluctantly, she answered. "Fael Themar. There's someone there who might push back against the High Elves. He won't be happy about it, but I think he will help."

"In the swamps?"

She nodded her head.

The swamps? Who or what was in the swamps that would fight the High Elves? I itched to get moving, picturing arrows pointed at me from every window. "Well, okay then. How do we get there?"

Her tears vanished, sucked back in through pure steely determination, I assumed. "Let's get back to the ship."

"Back to the ship?" I said, startled.

"We can't hide from him," she said. "But if he's here, looking for us, the Knoll is the fastest way downriver—we can get ahead of him."

I awoke confused, echoes playing into reality from a dream where I swayed, nestled high in a silvervein during a monstrous thunderstorm.

Low thunder rumbled, and my bed swayed, but I was on a ship, not in a tree. Did a storm shake the boat? I tried to recall my meditations from the night before—I vaguely remembered leaving my mother on deck with the Warder, then going below-deck with Hughelas. Excited tingles had dampened when I realized we weren't alone, but we'd held hands and I'd quietly walked him through meditations. The more I remembered, the more the dreamlike quality of my thoughts faded. Though I was still weary, sleep escaped my grasp.

My eyes sought the hatch and found it open and dry, but voices became audible as the thunder faded. I rolled from my bed, unsteady, as I continued to scrub the dream from my brain. My mother's hammock lay empty, as did the Warder's and all the crew's… but Hughelas still slept. *Better take advantage of a moment alone.* That we would soon part ways, he continuing to the Heartland while my mother and I dashed to the swamps, gave me pause. Was it wrong to pursue Hughelas when our time together was short-lived? But I didn't pause for long.

The wiry muscle in Hughelas's arms tensed as I slid my hands up under his sleeves to his shoulders. When his eyes opened, I pressed my mouth against his soft, warm lips, and he responded with a quiet moan that made me pull away and double-check that no one was near.

"Mmmm," he murmured. "That is the best way to wake up," he said hungrily.

"Woken to a kiss often, have you?" I said, pulling back.

"Bjah," he sputtered. "No! I didn't mean *that*—"

I laughed, well aware that I'd misconstrued his statement. I leaned in for another kiss, but the voices from above had turned to shouting. I easily picked out the familiar voice of my mother yelling, but couldn't discern the words over the grumbles of thunder. I sighed, and Hughelas tried to keep me there, to pull me back down for another kiss, but the magic of the moment had vanished… as magic longed to do near me. I left Hughelas's sighs to climb through the hatch.

I emerged to a confusing tableau. Dark clouds swept in from the east, promising rain, and a dark scowl decorated my mother's face, as she stood with her back to the Warder. He looked frustrated, his face red, but lightening, his fists unclenching by his sides. The crew of the ship simulated busyness, but they paid more attention to the show before them than the river they floated down.

The night before had gone so well! When we'd reached the ship in the dead of night, the Warder had been standing on the deck, hammer ready, just as we'd left him. "Back on duty?" my mother had asked him, her smile glued on tightly.

"Never left," he replied.

My mother shook her head, her smile becoming less forced. "You fool."

To which he replied:

"A fool, in truth, I may well be.
A ship that wanders through the sea.
But I know peace, and love... doth thee?
If not, then e'er the fool I'll be."

The captain's intent had been clear enough, and he'd told her no. Hughelas and I had exchanged a look, and he whispered, "He recited that poem to my mother *a lot*."

My mother kept shaking her head, but her words were gentle. "May I keep you company on your watch then?"

Hughelas and I, we'd left them there talking as we'd joined the crew in the hammocks under the decks.

But that was the night before, and the morning revealed my mother's bloodshot eyes, like she hadn't slept, or she'd cried, and when she saw me, she turned away and ducked her head further, so that she faced neither me nor the Warder.

"What's going on?" I asked her, approaching slowly like she was a fawn that might bolt at the least provocation, though there was nowhere for her to run save over the edge of the ship.

"Grugh," she said, shrugging.

I turned to the Warder for more answers.

"She said I..." *What?* I wanted to prod him. "... did what I did..." Turned away the captain's advances for my mother? "... just to get her to stay with me so that *you* would continue with us to the Mother of Trees."

I hadn't considered that. I supposed it was possible. But what did it matter?

My mother turned one eye to me, revealing the weariness behind it. She *cared* for the Warder, just as I cared for Hughelas. And the betrayal from thinking the Warder had tricked her had spread like algae on a still pond.

When I was little, I'd often wondered why I didn't have a father. Recent decades had shown me that my mother could be… a lot. She seemed to spoil even casual friendships with barbs and silly rebukes, creating a comfortable nest for just the two of us.

I pondered the predicament. I'd spotted no indication of guile from the Warder, nor his son. But that was exactly how people were suckered in. I moved my tongue from side to side, thinking. If the Warder genuinely wanted to protect us, his behavior would be no different from if he were trying to trick us into coming with him.

Stupid men and stupid us.

"Gah!" I declared as I stomped to my mother's side. "Come on, Mom." I pulled her forward, away from the Warder and his son, where we might stare out over the horizon at the approaching storm.

I glanced back, not missing Hughelas's open hand, like he involuntarily grasped for me. The puzzled look on his face rent my guts.

The day, ignoring its basic purpose, grew darker. Storm clouds billowed and rolled as lightning churned through the sky with distant rumbles. Perhaps it was the flashes of light that made their absence darker. Either way, the rain held off.

I watched the lightning dance through the clouds. I'd always liked a storm when I was safe in a silvervein. There was no warmer feeling than sitting cozy and safe inside a tree while the elements raged. But resting on the steps that led to the helm, watching the weather rage, knowing we headed into it… that provided a different thrill altogether. Something inside me longed for the coming storm, the outward elements reflecting my inner drive to confront whoever it was that threatened me. To have the fight I didn't want to have with my mother or the Warder or Hughelas.

Who was right? Who was wrong? I suspected they all were. My mother had picked a fight because she was afraid to get close to people. She slumped against the ship's rail at the bow, staring into the water below like it held the answers to her troubles. The Warder, sleeping after having stood guard through the night, had no long-term intentions toward my mother; he intended to pursue his godly mission. What right did he have to bend my mother's heart? And the same for Hughelas! We would part ways as soon as our goals diverged, so why pretend otherwise? Nevertheless, my eyes drifted to the hatch, where he'd disappeared with his father, probably reading. Was he thinking at all about me and the kiss we'd shared?

"Captain!" Kharis yelled from his position near the mast.

The captain raised an eyebrow from the helm, and Kharis beckoned her over. Handing off the wheel to Liandra, the captain sauntered down to join Kharis at the mast. I pretended to brood, but like the crew listening in on our earlier dispute, I paid rapt attention to their words.

"There's something up there," Kharis whispered.

The captain paced back and looked up, as though checking out the mast. Then she walked back. "I see nothing. Thallan?"

"I don't either, but Kharis's magic reaches farther up than mine."

"A threat?" she asked.

"Not at that height," Kharis said, "but I thought you should know."

The captain nodded and climbed back up to the helm. She re-cast her spells, presumably to watch the water through her magic, but her eyes wandered to the sky, searching.

I made my way to the hatch and the sleeping Warder below deck. After a day of being sick, and a sleepless night, his body hungered for rest. His hammer lay on the floor near his side. Hughelas, as expected, read a book under a dim magelight. He looked my way, and I grimaced. I shook my head no, so he returned to his reading. I wasn't even sure what I was saying no to, exactly, except that I'd decided not to wake his father—surely, my speculation was wrong. We couldn't be due for another dragon attack.

Before midday—a time difficult to pinpoint, since the clouds hid the sun—we reached the Flawless proper. I'd crossed it once a decade prior, but far to the east, at the edge of the Witless Mountains, where Roamers guarded the forest from troll attacks. The river was thinner there, carved into the mountain and not yet joined by its many siblings who communally sought lower ground. In the dim lighting of the storm-laden sky, I could not judge the distance to the far shore, but when the Amyla joined it, the Flawless became so wide that many tens of the Knoll would have stretched bow to stern across it. Quite the difference!

In joining the Flawless, the ship turned from a northwest course to southwest. I'd learned from maps in books that the river would eventually turn due west and head straight through the Heartland. The vein of water brought me closer to my chance to move freely among elves, but also to the same forces that might decide my life had been forfeit long before, and hence, pluck it, like a hair with split ends.

Celebrating our arrival on the Flawless, the dark clouds dumped their long-held reservoir of rain. In an instant, we went from being chilled by a whipping wind to sodden messes. The former invigoration of the wind turned arctic.

"Gaaah!" I screamed. Would we continue on? I could not see the captain, who had stood no more than five strides from me at the helm up the stairs. *I'd wanted this storm?* From memory of the location of the stairs, I darted under them for protection.

Surely the captain will anchor and we can wait out the storm below deck!

I'd been through gully-washers before, though always safe in a silvervein. The first waters would burst forth like a river breaking through a dam, but within minutes, the rain would subside to a heavy but lesser flow. Footsteps pounded up the stairs, and after several seconds, came pounding back down. How could they even see where they were going? The crew didn't need to see, though, did they—any home we stayed in for a year, I would have been able to find my way around in the dark. The ship was their home, and by all accounts, had been for many years.

I waited out the initial deluge under the stairs when, suddenly, the rain stopped.

Rain petering out was normal—the sudden stop was not. I extracted myself from under the stairs to find that the rain had not, in fact, stopped. Magical shields covered the Knoll. One, two, three, four... five. Red, translucent, curved domes covered the ship like mushrooms. To have five, each shipmate must have cast a shield, the captain included. They all stared up, concentrating on their spells to maintain our shelter. They must have practiced often to create half-bubble shields just so, with rain pouring off in ways that mostly spilled overboard instead of onto the ship.

The crew had somehow furled the sails during the deluge. I suspected they had done that without the aid of magic, but the speed with which they'd done it was supernatural.

"That's a nice trick," my mother shouted. She'd made her way across the ship to duck beneath the stairs opposite me. Hughelas had emerged from below deck. He stood in the open, watching the spell-casting elves, puzzled. "It seems a bit of a waste of mana," he shouted back. "Protecting us from the rain."

Then a screech ripped through the pounding of the rain against the shields. Something big hid in the clouds, and I regretted my earlier reluctance to warn the Warder.

"I don't think," my mother yelled, "that the shields are there for the rain."

The hatch popped back open, splashing against the floor of the ship with a sodden bang. The Warder bounded out, searching the sky through the shield, but the battering rain turned the outside of the shields into a wall of drumming darkness. We huddled in a roaring, rocking cave.

Lightning shot through the front shield, zipping past the foremast and landing on the mainmast, where it sizzled and popped, but did no real harm. The shields all shifted, moving toward the prow of the ship. Why move the shields when the lightning had gone right through?

Another bolt shot past, lighting the night, as Beldroth leapt to the front of the ship. The lightning narrowly missed him, raising steam from the floor of the ship, and the foremost shield collapsed, shrinking our cave. I took a step back, even though I stood far from what came barreling through. In only a moment, it reached the ship and Beldroth's eager hammer swing. The hammer connected with the jaw of the swooping monster, snapping its head back and redirecting its course to the port side of the ship. A wing of the beast knocked Beldroth sailing to my right. The tail end of the creature snapped the Knoll's rail with a mighty cracking, heard even over the drumming of the rain on the shields, and then the beast's back legs and tail slid off the side.

Its black, lizardlike head was the size of my torso and rested mid-ship. Its scaly body would have reached half the length of the ship if the tail end weren't dangling overboard. Leathery wings the size of our mainsails stretched out on either side. The tip of one reached past the foremast and the other was likely underwater. Our ship, with the dragon's weight, tilted dangerously, and the river dragged the monster into its hungry depths.

The ship lurched wildly as the winged creature's weight departed, sending me onto my backside, then rolling me forward, where I impaled my hand on something sharp. I looked up to find that only three shields remained.

I climbed back to my feet as someone called out, "There are two more! *At least* two more!"

Mother of Trees!

Another screech burst from the clouds—I tried to look everywhere at once, but our shield-crafted cave had only shrunk. I tried to evaluate the damage to the ship. It was obvious the rail had smashed off, but was the ship sinking? I didn't know.

Lightning danced behind the clouds, and I tensed for another diving attack. Instead, the lightning did not stop, but bounced through the dark clouds, revealing the rapidly growing outline of a shadow diving straight down from above.

The shields lined up between the dragon and the ship, leaving me unsheltered from the pelting rain. There was no way the shields would be enough—our destruction was guaranteed. My brain fried, trying to tell me to hide under the stairs and jump from the ship all at the same time.

A distant shriek tore the air, and the dragon shifted to the side, crashing down into the water with a cracking splash that sent me once more rolling across the deck, sliding rapidly toward the edge with no railing, across a deck slick with rain and blood. With my one good hand, I dug my fingernails into the wood of the deck, but they didn't catch, and I held my breath as I flew past the edge.

My outstretched arm snagged.

I flew back up as the ship righted itself, and my shoulder screamed that it would rip out of its socket.

But it didn't.

After a few more precarious moments, which included banging my hip against the hull of the ship, the tether on my arm pulled me on deck.

Hughelas. Hughelas had saved me from a watery grave. If my arm weren't numb, I might have overcome the screaming pain in my hip and the fact that whatever had impaled my hand remained in it, and kissed him right there.

"The other one has flown off!" a voice shouted. "All clear! Port side harbor!"

Other one? Harbor? And before I could even decide whether Kharis or Thallan had spoken, rain poured down, and the world contracted to a very wet and tiny space around me.

Hughelas hauled me away from the edge in jerky motions on all fours. The rocking ship and driving rain couldn't decide whether to compete or work together, and my numb arm and wounded hip made every inch a battle.

How do they steer the ship in this?

But they'd shown me how they steered it. Magic that enabled them to sense the surrounding air and water. Did it change things that so much water was in the air? I had no idea, and suspected I never would.

We reached some part of the rigging and huddled there. Safer, I wondered what was next. Someone had shouted that there were no more dragons. But what had happened to the one diving at us? I tenderly touched my injured hand and the thing that poked through it. The sharp end protruded from the top of my hand, and the bottom side was wider, like a thorn. Hard, like bone. A dragon's tooth? I'd fallen on a dragon's tooth.

Lights came from the port side, barely bright enough to pierce the gloom. Magical, for what fire could have withstood the brutal rain. The yell about a harbor jumped to the forefront of my mind. I tugged at the tooth in my hand while trying to make out the harbor as we neared. As we drew closer, the lights formed into squares, glowing from windows along a wall. Lights inside a building suggested fire and blessed warmth.

We huddled there forever, Hughelas ineffectually defending me from the rain. I worked the tooth free, adding to the mess of blood on deck. With cold fingers, I tucked it into my belt pouch to examine later. Feeling returned to my arm with searing tingles, but almost immediately lost ground to the slithering numbness brought on by the chilling downpour. It was almost pleasant to lose the pain in my hip to the cold, though I knew I would pay the price later.

By the time shields reappeared, and stomping boots accompanied unfamiliar shouting, the activity made no more sense to me than a dream after waking.

Overwhelming gratitude flooded me when strong arms lifted and carried me off the ship, with just a dollop of irritation about my weakness and need for help. When we passed under a stone arch, providing a reprieve from the rain, my gratitude vanished like a wisp's light in the morning. On the wall of the arch hung the symbol that had panicked my mother at the library. What had the librarian said? *He's in the library quite often, staying at a place he built downriver…*

Zoras!

Fear overcame weakness, and I rolled from the arms of my captor. I reached out to catch myself and spring away, but between the chilling numbness and physical injuries, I landed badly and jolted my injured hip.

I grunted in pain, but when a hand touched my shoulder, it found my bone knife ready to greet it.

The hand jerked away, and I scuttled back to get the wall behind me. The floor was wood, but the wall was stone. A large arch would allow an escape back into the rain and ship, but then what? A plunge into the river? The room was large, reeking of combat, housing contraptions of wood, metal, and stone that pointed out toward the river. A stairway climbed the wall I'd hunkered against. A large sliding door, presently closed, barred the exit at the side opposite the arch, and a fiery hearth fought back the chill of the storm on the wall across from me.

"Should have left them to the dragon," a golden-skinned High Elf mumbled with his finger in his mouth. Garbed in brown leathers with a gourd-like face that looked like it knew a smile as well as a worm knew the stars, he scowled at me with dark intent.

"She's just frightened," said another High Elf, standing by a table with books, papers, pen and ink before him. Though garbed similarly, his smile fit like a well-worn glove, comfortable and secure in its role. "I've seen you cut yourself worse on your own fishing hooks." Under better circumstances, he would have put me at ease. As it was, I wondered where my shipmates were, and why they had let strangers cart me off without accompanying them.

A grunting beast moved loudly and slowly toward the arched entrance, and I shifted my knife and scooted back along the wall. Had one of the dragons survived?

Lightning lit the night with a peal of rolling thunder—the storm still camped directly overhead. But worry of a different sort replaced my fear of attack under the lightning's glare. Hughelas and my mother each had one of the Warder's arms, while two more High Elves carried his legs, grunting as they hauled the hulking elf toward shelter. I jumped up to help, resheathing my knife and running out into the night. For a few seconds, rain doused me. Then I entered the cover of magical shields holding back the onslaught, and a weak magelight hovered over the group.

My eyes darted around, taking in the blood that soaked the Warder's clothes and covered his head. Head wounds bled fiercely—it wasn't necessarily as bad as it looked. Hughelas moved awkwardly, and I realized he'd stuck his father's hammer through his belt loop. It had twisted around, the handle sticking up and bumping his arm as he walked. I could at least help with that. I grabbed the hammer's head and, flipping it over, pulled it free.

My shoulder screamed at me, but it followed orders. The hammer weighed more than my full travel pack, or so it felt. I trudged behind, staying under the shield that followed the group, but with my sore shoulder and hip, I struggled. The Warder made it look so easy... but his arms were as thick as my legs.

I trailed behind my mother and Hughelas; the two High Elves who carried the Warder's legs walked backward. My mother's worried eyes were glued to the Warder. I wanted to prompt her, nudge her so that she saw the emblem on the wall. But as soon as they could set the Warder down, they did, and my mother immediately began Healing. She didn't comprehend the danger we were in.

She worked on his head first, encouraging the wound to close. It went so much more swiftly than when she worked on me. I grimaced, realizing how hard she had to work when I was injured. Diffusing the knot on his head took longer, and she stopped before it was fully Healed, shifting her attention to cuts on his chest. He would have a bruise and a bump on his head to remember his adventure.

I walked deeper into the building and set the hammer down. Hughelas joined me, pointed at the bump on his father's head and whispered, incongruently, "You saw the symbol on the wall? This place is marked for Zoras."

"I saw," I whispered back, waving vaguely at the wounds my mother continued to work on.

"Well, let's not panic. There's no reason the guards on his dock would think anything is amiss."

He was right. They might report a ship being attacked by a dragon, but there was no reason to bring up the passengers. Nothing specifically should have called attention to *us*. To *me*.

I relaxed just a hair. We might walk right under the sleeping dog's nose.

My mother sighed, plopping on her butt after having done so

many castings on her knees. She looked up at me and Hughelas, nodding with a satisfied smile—the Warder would survive.

"You always were good at Healing, Illiara, but in our years apart, you've gotten so much better."

My mother's head jerked up, her eyes going wide at the sight of the High Elf who still wore the most comfortable and understanding of smiles.

She flew to her feet, her dagger appearing almost magically in her hand. Jumping over the slumbering hulk, she placed herself between me and the High Elves.

I moved from behind her, positioning myself by her side with my bone dagger drawn. Hughelas placed himself beside me, his father's hammer looking unwieldy in his hands.

Three swords slid from scabbards with soft whispers, separating us from the High Elf who looked… mildly put off? Like his favorite meal needed just a hint of salt.

He casually walked in front of his men, waving down their swords with a gentle motion.

"Illiara," he said. Though he still smiled, up close I realized the smile didn't reach his eyes. No, his golden eyes looked… sad. He turned to me, then back to my mother. After a second of awkward silence, he turned back to me. "My name is Zoras."

"Ugh," grunted the Warder, taking advantage of the awkward silence to return to wakefulness. My mother was closest and nudged his hip with her boot. "Ugh," he repeated. "What hit me?"

"A dragon. But you hit him first, so you had it coming. Get up, you great lunk, we need help."

"Nonsense," Zoras said. "You're in no danger. I've searched for you for eighty years, Illiara."

"You will not take my child!" she hissed vehemently.

The Warder rolled to his side and pushed himself up on his hands and knees, slowly and carefully getting his feet beneath him. Still, even at his worst, he was a very large man. The High Elves had lowered their swords, and the eternally frowning man had even sheathed his. But at the sight of the Warder, they all tensed.

Zoras looked pained. "I have no intention of harming a hair on her head." He looked at me again, sadness in his eyes. "She looks like you. Good thing. Beauty was not among her father's redeeming qualities." My father? He knew my father?

He turned his back on us, collected some papers into a book from the table, and walked to the sliding door. "Drexus, when the rest of them arrive, please escort them all to the keep. I'll have Raeinna prepare rooms." He slid the door open, revealing a covered walkway. The rainy night swallowed any other revelations.

"What if the other dragon returns?" a High Elf asked.

"Dragons collect their dead," Zoras said. "Let it, or we shall see even more. I built the Keep to hold off trolls, not dragons. I just needed to send a message."

My mother grunted. "That sounds more like the Zoras I remember. Always sending messages."

"Indeed," Zoras responded, grimacing. He commanded the frowning man, "Bring the ship's captain to me when they are ready." He walked through and closed the door behind him.

The Warder finally made it to a standing position. "Are we fighting?" he asked my mother.

She looked at the High Elves, two of whom had been in the act of sheathing their swords when they paused at the Warder's question.

"No," my mother decided. She let out a frustrated puff of air. "No," she repeated, sheathing her dagger.

"Good," the Warder said, and collapsed back to the ground.

***

Zoras's keep turned out to be much greater than a waterfront warehouse equipped to fling gargantuan metal spears at dragons. Once the Knoll's crew had secured their vessel, and the Warder woke back up, Gourd Face escorted us out of the warehouse. He cast a thin shield that didn't keep us completely dry, but held off the worst of the downpour. Someone's magelight gave us a small circle of light to find our footing. Forks of lightning revealed a wall of stone that rose three times the height of an elf. Monstrous contraptions atop it suggested a breadth to the wall that defied the senses.

Anxiety strummed through my bones and popped with every dance of lightning. Were we walking into a trap? Was the man who created that monstrosity the person who had hunted me my whole life? By following the Warder and Hughelas, had I walked right into my pursuer's waiting arms? At best, the fact that dragons hunted them had resulted in my getting caught. At worst, they'd purposefully led me to a stone prison. When Hughelas touched me, I jerked away.

He looked at me with a puzzled expression, holding out a rolled up cloth bandage and nodding at my hand. My cut dripped, unnoticed by me, as we climbed the switchback stone path to reach the keep. I snatched the bandage from him and wrapped my wound, like my blood on the stone of the keep held an ominous portent. I wouldn't have been there if not for him and his father. Was he trying to convince me my capture wasn't his fault?

Finally, a wooden overhang protected us from the rain. Our group marched right in, though like me, my mother hesitated. She looked back out to the river, and I followed her gaze. In the storm, one couldn't see even past the length of an outstretched arm. She shook her head, not finding a way out. We shared a look of resignation and entered our prison.

***

Raeinna turned out to be a half-elf like me... more or less. Her skin was golden like a High Elf, but she was even shorter than I was. Also, the way she found opportunities to touch every male... she leaned into the Wood Elf stereotype more than any Wood Elf I'd ever met. It was off-putting, seeing her fawn all over the men. Only the Warder seemed unhappy about her attention. It irritated me that, while I walked into a prison, even Hughelas embraced it with open arms and a stupid grin.

She quizzed us to understand our sleeping needs, and while I dreaded seeing my prison cell, I itched for privacy to confer with my mother. Plus, I was beat up and exhausted, so even a bed in a cage was appealing. Though wrapped, my hand throbbed like the fires of Cenaedth burned inside it. I hoped my mother's mana would recharge enough by the time we reached our rooms for her to Heal it. They wouldn't separate us, would they?

The entire structure reeked of unnatural stone walls and cut-lumber floors. Air moved through the corridors, like I sat in the lungs of a great beast that only inhaled, for the air never shifted directions. Candles freckled the hallways, but Raeinna kept a magelight hovering before us, rendering the candles moot. Still, *I* would need them. The candles burned good wax, emitting no foul odor, and I wondered at their expense. Who could afford to place nice candles in a prison?

We entered a well-furnished common room through a door next to an unlit fireplace. Couches and chairs filled the interior, while shelves of decorations and books shared the walls with a few paintings. Raeinna declared that bedrooms connected through short halls off the long ends of the room. Those halls, and the door by the fireplace, were the only exits to my gilded cage. I didn't stay to watch her prance around for the men. No one tried to stop us when I led my mother to a room at the end of one of the two halls. She summoned a weak mage-light. I needed to talk with her, understand what had happened. Why hadn't the High Elf killed me if he'd wanted me dead? My mother was the only one I trusted, but did she have a plan at all?

***

Unfortunately, though my mother had mana, she couldn't get a Heal to take. We'd lit candles, and she'd dropped the magelight to focus on the Heal, but it didn't matter. She was exhausted. I understood and echoed her state. Her eyes, hollow in the reflected candlelight, told me she didn't have answers. She didn't have a plan. We were trapped.

I had one burning question. "Do you think the Warder and Hughelas were in on it?"

She closed her eyes, sighed, and shrugged. "The possibility crossed my mind. My honest answer is no." I relaxed just a hair. "But once you've paid for the rock, you will convince yourself it's a golden egg." Her reference to one of my Talena Talenforged stories yanked away my modicum of comfort. It didn't help that High Elves were always portrayed as crafty in Talena's adventures. On the other hand, Warders weren't tricksters in *any* stories.

We sat there side by side, questioning our judgment, worried about our fate. My shoulder ached and my hand throbbed, piling onto my mountain of failure.

Faint voices and laughter crept in from the distance. My mother eyed the door like it was something new and curious that she'd never seen. She turned to me with an eyebrow raised. I'd wanted nothing more than to be alone with my mother, but she had no answers—what's more, no spirit—and loneliness hit me hard. She wasn't the comfort I'd expected. I wanted, stupid as it was, Hughelas. And she wanted some-thing or someone out there too. I nodded my head, then we stood and left.

Someone had lit a fire in the hearth of the common area. Almost everyone from the ship lounged somewhere in the room: the captain and her daughter shared a flask at a small table in a corner while the crew circled the hearth. Hughelas and the Warder lounged at a long couch across from the fire. Kharis was noticeably absent.

Hughelas smiled and waved us over.

"… and you smashed it right in the head!" Thallan was saying, catching one fist in his other palm with a slap. The motion he described bore little resemblance to the one he demonstrated, but it drew the event to my mind anyway. Drowning in my own concerns, I'd not truly considered the fact that the Warder had charged in to fight a dragon!

Hughelas stood and walked to me, and my mother took his vacated spot on the couch.

"I thought it would feel better," the Warder said, looking down at his hands. "I'd carried so much resentment for so long." He rolled his massive shoulders. "But I think something inside me has broken." My mother cocked her head, curious about what injury she'd missed. "I feel no better for having taken some measure of revenge."

"Revenge?" The voice at the door surprised everyone. Had Zoras stood there when my mother and I left our room, and I'd missed him? I didn't think so. The sliding door that led to the rest of the keep had been open, but only darkness had filled it.

My mother leapt to her feet, and everyone else froze.

"I heard voices," Zoras explained with a shrug. He waved to the dark hallway behind him. "No guards. Just me. You're safe." Though his words sounded like he meant us all to hear them, his eyes never left my mother.

He took a step in, closing behind him the sliding door we had all left open.

"What about *your* safety?" my mother asked, her voice grave.

The man who had hunted me my whole life stood with his back to the room, leaning against the door he'd closed. No sound save for the crackling of the fire accompanied his slow turn. We could kill him. One death, and I would be free. Free.

But that wasn't true, was it? I would simply be pursued by others, both for my original sin of existing… and to collect on the debt of murder.

"We have much to discuss, Illiara." Zoras's words sounded too weary to carry themselves forth. "But not tonight."

Like a switch had flipped, he turned and smiled encouragingly to the Warder. "Tell me, what revenge would you seek against a dragon?" He strolled over to a bookshelf while producing two bottles of wine from deep pockets of his robe. He set one on the shelf, uncorked the other, and purloined brass cups from the shelf. He walked first to the Warder and then to the crew of the Knoll, handing out cups and pouring wine. He waved for the Warder to begin his tale, but Thallan jumped in instead.

"Are dragon attacks common here now? You seemed ready for them, but I've traveled this way before and never seen one."

Zoras opened the second bottle while he answered. "No. No,

they are not common. Very rare indeed. This fortress was built to stop *trolls*." He held up a hand to forestall questions. "Trolls don't get this far west either. But while I hope for the best, I prepare for the worst." My mother snorted loudly. The corner of Zoras's mouth twitched. He approached my mother and me last with the freshly opened bottle, and when my mother rejected his offer, I followed suit. "But just a month ago, a dragon flew in from the west and circled above the keep. It looked huge, though it was difficult to judge distance and size since it was so high up." He shrugged, whether about the dragon's size or our rejection of his wine, I wasn't sure. "After circling for long enough to send the keep and Telloria'ahlia into a panic, it flew back east." He poured himself a cup of blood-red wine. Speckleberry. Good stuff. I regretted my decision just a little—I'd never had high-quality speckleberry, and I imagined Zoras would have the best. "But I *prepared* in case it should return."

"The bolt you shot at the dragon was massive!" Thallan held out his already emptied cup for more. Zoras raised an eyebrow and set the bottle in front of the captain. "I'm glad you prepared for it to come back, because it returned with friends."

The captain shook her head no when Thallan put his cup by the bottle. "We'll be lucky if Kharis can walk tomorrow. I need one of you ambulatory."

Thallan looked at the closed sliding door and mumbled something like, "You've stolen the wind from my sails *twice* today, Kharis."

"*Not* the same dragons," Zoras replied, attempting to regain control of the conversation. "The one that flew over us a month ago was white. These were black, and very intent on your ship."

The dragon was our fault—well, specifically, the Warder's fault. I willed him to keep his mouth shut, as I didn't relish the thought of how many years we would have to work on the Knoll in order to pay off the repairs. But that would be ludicrous too, as having the hammer on board would incur more attacks and more damage.

But, as the world had taught me many times over, my will had no bearing on reality.

"The dragons hunted *me*," Beldroth said, drawing all eyes. "I will find some way to pay for the damage."

Damned noble fool.

"Why did the dragon hunt *you?*" Ghirsel asked, her tone... skeptical?

"Dragons and Warders have disputed land for centuries,"

Hughelas asserted. "To be more accurate, dragons do what they want, where they want, and sometimes they find elves in their way."

The crew harrumphed in agreement with Hughelas, but I noticed Zoras biting his tongue, holding back something.

"One took a liking to our home," Beldroth said.

"What kind?" Thallan asked.

"One of the Ancients," the Warder answered.

That got Zoras's attention. "Which?" he asked. "Which of the Ancients?"

"Do I know dragons?" Beldroth asked, his tone, for the first time I'd ever heard, cold. Cold as death.

"It was a white," Hughelas interjected. "It arrived wounded, and it was not our intent to fight it." The Warder took a long pull from his wine. "But it... forced our hand." He paused, struggling for his next words. "Like I said, it arrived wounded. All we did was push it over the edge."

We? What had Hughelas done?

Zoras looked pensive. "And no other dragons saw this?"

The Warder shrugged. "No. But my hammer," he said, raising it a finger's height from where it sat next to him, then dropping it with a thud, as though we hadn't understood which hammer he referred to. "It's made from a bone of that Ancient, and a dragon saw me with it. A big..." He raised his arms at his sides like wings and flexed them. On the small couch with my mother beside him, the Warder looked absolutely enormous. "... red... dragon. We were quite far, but I think it was another Ancient." Zoras looked incredulous. The Warder's story did appear somewhat fanciful, with not one, but two legendary dragons. "Not long after that encounter, the attacks began."

"Dragons collect their dead," Thallan murmured.

"I don't understand," Zoras said.

Thallan started to speak, but Zoras waved him quiet.

"I mean, if the red saw you, and recognized the hammer as a dragon bone... which is not obvious... why didn't it retrieve the bone right then and there?" I cringed. Zoras didn't know about the dragon bone lighting up under a certain spell, and I didn't want it discussed. If a dragon's vision enabled it to see the magic of the bones, then the hammer *would* be obvious. But, the topic hovered too close to my opposing nature of *devouring the light*, and while I'd decided to be more open and intentional about who and what I was, the idea of mentioning that in front of Zoras terrified me.

"I don't know," Beldroth answered. "We were very far away, with terrain impeding its view."

"We hid behind a rock," Hughelas added with a small grin for me.

"I'm only guessing," his father continued, waving away his inability to explain the motivations of dragons. "The dragon attacks started on our return trip after spying on the trolls. After the Ancient looked in our direction. I would swear it saw us, even hiding behind the rock, and looked—"

"*Spying* on trolls?" Thallan blurted. "You lead an interesting and dangerous life, Warder of the elves."

"You returned to your home?" Zoras asked quietly. "After you saw the dragon—after, perhaps, it saw you—you returned to the remains of the white dragon?" Was Zoras implying that the red dragon had tracked the Warder and his son? *Dragons collect their dead.* Were dragons smart enough to play a long game to find their dead rather than just grabbing a bone in front of them?

"I grew… morose… after Lyrei's death," the Warder said with resignation, responding to Thallan and not Zoras. Hughelas pinched his lips and looked down. "The Lamenter's Vigil exists for good reason. My son needed better." Beldroth looked over at his son and smiled. "So, I made the hammer—". He sounded more his usual jovial self as he continued. "I suspected it would be the perfect weapon for smashing a troll's rocky excuse for a brain." I pictured Hughelas stuck in a cave with a heartbroken version of his father, the putrid remains of a dragon keeping them company. That couldn't have been the reality, could it? But it wasn't the right time for me to ask for details.

"Troll attacks had grown infrequent over the last decade, so I went looking for them." Hughelas's words from one of our earliest encounters, when he'd been mocking his father, popped into my head: *peace and prosperity have broken out like a plague*. "But what we found east of the Witless Tarn sent us on a different path."

"What did you see?" Zoras asked, leaning forward with eyes wide.

"A Warlord," Hughelas answered. The room grew quiet. "They have a Warlord." A collective groan launched a babble of discourse between people with stories to tell of the last, or prior, rounds of Warlords.

I didn't have a story to tell of Warlords past, nor did Hughelas. He looked at me like he'd just had an idea he wasn't sure he should share.

"What?" I asked, hesitantly. He inched over to my side, and we pulled away from the larger group. There was nowhere to go in the room that would have offered privacy, but I had no trouble hearing him above the noise of shared stories.

"I have an idea," he said. Holding his hand up to tell me to stay put, he retrieved his pack. I noticed that Zoras wasn't taking part in the exchanged stories, but he listened, keeping his eyes on me and Hughelas. Hughelas handed me the scroll case he'd purchased from my mother, then had me wait again as he retrieved his father's hammer, earning a stink-eye from his dad. "I want to try something," Hughelas explained, setting the hammer down and taking a step back to join me.

If he or the Warder were in league with the scheming Zoras, they'd covered their tracks well. They'd done nothing to make me think they'd communicated in the past. But wouldn't they hide any prior connection? I wanted to trust Hughelas. But, as my mother had mentioned, I'd already bought the gold-painted rock. *Gah!*

Hughelas took a scroll from the case and activated it. Eyes turned our way—how could they not when flame licked paper to ashes? He cringed, and my mother followed suit, embarrassed about the failure of her scroll. He pulled out another, and when it failed, a third. Stories petered out to watch the new curiosity unfold. I blushed, trying to make myself smaller. Scrolls were notorious for their inconsistency: it wasn't that which embarrassed me—I just wasn't sure what we were doing and the attention made me uncomfortable.

I distracted myself by thinking about my mother's efforts at writing scrolls. Practice at writing them helped their efficacy, and my mother had practiced for many long years. Scrollwriter's Ink also helped, but the latter we had never been able to afford—and I had never stolen any! Her most common scrolls were for Healing. After all, she'd worked the spell on me countless times, and people always liked having extra Heal spells on hand.

On the third scroll, Hughelas's eyes lit up. He looked around the room, his eyes lingering a moment on Zoras. Then he turned back to the hammer.

"Now," he said to me, "pick it up."

I hesitated. Deciding I was going to be open about what I was versus actually doing it… they were two entirely different beasts. Especially in front of Zoras.

"Hurry," he said. "Before the spell fades."

I did as he asked, noting that the hammer, though heavy, was lighter than I expected. My injury and exhaustion when I'd lifted it on the dock must have hampered me more than I'd realized. Still, it wasn't something I could lug around all day the way the Warder managed. Hughelas smiled. "That's it!" he whispered with conviction.

"What's what?" my mother asked, concerned.

"They…" Hughelas struggled for words, "balance? Cancel? When she carries the hammer, I can't see it."

My mother grimaced. Hughelas gave a nod of apology, but continued. "If we want to hide the hammer, we are well equipped to do so."

What? So I have to lug this thing around? The hammer weighed more than it had just moments before.

"Maybe so," Zoras said, less confused by the conversation than the ship's crew. "Nevertheless, I think we should head into the Heartland, and I do not think we need to worry about dragon attacks while we are there." I could practically see the puzzle pieces assembling in Zoras's golden eyes. He turned his gaze to me. "*You* might be safer though."

I set the hammer down and took a step away from it, frowning at its imposition. My mother stared daggers into Zoras, while Zoras looked at me like a game-piece he couldn't decide where to place. The Warder frowned like I'd nabbed his favorite toy, not noticing that the captain and her daughter scowled at the man who had brought harm to their ship.

I left the lousy lot of them, preferring to lie awake in solitude rather than suffer further betrayal at the hands of the duplicitous rock I'd allowed myself to believe to be a golden egg.

I awoke to a throbbing hand and a muffled peal of thunder, and found the room dimly lit from a sun that managed to push a few rays past the defending clouds and illuminate the outline of a curtain. My mother slept beside me, between me and the door, though I hadn't heard her come in. A brief alarm coursed through me at the thought, waking me further—*anyone could have snuck in!* I sat up, wondering where one relieved one's bladder in a stone construct. I tried to get up without waking my mother, but failed. It was just as well; I needed an answer. "Where do I pee?"

She rolled over to face me and smiled. Yawning, she nodded toward the window.

"I pee out the window?" I tried to picture that, wondering how hard it was raining on the other side of the shutter.

She laughed. "I need more light."

I pulled the curtains open to find brown, wooden shutters behind them. Drawing the shutters open revealed more light than I'd expected, but also the material we'd seen in the library. Glass! I tapped it with a fingernail using my good hand, creating a pleasant "tink" sound. Light shined through, but the foggy glass hid what lay beyond.

I turned back to my mother, who peered into a dim corner of the room. I followed her gaze to a pot that sat in the corner. I looked back at her in question, and she smiled and nodded at it.

"I pee in a bowl?"

She nodded again, rose from the bed, then walked over and proved her point.

I found the whole idea quite disconcerting.

But my bladder didn't care whether I liked the idea or not.

"You've done this before?" I asked my mother while she swapped with me and took her turn tapping at the glass of the window.

"I wonder how they made it flat," she remarked, ignoring my question and running a finger along one of the squares of foggy glass, each section a little bigger than my hand with wood running between them. Why did it feel like air pushed through the room when the window was blocked? It looked like my mother stared outside, though I thought the glass was too cloudy to allow that. When I finished my business, I joined her. Indeed, there was nothing to see but the glass itself, yet her eyes stared past them.

"Mother?" I said, unintentionally reaching for her hand with my bandaged one, then jerking back when pain lanced through it.

"Time to take another stab at Healing that," she said, sitting back down on the bed and patting it. I dutifully sat beside her. She took my hand, unwrapped the bandage, and looked it over. Overnight, the wound had swollen and purpled to a state much more difficult to Heal than the original puncture. It also thrummed with pain to the beat of my heart as she flipped it over, pulling back skin to be sure the cut was clean. "I suppose we are lucky this is the worst of it," she said. "You could have been drowned, eaten, ..."

"Taken prisoner by the elf who has wanted me dead my whole life," I suggested.

"Yes, we're lucky *that* didn't happen, aren't we?" She sighed and began casting her spells.

"We *are* prisoners, aren't we?" I asked.

My mother shrugged in the middle of her spell, never stopping. She completed her spell, but the spell didn't take. "He wants us to think we are not," she said. "But we are in his keep, under his care. I suspect we will find his *assisting eye* fixed upon us now. Frankly, I'm pleased we lived through the night." With those chilling words, she began her spell anew.

"I don't understand why he wants me. Why he wants me dead, or locked up, or whatever his goal." I would have to wait for her to complete her spell before she answered. "I'm eighty years old. Hunted. Caught. Maybe it's time I understood why?"

My mother had cast Heals on me thousands of times in my life. She was a Healing machine. So she didn't stop, even as her tears plopped onto my hand.

The Heal took, not returning my hand to complete health, but the swelling went down and the opening shrank. The throbbing subsided. It would be tolerable, though I suspected she intended to try again.

"Zoras is very old," she began, like she was telling a story. "Older than the silverleaf we called home in E'anashys. Probably the oldest elf in the Heartland." Oh. Wow. I couldn't imagine being older than a tree that towered into the sky.

"Yeah, that's not the weird part." She grimaced. "He was like a father to me." She laughed scornfully. "At one time, I actually thought he might *be* my father. It was the only way I could make sense out of being cast aside by my family, sent to live with 'Uncle Zoras.'"

I was absolutely speechless. So many emotions dashed around that I couldn't pick which one to follow. Was I angry that she'd never shared that with me? Was I excited to learn? Did I feel sad for her? Happy that we shared daddy issues?

She started another casting, leaving me hanging, puzzled... no, bewildered! We had spent my entire life on the run from a man who might have been her father? Were her daddy issues worse than mine? I didn't think I'd completed a single thought by the time she finished her casting, the Heal failing.

"What in the tangled roots of the Mother?!?" I blurted, and my mother scowled, despite her having said much worse in her own lifetime.

"Zoras is cold. Calculating. I saw it many times. He does what must be done. His reasons always sound good, sound high and lofty, but elves *die* from his actions." She looked at the clouded glass like she could see beyond it. Could she? Was she using some form of magic I didn't comprehend?

"To make a long story short—"

"I want the long story!"

"—I gave him reason to want you dead. I defied his machinations. I put his plans at risk by having you at all, and your being Bereft made his situation... impossible."

"What? How?"

"So I took you and *ran*. I hid and moved and secreted you away for decades."

"What are you looking at?" I finally blurted, wondering what special magic involved clouded glass that I missed out on because I was Bereft.

Her eyes shifted to mine. "The past, dear. I'm looking at the past. Eighty years is a long time. I look back and see someone else entirely. Sometimes I wonder why we live so long. I think about how I've changed, how different I am from the person I once was, and I wonder if anyone else feels the same."

She launched into another round of Healing.

My thoughts began to organize themselves. She had run away with me to save me from someone she had thought of as a father. A cold father, but a father nonetheless. It must have been terrible to flee from one's family, and beyond scary to believe her infant's life... my life… was at stake. But if it were so distant to her, as though it had happened to someone else, shouldn't it have been easier for her to talk about?

When her Heal landed, a calm fell on me like a warm blanket. It was more than the soothing balm of pain disappearing; there was something oddly comforting in the recognition that one might get so far from one's past that it became a distant memory. Not forgotten, but tucked safely away behind clouded glass. I suspected I was being a little silly about it. I was young; the monsters that plagued my dreams were those of a child. I understood that. But I'd lived a hard enough youth to recognize the comfort of leaving ghosts behind. Wasn't that part of what I sought when I had wanted to depart from my mother and live on my own?

"Is it possible…" my mother mumbled, again staring at the window. I sat, waiting. "Do you think it's possible *he* could have changed too?" The question came from a much younger version of my mother… one that sat on the other side of the window.

I put my newly healed hand in hers. "He may be older than our favorite silverleaf, but he could still change."

Her eyebrows bunched together in a scowl. "Gods! *He'll* never change." The way she said it… she hadn't been wondering about Zoras. Who then? "Come on," she said, becoming her old self once again. She rose, grabbed her pack, and walked to the door. "Might as well get going. We're still headed to Fael Themar."

"Wait, we are?" I rose and grabbed my pack. "You said Zoras wouldn't let us out of his sight."

"He won't," my mother said. "He'll go with us."

Beldroth : 3

The hollow ache was far too comfortable, far too familiar. But it made no sense. I'd hardly slept, and when I flipped over and saw light peeking from behind a curtain, I latched onto the opportunity to give up on sleep. I sat up and walked to the window, pulling back the curtain. Some unfamiliar material sat between me and the outside. I frowned and tapped it with a knuckle, causing a fragile sounding "thunk." Being encased in stone walls had at first comforted me, reminding me of home. But reminders of home were not all candy-flavored snow.

"Dad?"

Even Hughelas's sad query reminded me of my dark times during my Lamenter's Vigil, a decade in a cave where I mourned the loss of my beloved Lyrei. Why had I sunk back to that dismal state? The vigil was meant to flush one's system, so that the widowed could move on renewed, excited once again to experience life. I had done what I was supposed to… why wasn't I feeling the correct outcome?

"Yes, my son?" I answered.

"What's wrong?"

So I hadn't hid it as well as I'd thought. "Something troubles me, but I know not what." It reminded me of when my Vigil ended. I'd completed my years of mourning, anticipating with some eagerness my return to the world. I'd crafted the hammer from a bone of the one who'd taken my beloved's life, and I'd cherished the dream of opportunities to use it. *There's nothing quite like hitting things to renew one's spirit!* But when the time had come to leave my home, I'd balked. My heart had remained encased in ice.

"It's okay to miss her." My son sounded so reasonable.

But, it wasn't okay. For a number of reasons. First, I'd performed the Vigil and thereby, moved on. Perhaps I'd faked it a bit at first, clumsily going through the motions of living. But the mask had begun to fit. Unbidden, memories of walking through the forest with Illiara, laughing and exchanging stories, leaped into my mind. My spirit lifted, but then guilt swept over me like an avalanche and my heart became even more grim than it was before. Illiara was the second reason it wasn't okay to miss Lyrei. Illiara made me laugh, and her fierce bursts of temper lit a

fire in me like the legendary lava in the veins of Cenaedth. From our
very first encounter when she'd chewed a hole in me about scrolls! I
couldn't long for Illiara's company *and* miss Lyrei. Could I?

Regardless… "I don't think that's it," I said, my words ringing
true once I'd uttered them. Yes, all that business with Illiara was confusing and not nearly as clear cut as our traditions and teachings had implied, but that wasn't the bones of the matter, even though it had been a
piece of what had kept me awake. The light from the window had
chased the lesser demons from my mind, sending them scurrying into
the darkness with their little distractions.

"Then what is it?"

I hated to admit it, even to myself. "I think I feel bad for killing
that dragon."

There! I'd said it. It was out there. No taking it back. Slow seconds crawled past. Why wasn't my son saying anything? He was embarrassed. Who wouldn't be?

"You *what* now?"

I couldn't even look at my son. I shrugged. The proverbial cave
had already sealed off. Might as well drink the ale I'd been trapped with.

"I feel bad about killing that dragon!"

Footsteps approached slowly from behind. Then my son was
beside me, an arm on my shoulder. "You've killed dragons before." He
sounded like the very voice of reason. "Why do you feel bad about killing *that* dragon?"

He was right, of course. I'd killed dragons. They'd flown,
crawled, or swam into the mostly abandoned area near the former met-
ropolitan of Bellon. With self-righteous anger, I'd defended our home.
The dragons hadn't attacked out of malice, unlike the trolls. They'd
simply looked for opportunistic gain. I'd never been able to convince the
Lithos Synod of the danger to the downstream Warders should dragons
inhabit the mouth of the Contentious River. So those of us who couldn't
forsake the burned-out land that had once been our home kept the
dragons at bay.

And we always let one live so that they could collect their dead.

"I shouldn't have done what I did," I said. My hammer sat by the
bed, and I looked at it askance. "Not then and not yesterday."

"You… shouldn't have made the hammer?"

Daft boy! "Nothing's wrong with my hammer!" For someone so
smart… "I hit that dragon yesterday after it was already dead! There is
no honor in that." Untethered anger. The Mother would frown. "And I

should not have collapsed our cave."

"Ahh," breathed my son. We stood in silence for some time. He understood what I meant, though I suspected he could not relate to what had driven me to bury the dragon that had killed my wife, to block it from its kind. My boy had always had a gentle spirit. He both looked and acted more like his mother than he did me. I had no delusions that his massive intellect came from my side of the family. Had he inherited *anything* of me?

"When this is done," he finally said, "we can go dig her out. Then they can collect her."

I nodded, breathing out my darkness, then inhaling the Mother's love for the living embodied in the wisdom of my offspring.

Elliah ~ 32

"Fear is one of his many tools," my mother whispered to me as we waited in the dry warehouse to board the Knoll. She hadn't been kidding about leaving—after I'd stormed out of the common room the night before, they'd solidified plans to move on to the Heartland, Zoras included. Our group met in the commons and journeyed back to the warehouse, where the crew of the Knoll continued to their ship in the drizzling rain, while the rest of us remained under cover. Zoras and several High Elves discussed logistics of the keep, and when Zoras frowned, I realized my mother had meant for him to hear her whispered warning. "Is the Knoll really safer out on the water, or near the ballista of the Keep?"

"The dragons will come for their dead," Zoras said to his men. "Let them. If they attack, return the attention. Hire some elves to handle the ballista, and bring in some of those students whose work I've funded at Silvendir—they can test their theories, if it comes to that."

"See the way he toys with lives?" my mother faux-whispered, louder than her previous words. Hughelas and the Warder stood with us, and they both fidgeted, uncomfortable after my mother's verbal jabs.

"But don't let them start a fight," Zoras cautioned his men with a quick eye roll for my mother. "They'll be overly eager. I suspect you will encounter nothing more alarming than a show of dragons fishing their dead from the river."

My mother didn't let it go. "It's amazing how he can sound protective when he's really setting a powder keg near an open flame."

Sighing, Zoras told his men, "I've sent word to Heartshield Hall."

My mother stiffened at those words.

He tapped a paper on the desk. "Expect these shipments, though I *do not* think you will need them. Better safe than sorry." He looked at each in turn. "You've got this," he told his leaders, then he walked around the desk and approached our group.

"To whom did you 'send word?'" my mother hissed. She looked near to panic.

Zoras raised an eyebrow. "Axilya, of course. She will be discreet, as always."

"Via message crystal?" she asked.

He nodded. "I did not inform her *you* were coming. I only discussed *my* return, and that I wanted it to go unnoticed."

"You knew we were coming," my mother stated, like she'd just puzzled something out. "You're far too prepared to leave."

"Come now," Zoras said. "Do you see other ships at the dock? You know I have ships. If I were prepared to leave, wouldn't I have one here? *You've* brought this danger to my door, and when I try to help, you accuse me of somehow fabricating the entire situation."

"Varitan," my mother said. "*Professor* Varitan from E'anashys." She spat out the word "professor" like it was poison. "He sent you word when we left. You share a message crystal with him. I thought I had enough dirt on him to keep him quiet." What? Dirt on my old teacher? "There were other ships in Anysa. You commissioned them—you were looking for *us*."

"Interesting theory," Zoras said, his smile and chuckle genuine.

My mother stared him down.

"What are message crystals?" I directed the question to my mother, mildly irritated that the topic had never come up. More secrets?

Hughelas the Deceiver answered instead. "I've heard of them, but didn't know whether they were real. Crystals that two mages can use to communicate over long distances. Their basis is a spell that each mage can use to listen to another's thoughts." He whispered the next, as though his father and Zoras weren't right there listening. "It is considered a highly unscrupulous spell in a field called Empathy." Zoras raised an eyebrow, and Hughelas returned his voice to a normal level. "If two wizards use that spell, and somehow bind the spell to a pair of crystals?" He looked to Zoras for confirmation, but received only stoic silence. "They can communicate over great distances."

Well, add that to the list of things I will never be able to do. I'd long ago reconciled myself to the fact that I would never cast a spell… only rarely would a spell even land on me. But… but possibly that also meant no one could spy on my thoughts with a spell? A spell Zoras was not denying he knew.

"Empathic spells are not all bad," Zoras said quietly. "Even listening in on another's mind can help someone dealing with trauma."

My mother scowled at him.

"I'm not wrong," he said, "though I concede the spell can be used for nefarious purposes as well."

"Can be?" my mother scoffed. "One person's good intentions

can be anathema for another."

"I've missed you, Illiara." He shook his head. "For the record, I do *not* share a message crystal with Professor Varitan. Honestly, Illiara… Varitan? However, he *had* sent word that you took up residence in E'anashys. He undoubtedly hoped to win my favor. Just be happy with whom he chose to inform."

My mother cringed.

"In fact, I had just missed the Knoll on its upstream journey—I'd considered paying you a visit, but got held up with a complication at the Barrakrea. Ironically enough, preparing the keep should a certain dragon return. And, yes, some of my ships traveled upstream, but not in search of you. Trolls have been spotted at the edge of the Border Woods."

The Warder's eyes lit as his co-conspirator reinforced his story. Pathetic.

"I sent weapons upstream to the Wood Elf troops. But I dallied too long in the keep, and when the rains began, I realized I'd missed my chance to catch a ship for the season. But it was fate—if I'd left, I likely would have missed you."

"Fate," my mother scoffed. "Only Warders and their sheep believe in fate." She had the decency to blush as she uttered the derogatory but oft-repeated comment, though neither the Warder nor Hughelas showed signs of taking offense.

Zoras only grinned and shrugged, looking around the room as if to say, "What else than fate?" Challenging my mother to prove him wrong.

"Why, Zoras?" my mother asked, her voice cracking. "Why search for us? Don't get me wrong, I'm grateful you didn't kill me or my daughter on sight."

The Warder and Hughelas both tensed, the Warder going so far as to ready his hammer. Fake!

My mother charged ahead. "But what are your intentions? The Warder seeks a Blessing from The Mother."

Right. I rolled my eyes.

"My daughter seeks freedom. What do you seek, Zoras?"

"There really is no more to it than wishing to amend a past mistake. I know this will sound… well, nasty… and perhaps contrary to what I've said so far, though I don't mean for it to—I hope you don't live as long as I have."

My mother scowled at him.

"A thousand years brings many opportunities for regrets. Some weigh heavily. Lightening one's burden becomes more motivational than I would have understood in my youth."

"We've all made mistakes we wish we could undo," the Warder said. Was turning us in to Zoras one such mistake? His words, though very similar to Zoras's, calmed my mother where the High Elf's had not. The Warder was so sincere. Always.

Was it possible only Hughelas was involved in handing us over to Zoras? It made some sense. His father wasn't the smoothest rock in the stream, and Hughelas was exceedingly bright. Perhaps the Warder was just as manipulated as I.

My mother still prodded, but with less accusation. "You still haven't said what it is you seek."

"But I have," Zoras replied. "I seek redemption."

With an exasperated sigh of utter disbelief, my mother turned and walked out into the drizzle.

We limped down the river, stopping frequently to re-patch the damage to the hull from the dragon's attack, bailing water from the hold, ultimately stretching what was supposed to be a three-day journey into ten. The crew grumbled that, if the rain would only have held off for a few hours, they could have repaired it better, then moved on more quickly. Unfortunately, the weather worked as it was meant to—heavy spring rains, occasionally reducing to a drizzle, followed us. I wished the crew would cast shields to stop the downpour, but shields took a great deal of mana, and they conserved their magic in case another emergency screeched from the sky. The dragon which had flown off had presumably returned for the ones killed—*dragons collect their dead*—but would it, or they, attack again?

As soon as my mother had walked out into the rain, Hughelas placed a new, and considerably hefty, burden on me. "I think you need to carry the hammer." Not surprisingly, Zoras backed him up. The Warder pretended not to like it any more than I did, but obliged them. Possibly the Warder didn't like it—he might not have been in on their manipulations. How did my holding the hammer aid them in their schemes? I couldn't work it out. Not wanting to reveal I was on to their connivery, I played along. Zoras even supplied a harness, much like the Warder's but made for my smaller build. Though the bone weighed slightly less than a rock, the hammer still threatened to spill me backwards at any moment.

Outside of that, the days passed without event. Truly. The ship was fraught with tension—the crew was on edge from the rain and the possibility of a dragon attack. My mother stayed clear of Zoras, which proved difficult in our confined space. The Warder followed her around like a lethargic shadow, drifting behind but never letting her out of his sight. Hughelas and Zoras spent a great deal of time talking. I'd lingered nearby once to listen, and Hughelas had asked questions, jumping from topics historical to magical, prodding Zoras on subjects from old books. It didn't take me long to realize Hughelas was quite enraptured with his arrogated teacher, and Zoras enjoyed the attention. They truly had a great double-lie going: Hughelas having played his part in capturing me for Zoras, then acting like they had a burgeoning friend-ship instead of a long-standing agreement.

I spent much of the time hunkered down in the hold, rereading old stories from Talena Talonforged, having a new appreciation for her visits to the islands of the Salts or the stone gardens of the Warders. But I depended on light from the hatch, or magelight if anyone entered the hold for other reasons, which they often did—Zoras and Hughelas each had their own books. I read alone; I meditated alone; I fumed at the injustice of my solitude... alone.

Weary of the crowded loneliness, I approached my mother while she attempted to create scrolls in a section of the hull where, other than the high humidity, the ship remained dry. The Warder generously kept a magelight aloft to enable her work. Unfortunately, my timing couldn't have been worse—just as I'd walked over, the ship lurched. I wasn't close enough to catch the inkpot, but my mother's reactions remained sharp... as sharp as her pen.

"Rotting vines!" my mother blurted, bringing her cut finger to her lip. Then her eyes grew even wider. "Stinking, rotting—" She mumbled curses from around the finger she kept in her mouth to prevent blood from dripping on her scrolls, but I spotted the source of her anger. Blood had clearly run into her inkpot. Beldroth Healed her finger, but couldn't slow her rant. "It's the only ink I had left," she eventually com-plained, her anger burning out. Not wanting to be the target of her ire, I slunk out of the hatch instead of approaching her. As I exited, she sighed and continued her scroll. "I might as well finish this one."

"What was it?" Beldroth asked.

"Slow spell," she muttered, staring at her partial scroll and bloodied ink with irritation.

"Always handy," Beldroth said approvingly.

"If they worked with any consistency," she complained, then set back to finish her work, even though it was clear she believed it to be ruined.

During the lulls in the rain, when the sky merely drizzled its con-tents, I'd done one of two things. The Warder still pushed to train me. Beldroth declared the slippery deck to be an ideal training ground. He spoke to me when the topic related to fighting. It was brutal, but it filled my time.

The other way I burned away hours was scoping out the plains that separated the Heartland from the Border Woods, but I had no one to answer my questions. What race of elf lived in the little towns we passed? Why did we moor in the river instead of the small town docks? What did one do for food on the plains? What were its dangers?

It rankled, but… eventually… I missed Hughelas. I mean, he was still on the ship, but knowing he danced to Zoras's tunes changed everything. I missed what I'd thought I'd had. Truthfully, I wanted things back the way they were, even though it wasn't real. I was no different from the Warder, who wanted to believe a Blessing from the Mother of Trees would change the world.

Was it possible Hughelas *wasn't* in league with Zoras? He had called me out in front of Zoras, a damnable piece of evidence for sure. Why had he done that? He could have just told Zoras. And if he'd actually known I concealed the hammer's magic from dragons by carrying it, it was awfully convenient that he didn't tell me until *after* the dragons had driven us into the waiting arms of Zoras. But, if it had been a conscious choice, then he'd risked the lives of us all—his father, who carried the hammer, in particular.

The more the days stretched on, the more I wanted to believe Hughelas was innocent. The golden egg, for once, was actually a golden egg. Yet I kept myself distant, pulling away in the rare moments we found ourselves alone, missing his laugh and the way he listened and his touch. But being miserable, as my mother said, is something of a self-fulfilling prophecy. It lends itself to isolation and more misery. And those long, slow, lonely days in the rain were the most miserable I'd ever been.

Quiet, tense, wet, and irritable, we floated into the Heartland. It was supposed to be so different. I'd imagined, before the dragons had set us on a different course, that I would be overwhelmed with awe, Hughelas at my side as we pointed—with our free hands, of course, because he couldn't let loose the hand between us—and marveled at the sights. I wasn't sure what I'd expected those sights to be, but they were going to change my world.

Okay, maybe that was too much pressure to put on a parcel of land. *But surely it can do better than this!*

I stood port side, ignoring the drizzle, a little toward the stern where the railing remained intact, though I made a point not to lean over the side and risk breaking more of the ship.

"Faellon lies on the starboard side."

"So you're speaking to me again?" I didn't turn around. My statement wasn't fair. I'd been the one keeping Hughelas at bay, not the other way around. But I couldn't tell him that.

"I'm sorry," he said hesitantly, sounding unsure of what he had to apologize for.

He moved to stand beside me, touching the rail as cautiously as I did. We stood there in awkward silence. Finally, something gave within me—stupid as the feeling was, I missed him. "I'm sorry too," I said, and I finally looked directly at him. He looked so sad and alone. The corner of his mouth twitched just a little with my apology.

He scooted closer and his hand brushed mine on the loose rail. "You know, I'm very good at puzzling things out… until it comes to people." He looked out at the land passing by, trees and occasional homes nestled in them. "Perhaps it's because we didn't have many people around as I grew up. Or because the missionaries who arrived in Bellon tended to be zealots." He sighed. "But I think I'm simply not inclined toward understanding people. Not like Zoras. He really understands what makes people tick."

I scooted my hand away from his, and he looked down at the space between our fingers.

"Ah," he said. "You don't like how much time I've spent with him."

I scowled and hissed. "*I don't like* thinking you were involved in his *catching* me!" I hadn't meant to say it. I'd opted to play the game, hadn't I? Play along, live in the illusion that Hughelas was actually my friend. I wished I could take the words back.

Hughelas cocked his head. "How could I even have done that?" he mumbled. Then, surprising me, he said. "I suppose I could have carried a message crystal and warned him we were coming, but if the dragons hadn't attacked, we would have coasted right past his fortress. And I honestly didn't know message crystals were real, though that's easy enough to lie about. So wouldn't I have to be in cahoots with the dragons as well? Or at least have had some way of drawing them out when I wanted them?" He pursed his lips. "Now that's an interesting idea. Now that you're carrying the hammer, I suppose there is a way to cover the candle's flame until such a time as we wish to let it shine."

What? He was actually solving the problem of how he might have colluded with Zoras! For me! Was it some kind of trick? Some double-agent mind game? Lay the truth out before me and convince me that he'd just thought of it, so that I would trust him? All while telling me he wasn't good with people so that I would believe in his innocence?

"Gah!" I yelled, and pushed him away. He used the rail to stabilize himself, caught his boot on a board loosened by the dragon attack, then stumbled sideways, pinwheeling his arms with all the enthusiasm of the last male trilla bird desperate for a potential mate to choose him. I gasped and almost laughed… until a sudden shift tilted the ship and Hughelas's hip hit the rail.

The whole rail shifted and Hughelas's weight went too far. Even if the rail held, Hughelas would go over it. Before I even grasped what I'd done, I had a fist full of Hughelas's shirt in my hand, leaning back hard into the ship.

In seconds, we stabilized.

I let go and wiped my hands on my skirt, like that would clean them of the guilt and embarrassment of having pushed him in the first place.

"I'm going to consider that an indication that you think I *might* not be involved in your capture by a life-threatening pursuer who seems, to my naive eye, to be taking you exactly where you wished to go." He grinned wickedly and held out his hand to me.

And he was right—I was still headed for the Heartland, where I'd wanted to go. Except I'd intended to get there ahead of Zoras and sneak past to the swamps.

"Come on," he said. "Let's at least watch the more interesting bank."

I grimaced, joy and foolishness mixing together. Not the good foolish I'd felt before when I'd first been heart-struck, which was a sudden revelation of its own. No, rather, I genuinely accepted a foolishness that bordered on weakness, because I wanted to hold Hughelas's hand, despite not being able to rule out that he might be tricking me.

I berated myself for my imprudent feelings. How could I cloud my eyes like the glass in Zoras's keep? The new Elliah, the one who intended to see the Mother of Trees and clear her name, *that* Elliah deserved better. *Well, maybe she didn't... she messed things up pretty good.* I beat that thought back as well—I would learn from my mistakes. And would that girl ever have come to exist without Hughelas's encouragement? Perhaps... one day... but it would have taken much longer. That realization brought a second flavor of guilt—I owed Hughelas for believing in me when I did not. With an awkward emotional swirl of guilt and pride, I placed my hand in his.

He backed up a step and spun me around like we danced. My anxieties flew away like water droplets shaken loose from the fur of a wolf. He swapped hands above my head so that when we faced the opposite shore, not only was he holding my hand, but it was both of our right hands, so that his arm wrapped around me. The sensation of his fingertips on my waist—even with my hand in between his palm and my skin—sent a tingle of excitement coursing through me.

I laughed. "Smooooth, halfbreed."

He grinned, but didn't reply. My mother and Beldroth stood where we headed, looking out over the rail. "Over there," she said, pointing. Through the drizzle and the mist rising from the river, I thought I could make out the tops of silvervein trees poking through. "All the cities surrounding Alenor have large Wood Elf populations, but Faellon has the largest, probably because it lies closest to the Border Woods. Or possibly because the silvervein grove in Faellon is the oldest and largest... outside of the Border Woods, I mean."

"Well, what do the High Elves live in?" I asked, wondering what I should expect of Alenor.

"Buildings," my mother answered. "Like what we saw in Telloria'ahlia, only... more grand."

More grand than the buildings in Telloria'ahlia? I bit my lip as my mind spun trying to picture grand buildings, wondering whether I might see any in Faellon.

"There are silverveins too, including the biggest one in the land, where the Mother lives."

"Wait, the Mother of Trees lives *in a tree*?" I made a noise of disbelief, and my mother's cheeks tinged pink with embarrassment. "I'm sorry, Mom. But until you told me you'd seen her, which was only recently, I hadn't believed she was even real. I have trouble… internalizing… that there's a goddess living amongst us *in a tree*."

My mother's cheeks reddened further.

"Of course the Mother of Trees is real," Beldroth said, the words coming out slowly, like he couldn't believe he had to utter them.

I stared daggers at my mom. "Everyone talked about her in stories. Legends. Some read like she is a god who created us all." In contrast, my mother had spat the phrase "Mother of Trees," like it was a curse; she had never behaved as though the Mother were something living and breathing, nor someone to be revered. "Others talk about her like she was a warrior-wizard. I'd come to believe they were just stories—no one talks like the Mother is a god who plays a daily role in their lives!" Well, that wasn't completely true—there was one who talked differently, but he sounded crazy. "Except the Warder, who talks like they're old friends."

"The Mother of Trees *is* a god," the Warder spat, "and she *did* create us. She still listens to our prayers. Any endeavor she blesses will succeed—that is why we seek her out." He grew weary as his words dragged out, like I'd burdened him with unbelief.

Hughelas came to my defense. "To be fair, I've never been sure. I mean, creating life, stopping floods, fending off Warlords of the Father of Stones—who also seems rather fantastical to my mind—fighting alongside Roamers… but no one talks about her like she walks among us, dining on eggs or berries for breakfast, shopping for a new tunic, drinking too much speckleberry wine and singing obnoxiously, passing gas after—"

"The Mother of Trees does not pass gas!" shouted the affronted Warder.

"Probably true," a calm voice added, and Hughelas pulled me closer, tightening his grip on my hand. Zoras had appeared from nowhere. "But I assure you, the Mother of Trees is real, and, at one time, was very involved." The High Elf directed his piercing gaze at the Warder. "She said elves were her 'first creation meant to further creation.'"

"On the sixth day," Beldroth said, as though quoting something he'd heard or read, "the Mother created helpers."

"And one thing we, those whom She created, went on to invent were stories of our own creation," Zoras said. "The Mother enjoyed the stories we devised. She said they sounded so much more brilliant than reality."

Beldroth looked mortified.

"That was recorded by Beluar Zinric, the leader of the Warders affectionately known as the Sheep King." Zoras's statement took the wind from the Warder's sails. "He wrote that particular epiphany in a collection of works, mostly poems, called 'Of Mothers and Sheep.' Let me ask you this." Zoras spoke politely, but with force. "She created life, correct?"

"Yes," Beldroth answered.

"So elves?"

"Yes!"

"Dragons?"

"Yes," Beldroth answered, but with a slight hesitation.

"Trolls?" Surely that was a question the Warder had encountered before. I had interrogated my mother with such questions as a small child, and I couldn't imagine Hughelas being less inquisitive than I.

"The Father of Stones corrupted her creation," Beldroth answered with conviction.

"After?" Zoras asked.

"After the Mother and the Father brought their fight to our world."

"How much time was there between the creation of the elves and the time of the gods' fighting on the material plane?"

"Elves wrote those stories," Beldroth said slowly, looking out over the rail at the world we passed through. "Elves entrusted with the holy work of capturing the essence of her stories accurately."

"Divinely inspired, without a doubt," Zoras threw in. His tone sounded sincere, reassuring the Warder, but Hughelas squeezed my hand. Insincere? "But how long of a time period was that?"

"The time?" the Warder said, turning back. "I don't know. Why does it matter?"

"Maybe it doesn't," Zoras said. "But where was she? What was she doing? How long was she doing it?"

"What?"

"She fights the Father of Stones. Here, on our world. So where was she before then? Where was he?"

"She was here, of course!" Beldroth proclaimed.

"I'm only a thousand," Zoras said. "I wasn't around for the great flood. But even now there are a few elves, ancient elves, that remember a time before the flood."

"The Old Guard," the Warder whispered with reverence.

Zoras continued. "A time without the Witless. Before Warlords. Before the Father of Stones decimated our world. And you know what they said?"

The Warder stared, lips pursed and veins popping from his neck. But he said nothing.

"They said," Zoras whispered, "she wasn't *here*."

"Blasphemy!" Beldroth shouted. The two elves stood of a height, but the Warder had to have been three times the girth of Zoras. Still, Zoras didn't back away.

"Why? Why couldn't she have been somewhere else? How does that contradict anything else you know?"

"We are her created! She would not abandon us."

"Do you think it abandonment when a mother bluetail swims away from her chicks, leaving them to either swim or be eaten by a predator? Or is she hoping and expecting that her chicks will follow and learn?"

The Warder's jaw moved, but no words came out.

"What if she created us to be like her, but when she left, we didn't follow? What if we were the chick who decided the land was safer than the water, safer than the protective wing of our mother?"

The Warder's eyes pinched in concentration. He wasn't dumb—I knew that. Though he wasn't as sharp as his son. But he was rock solid in his beliefs. And Zoras was prying at the door that housed them.

"What if the Mother came back to save us after we were too afraid to be what she meant us to be?"

The Warder's face softened. "I like that analogy. Why have I never heard it before?"

"Because," the High Elf said, still calm, "the conclusion is frightening. What if, like with the mother bluetail, the predator was one even the Mother could not fight off, despite wanting to save her chicks? What happens when the Mother *loses*?"

As we closed in on Faellon, the river filled with activity. First small boats, and then ships smaller than the Knoll. The Faellon docks—Faello'dajor, to be precise—held several ships the size of the Knoll. Like Telloria'ahlia, a small city of its own had grown on the river near Faellon. The name, Faello'dajor, was more poetic than Telloria'ahlia, meaning the nature of mushrooms to sprout new mushrooms nearby. The docks even had the look of fungal growth along the shoreline, beautiful in its way. It lacked the elegant and thought-out organization of Telloria'ahlia. Instead, it sprawled along the shore, boasting sections that rotted yet also fueled fresh growth. Or so I imagined.

We left the Flawless at that point, heading up the slow-moving Fael'anor, and I wondered about the story behind a river whose name translated as elf-blood, but I didn't ask. The Knoll moored in a less-used—so I presumed cheaper—area at the north end of the docks, on the ominously named tributary of the major river.

The captain gathered everyone as we moored. "We are *not* docking here for the night!" she proclaimed. "No one leaves the Knoll except on my order." Then she nodded to Liandra, who leapt off the boat to the pier and disappeared into the darkness.

"Why can't we leave?" I asked, curious and excited to see another new place. I'd caught glimpses of every race as we'd coasted past—lots of Wood Elves and High Elves, many Salts, but also an occasional Warder or Alluvium. Wood Elves sometimes sported dark brown skin, but elves with gray to black skin were entirely new to me. Their builds resembled Wood Elves, athletic and lithe, but at a distance, in the drizzle, I might have been fooling myself. I wanted a chance to see everything up close.

"Because I'm the captain," Captain Edraele said in a frosty tone, "and I said so." She turned and entered her cabin, slamming the door and ending the conversation.

"Don't overthink it," Zoras said, and even though he'd stood nearby, his breath on my ear startled me. "We will press on to my home in the night."

"The Barrakrea?" I turned red as soon as I uttered the question—the Barrakrea was days away, back upriver. Dumb question.

"No, my original home. It lies northeast of Alenor, another hour upriver. The Knoll will undergo repairs there, which means it will be in dry dock for some time."

"You have a dry dock large enough for the Knoll on your *property*?" Hughelas asked, glued to my side as magically as Zoras's sudden proximity.

Zoras ignored the question. "Which means they can't deliver their cargo as intended. It's a prize cargo pulled out of the Border Woods on the last ship until the spring rains subside."

He paused then, giving me time to consider. The Knoll's trip upriver had been risky, and they'd taken the risk in order to get merchandise that would be more valuable for the scarcity of those goods over the rainy season. I'd hauled barrels and barrels of something into the hull of the Knoll. Well, technically, Beldroth had hauled them in… I'd merely shifted them around.

But where had the captain intended them to go? Clearly, Alenor hadn't been their destination.

"She has to trade with other Salts," I concluded. "The Knoll carries casks of speckleberry wine, and they were meant to go out of the Flawless to some other part of the world. The only ships that can make that journey are Salt ships."

"That's right," Zoras said, smiling at me. "The captain sent Liandra to charter other ships to deliver goods under contract, and we can store the rest on my property while the Knoll is being repaired." He looked from us to the city. "You'll have time to visit Faellon during your stay, should you wish it."

The Warder stretched, popping noises crackling from multiple joints. "I shall start hauling barrels above deck."

We kept busy for hours, the lifting requiring more effort than when we loaded, but proving simpler as the goods no longer needed organizing or securing. Zoras didn't have Beldroth's muscle, but his tall frame and long arms were useful in reaching knots, and his fingers nimbly untied them.

Beldroth, quiet for a long time, spoke to Zoras as Hughelas and I rolled a barrel away from the hatch. "The Mother of Trees involves herself in our affairs less than she once did. Is that what makes you worry she loses the battle?"

"The Mother of Trees has not moved or spoken in the last eighty years," Zoras confirmed, glancing my way, then quickly turning back to a troublesome knot. "And some fifty years prior to that. She becomes more like a Rooted and less of a Roamer with each passing year."

I rolled another barrel from the hatch to the ship's side, passing Hughelas on his return trip from moving his last barrel, and lost the conversation. The legends told of the Mother of Trees fighting alongside the Roamers. I'd pictured her as a giant Roamer, a tree who walked and fought and, in her case, cast mighty spells that devastated ranks of trolls. Trolls may have been thrice the size of elves, but Roamers grew as tall as two trolls standing atop one another. I'd never seen either—my mother mostly kept me clear of the east side of the Border Woods, where we might encounter them. Still, Roamers were made of wood. A gang of stone-skinned trolls could take down a Roamer, and trolls often traveled in groups, where Roamers worked solo. I'd read about their battles, even if I'd forgotten the detailed dates and names of those campaigns.

I returned to the hatch in order to retrieve another barrel, smiling at Hughelas as he carted one to the growing collection on the dock.

"… believe the story of the flood and the origin of her nemesis are connected." Zoras's voice rose from the hatch. "Origin is perhaps the wrong word—I really mean the transmogrification of the Father of Stones into his current form." Transmogrification? I glanced into the hold and Zoras seemed busy with a stubborn knot—he didn't *appear* to be trying to use words that made him look smarter.

"I don't understand your meaning," Beldroth said. "Are you implying that the story of the Creator of Worlds speaks of the same entity as the Father of Stones?"

"Might be," Zoras answered. "There are three creators in that story. One who orchestrated the creation of planets from matter. Another who placed life on those worlds. Some believe the former and latter are the Father of Stones and Mother of Trees in their original forms."

I could not justify lingering—more barrels needed to be moved. My mother worked with Thallan to take them from Beldroth, who did the heavy lifting from the hold. I considered asking her to switch jobs just so I could hear more, but I didn't. As I walked away, I heard Beldroth saying, "I don't see how the stories connect. And the Deities' Descent says nothing of a third creator…"

I hurried my barrel over and rushed back, flashing an irritated smile toward Hughelas each way. My haste closed the gap between us, so that we both were near the hatch as Zoras said defensively, "… just trying to prepare you for the reality of what you will see. Even if she animates, you need to understand what her blessing looks like."

A loud bang caused my mother to grimace, and Hughelas stopped rolling his barrel away, hurrying back to the hatch with me. Beldroth stood opposite Zoras with a barrel between them, where he'd slammed it back to the floor.

"I… am… not… a… child," Beldroth said softly, his popping veins counterpoint to his quiet words. "I have a few centuries under my belt, and I remember the days of old, when the Mother blessed campaigns, and the glory of those battles still sings in my heart." He beat his chest once with both fists. "But I watch my people losing hope, decade after decade… forgetting. We never recovered the ground we lost to the trolls in The Burn, and the dragons eat into our flanks. You do not see it, so deep in the Heartland, but you will. When the Warders fall, and the Border Woods succumb to the forces of the Father of Stones, you will see, but by then it will be too late."

Angry, the Warder heaved the barrel up high over his head, and my mother and Thallan backed up as he thumped it onto the deck.

"Keep antagonizing him, Zoras," my mother shouted down. "It makes our job much easier."

A grin crept across Beldroth's face.

"I'm not trying to antagonize you," Zoras complained. "I just want to prepare you. If you've seen her in battle, the sight of her now… you may find it unsettling. Besides, I *do* see the future you prognosticate. That's why I built the Barrakrea."

My mother popped her head next to mine, catching Zoras's attention in the hold. "You don't have to *try* to antagonize. You are a master who can irritate effortlessly."

"So it seems," he sighed, working another knot.

I'd been led to believe Zoras was a sly and crafty manipulator, always a step ahead and always prepared. Either he was incredibly clever and had steered the Warder toward some unfathomably useful outcome, or… he wasn't as smooth as I thought and he'd just fumbled a conversation where he'd intended to be helpful. It wasn't until Hughelas bumped me with a barrel, reminding me of my work, that I finally took my eyes off the High Elf.

Elliah ~ 36

I awoke to a disturbing sense of stillness, my mind not recognizing the barely discernible surroundings. *Why isn't the river moving?* Walls and a ceiling, all too far away, light peeking in from around a large cloth or blanket. My hands slowly explored my surroundings of their own accord, my brain spinning in confusion. My hands figured it out first—bedding.

I lay in a bed, in a room… on dry land. Pieces clicked into place. We had worked into the night unloading the cargo of the Knoll. Then we had made our weary way upriver and docked, and I'd trudged, exhausted and half-asleep, into a building, then a room, then…

I turned my head to the side and found my mother there beside me, the bed so large that we slept comfortably without touching one another. Calmer and more oriented, I tried to piece together the memories of how I'd gotten to the bed. I couldn't. My recollection of the night comprised fuzzy images of moving boxes and barrels, over and over, and the more I tried to tighten my hold on details, the faster they jumbled.

Discarding the effort as pointless, I let out a silent sigh, wondering where Hughelas was, how long my mother would sleep, and whether it would wake her if I tried to leave and explore on my own. I slowly extracted myself from the bed without waking her, noticing every sore muscle and tender bruise as I went.

The wooden floorboards did not creak, and the door slid open silently, letting in abundant light. I slipped through it and shut it quickly and quietly behind me, recognizing the familiar outside-ness even before I turned around to take in the view. The rains had stopped, laughing at the mess they had made of our downriver journey. I stood in a square courtyard with doors like the one I'd just used decorating the inner gray stone walls. The square was grass-covered with a few trees and no brush, so that one had full visibility of the open ground. A wooden overhang covered a stone walk around the rooms, to allow one to travel the ring and remain dry in a storm. Or stay out of the muck caused by spring rains. More trees stretched off in the distance behind the single-story rooms that surrounded me. The side to my right was missing a room in the middle, so that one could enter and exit the courtyard, and I bee-lined for it across the grass, enjoying the ground squishing between my toes.

The morning sun had risen before me, admonishing me with its glare, but it hadn't spent half the night hauling around heavy cargo, so I snarled a rebuke. But when I saw what lay on the other side of the courtyard, I stopped and stared. The grounds before me were *massive*. Directly in front of me lay a cobbled road leading to a four-way intersection. Far opposite me in the distance, the road led to hills. To the right, I spied masts and a tower that suggested where I would find the river should I want to, but it lay far enough away that I could not hear it. And to my left? A walled-in enclosure the likes of which I had never imagined—a gatehouse that resembled an open maw invited one into a courtyard large enough to house two silvervein trees with a mansion in between. Rope bridges connected the silverveins to the upper parts of the primary structure. Silverveins took hundreds of years to grow to that size. Had Zoras planted them as a child? Had the structure between them stood as long? Flabbergasted, I couldn't move—it was all too astounding, and too many curiosities tugged at me.

"Elliah!"

It took me a moment to find who shouted, though he stood dead in front of me. Zoras waved from the crossroads, helping me pull his figure out of the craggy hills far behind him. Another elf stood with him, and they returned to their conversation as I walked to the crossroads.

I let the beauty and majesty wash over me as I ventured up the cobbled road. Chirping birds relaxed me while an inner excitement built at the idea of exploring the area, creating a… euphoric pressure.

"I'll see it's done," said the other elf, a male who could have been a hundred or a thousand, who then nodded at me and left, heading for the river.

"Good morning," Zoras greeted me.

"How?" I asked. "How did you create all of this?"

"I've… had a lot of time," he answered, looking around.

"You've had more than that," I said. "Normal people don't have lawns manicured with silverveins." I waved at the two that flanked the main house. "Normal people don't construct safe houses for an apocalypse." I waved vaguely toward the river and the Barrakrea we'd left behind. "What you have… is vision."

Zoras smiled proudly, but something in his eyes looked not-so-proud.

"Come," he said, "let me show you Heartshield Hall." He turned toward the building cradled between the silvervein trees, holding out an arm as though he meant me to link an arm in with his. I cocked my head at the gesture. Was it some High Elf thing? It wasn't something I'd seen among my people. I pursed my lips, an intruding thought reminding me I was only half Wood Elf. So, if it *was* a High Elf thing, it was at least half *my* thing.

He was practically laughing at my indecision when I finally stuck my arm in the loop created by his. I wasn't sure what he meant for me to do with my hand, but he took it in his other hand and placed it on the cloth-covered forearm that formed the loop. Weird. When he started forward, I had to leap to keep from getting pulled off-balance. How in the world was this a good thing? Not that I expected an attack out on the lawn, but I holstered my bone-knife on the right, and I couldn't get to it with my hand on his arm. As we walked down the long cobbled street toward his home, I considered whether being unable to reach my knife was the point. Did that form of walking show how comfortable I was in my surroundings? That I didn't need access to my knife? How stupid.

The road was long enough that I had enough time to decide that the gesture was, indeed, pointless and a liability to combat, but I hesitated to remove my hand, thinking it would offend Zoras. I would endure the situation for the walk, but my hand twitched every few steps with the need to be free. Zoras turned his head to me with a mischievous smile, and released me, pointing off into the trees to the left of his home, forcing me to drop my hand from his arm. *Whew!*

"Alenor lies that direction," he said, pointing to a path leading into the trees. "Travel by river is faster, but more exposed. Like Deara, the trees keep secrets."

I chuckled at a phrase I'd heard from my mother often enough over the years as we'd snuck out of town. But Deara? I hadn't heard that part before. *Isn't that the legendary island of pirates?* My hand settled on my knife's hilt, keeping itself occupied so that it didn't have to deal with the previous nonsense, and we walked on.

"You, your mother, the Warder, and his son are staying in a courtyard set up for guests. Over the centuries, I've hosted some large gatherings." Large? I'd lived in villages smaller than that courtyard. "The crew of the Knoll stayed on board, and once the ship is in dry dock, they will undoubtedly find a place to stay on the water. So you all have the courtyard to yourselves. I also have some rooms carved into those caves," he said, pointing down the path opposite the courtyard, but they were too far for me to make anything out. "Some Alluvium and Warders can't sleep without the comfort of cave walls." Hughelas had expressed such discomfort, but Zoras had already said they chose the courtyard near us. Reminded of Hughelas, I was doubly glad I'd removed my arm from Zoras. We neared our destination. "The manor, with its gatehouse and courtyard wall, is relatively new. I built them about three hundred years ago."

Oh, that's slightly less impressive than what I expected. It was a silly notion—his manor was still more than three times older than I.

"The old manor was in the same location, but the silverveins had outgrown it."

He rebuilt to match the silverveins? More impressive.

"There are paintings of the prior structures that stood here in the gallery on the second floor."

We walked through the gateway. "Why did you make it look like one is walking into a mouth?" I asked, amused.

He shrugged. "In the High Court, I used to argue a lot, and behind my back, they called me The Mouth. This was my way of poking fun at myself. And letting people know I knew, I suppose."

"The High Court?"

"That's right. The leaders of the High Elves who have taken it upon themselves to administrate… everything. Including access to the Mother of Trees."

We exited the back side of the mouth, fortunately with no throat-related surprises, giving me my first up-close view of the manor proper. Stone curved up and around in twisting spirals that appeared to defy logic. They seemed too long to be of a single piece, but I didn't see how separate pieces would have remained stable in a storm. The stone color varied from pink to gray, with sections that sparkled in the morning light. My skin prickled as I stood there, just drinking it in, but Zoras didn't hurry me. In fact, his satisfied smile told me I'd given him exactly what he'd hoped for.

"Would you rather see the silverveins first or the—"

"I've lived in silverveins. Show me the manor!" The only fancy building of stone I'd ever entered was the library in Telloria'ahlia. My stomach bubbled with excitement, but my curiosity didn't end with the manor. "Tell me about the High Court. How many people are in it? How does it work?"

Zoras laughed merrily and led me into the manor through a wooden door twice my height. A massive open area sat just inside, with an enormous oval table in the center, decorated with a white cloth that sported a red trim. Open shutters along the wall behind us let in indirect morning light, but sconces lined the room, there to hold torches or house magelight. A set of large gold rings hanging from the ceiling lit up with magelight at a spell invoked by Zoras. Two wide staircases climbed the back wall in a symmetrical pattern, creating a landing at the top of the wall that looked down upon the space where I stood, gawking. The infamous Zoras crest, the one that had first scared us out of the library in Telloria'ahlia, decorated the wall under the landing.

A blond-haired high-elf woman popped out of a side door on the left that had glowed with light. "Good morning, Lord Zoras. Shall I keep these alight for you?"

"Good morning, Axilya. Yes, please. I expect our other guests will be along soon, and we have work to do. Can you arrange for food?"

"It's good to have you back, my lord," she said with a smile, her gaze drinking the two of us in like a lioness stumbling upon a hidden spring. Her eyes followed us as we crossed the room to climb the stairs, and it was all I could do not to turn my head and stare back.

Without pause, Zoras climbed a staircase, saying, "The High Council, at its creation, comprised thirteen High Elves who voted on topics that reached them to create law. With an odd number, the vote would always have a decisive outcome. But, over time, the system evolved into something more... complex." He pointed at a picture at the top of the landing that depicted a house very different from the one we explored. With the twin silvervein trees, it must have stood in the same place as the current mansion. Feeling eyes on my back, I looked behind me, but the woman was not there—I was imagining things. "That was the previous manor," he said. "The mix of stone and wood was very common in that era, illustrating how the High Elves worked in harmony with the Wood Elves and the Alluvium. See the fountains—for the Salts. The Warders don't have a material associated with them per se, though some say weapons or blood. Personally, I think their contribution is something more like spirit or hope, which I believe I captured better in the current incarnation of the manor."

There was an open doorway in either direction off the landing. He walked me through the one to the left and cast another spell to summon magelight. The magelight below us flickered out then lit back up. What kind of life was it for your job to be keeping the lights running in someone else's house? Though the woman... Axilya... probably lived in the manor as well. Still, tending even a pretty cage meant being caged.

Paintings decorated the walls, and statues stood between them,

all tastefully arranged to pull the eye. Some showed buildings or landscapes, but most held people. While the majority were High Elves,
many depicted Wood Elves, Salts, Alluvium, and Warders, both men
and women. All had name-plates under them, but they meant nothing to
me.

"They were all friends once," Zoras said. "Many have passed
on. Others, I've lost touch with… a thousand years is a long time."

I stopped when I recognized someone. My mother looked out at
me from the canvas, an unfamiliar but joyous smile on her face. Though
elves don't grow old, the girl in the picture looked younger than my
mother—less jaded, less tired. I'd caused that loss of innocence.
Though I had sometimes bristled under her controlling influence, the
picture stood as a stark reminder of how much she had sacrificed for
me.

"She told me you were once like a father to her," I said quietly.
She had said more than that—that he might *be* her father.

Zoras sighed, nodding. "Unfortunately, I've never let bloodlines
interfere with my plans. I voted against her, so to speak. Against you.
And she ran." He stared at the picture. "I am grateful for her stubborn-
ness."

I didn't have the complete story, but I'd caught enough implica-
tions, and it stung me to hear my life or death glossed over as a vote.
"So you voted I should die."

"It never actually came to a vote," he said haltingly. "Regardless,
that's not the way we would have worded it. We were voting for the
preservation of our magic. What was the phrase? The Mother created
elves to reflect her nature, and a being without magic was not an elf."
Under his breath, he mumbled, "For the love of words."

"So I'm not an elf." The words hurt, even though I'd thought
them myself on many occasions.

Zoras sighed. "Like I said, I was wrong."

"What changed your mind?"

"Time," he answered with a grimace. "Solemn reflection. The
Mother created life. She created both elf and troll. She had her reasons.
Who am I to define an elf?"

He had stared at the picture of my mother as he spoke, but then
turned to me. "I don't… I can't… there's nothing I can do to take back
what I've done. But I am… sorry."

He looked sincere. He looked repentant. Was I being played?
Because I'd seen my mother distance him, I didn't trust him, or perhaps

I didn't trust myself. If he'd condemned me to death as a baby, I understood why my mother would not forgive him. Was it wrong that I wanted to exonerate him?

"There's a spell," he said. "It would let you see into my mind, test the truth of my words. May I cast it?"

I thought about it. "Would you know my mind as well?"

He smiled. "No, that is also possible, but a separate spell. And you won't literally know my mind—it lets you see my sincerity. Think of it like a truth-detection spell."

I nodded; it was likely the spell wouldn't even work. "Okay."

"This will be a little weird, I'm afraid. Put your hands on my head."

"Umm…" I moved hesitantly closer and slowly placed a hand on each side of his head. The proximity unnerved me. He was a handsome elf, if a little odd and cold, and I was overly conscious of reaching up to place my fingers on his skin. Wearing a smile, he closed his eyes and started murmuring an incantation. In my peripheral vision, he gestured, casting a spell.

He stopped and opened his eyes. "It didn't work. Let me try again."

Awkward, I spouted the first thing that popped into my head, "Maybe if I looked more like Raeinna." *Okay, what made me think that would help the awkwardness?*

My cheeks burned, but Zoras just chuckled, closed his eyes, and began casting. *Thank goodness!*

He peeked out one eye, having clearly failed a second time. "Wishes come in threes," he said.

"With death as brides," I responded. He raised an eyebrow in question, then nodded and closed his eye. I'd read that in a poem once—*Wishes come in threes, with death as brides*—and it had stuck.

Zoras's head took on a soft glow between my hands. The spell was not one my mother had ever cast, and I wasn't sure what to expect. Or what to do. But it had obviously worked. I presumed something would show up if he lied.

"Hmmm," I murmured, thinking. "Are you a troll?" I asked.

He smiled, his image already darkening with shadow before the "yes" escaped his lips.

"Are you an elf?"

"Yes," he answered again, a slight glow, like reflected light, emanating from his face.

Okay, paradigm established. *Now, what do I do with it?* He wanted me to trust him.

"Do you wish me dead?"

"No." He continued to glow.

"Are you planning to hurt me or my mother or friends?"

"No," he said with a sigh, and shadows crept over his visage. "Not directly," he amended, and the glow returned. "But bringing you before the council has inherent risk." The glow remained.

Okay, that seems fair.

"Why do you want to help me?"

"Because I was wrong, and your life is important, and I want to make amends."

Parts of his face glowed, but shadows crept in.

"Try again. Why do you want to help me?"

"It's complicated," he said, his aura still glowing. "The spell doesn't do well with complications or partial truths. I should have prepared better." Sighing, he started again. "Because I was wrong, and your life is important, and I want to make amends, and..."

His face glowed with pure truth, and I perceived I was finally going to get answers. Then hot blood splattered my face, and I jumped back with a gasp.

My first thought was that my magical defenses had triggered, causing Zoras's spell to go haywire, and blown his head clean off.

But Zoras's head remained attached. Blood pumped from his neck in spurts, dousing me and then the painting of my mother as I danced to the side. He crumpled to the ground, revealing my mother, knife in hand, fury etched on her face. The Warder stood behind her, grim-faced.

"Keep your hands off my daughter!" she hissed. Which struck me as odd, given that he hadn't had his hands on me. Had he?

"Guard the door," the Warder said, and only then did I spot Hughelas closer to the exit. He nodded, looking at me with a frown and distant eyes, then disappearing.

Zoras crumpled, and my eyes darted back to the immediate dilemma. Blood surged between the fingers Zoras held to his neck as he lay on the ground.

"Mom!" I shouted. "What are you doing? Heal him."

"Swear that you will not pursue my daughter," she said, less loudly, but firmly.

He gurgled and choked.

"Swear it!"

"I swear by The Mother of Trees," he croaked out. "I will not pursue Elliah."

The pool of blood grew frighteningly large. I looked past my fuming mother to the Warder behind her. "You know how to Heal. Do something!" I shouted at him.

"If your mother so wishes," he said.

I growled, grabbing my mother's shirt. "Heal him!" I pleaded. She still just stared at his bleeding body. "Heal him, or I'll…" Inspiration struck. "I'll confess to his murder."

She twitched like I'd struck her, but she kneeled down and began her Heal spell. She had to cast twice to get the bleeding under control, validating my sense that the situation had called for action.

"Innocence attracts Zoras," my mother said, her voice still holding an edge of anger, but not the gale of fury from before. "And the thing about innocence is that once it's gone… you can't get it back."

"You're wrong," Zoras said, pushing himself up into a sitting position. What was my mother wrong about? What was she even saying? Zoras was attracted to me?

My mother snarled, but he snarled back. "Look at her," he barked. "She's been running away her whole life, raised by as cynical an elf as walks the land. She's hardly innocent."

Proud yet insulted, I added my snarl to the conversation. I'd lived a hard life, and since fleeing E'anashys, I'd consciously worked to take pride in who I was and how life had shaped me. While that wasn't the goal of the Warder in dragging me before the Mother of Trees—and apparently the High Council—it was mine. I would stand before the Mother herself and declare I was worthy of life, for all the High Council to see. I was damaged goods, but I would be damned if I'd let that define my limits. At the same time, hadn't I shown wonder as Zoras had escorted me around his manor? Wasn't I innocent?

My mother made a noise of disgust in her throat.

"I'll never get all the blood out of this stone," Zoras mumbled. "I'm going to have to rebuild to get rid of this."

"Ever heard of a rug, genius?" my mother snarled. "You've had more money than sense for too long, Zoras."

Zoras climbed to his feet, stepping away from the pool of blood, but looking at his ruined clothes. "If you'll pardon me, I'm going to change," he said. What, we weren't getting kicked out? Sent packing? "Meet me back downstairs. We still have plans to make."

He gingerly exited the room while trying not to drip blood as he went. I turned my wide-eyed look to my mother.

"I'm hardly the first person with their portrait on his wall who has threatened him," my mother said. "Elliah, don't buy whatever he's selling you. We should leave now and find our way to the Mother on our own. He's trying to gain your trust because he wants something, and if that were just your body, that would be bad enough." I blushed. "But it won't be that." She waved at the mansion. "Zoras plays a long game." She looked thoughtful. "He wants something," she said again.

While I couldn't argue with her reasoning—the mansion and grounds spoke to Zoras's ability to plan for the future—the hint of an insult irked me. He wanted me to trust him, and he'd shown me through his spell that I could. Why did she rule out that he might be genuinely attracted to me? I mean, he was old, but was I so ugly? "You don't think anyone could just *like* me?" I accused. "Because of what I am?" She may have kept me alive, but she still thought of me as being broken.

She stiffened, then sighed and softened. "No one loves you more than I do. But it is time for you to make your own mistakes. I will stay, and we shall meet with Zoras." Then she turned and walked out. The Warder gave me a look that reminded me of the one Hughelas had sent my way earlier—a frown, concern in his eyes. Resignation? The identical looks raised alarms. The Warder nodded once and then followed my mother out. Hughelas was nowhere to be seen.

I wanted to shout for her to wait, torn between my knowledge that she only did what she believed was best for me, and my need to be my own person. I stared at the blood she'd spilled for me. She was wrong about Zoras—his spell had shown that. Plus, he understood what I was, but still found me… appealing? But the person with whom I truly wished I could talk through it all? Hughelas.

"So I must convince the High Council to let me have an audience with the Mother of Trees?" Beldroth asked.

"That's what's expected, yes," Zoras said, fingering the healed cut on his throat, though it lacked even a scar, as he glowered at my mother. "But that could take years."

"Years?" Beldroth sounded affronted. "I plead my case. They decide. Where are the years in that?"

"Council members not around for the vote. Research requested. Information checks. New research requests. More council members away." He waved his hands in exasperation. "Years."

"You helped create that system," my mother pointed out.

"Yes!" Zoras blurted, standing and pacing. "When the Mother of Trees began her decline, we wanted to protect her, to preserve our way of life and slow down her... deterioration. So we gummed up the works—I wasn't the only one, but I played a role in it. I hoped it would slow changes, keep the status quo. And it helped, for a time."

"But there came a time when it certainly did not help," my mother stated, her tone cold.

Zoras nodded. "Agreed, but I was stubborn. I thought... it doesn't matter what I thought," he said, relinquishing the ghost of his self-justifications before my mother. "But I can help you get in to see the Mother of Trees."

"How?" Beldroth questioned. "You'll speed up the process? Use some kind of Council Member Pass to get me through."

"Sort of," Zoras said, his mouth twitching. "I'll call a meeting of the Council as a distraction. They'll expect that's why I returned. 'The Mouth has returned! Let's hear what word it brings.' It will be very natural. And once they are all gathered—"

"You expect me to sneak in again," my mother concluded.

"You snuck in before?" Beldroth asked, sounding both amazed and affronted. The question was on my lips as well, but the Warder beat me to it.

"She did," Zoras answered, "And with a baby in her arms. It must not be *that* hard."

"Unless she's changed locations," my mother began, and Zoras shook his head no, "then she resides away from the heart of Alenor. She was in a silvervein surrounded by other trees, and I am a Wood Elf. It was easy to bypass the High Elf gates on the ground. Are you telling me that the High Council did nothing to correct that?"

"They trimmed back the surrounding trees," Zoras answered, nodding his head in acquiescence. "But I have confirmed that they did that only once, after... the incident. It has been eighty years."

"Nature will not have honored the Council's decision," my mother concluded.

Zoras shrugged with an eyebrow raised. "That's my hope."

My mother clicked her tongue in irritation.

I glanced at Hughelas, who had reappeared when we'd gathered, but kept himself apart, aloof, and unavailable. He sat deep in thought, not hearing a word. Would he even listen if I tried to explain what had been going on in the gallery? I needed him to listen.

"I," declared the Warder, "am not a Wood Elf. Though I'm sure my delicate physique has confused you."

My mother smiled. "If *we* can get in, we can get *you* in." We... she said we. Meaning she intended me to be with her? She cocked her head and pursed her lips. "Might need some pulleys, and the rope will have to be good quality."

Beldroth laughed. "If you fail, I shall make quite the impression." Then, more somberly, "I hope I can make as much of an impact should you succeed."

"What about me?" I asked. The morning had left me unsure of myself, and I hated how pathetic I sounded.

"You will be with me," my mother said. "Pulleys or not, I can't lift that lump of a Warder on my own." Beldroth chuckled, but it wasn't the manual labor that concerned me.

"But how does that help me?" I couldn't let it go. "It's the Council that declared my life forfeit. It's them I have to convince in order to live without hiding. How does bypassing the Council, probably getting further on their bad side in the process, help me?"

"Convincing the Council will take years," Zoras answered. "That's my goal. I can keep you safe at my manor while I work through it."

My mother scoffed.

"She would be safe here," Zoras said again.

"Safe from the rest of the Council? Perhaps. Safe from you?" she asked.

But he'd been trying to show me I could trust him. Didn't that imply safety? Or was he angling for captivity?

Zoras glared at my mother. A chasm had opened up beneath me—the prospect of being confined to Heartshield Hall, while a pretty cage, left me hollowed out inside. I stared at Hughelas, willing him to look at me, to tell me it would be okay, that he would keep me company while I waited, or that he had a better idea. But he still stared at nothing, not looking at any of us.

"There is a riskier gambit," Zoras finally said.

"Here it comes," my mother said, pacing. She pulled out her dagger and gestured for Zoras to get on with it.

"How confident are you in this quest of yours?" Zoras asked Beldroth.

"Extremely," the Warder answered.

"What difference does confidence make?" my mother asked. "He will get the Mother's Blessing or he won't."

Beldroth grunted his offense, but my mother waved him off with her dagger, and his grunt turned into a chuckle.

"If he can get a blessing out of the Mother of Trees," Zoras explained, then pointed at me, "and *she* is there, I could push a change through the council quickly."

My mother stopped pacing. "They couldn't ignore her being involved in the Mother's Blessing," she whispered.

Zoras grimaced.

"What?" my mother questioned.

"The catch is, they have to know that the Mother Blessed his cause," he said. He let her think.

"We need a witness," she said. "Someone the Council will believe."

Still grimacing, he told her, "I have an idea. But you will not like it."

And, indeed, my mother did not like his plan. It put us all at risk—even Zoras, to his credit. But it at least would keep me from having to haul the Warder up a tree.

Elliah ~ 39

Hughelas left once we sketched out the essence of our plan, but for the hours we spent discussing what-ifs and contingencies, I kept looking at his empty seat, at the door, twitching with the need to talk with him. He'd claimed he wasn't feeling well and wanted to rest, but both of our parents had conspicuously looked at me. The whole time we worked out the plans that would determine my fate, I couldn't stop thinking about him and how I wanted him there. I wanted the elf who liked me for who I was, not just how I looked or what I represented. When we finally pinned down something we all agreed to, I departed to find him.

I walked through the evening light to the cabins, in mild wonder that the day had already passed. Zoras had supplied food, but I hadn't realized just how long we'd sat in that room. A quick perusal of the rooms we'd slept in revealed they were replete with emptiness.

Remembering how much the water calmed him, I thought I would find him by the river. I thought wrong. In the dying light, there were a thousand little places he could be and I would not see him. He wasn't necessarily hiding, but I couldn't shake the idea that he avoided me.

Had he gone exploring toward the caves? I'd never find him! I looked up to find the first stars painting their canopy. I wanted to scream my frustration at them, but I imagined my mother and the Warder running to my rescue, only to find a pathetic, lovesick child.

Disappointed, irritated, and just a little worried for him, I returned to the cabins. I wanted to find my mother and his father and see if either had seen him. But I stopped when I heard Zoras's voice in my cabin.

"Still, slitting my throat, that was a bit extreme."

"You wanted her trust." My mother, slurring her speech slightly, like she'd had a glass or two of wine since I'd seen her last, answered belligerently. "Believe me, at her age, there's no better way to gain it than pissing off her mother."

What? I replayed the morning's events in my head. She'd slit

Zoras's throat. That couldn't have been a ruse. Couldn't have been.

Could it?

Zoras chuckled quietly, but my mother spoke. "You long for innocence, you know. And an alluring figure."

"The heart wants what the heart wants," he replied. "But I don't agree with your assessment. I'm attracted to curiosity—it often overlaps with innocence."

"And an alluring figure," my mother repeated.

"Did you get it out of your system?" Zoras asked. Irritation washed over me—he hadn't agreed to finding me physically attractive, even though I appreciated how difficult it might have been to say so to my mother.

"I think I could slice your throat a few more times," she answered.

Zoras laughed ruefully. "I'm sorry, Illiara. I truly believed I was doing the right thing, and I truly fouled things up."

Footsteps behind me caused me to spin. Beldroth and his son had entered the courtyard. I tried to lean against the wall and look casual, which had to have been a complete success, because who doesn't lurk outside their own room?

Completely self-conscious, cheeks flaming red, I stared at my feet—after searching the grounds for Hughelas, he'd caught me eavesdropping on my mother. My heart and nerves muddled in a potion of awkwardness, and I wanted to slink away, but it wouldn't have resolved anything. "Hughelas, can we talk?"

He jumped like an insect had stung him. "We were just going back to our room to turn in for the night."

"I need to talk to Illiara," the Warder said, and he walked into our room, leaving Hughelas squirming in the courtyard, looking at the stars, the trees, the grass... anywhere but at me.

"Hughelas, look at me," I whispered, cognizant of the fact that, if I could hear my mother when she spoke at a normal level from our room, she could hear me too.

Sighing, he held himself still and looked at me.

"I'm not interested in Zoras," I said. "I like *you*."

"What?" he asked stupidly.

"I like *you*," I repeated.

He squinted at me, perplexed. "I like you too."

Why was this confusing for him? I closed the distance between us and kissed him... a long, sloppy kiss that stirred my blood.

But apparently not his, because when I pulled away, he still looked confused. I pursed my lips. "What?" I asked.

"What what?" he responded, his eyes big.

"Look," I said, frustrated, but trying one more time. "I understand what it must have looked like in the gallery." Hughelas squinted. "But I just wanted to see whether I could trust him."

"I... know," he said with hesitation.

"Then why have you been so weird all day?"

"I haven't been weird!" said the half-Warder half-Salt who rattled off theories that took most elves hundreds of years of study, who had drawn me out of hiding, who had even apologized to me, but who had spent the day distracted and alone when we'd needed his wits the most.

"You've been checked out all day," I complained. "We've been planning how to achieve your *father's* goals—the whole reason you're here—and *mine* as well. Yet you've said almost nothing. You should have been *helping*."

"I'm... sorry," he said, genuinely considering my words. That was one thing I had learned to love about Hughelas—he actually listened to me. "I promise you, it wasn't because I was angry with you about Zoras."

"What was it then?"

He grimaced. "I can't tell you." When the silence dragged on, he added, "I made a promise."

"To whom?" I whisper-yelled.

He didn't answer, but his eyes darted to my room. Beldroth, Zoras, and my mother were all inside. They'd tricked me. My mother had slashed Zoras's neck just to push me toward trusting him. *Why?*

Beldroth's laugh escaped the room. Some joke at my expense, no doubt. *See how easily we fooled her?* But why? Would I have bought into the plan we'd drummed up if I hadn't believed I could trust Zoras? Maybe not, but I thought I would have—because I trusted my mother. Or I *had* trusted her.

It crossed my mind that, if they intended to trick me, I should play along until I figured it out, and turn the tables on them. But I was too angry, and the sensible move flew out of the cage.

"I know what you're up to," I said to the room, not sure how I'd even gotten there. The room hushed in an instant. Eyes flicked to Hughelas a second later when he followed me inside.

My mother frowned at him. "Let me explain—"

She stopped mid-sentence and cocked her head in question. I whipped around in time to see Hughelas slap his arms down by his side. What had he been doing?

"What is going on?" I demanded.

My mother's face became stoic. "Not now, Elliah," she said. What in all the burning forests was going on?

"Now, Illiara!" I demanded, using her name to be sure she knew I meant business.

She narrowed her eyes and stormed out, murmuring, "Come with me... daughter," as she went past.

I stood there, holding my ground, even after she'd departed. Hughelas and his father turned their gazes at anything but me. Only Zoras dared to look, and his ever-so-understanding smile aggravated me further. Grunting, I left the lot of them behind to find my mother.

She stood in the entryway to the courtyard, but as I approached, she turned and walked away, moving slowly enough that I caught up with her. She headed straight down the road from the courtyard toward the crossroad.

"Something's got a bee in your britches," she said, sounding irritated, but in a voice I recognized as her attempt to sound calm when she wasn't. "Whatever it is, you are probably wrong." Her callous disregard for my sleuthing skills angered me. "But possibly not," she said, more to herself than to me, and that took the edge off my anger.

"You slashed Zoras's throat as a ruse," I said.

She missed a step, then resumed walking. "Why would I do that?"

"I don't know, but I heard you in there before the others arrived. You said there was no better way to gain my trust than to make you angry."

My mother sighed. "Elliah, that was just an ironic observation, and, sadly, one that has held true through the ages, at least in our family line." I didn't know our family line, but the fact that she'd shared no family history with me was a maddening topic for another day. Her *ironic observation* irritated me. Hadn't I just come to terms with how much she had given up for me? Of course, I hadn't mentioned that to her...

"I... appreciate... how much you've sacrificed to keep me safe," I said, meaning it, but also using it as a weapon to show her I wasn't the person she thought me to be, someone who would hurt or anger their own mother. Like I'd just done by maliciously brandishing kind words. *I am a terrible person.*

Her shoulders slumped like she'd lost the energy to control them. She breathed out a slow, loud breath. "Ghch," she choked out. To my knowledge, that was not a word. *What in the rotting fungi?*

"Mom," I said, a worry creeping up on me from the base of my spine and quickly causing tingles on the back of my neck. "What's going on?" Had she fled for more reasons than just keeping me safe? Maybe Zoras's throat-slashing hadn't been the first. She had been rather good at it. Of course, she'd killed a lot of animals…

Or had she realized our gambit risked too much? She wasn't going to do it. She would not support me. What would I—

"I'm pregnant," she spat out.

Like a fox had dropped from the sky into a group of finches, my thoughts darted off in a thousand directions. With slow, calming breaths, I lured them back. Some indefinite time later, I realized she was babbling. "—and I really have grown to care for him—"

"Mom," I said, quietly.

"—plus he really is quite gentle for such a big—"

"Mom!"

She shushed.

"Did you say you're *pregnant*?"

"I did," she chirruped, then resumed her silence.

Pregnant. My brain couldn't decide where to begin. It was uncommon for an elf to have a child before the previous one had fully grown, a span of about a hundred years. It wasn't unheard of. And I was eighty. Mature for eighty. So, pretty close. People had babies. Some day, if I lived long enough, I might have a baby. I could wrap my mind around that. But the other end of the equation…

"You mean the Warder is the father, correct?" My wits wouldn't cooperate, and I needed to take—haha—baby steps.

She nodded her head quickly, still unable or unwilling to speak.

"The Warder we've known for two weeks?"

The earliest an elf might realize she was pregnant was two weeks into the pregnancy. To my understanding, it would take some special spells to be sure, though they were spells I expected my mother knew. And she wouldn't tell me she was with child if she wasn't sure.

"Moooom," I groaned. "When?" But then I held my hands between us, telling her not to answer. She'd just been saying something about the night it rained along the river. I couldn't stop my brain from doing some rough math, and even that seemed too recent for her to *be sure* she was pregnant. I slapped my hand to my face. The morning after we'd met them, she'd come into our home to gather the last items before we left. I'd assumed she'd gone out foraging.

"The night we met him?" I didn't really want it confirmed, but I couldn't stop myself from asking.

"I had second thoughts about traveling together. To learn what kind of person he truly was, I went to spy on him, but he wasn't at the mill. I followed his trail and found him, watched him pray by the stream. He was quite the sight, praying, shirtless, in the moonlit glade, and… I remembered… other ways to learn about what makes a man tick. I justified my actions with the thought that, if I wore him out, he wouldn't follow us. He's a man. They get sleepy… after."

I rubbed my face with my hands.

"That didn't really work out," I said. And I had to admit, I was glad it hadn't worked out. If we hadn't traveled together, my mother and I would have kept running, as usual. We wouldn't have broken the cycle, and I wouldn't have come to terms with who and what I was.

"He doesn't tire easily," my mother said with a twitch of a smile, and my hands moved over my mouth as a bark of laughter escaped my lips.

"That's not funny," I said, as tiny little giggles escaped from both of us.

"It's a good thing you gave me so much practice Healing," she said, drawing me out. Then, with a wink and a chomp, "I like to bite."

I laughed, appalled but curious, and feeling more adult by the way my mother had spoken to me. I could talk to her about all the questions I'd had, the sensations that were new to me—that hunger for something not food. But also…

"Aren't there spells?" I asked. "To prevent that?"

"Good girls don't use those spells," my mother said. She looked down at the ground, whispering mysteriously, "Even with the protection of mental barriers, his words worm their way into my head." More loudly she said, "Yes, there are spells to prevent pregnancy. I didn't use them." She sighed, looking at me crookedly and half-smiling. "And obviously you cannot, so you'll need to be more careful than your mother."

Yes, she was treating me like an adult. Finally.

"He's a great lunk of a man," my mother said, her eyes casting over my shoulder back toward the courtyard. "But I find myself drawn to him." She returned her eyes to mine. "You asked me before whether I believed in his quest. I didn't. But I want to trust him. I want to trust him *so much*. It's been so long since I've had something to believe in, something beyond just staying alive and keeping you alive. Maybe I'm a fool—"

"You are," I said, smiling, "but that's okay." I'd caught a little of the same sickness from Hughelas. Hughelas. That's why my friend had been acting weird. "Hughelas knows?" I asked. Why would she tell him before me?

She nodded. "He overheard me telling Beldroth this morning. It wasn't intentional."

Okay, it made sense that she'd tell Beldroth first, even though that stung just a little.

"I made him promise not to tell you until I spoke to you. We looked for you, and found you with… well, events went a little sideways."

Sideways. She'd slashed a man's throat, then Healed him. After that, we'd spent the day creating plans alongside the same elf. Not just sideways, but over, under, through, and back again.

"How did the Warder… how did Beldroth… take the news?"

"He's sad." Anger flickered and I scowled, but my mother waved it away. "He seems to think my being pregnant means I can't travel with him anymore."

"Why?"

She shrugged. "I don't know. Maybe that's the custom with Warder women? Or the Salt wife he lost."

"They married?" Few elves declared the intent for a lifelong bond, given the potential eternity of an elf's lifespan. But we often used the term wife and husband to convey even a temporary partnership if it lasted a few years. Couples sometimes performed an actual wedding ceremony—some elves appreciated that the opportunity for death abounded, and a lifelong commitment might not be so long at all.

"No, not officially," she said. "And I've told him I didn't sit still while growing you. I'm not sure he believes me yet. It may not matter—it all depends on what happens with the Mother of Trees."

I nodded and shrugged, hoping to convey that I did not know about any culture differences regarding Warders or Salts and babies. It wasn't something I'd ever paid attention to if it had come up in any of the books I'd read.

Feeling closer to my mother than I had in decades, I jumped forward and hugged her. "Congratulations, Mom."

She hugged me back, snuffled, and said, "I cannot believe I'm doing this again."

"You've got this," I said. "I'll be here to help." Not wanting to let go of an opportunity I'd hoped for to talk to my mother about sex, I forged awkwardly ahead. "Now, I have some questions for you."

Beldroth : 4

It was ironic that I was given the task that Hughelas wanted, heading into Alenor, while he traveled with Illiara to the Mother's Den, where I wished to be. It wasn't just that, being closer than I'd ever been to the goddess, I longed to take the final steps and see her. Nor that I missed hearing Illiara's fiery temper and sudden laughter. It was also that I had little interest in the city of High Elves.

My son would have looked at that floating cloth bubble the size of a small room, carrying beneath it a basket large enough to hold a flame-wielding High Elf with some room to spare, and marvel at its in-genuity. Whereas I saw a race determined to grab more than the Mother meant for them. Or the large yard—*what had Zoras called it? … factory?*—which produced sheets of the clear material I'd encountered in the window of Zoras's fortress. Multiple buildings inside the cleared out area puffed black smoke into the air. It reminded me too much of the devastation of my homeland, only the High Elves had done it to themselves.

"I'd heard Alenor held the oldest silvervein grove in the world," I said to Zoras, seeing small, spindly silvervein, not fit to live in, scattered among the buildings. They looked… unhappy.

"It does," he answered. "But unlike elves, silvervein age. They grow old and die. There was money to be made in the selling of the trunks, money that went into growth of the city and its economy."

"But new silvervein should have grown from the old," I pro-tested. Who would buy a silvervein trunk?

"I suspect that the new trees needed the nutrients from the old in order to thrive."

Zoras seemed not at all bothered by his own statement. Though, truthfully, I found the High Elf to be unconcerned about most topics. I may have lived most of my life in a cave, but Zoras's heart rot-ted in a tomb. How could they not care that they'd killed off a silvervein grove?

Whispers of seeing a Warder raced ahead of me. Then another murmur arose when they recognized the High Elf I accompanied. That was part of our gambit. We needed attention. And according to Zoras, nothing created more attention than fame trying to go unnoticed. He'd utterly confused me with his declaration that, "of course, I'll need *you* there for people to notice that I'm trying to enter the city unnoticed."

"Why me?" I'd asked. "Of everyone here, I'm the least interested in your High Council."

"Because it has to be someone that will draw attention," Illiara had answered. "But not because there's a bounty on their head." She'd actually smirked as she'd said that.

"Plus," Hughelas said with a crinkled face as he puzzled out Zoras's motive, "it will make sense to go see the Mother of Trees with a Warder."

"Are you certain you have no High Elf blood?" Zoras had asked, as though only High Elves had a right to brains.

For the thousandth time, the absence of the weight of my hammer asserted itself. The eyes of so many High Elves made me especially self-conscious. I still had my sword, but swords did little good against trolls, and I didn't have the skill with it that I had with a hammer. High Elves used swords. Salts used swords. My son was built for a sword. Warders carried hammers. So, essentially naked, I approached a tall building that reeked of High Elf pretentiousness.

At a distance, I mistook it for a white silvervein, but as I neared, I realized it was not wood at all. The main edifice rose into the sky, a blend of graceful spires, elegant buttresses, and sweeping balconies. The facsimile of a trunk ran like a massive column in the middle, with upper floors protruding away, and supported by thin "vines" of shimmering metal that reached to the ground, somehow supporting the massive weight of the rooms that extended from the center.

The white stone of the tree, and that on the ground beneath it, shimmered with a faint iridescence, and glimmers of color drew my eye to gems that refracted the dappled sunlight, bringing light in under the canopy of rooms.

"I thought Wood Elves lived in Alenor too," I said.

"They do. Just not among the High Elves." He pointed to trees in the distance. "That's the Wood Elf district."

Buildings prevented me from seeing clearly, but… "Is that a wall?"

"Technically, it's an aqueduct, supplying fresh water from the river. Remember that giant wheel you asked me about as we docked? It pushes water up, and the aqueduct carries it throughout the city. The river and gravity do all the work."

The wheel had been impressive, its paddles the width of the Knoll. Still... "It looks like a wall to me."

"It's an aqueduct," he assured me.

"That separates the Wood Elves from the High Elves. Can one walk through it?"

"There are roads and gates that allow passage. Guarded for the safety of the people."

"Which people?"

"All people. Each race deserves safety and a place they can call home. Everyone is happier when surrounded by people *like* them."

My world had grown larger when I'd met my Salt wife. Before Lyrei, my world had grown monotonous—train mercenaries, fight trolls, push dragons back over The Perils. Illiara had opened my eyes to even more of the world. "I'm not."

"Look," he said, nodding ahead as we walked into the shade of the fake silvervein. "See. Wood Elves."

Sure enough, a family of Wood Elves approached the entrance to the building, but they halted when two spears suddenly formed an "X" in their path. The father Wood Elf tried to push a spear out of the way and found himself shoved back instead. The guards' golden faces remained fixed, bored, as the mother Wood Elf yelled at them, their small daughter helping her father off the ground.

I didn't realize I'd started running, or yelling, until I reached back for my hammer and found it absent. It only then dawned on me that rushing toward High Elf guards in the capital city of the High Elves might not have been the wisest move. For all I knew, there was a good reason those particular Wood Elves should not be allowed in the governing building of the Heartland. Perhaps neighbors' sheep had mysteriously appeared amongst their flock one too many times. Or they'd stood outside a council chamber, singing bawdy songs at the top of their lungs, like Queereye Allister whom I'd met in Aendolin. I glanced over my shoulder at Zoras, feeling like an idiot, but he just nodded his head.

Oh, that's right. I'm supposed *to make a scene.*

My inelegant sword got the point across. *Ha!* The Wood Elves moved aside and the High Elves took a step back, directing their spears at me. They made it easy to lop off the tips, leaving them with much less threatening sticks. More guards rushed from the building... two, three, four! All with swords. Six total, but two held only broken and unwieldy spear shafts. Still, I missed my hammer.

"Do you intend to stop me from entering this building just because I'm not a High Elf?" I asked, my blood heating as it always did during battle. The Wood Elves wisely backed outside of the High Elves encircling me.

One of the newcomers answered. "We intend to stop you because you're a very large and angry man waving a sword."

"I just intend to slow him down a little," said the guy next to him.

"Trentius!" shouted the first speaker.

"I'm just being realistic. I mean, look at him," said Trentius.

"Hold your ground!" barked the first guard.

"I didn't say I wouldn't. I just don't expect I'll be holding it for very long."

"Then hold your tongue, for once!"

I had trained countless missionaries to fight in the Blasted Lands. Occasionally, a recruit like Trentius came through, one who talked when anxious—their mouths spilling forth all the worry they kept locked up when the pressure intensified. I sympathized with his leader, but Trentius would do better once he saw combat… assuming he lived.

"Why did you stop the Wood Elves from entering?" I turned slowly as I spoke, looking each of the High Elves in the eye, judging their stances, their confidence. Two had fought before, both wielding swords. One was their leader. I focused on the guard who had pushed the Wood Elf. He gulped and stepped back. *Good.*

"They were under orders," said the leader. "The Council is not in session. There is no reason for Wood Elves to enter."

I kept my eyes on the guard with his broken spear. "Is there a reason they should *not* enter?" He'd *shoved* the Wood Elf.

The guard I stared at twitched. It wasn't their leader who responded, but rather the nervous Trentius who spoke up. "See, I'm not the only one that doesn't understand. I get that it's a rule, and our job is to enforce rules, but why—"

"Shut *up*, Trentius," barked their commander, "or you'll be shoveling Mucker shit for a month."

After a very brief pause, Trentius remarked, "Did you know that if you mix Mucker shit in with the dirt of a garden, the plants grow faster? Sir."

"By the fiery pits of Cenaedth, if you don't shut up—"

"Gentlemen," injected the elf I'd been stalling for.

"Step back!" shouted the leader, and I finally disengaged from the guard who'd shoved the Wood Elf. In my peripheral vision, I'd witnessed the crowd gathering, keeping a safe distance, but jostling each other for a view. I turned to the leader, whom Zoras had approached from behind, and I heard his name spread in a hushed whisper. The leader turned and saw who he'd yelled at, and his golden face paled. "Zoras," he said, losing all other words.

"I'll take him off your hands," Zoras said, brushing past the leader. "Sheath your sword, Beldroth. We are all on the same side." He looked over at the leader with his final words.

Grunting, I did as I was told, and the High Elves reluctantly did the same.

Zoras started toward the building, the guards parting to let him through. He paused when I didn't follow. He raised an eyebrow at me, and I looked over at the Wood Elves, who were caught somewhere between the guards and the larger crowd that had kept a modest distance away.

"You too," Zoras said, raising his voice, presumably so the Wood Elves could hear, but loud enough that everyone would hear. "We are all in this together."

The father pulled his daughter forward, while the mother scowled but joined them. I casually bumped a High Elf guard as I passed. I didn't like throwing my weight around, but he'd done the same and earned the right to know how it felt to be casually belittled in public.

As I joined Zoras and the Wood Elves, I smiled at the crowd that had gathered. It wouldn't have been right to condemn them all—in fact, that Trentius fellow had shown that even some of their officials had open minds. Zoras mumbled something about the truth being big and simple, but I didn't think he was talking to me, so I continued smiling. After all, I had created a scene that drew attention to Zoras—step one was a success!

Mother's Den was not a town per se. Officially, it had no name at all.

"The High Elves prohibited a town from forming," my mother explained, then chuckled. "They set up a garrison to prevent elves from visiting the Mother of Trees. Garrisons attract suppliers. So, the very act of secluding the Mother drew attention."

The not-town reminded me of the outskirts of a Wood Elf village. Not-shops and not-homes hid discreetly in trees and small caves that connected through little more than game trails. Each of them looked like they could fold up and move at a moment's notice. There were no stone buildings, no silverveins, and little to declare it more than a random spot in the middle of nowhere.

But for a Wood Elf, signs of elf habitation abounded. Most notably, elfbloom sprinkled the terrain. It was obvious an effort had been made to remove it, but the pernicious eavesdropper still protruded from hard-to-reach nooks and crannies. We followed clues until we spotted a Wood Elf woman washing clothes in a tiny stream along a game trail. The noise of the stream covered our approach for a time, but she bolted when she heard us.

"We are on a pilgrimage," my mother called out, "seeking shelter for a time." Not travelers… pilgrims. Those who sought to be near the Mother of Trees, hoping for enlightenment through proximity, despite the prohibition declared by the High Elves.

The woman paused, looking at Hughelas with particular interest and slight suspicion. "I've never seen a Salt on a pilgrimage to the Mother."

"My father is a Warder," Hughelas answered.

The hostess's face lit up. "A Warder?" She began to walk back to us, cautious but curious. "I'm told Warders originated the Pilgrimage to the Pristine Patroness."

"The what?" I asked, regretting it immediately, since that obviously explained our being there. Blushing, I quickly added, "I didn't know the pilgrimage had a name."

She nodded, accepting my blunder. "Anfelan says the Warders used to come all the way from the Contentious, bearing sheep and appeals for Blessings. They stopped when the mad Alluvium burned their land. There are rumors of a Warder visiting Alenor. Will we see their return?"

I smiled—we recognized that our trek through the woods would take longer than it would take Zoras and Beldroth to reach Alenor by boat. It seemed whispers had made the return trip from Alenor more rapidly than our small band had managed.

Hughelas cocked his head in that thoughtful way he had. "I suppose it depends on *our* experience and the story we return with. Is there someplace we can stay for a time?"

"There are rooms in my tree. It's no silvervein," she said to me and my mother, "but it suffices."

***

Once Zoras and Beldroth had drawn the attention of the High Elves in Alenor and, specifically, called the Council to meet, they intended to join us at the Mother's Den. It would take days to notify the Council members and pull them together—and Beldroth, as a Warder, provided the perfect excuse for the two of them to visit the Mother of Trees. Zoras would tell the High Elves that he intended to "check on the security" of the Mother of Trees, so that the Warder could report back to his people.

My mother worked on scrolls while we awaited their arrival. Hughelas and I practiced the combat lessons his father had left us with, occasionally resulting in a sprawl on the ground that ended with a kiss—not something either of us had learned from the Warder. Though, if I thought about it—and I tried not to—it might have been among the lessons the Warder had shown my mother. *Pregnant!* The visceral reminder of untethered passion had cooled my furnace; Hughelas and I slowed our ardor, keeping the fire at a low burn.

We practiced meditations as a group in the evening, my mother teaching Hughelas harder exercises, ones that had become a habit for me. The effort played in well with our deceit of being on a pilgrimage, as meditations and prayer looked very similar from the outside, and our hostess even joined in one evening. She called some of our exercises by different names, and my mother would nod begrudgingly each time, like she disagreed, but didn't want to argue.

"These exercises, I see how they help with spell-casting," Hughelas pondered aloud during one of our sessions. "Focus, clarity, but some of them perplex me. Why work on locking in ideas, making them rigid? Doesn't that make it hard to learn new things, for fresh ideas to come in?" He looked at me sideways. Was he calling me rigid?

"It does indeed," my mother said with a wan smile.

"Then why? Watching your own thoughts, like a sentry, as though you must guard—"

He stopped, looking at my mother cock-eyed.

"Must guard your very thoughts," my mother finished. "Yes."

"Against whom do you protect your mind?" he asked. Protect our thoughts? They were just exercises. Rituals. Performed to enable health and well-being.

"Everyone," my mother answered. And another naïve childhood idea vanished. Zoras had mentioned spells that let one listen in on another's mind, and he'd hinted at spells that let you speak into someone else's mind. My mother had trained me my whole life, not in exercises meant to calm and clear one's mind, but to protect it against eavesdroppers! Did it really matter, with my natural protection against magic? I didn't know, but she'd prepared me, nonetheless. With a quiet sigh, I resumed the exercises, and Hughelas embraced them with a newfound enthusiasm.

Lairras, Last of the First

It was time. With a mix of wonder and dread, I sighed, recalling past occasions of hope and joy, but knowing loneliness and oblivion awaited me. The combination of natural instinct and memory weaved together to inform me that time was not my friend.

Time. In my youth, it had stretched on with eternal promise. Since the Breaking, it had rushed toward the finality of my death, while creeping forward in the vacuum of loneliness. I missed my sisters, but they had forgotten everything but my name. Still, I missed them. Their lazy children I could do without, particularly the blues, who'd lost the distinction between peace and indolence.

Still, my successor was coming. She would be among my next brood, housed in a smaller egg, then breaking forth ravenous, hungrier than the rest. Her magic, stronger and more refined, but… ultimately broken. I'd tried to help the other Lost—at least she would have the advantage of what we'd learned did *not* work. But there was a chasm between knowing what didn't work and knowing what did, and we had yet to cross it.

Nostalgia spread its wings, reminding me not only of my Lost sisters, but of the creations once entrusted to my care. I'd spent lives, my entire existence, raising them. Then everything had flown off course. The only elves I'd seen in the last century had been raised by others. I wanted the old times back.

I slunk through my cave until I reached an opening to the sky. Timeworn anamnesis drew me to the stars, reminding me of a time when I was just me, of how much I once wished to be among the glimmering speckles of magic in the heavens. How I'd wished to be free of the burdens of raising another species, free of familial bonds, free to pursue my own dreams. Journeys on the winds of memories reminded me of how painful it could be to get what one wished for.

The clouds darkened with my thoughts, dimming with the context of memory of the Breaking, when everything went wrong, when the sky had darkened for years—the elves claimed they could not see the stars at all. Then, after millennia of caring for them as one would care for a mewling baby, after keeping handfuls alive during the dark years, I became redundant.

I'd secluded myself, interacting only with my children, and casting them, *even them,* out as quickly as I could.

I jumped off the cliff edge and took to the sky. There were inoffensive ways to supply my body with what it craved, but I didn't see the point in pursuing them. I would catch some of the lazy blues, maybe even some of my own children. I wondered if enough elves would assuage my hunger. Doubtful.

With the passing of years… *hundreds* of years… curiosity finally got the better of me. I'd seen elves nearby, but not the golden-skinned elves who had been under my care. I hadn't seen them since just after the Breaking. What had become of them? Had they survived? Ultimately, we were all doomed, but… it might be nice to see them one final time before the stars no longer shined upon me.

My mother didn't know the exact paths to reach the silvervein that housed our goddess, even though she'd visited before. Though it was true that *I* had also met the Mother, I deserved a little slack for not remembering the way. After all, at that time, I'd only just entered the world, the "Mother's Creation." I still rolled my eyes at the very thought that a being who lived in a tree had created our world, the belief that Beldroth clung to and lived by.

We scouted out the silvervein, following directions from our hostess, and found, to our dismay, that the High Elves *had* cleared the woods around the silvervein. They hadn't cleared them terribly far, leaving about a tree's span of bare ground around the silvervein, but they'd made it impossible to reach the silvervein by sliding in from a rope attached to a nearby tree.

The High Elves, however, had not cleared out more than they had to, preserving the forest and enabling the Mother of Trees to hide amidst a difficult-to-find clearing in the forest. Due east of the silvervein, a small stone building of clean lines stuck out like a sore thumb amidst the sprawling growth. It hosted a second story with a clear view of the silvervein and the surrounding grounds. Clinging to a tree at the edge of the clearing, I spotted occasional movement in that second-story window—the High Elves watched over their prize.

They'd constructed a stone wall around the base of the tree, with pointy bits of metal atop the stone. It would have been next to impossible to climb without being spotted by the High Elf patrols or the watchtower. Oddly, they'd left an entrance to the wall—an archway that faced the watchtower, and said archway had no door nor gate. Yes, it had three armed High Elves defending it, one that stood by the opening, and two that paraded around the wall, but the simple addition of a small metal frame with a lock on it would have prevented any mad dash to the silvervein and the slumbering goddess we assumed it contained.

Pilgrims, mostly Wood Elves, knelt on the grounds in the clearing, well clear of the wall and the High Elf patrol. It surprised me that a High Elf occasionally joined the pilgrims. Praying.

If more guards waited inside the circular wall, we never saw them. None of the High Elves ever entered or exited the archway that separated the silvervein from the rest of the world. The silvervein itself had something odd about it that took me a while to pinpoint—it was too still. Yes, it was isolated from the rest of the forest, but that should not have stopped birds from visiting. In fact, with the protection from below, that silvervein should have been the delight of every sparrow! Yet the tree was quiet, still... isolated and lonely.

We came up with a simple plan, though communicating that plan to Beldroth and Zoras had its challenges. It was unfortunate we could not set up a communication crystal for Hughelas or my mother to talk to Zoras, but I learned that creating a set took weeks of work from each elf.

Despite the Mother's Den's official non-existence, its discreet community spread rumor as quickly as any other. Our hostess interrupted a meditation session with barely concealed excitement. "I hear the Warder that went to Alenor is headed to Mother's Den." All it took was a raised eyebrow from my mother to get her to continue. "Rumor has it—though I don't believe it, of course—that he travels with Zoras. Wouldn't that be something, were The Mouth to pay Mother's Den a visit?"

I looked at my mother, who bit her lip in some semblance of worry.

"You're lying!" our hostess gushed, though my mother had said not a word. "You were expecting The Mouth, and the Warder, and you kept it to yourself?" She turned to Hughelas, who still sat with his eyes closed, attempting to concentrate on his exercises. "The Warder *is* your father."

Hughelas opened his eyes and sighed. "So my mother claimed."

"Well, we have no more room here!" Which was true... my mother and I shared a bed, and Hughelas slept on a hammock outside her home in the open air under an overhang. "Besides, I couldn't have a High Elf stay here. Think of the scandal!" I couldn't tell from her expression whether she was genuinely appalled, or perhaps a little excited, by the idea.

"I'm sure they will stay with High Elves," Hughelas offered.

Our hostess nodded, but her face fell.

"Would it be all right if I stayed here?" he asked.

The woman's smile returned a fraction.

"And perhaps my father could come share a meal?"

Excitement bloomed in her eyes. Clapping her hands, she

looked around at her modest rooms. "I'd best tidy up." She evaluated her opportunities for improvement, mumbling, "Now don't mind me, dears. Go on about your prayers."

My mother rolled her eyes and grinned impishly, but only I saw it. "But how would we find him? We don't know any High Elves, and I wouldn't be seen with one even if we knew where they were."

Our hostess waved her concern down. "Leave that to me. Leave it to me."

My mother pretended trepidation. "I…" Our hostess licked her lips, hungry for my mother's next words. "I would… prefer… the High Elves *not* know I'm here."

Our hostess put a hand to her mouth.

"You see, my last visit wasn't a century ago. It was closer to eighty years, just after that… incident."

The hostess gasped.

"I got too close to the silvervein, and the High Elves… banned me from returning."

"Ooo!" our hostess crooned. "Returning for a pilgrimage after *that*." She made a clicking noise with her tongue. "So brave. Don't you worry, dear. Your secret is safe with me."

I supposed the safety of our secret depended on whether our hostess thought she would get more mileage out of hosting an outlaw or having a Warder in her home.

In the end, our hostess overcame her fear of social barriers, or she embraced her love of being the in-the-know person and approached the High Elf garrison, returning with Beldroth.

Our hostess also enjoyed the scandal of the kiss Beldroth planted on my mother. And later, when my mother put her hand on her belly and the Warder looked down at it and smiled, our hostess gasped. We provided her seeds for a thousand gardens of viney tales. And whether we succeeded or failed, the next day would plant a thousand more.

***

When dawn broke, the sun's first rays found the three of us praying in the clearing. Other pilgrims knelt around us—morning prayers drew the biggest crowd. We didn't group together… we did nothing to draw attention.

Time stretched on, and I did as my mother had suggested—I

practiced my mental exercises. It was difficult, with all the adrenaline thrumming through me, but she'd assured me that such conditions required the clearest of minds. As the sun rose, I repeatedly returned my mind to calming exercises after each distracting addition or exit of a pilgrim. I set a finger to my neck, concentrating on the beating of my heart. I took long breaths. My heart slowed, my mind influencing the autonomic systems of my body. When the distinctive form of the Warder appeared at the east end of the clearing, I felt grounded. Ready.

Thump-thump. Zoras walked beside Beldroth, and they beelined, direct but unhurried, to the silvervein.

Thump-thump. We'd learned from Beldroth that he wouldn't be allowed inside the stone perimeter around the silvervein. Those were the High Elves' standing orders, and even Zoras had not convinced them to disobey their directive.

Thump-thump. It didn't matter. Our plan assumed as much.

Thump-thump. Hughelas had planted himself near the center of the path between the garrison and the arch that led to the silvervein. The Warder paused for a word and let Zoras pull ahead.

Thump-thump. I watched, waiting for Zoras to hit his mark, somewhere far enough from Beldroth and closer to the archway… but not too close.

Thump-thump. On cue, with as much mental clarity as I could wrangle, I charged Zoras, screaming and waving my bone knife like a madwoman. I started near the forest's edge, allowing a fair distance to perform my show.

Thump-thump.

"Protect Zoras!" shouted the Warder, running with exaggerated slowness to defend the High Elf, who had frozen with fear. "Defend the High Lord!"

Thump-thump.

The guards raced from the silvervein to secure Zoras… leaving the gateway wide open.

Thump-thump. Thump-thump. Thump-thump.

The High Elf guards reached Zoras before I did. One of the scattered High Elf pilgrims joined them. Was he really even a pilgrim? It didn't matter. With Zoras thoroughly protected, though Beldroth had not quite reached them, I pivoted.

Thump-thump.

I charged toward our true target. My mother, positioned closest to the archway, had already made it, her scrolls out, burning through a first.

Thump-thump.

She lit a second.

Thump-thump.

"Rotting fungi!" she snarled, down to her last scroll. She was supposed to Slow the guards. Slow scrolls were a lot of work to create, and she'd only managed two while we stayed in the Mother's Den. She'd burned them to no effect.

Thump-thump. I recognized the remaining scroll. All she had left was the one with tainted ink that she'd written on the Knoll.

Thump-thump.

She ignited it… and luck smiled upon us. The guards, Zoras, even Beldroth and Hughelas slowed like they moved through molasses—the scroll had performed admirably!

I would have laughed if I hadn't been so professional and focused, and with that thought, my clarity scattered. Time returned to normal, sounds became jarringly loud, and my heartbeat dashed forward like a loose wolf.

With my mother at my heels, I darted through the gateway. I didn't slow but charged toward the stairs, when I heard a thump behind me.

We had noted that, though they carried bows, the guards seemed unprepared to use them. I spun to find my mother down, and I jumped aside to prevent myself from getting skewered, thinking we had been wrong, and an arrow had pierced her from behind. Hiding behind the protection offered by the stone wall, I looked at her more closely. No arrow poked from her, and none flew past. Staying out of eye-shot behind the wall, I peeked my head through the archway.

The guards ambled toward the opening, the Slow spell wearing off. Yet, they didn't hurry even when they could. They approached with swords drawn, but bows still over their shoulders. They hadn't shot my mother.

"What's going on?" Zoras questioned, walking with them, as Beldroth jogged past them to get in front.

"Stop!" another guard yelled to Beldroth, who didn't listen, but dashed through the archway with his hammer drawn, only to collapse on the ground beside my mother, hammer clattering forward until it hit the wooden stairs I'd intended to climb.

"Father!" Hughelas exclaimed, creating his own less aggressive variation of Beldroth's maneuver, and landing near his father.

"A novel form of security," a soldier shorter than the rest commented to Zoras, smirking. Then he frowned. "But I'll have to tell Iolas that it didn't knock them all out."

"I guess the magic can only handle one at a time," said a guard with long golden hair. They all stopped outside the entrance.

Knock them out? I looked around, but couldn't find what had done it.

The magic… it was a *spell that had dropped them!* Somehow. None of them had cast it, so who had? But knowing it was a spell told me enough—the magic hadn't failed because of the number of assailants, it just hadn't worked *on me.*

Do I dart up to the Mother of Trees? Were the guards stuck outside, or did they have some way to bypass the spell? Was there any value in my getting to the Mother of Trees without Beldroth or any witnesses? Zoras pushed forward, arrogantly examining the space beyond.

Then he looked me in the eye and said, "I hope you're not as foolish as she." He glanced down at my mother's prone form, then back up. "My *image* of her is forever ruined, and now she's really *painted* herself into a corner." Then he winked and turned his back on me. "You must have some way of deactivating the spell," he said to the soldiers. "How else did you let in a High Lord?"

His words drew me back to the day in his painting room… she'd gotten blood on her painting, ruining it. The pieces clicked, and I understood exactly what Zoras intended me to do.

"Get back!" I yelled, my bone knife appearing at Zoras's throat. *Wow, it hadn't looked awkward when my mother had slit Zoras's throat, but she and I are the same height, and he is waaaay taller.* He helpfully bent his knees just a hint.

The soldiers backed up. "You don't want to do that," the talkative one said.

I backed Zoras into the doorway, my free hand moving under his arm to catch his weight should he pass out. I walked him backwards under the stern gazes of the three soldiers.

His weight collapsed backwards into me, and just to catch him I had to push my hand against his neck, skin-to-skin. He jerked and popped open his eyes, then breathed out deeply, like he'd just finished a long run. So skin contact helped others resist magic… or hurt them by warding off good spells; I would have to be careful not to touch someone while they were being Healed.

"The spell isn't working," a guard said, and I realized for the first time that one guard was female. She charged in and... bam! She fell atop the Warder like his butt was a cushion, and we all watched dumbly as her body slid slowly off him. Not completely dumbly, as I'd snaked my free hand down and pressed it onto my mother's face.

Zoras didn't fall back asleep, and my mother stirred.

"Turn off the spell!" the short guard shouted.

"Yrneha has the key," Long-hair said.

Shorty pulled his bow off his shoulder.

"Mom!" I hissed urgently as she struggled to wakefulness.

Even from a dead sleep, my mother was faster with a bow than the High Elf—it moved like an extension of her body. Shorty dropped his recurve with a startled yelp as my mother's arrow nicked his hand and flew off.

"No," my mother said simply.

That left Hughelas and Beldroth to wake up.

***

Even the sensation of Zoras's warm blood trickling down my fingers didn't detract from my elation. Nevertheless, I pulled my hand a hair's breadth away—Zoras didn't deserve another near-fatal neck wound. "What now?" I mouthed to my mother.

Intentionally waking Beldroth like I had my mother would blow his cover as a protector of Zoras. In the guards' eyes, Hughelas would be associated with Beldroth, so a similar problem. Did blowing their cover matter now?

She leaned over and whispered in my ear. "Step on his hand as we climb the stairs."

Ah! My bare feet on his hands—I hoped the minimal contact would work.

I backed up with Zoras, holding him at knifepoint. It was clumsy, and without the aid of Zoras playing along, I would surely have flummoxed it. I stepped onto Beldroth's outstretched hand, then Hughelas's. It was quite difficult to manage that level of clumsiness without actually tripping up.

"The Warder stirs!" my mother shouted. "Drop the High Lord and let's go."

For show, I shoved Zoras away... moving my knife out of the way, of course. Then I turned and darted past my mother, who kept us covered with her bow until we climbed out of sight up the stairs.

"Let's try to pull Yrneha back out," Shorty said.

"Rouse yourself, Warder! We must stop them!" Zoras shouted. Beldroth, Hughelas, and Zoras would not trail far behind us.

Then, as with any silvervein, we embarked upon a great deal of climbing. But my excitement didn't fade—I was going to meet a god! Well, *see* a god, anyway—my confidence that Beldroth would stir the sleeping numen had never pushed out of its seed pod. The ground it sat in had been salted long before, and the pod's shell had proven thick. Still, the embryo lived, and at the top of the climb, it would either take root or die.

I heard another shout from Zoras below. "Follow as soon as you can! We will try to stop them!"

Our comrades caught up along the way. My mother and I could have gone faster, but I wasn't sure Hughelas would have managed, and we wanted them to catch up. No one spoke. We just jogged up the winding stairs that sometimes circled the trunk and sometimes ran off through the wide limbs before finding their way back to the trunk. Whoever had grown the stairs for the Mother of Trees had tended toward an artistic, curving meander up the tree, but each step was both wide and long, as though crafted for something much larger than an elf—it made the climb gradual and long.

Finally, my mother stopped. We had passed a few room-like spaces—flat, open areas that sometimes had canopy coverage very high overhead, and sometimes did not. The one we stopped in had no magically grown ceiling, and sunlight leaked in through the natural branches above and around.

"Why are we stopping?" I asked, seeing more stairs lead out the other side.

She pointed toward the confluence of branches at the trunk, and I stared, searching for some danger hidden in the boughs. Then the image clicked into place, and I realized nothing hid in the limbs—the limbs were something else. The Mother of Trees.

She sat, her back against the trunk, legs bent, with her forearms crossed over her knees and her head resting atop her arms, like an elf relaxing after hard labor, only several times bigger. Her knees, even partially bent, stood higher than my head. I had the incongruous thought that there was no way the being before me could have climbed up and down the stairs I'd just traveled—she was too tall. Had the opening been bigger at one time? I frowned—had she sat there so long that the tree grew around her?

Beldroth wasted no time. He approached the sleeping goddess and knelt by one of her enormous feet.

"Mother of Trees," he began, "our people are battered. Trolls and dragons feed on our dead." His patron remained still. "They have a Warlord." Still nothing. "I see a way to strike back. A decisive move that will save the elves from slow demise. I seek your Blessing. Please, Mother. Bless this effort."

He put a hand on the still foot of the Mother of Trees. Long seconds passed.

"Please," he begged. "We need this. We need you."

But need did not change the world. It never had. I knew that well enough.

My mother and Hughelas approached Beldroth from either side. They looked at one another, then each placed their hands on the Mother's bark, closing their eyes in silent supplication. My mother wanted to believe. She put her other hand on Beldroth's back, a living conduit and amplifier of hope.

Yet the Mother didn't budge.

Beldroth needed his god. Truth be told, so did I. I so wanted my life to change. I wanted to stop living on the run. I needed it. But need did not change the world.

Zoras held back, looking down the stairs at the two guards that ran up behind us. He nodded to me to go. "I'll slow them."

"Rotting curses," I barked, stomping over. We were out of time. "Wake UP!" I shouted, slapping my hand on the leg of the Mother of Trees like she was a recalcitrant child.

And the world broke.

Elliah ~ 42

The noise of a thousand trees falling bellowed forth as lightning surged through my fingers and mind. Memories flashed—a world of water where I unlocked the first aquatic life, a world of fire where gelatinous creatures splashed and played in molten pools, a world where trees pushed forth from the ground into full height with the speed of an arrow. World after world flashed by, a vast history of the universe screaming through my mind, filling it beyond its meager capacity with memories from an infinite amount of time.

I heard my own screams among the roaring snaps of a falling forest. Decades of training snapped into place—I locked down incoming thoughts and perceptions, shutting out input to stabilize my sense of self. With a Herculean effort, I pushed everything *not me* away, creating space to form a watcher, a piece of my mind set to guard the expanse between me and not-me.

Breathing like a furnace, I reopened my perceptions and tried to understand where I was—crouching on all fours atop wood that undulated beneath me like the Knoll during heavy weather. My mother crouched over me, protecting me and…

"Gaaaaaaaah!" screamed the Mother of Trees, pushing herself upright against the trunk of the silvervein. She flailed her arms in front of her. "You'll not take them!" Her voice was that of beasts and birds, roars and chirps and creaking of branches all at once, yet I understood her. One arm struck a branch and snapped it off well behind us.

"Mother!" Beldroth shouted, as the limb thudded onto the platform. "Mother!" He wrapped his arms around her lower calf, though they only reached halfway.

I didn't know how, exactly, he expected to calm her. Her eyes—panicked, frightened green eyes covered with cobwebs—stared straight ahead, though she feebly raised her leg, then slammed it back down. But the force was insufficient to dislodge Beldroth.

"Mother!" my mother shouted. "It's Illiara. I've brought my daughter, Elliah."

The goddess slowed her swinging arms, squinting down at us.

"You held her as a baby," my mother reminded her. "You told me to name her."

Hughelas moved to cover my back from the High Elf guards. Where had Zoras gone? The guards weaved around the fallen limb. I climbed to my feet, the floor stable—had I only imagined its movement? What were those images I'd seen when I'd touched the Mother? Memories that were not mine, like long forgotten dreams pulled forth by a scent.

"They come," the Mother said. "*He* comes to destroy you all. Death. Death. Everywhere death. *Worlds* dead."

"Yes!" Beldroth shouted, and the Mother looked down at him as he clung to her leg. "But I have a plan. We can stop them. Please, Mother. Bless my plan so that we may end the scheming of the Father of Stones."

She stared at him curiously, studying him for a long moment, her eyes sharpening and growing brighter. "Your plan will work, but it will not save you."

"All men die," Beldroth declared, smiling. "I would gladly give my life to your cause."

"I would that I could stop you from achieving that particular happiness," the Mother said, gaining coherency like one rousing from deep slumber.

The Mother of Trees, gargantuan, bent down on her unoccupied leg to place a knee on the ground, bringing her face closer to mine. "As it was before, I cannot See you," she said to me, turning her head this way and that, as though she might catch a glimmer of something she expected to be there. "May I?" She held her enormous hand next to me, finger pointing like she meant to poke me in the belly.

"Okay?" I said, cringing.

She moved her hand forward.

Lightning coursed through my mind, bringing a vision of a world dancing with fire. The memory of excitement flared at the light of a star blinking into existence. The vision shifted to the flight of a creature I had never seen—a thin silver disk with a hole in the center and a translucent ball of purple dangling beneath—as it glided on drafts of air with nothing around save clouds. The air morphed to water, and a thing made entirely of tentacles pushed itself gracefully amidst others of its kind.

The world returned around me. The goddess's finger had withdrawn.

"Such a dangerous game, Seeing," she said mysteriously. "I must restrain my interest, or risk pushing you off course. But your thread goes on. You will survive."

"What was I seeing when you touched me?" I asked, impertinent but curious. Who did I think I was, asking questions of a god?

"I don't know," she said, half-smiling. "What were you seeing?"

"Different worlds," I said. "Creatures I cannot explain."

"How interesting," she replied. "And before you ask, I do not know why you saw those things. *My* memories. I wish I could stay awake long enough to discuss it, but my energy is almost gone." With a thud, she parked her bottom on the floor, dislodging Beldroth in the process.

"But my plan will succeed?" Beldroth asked, picking himself up off the floor. "I have your Blessing?" The two High Elves had made their way around the branch, but stood, swords drawn, unsure of their next move. Undoubtedly, they'd never received instructions on what to do should the Mother of Trees awaken.

"My Blessing?" she laughed, a weary self-mocking noise. "If you ask for it, you know not what my Blessing means. Talk to your elders. Still, you have it."

"Who else will die?" Beldroth asked. His question seemed odd, yet also an echo of my own thoughts. The Mother had popped out of her stupor declaring death. Like clouds dark with rain, the very air portended doom.

"Everyone here," she answered. "Everyone but her," the Mother of Trees said, nodding at me. "She will be here with me. I *Saw* that. The rest of you, everyone here, dies. I'm so sorry." She returned her head to her lap and breathed out a sigh.

"Wait!" I said. "What do you mean, everyone here dies?" A rising panic filled me.

"Be at peace," she said, not raising her head. "Without you, it is even worse—all life would end."

Why would that comfort me? She said no more, but I wasn't ready to give up. I wasn't done with my questions. My touch had awakened her before, so I reached out and laid my palm on her foot, letting down my mental guard, reaching out in some way—I *craved* her memories.

***

Images coalesced in the fog—Beldroth slashing at an enormous white dragon that lay wounded, then the white, with its gleaming scales, transformed into a dragon black as night, and Beldroth lay prone before a mouth large enough to swallow him whole. The black morphed into a red, and Beldroth stood before it, hammer raised, ready to fight. Why the obsession with the Warder? Because he asked for the Blessing? *No, it's not Beldroth that I want to see. I want to know why so many must die. Who are we fighting?*

The light fog faded to darkness, with a canopy of stars on one side and total blackness on the other. I tumbled deeper into memories, losing myself in them. Almost giddy with excitement, I bore witness as something pulled mass and energy together until a star blazed to life, blue and spectacular. Then a white sun lit up to dance with it. A cosmic show, not performed entirely for me, but *he* took pleasure in my appreciation. Matter collected and spun around the newly formed star, and I watched in wonder. Then *he* darted off. I wanted to stay and watch, to see what happened to *his* creation after *he* left it behind, but *he* pulled and I didn't want to be separated, so I followed *him* to where *he* lit up another pair, a red and yellow set, locked in a dance that would last their lifetime.

We had journeyed together for a very, very long time, and I'd watched enraptured for most of it. I couldn't remember a time before, but *he* had already created a brilliant canopy of light when *we* became a *we*. There was a time before me, when it was just *him*, I supposed. Was it just *him*? I had tried, more than once, to go look, to see some of the stars in the distance, from before we became a pair, but *he* always moved on. I didn't like the separation, being alone, and *he* drew me on, so I followed.

But... I would always know where *he* was—*his* lure tugged at me, no matter how far apart we were. So... even if I left *him* for a time, I would be able to find my way back.

Determined to understand more, I darted away, not so far as to find stars that were lit before I existed, but back to the blue-white pair. I watched them dance, following *his* pull as *he* moved on and created star after star after star. But the dancing pair called to me, begging for me to *do something!* They lacked a critical component... or they had it, but couldn't use it, like a candle that lacked flame.

I was sure.

The little planets that orbited the stars, balls of rock, absorbed the essence of the stars, but they did nothing with it. But, *he* and I, we fed off of the energy from those stars, and... maybe something else could as well. The stars' power danced within me, and it could do the same in others.

I moved in closer to one of the balls of rock, took a little bit of me, and left it there. Then I sat back and watched, resisting *his* tug, and waited. Something on the rock began to stir. No, lots of somethings stirred! Green covered the rock, absorbing the light from the star and transforming the rock. I bubbled with excitement. I was like *him*! I could create, and my creation enabled dances, similar to *his*, just on a different scale.

I followed *him*, trying to catch up, but pausing to leave a little of me at each of *his* creations. It took so little of me—*I am meant for this!* I learned how to leave a bit of intent, not just creating green, growing things, but the seeds of things to swim, crawl, and fly, enabling fantastic colors and dances of so many things. I could create more designs than *he*! Elegant variations of shades and movements, songs and dances!

It brought me so much joy that I wanted my creations to feel the same. So I took my time on one of the planets that orbited a single star. I stayed longer and created creatures that would one day be able to create things of their own—to use the power from the light of the stars to form their own creations, to weave the magic and orchestrate their own dance. I created some like me, some in honor of *he* who created stars, and some that mixed the two. I used everything I had learned about life, limits, balance, and boundaries to create marvels. That planet would be a monument, a firm foundation for life and magic, and I wanted so badly to show the planet's creator.

But I had drifted farther behind.

I hurried, leaving most planets with simple creations, but it brought me such joy to create the seeds of something more complex, that I had to pause from time to time and populate planets with paintings more grand. It was enough for me to know *he* was out there, creating more stars so that I could create more... creations... more life.

I practically sang the next form of life into existence, its planet so thoroughly bathed in magic that I questioned my previous choice of a monument. Giddy, my mind danced with the possibilities, and though I sensed a change was coming, I ignored the feeling, embracing the joy of what might be. I didn't understand at the time—Seeing had never before shown me something discordant with the present. I didn't understand what I Saw.

My frolic halted when I came across something wrong. A star existed, and planets circled it, but... but... the light had no fuel. Or so little that I could do nothing with it. Why?

I jumped ahead, and the next star was the same. I leapt forward, skipping stars and planets, to catch up with *he who created stars,* and found *him* bearing the cosmic equivalent of a smirk. *He* had pulled me back, lured me with a pain much greater than the tug on our binding. I watched in sadness as *he* created a star with little potential for life. *He* moved ahead and I followed, appalled and hopeful that, with me present, *he* would start creating stars with power again. The dead stars did not even do *us* much good—the fuel from distant galaxies empowered me more than *his* newest creations. But *he* didn't stop. *He* kept creating dead stars. My mind turned to all the stars created before I started my own work, all the stars with the potential for life.

Disillusioned, sad beyond measure, I left *he who created stars.* I returned to the old stars, deciding I would have to make do. And it wasn't limiting, really. The Universe held a cornucopia of stars—it had always been folly to believe their count would be endless. Still, I mourned the future. If only there were some way to create life on those planets where the stars seemed... dead.

I wondered, if I couldn't create something original, might I use the life I had created on other worlds? I returned to one of the dead planets, needing to know, and I tried something new. I used my magic to make myself corporeal, to carry with me the very smallest forms of life. Then, I jumped to one of the worlds with a dead sun, bringing with me the seeds of life I'd gathered, and I planted them under the dead sun. Many didn't take, but some did! Oh, they didn't flourish. But they fought, and clung to life, with a beauty and fury reminiscent of the creation of stars and planets themselves.

I repeated the process, seeding more of the planets that circled dead stars, bringing the germs of life over from planets more conducive to creation—giving the planets a chance. After some practice, I even seeded a planet with a variation of the beings I'd created on my monument planet, creatures who would think and create. My actions touched on cruelty, as the transplants would never have the magic to create in the way I'd intended them to when I'd planted them on their original planet. But the dead planet needed them, and something in my very distant Sight made me think the strength born of their fight would be vital.

That time... the second time *he who created stars* tried to stop me... I believed it when I Saw the future coming. Still, I had no idea what to do. *He* jumped to a world I had just finished seeding; and snarling with a Galaxy-wrenching reverberation, *he* destroyed it. Wiped out the star with a fury that turned it to *nothing*, the hole left behind sucking in the light of nearby stars. The planet that had circled that star, and all the life it carried, disappeared in a blink.

He moved on, destroying stars, both the newer stars with their sparsity of life-giving magics, as well as the older ones, replete with magic and life. I fought back the only way I could, creating more life, trying to keep up, hoping to get ahead… but ultimately, since *he* created no new stars, but only destroyed existing ones, I would lose.

I didn't understand. Why was he destroying my work and *his* own? *He* needed those stars as much as I did, maybe more. *He* fed off the magic they created, and the holes *he* left behind diminished *his* supply even more than not having a star in the first place. Was *he* really so angry about my creations as to become self-destructive?

It didn't matter. I had to change my plans. I should have had time, but what I Saw urged me to act quickly. With only a few more stops, a few more stars destroyed, a few more worlds teeming with life that would cease to exist, *he* would reach my monument. *He* would destroy the planet where I'd first created fellow creators.

So I set a trap. I went ahead, calling *him*, pulling at *him* the way *he* had pulled at me for so long. Bindings had two ends. Our dance was not so different from those I'd learned to create.

Come see what I made you! Come see how I honor you! At one time, I'd meant it to be an honor. I'd meant one of the created beings to reflect *his* nature.

When *he* arrived, *he* did what I hoped. I'd never called *him* before, and *he* was curious. *He* came close, saw me on the planet, and joined me, becoming corporeal like me.

I sprang the trap.

I locked down magic, creating boundaries and limits like I did with the creations of life, but I did it with magic itself. To say it was risky would have been the understatement of all eternity. I couldn't See that my plan would work—there were too many possibilities, too many ways things might go wrong, and Seeing past the change in the boundaries of magic fractured the Vision even more. But *he* was destroying the Universe, and with my change, *he* would be trapped. Unable to leave… unable to destroy.

No matter that I would be trapped with *him*. A small price to pay to ensure my remaining creations would survive.

***

Two fiery eyes opened, giant in my vision. Raw and exposed, I cowered before an unexplainable fear that sank its teeth deep into my bones.

Slamming my barriers back into place, I quickly brought my watcher into existence, setting it on high alert.

Crack!

With crushing pressure, my barriers snapped. I'd not known until the last week that the mental exercises my mother had etched into me through decades of repetition were meant to provide a barrier against an actual threat, and the realization of just how poor my protection was… came too late.

"Who is this?" came a rumbling voice in my head. "Hmmmm. Sister. How did you get on the other side?"

I said nothing. I couldn't. Fear gripped me too tightly, like speaking would draw unbearable attention. *He* was anger incarnate. *He* burned with pain and resentment unending. Raw emotion ripped at my very being. The true enemy, the destroyer of worlds, wanted out, wanted *his* freedom, wanted to end… *everything.*

"I wish I had known about you. I could have used an ally on the inside." The red eyes blazed, and I knew I lived only at the whim of a monster. Only because I might prove useful… in something terrible. "But you can't be in here. Come find me if you wish to talk. I will watch for you. Now… begone!"

And I popped back to reality, broken.

Epilogue

I Healed my daughter, unsure what had happened to her. I cast again and again, not knowing whether my spells didn't land or if they landed but accomplished nothing. She wouldn't wake up. She breathed. If she'd hit her head… head injuries did not always Heal.

"Zoras!" I shouted. As much as I loathed the nature of mind spells, I needed to know she was okay. What would I do if she wasn't?

"Zoras!" I shouted again.

"He's over here," Beldroth said with such solemnity that I knew something terrible had happened.

It was still with great reluctance that I pulled myself away from my daughter. Hughelas was right there beside me, his mana spent. He would keep trying as he could. Rising, I jogged to Beldroth, who stood by a fallen branch.

The branch was huge. As wide as Beldroth, it would have made a decent tree on its own, and it had smashed through the floor in places. Everywhere it broke through, or even touched the floor, it had grown into the floor, connecting and forming something new. Zoras lay, pierced by smaller limbs of the branch, blood dripping through the floor and disappearing.

I saw no way to free him.

"Oh, Zoras," I lamented, kneeling beside him. Tears escaped for the man who had once raised me. "You *would* leave right when I need you."

To my surprise, he gurgled a laugh, and blood bubbled from his lips.

He tried to speak, but nothing came out. There would be no saving him. The tree was growing back into itself, connected through him. It would tear him apart. I looked up—the silvervein also regrew where it had broken, sealing off the opening above. The Mother's magic. Not always the kindness we wished it to be.

Hating myself for my cruelty, but needing to know if he

260

had any vital information, I prolonged his demise. I Healed him.

It didn't work… it couldn't work. You can't Heal a gut wound when the gut is still pierced. But it gave him a little time.

"Should I cut him loose?" Beldroth asked.

I didn't know whether he meant to cut holes in Zoras to pull him loose, or cut the limbs growing through him, but either would be too much. It was crazy that he wasn't already dead.

"It's okay," Zoras whispered. "I am ready to go. Illiara, hear this: to survive, elves need a catalyst."

"You're not going to catalyze anything…" I granted him a final tenderness. "Uncle."

Zoras smiled, though weakly. "Catalysts accelerate change without being consumed. You heard the Mother. Everyone here dies. All save one." He coughed out blood. He wasn't going to end his life with a soliloquy on how he wished he'd spent more time raising his erstwhile daughter, creating memories with those he loved instead of working.

His final words would echo his millennia of manipulation. "To survive, elves need a catalyst."

Acknowledgments

What a ride! Starting a new series, one that had to connect up to the previous series and explain… well, I can't tell you what all it is supposed to explain, because that would ruin the fun. My point being that the story is challenging. Finding splits for the story is also challenging. I'll have to restart book two and create a new cutline, because it is tooooo long.

But that's not really an acknowledgment. I think my biggest thanks needs to go to Edith Pawlicki. She writes the Immortal Beings series, the Unseen series, and a few standalones. She has become my WBF (Writing Best Friend), and provided fantastic and constructive feedback that made Mother of Trees so much better than it might have been. In the common interpretation of "iron sharpens iron," she's made me a better writer. If you're plagued by curiosity, and wonder why I mentioned the "common interpretation", go search for "'Iron Sharpens Iron' as a Negative Image," from the Journal of Biblical Literature. I definitely did not mean the negative interpretation of that phrase. Edith has made my writing better. Marla Taviano, my editor, also continued to shape me as a writer. I like that with each book she can create a new group of biggest mistakes. The fact that the old mistakes diminish means that I have ample opportunity to make new mistakes!

I had many other folks read alpha and beta versions and provide valuable feedback that made its way into the book. I really appreciate that help when the writing was still clumsy, the story discombobulated (and somewhat dull), and I hadn't yet found the current and the wind that would take us all where I wanted to go.

I want to thank all the creatives involved. First, my mapmakers, Veronika W and Luis Leopardi, whom I found on Fiverr. Yves Muench, also from Fiverr, created a fantastic cover, and I was not fun to work with on that. So, kudos to you for that effort. Jillian Yetter, who narrated my first book, helped me create an advertising plug for this one. Thanks, Jillian!

My at-home and virtual support system kept me going

when it seemed like I'd struck ground. Somehow, they pulled me out of the rocks before the hull suffered too much damage. My direct family, including my increasingly wise daughters, played important parts in that, encouraging me and also helping me carve out time. My mom remains my #1 cheerleader, and though she's moved far away, I can still hear her cheering when the night is still. The Fortezas acted like a second family, offering help when I needed it, and asking how things were going with such persistence that it kept me motivated. Finally, I had support from a group of very reassuring readers. I mentioned some at the start of the book, but there have been more who touch base now and again with a kind word or two, and most days, that is all I need. Their amplification on social media means the world to me. I truly appreciate all the folks who took the time to write a review at any and all of the places.

So, thank you, readers! I like writing enough that I might write into a vacuum, but it is so much more gratifying and fun to have readers.

Author's Note

Sign up for my *newsletter* (https://pages.sjmorriswrites.com/ebook-land-ing-page) to receive updates on my writing, as well as early views of artwork and exclusive short-stories that give you glimpses into characters from The Guardian League and Thaumatropic Roots.

If you enjoyed The Guardian of The Palace, please leave a review on GoodReads (https://www.goodreads.com/book/show/203075343-mother-of-trees) and Amazon (https://mybook.to/TRB1), Bookbub (https://www.bookbub.com/books/mother-of-trees-an-epic-fantasy-thau-matropic-roots-book-1-by-steven-j-morris), etc. Ratings definitely en-courage folks to give my books a shot, and reviews, even a few words, help people understand whether they're going to get the fantasy they're hoping for. Help other readers connect with the stories they want.

http://sjmorriswrites.com

Thanks,
Steve